Praise for *Love Sold Separately*

"Witty, clever and full of original characters, it kept me up reading way past my bedtime! A great romp of a read."
> —Candace Bushnell, *New York Times* bestselling author of *Sex and the City* and *Is There Still Sex in the City?*

"An absolute delight... Meister has created a complex and comic main character who pitches cool fashion (as well as some hideous designs) on a cable TV shopping network...all the while maintaining her smarts and satirical eye. What fun!"
> —Susan Isaacs, *New York Times* bestselling author of *Compromising Positions* and *Takes One to Know One*

"Completely charming! Wise, hilarious, and with a determined heroine you will instantly adore, the oh-so-talented Ellen Meister brings her special chemistry to this shopping-and-the-city delight."
> —Hank Phillippi Ryan, nationally bestselling and award-winning author of *The Murder List*

"A clever cocktail of mystery and laugh-out-loud humor with the perfect twist of romance. Great fun guaranteed."
> —Tami Hoag, *New York Times* bestselling author of *The Boy*

Praise for the other novels of Ellen Meister

"A quick, charming read that will delight Parker fans and stoke the curiosity of those unfamiliar with her great wit."
> —*Library Journal* on *Dorothy Parker Drank Here*

"Magical fun."
> —*Booklist* on *Dorothy Parker Drank Here*

"Meister reveals the pathos behind the pith... Classic Parker zingers sprinkled [...] [...] [...] rothy Parker

"What bliss to be [...] [...] hy Parker.... Meister's wonde[...] [...] d elegiac sass worthy of th[...] [...] mber."
> —Elinor Lipman on *Farewell, Dorothy Parker*

Also by Ellen Meister

Dorothy Parker Drank Here
Farewell, Dorothy Parker
The Other Life
The Smart One
Secret Confessions of the Applewood PTA

Love Sold Separately

ELLEN MEISTER

mira

mira™

ISBN-13: 978-0-7783-0931-4

Recycling programs
for this product may
not exist in your area.

Love Sold Separately

For questions and comments about the quality of this book, please contact us at
CustomerService@Harlequin.com.

Mira
22 Adelaide St. West, 40th Floor
Toronto, Ontario M5H 4E3, Canada
BookClubbish.com

Printed in U.S.A.

This one's for my sisters—
Andrea, Barbara, Donna, Melissa, Rozanne

1

Dana Barry took another long pull on her joint, gulped the smoke and held it. She needed this. Twenty-nine was too old to be out of work with no prospects and an agent who hadn't sent her on an audition in six months. And it was definitely too old to get fired by a barely postpubescent boss because of her attitude. But damn it, working at the pop culture clothing store had been driving her crazy. Every customer was worse than the last. There were just so many teenagers with a *Steven Universe* T-shirt and an infected nose ring a person could take.

"C'mon, Lucas," she had pleaded with her boss. "You *hired* me to be edgy. The kids like when I push them around."

"I hired you to ring the fucking cash register," he had said.

It was no use, of course. And once again, she was unemployed. Thank God for the residuals from those Olive Garden commercials she shot last year. But even that was barely enough to cover her student loans plus the rent on her pocket-sized Manhattan apartment, and would run out soon.

Dana exhaled and rested her joint on the ashtray, then picked up her wineglass and took a sip. It was a California cabernet, dry and rich. She let it rest on her tongue for a moment, enjoying the plumminess. She took a few more sips and went back to her joint.

By the time she realized that she had been lying there long enough to find constellations in the sand pattern of her ceiling, Dana's stress had dissolved. To hell with that job.

The bass beat from her headphones reached deep inside her body and she let herself merge into it. It was a song she had listened to dozens of times, but she became aware of a buzzing in the background. How had she never noticed that before? The buzzing stopped and started again. This went on and on in an endless, eternal loop. It was pleasant at first, but then the sound became faster and more acute. Dana's eyes closed and opened, and she realized the buzzing wasn't part of the music. It was her intercom.

She pulled off her headphones, floated across the room and pressed the talk button. "Who's there?" she asked, her own voice startling her. She wondered if she sounded as stoned as she felt.

"Jeez, I thought you were dead," said the woman on the other end. "I've been ringing for ten minutes. Let me up."

"Who is this?"

"It's Megan, you idiot. Are you high?"

"No, I'm low," Dana said, which struck her as so profound she felt as if she had just ripped a hole in the cosmos. She leaned on the button that unlocked the outer door to her apartment building, and was still holding it when her bell rang.

Dana opened the door and her best friend, Megan Silvestri, burst in wearing a cinnamon-colored suede jacket Dana hadn't seen before. It was beautiful. So beautiful. Magnificently beautiful, like looking into the sun. And while Dana understood it was the weed that made it so intense, she believed the garment's splendor was real. She just happened to be enlightened enough—at that particular transcendent moment—to fully appreciate the wonder of it.

"I called your cell phone, like, twenty times," Megan said, unzipping her jacket.

Dana ran her hand down the baby-soft fabric of her friend's sleeve. "Is this new?"

"Seventy-percent off at Saks."

"It's what heaven would feel like if it were a side-zipper bomber jacket," Dana purred, and pressed her cheek against her friend's shoulder.

"Shit, you're wasted. You'd better get it together fast. There's an open call audition across town and we have to get there by two."

Dana didn't quite understand and looked deep into her friend's chocolaty eyes for clues. "What are you talking about?"

"The Shopping Channel," Megan said. "They're looking for new on-air personalities. We have less than an hour to get to their studio."

"Where's their studio?"

"West Side."

Dana was confused. "Of Manhattan?"

"Yes," Megan said, pronouncing the word as if it might be difficult to comprehend. "Now hurry."

Dana blinked, trying hard to focus. "I thought the Shopping Channel was in Pennsylvania."

"That's QVC."

"No wait, Florida. Aren't they in Florida?"

"That's the Home Shopping Network. This is the Shopping *Channel*. Very third tier and mostly fashion, but you've seen it plenty of times. Now take a shower and put on something pretty. I'll make coffee."

Dana hesitated. "I'm auditioning for the Shopping Channel?" She felt about ten steps behind.

"Yes, Dana. Yes. They need a new host."

"Like…one of those ladies who talks about earrings and shit for twenty minutes at a time?"

"It's perfect for you."

"What about *you*?" Dana asked.

Megan folded her arms under her head-size breasts. "Forget about me. I'm done with auditions. Besides, they're not looking for short, fat Italian girls."

"You're not that short."

Megan gave her the finger.

"I'm sorry," Dana said. "I'm such an asshole when I'm stoned."

"I'll forgive you if you get the gig."

Just one month earlier, Megan had announced that she was giving up on her acting career, but in the same breath offered to become Dana's manager. She insisted that she believed in her friend's talents, and was frustrated that Dana's agent wasn't getting her enough auditions. Megan's enthusiasm was contagious, and Dana agreed. Since then, whenever Megan wasn't at her job waiting tables at an Italian restaurant downtown, she was assiduously combing the listings in *Backstage* for the most suitable gigs. She was damned serious about the whole thing.

Dana sighed and leaned against the wall. "I'm really stoned."

"Well, get *un*-stoned," Megan said, pushing her friend toward the bathroom. "Cold shower, caffeine. You'll manage."

Dana paused. She was having a hard time following the thread of the conversation. "Why am I doing this?" she asked as Megan shut the bathroom door after her.

"Because you need to move out of this shithole. And you were born for this job."

"I was born for this job," she said to her reflection, and then called out to her friend, "Why was I born for this job?"

"Because you can describe the shit out of anything. You notice things on a molecular level. You're pathological."

Dana picked up her hairbrush, held it toward the mirror and spoke in an ebullient TV hostess voice to her own wide-eyed face. In the bathroom mirror, her gray-green irises were almost the color of celery. "The Dana Brush by Conair has fine nylon bristles that won't pull or tug," she gushed. "You'll notice that the tip of each one is carefully rounded for your comfort." Dana ran her hand over the bristles, mesmerized by the way they bent and bounced back. "And they're *flexible*," she added, punching the word as if it were a new invention. "Plus, the unisex handle makes it—"

"What are you doing in there?" Megan called.

"Rehearsing!"

"You don't need to rehearse. Just shower!"

As Dana stood beneath the velvety rushing water, the reality of her situation started to break through the fog. She really did need this job. Needed the hell out of it. And if she wasn't so stoned and drunk she might even have half a chance at getting it.

"Hurry!" Megan said as Dana toweled her hair.

"I *am* hurrying."

Dana opened the medicine cabinet, took out her moisturizer, put it on the counter and stared back at the narrow shelves, zeroing in on the prescription bottle wedged between the Band-Aid Tough Strips and Secret Solid. It was Dexedrine, the ADHD medication her ex, Benjamin, took every morning. She had promised herself she would make him feel guilty as shit before returning it to him. But once he left—at her insistence—she never heard from Benjamin again.

So now here she was, staring at the solution to her problem, and wondering if it was worth the risk.

But *was* it a risk? She knew Dexedrine was a central nervous system stimulant used safely by millions of people. She also knew that it was addictive, and meant for people whose brain chemistry required the kick.

Still, it wasn't like a single pill would turn her into a speed freak. She'd done it once in college to help her pull an all-nighter, and nothing bad had happened. Hell, she'd even aced the paper she had stayed up to write.

Dana took the bottle from the shelf, held it in her hand and stared at it. She needed to think. Not an easy task when she was this high. Still, she knew there was something else. Something relevant to this decision.

Then she remembered. It had been a vow. When she took the pill in college, she had promised herself it would be just that once, to help her through an emergency.

But this was an emergency, too, wasn't it?

Dana glanced at the door. The smart thing to do was to tell Megan to go away and just crawl back into bed. But then what? She didn't even have a lousy job.

It was all so confusing.

"Coffee's almost ready," Megan called.

"I don't know if I can do this," Dana said.

"I swear to God if you don't get your shit together and go on this audition I'll never forgive you. And you'll never forgive yourself, either. Remember what happened with the Yoplait commercial? Now get dressed."

The Yoplait spot was cast by Williams Mitchell Advertising, and Dana had been scheduled to read for it. She was a no show for the audition for reasons she couldn't even remember, and later found out the client had seen her in a Liberty Mutual commercial and specifically asked for her. The part went to the odious Lisa Ann Whitney, who now had a supporting role on a hit Netflix series.

Dana pressed down on the lid of the prescription bottle and

twisted it open. Fuck Lisa Ann Whitney, she thought, and tipped a small white tablet into her hand. Just this once, she thought. And then never again. Dana ran the faucet, popped the pill into her mouth and used her hand to slurp a gulp of water.

And then, as an afterthought, she tipped out one more pill to tuck into her purse, just in case.

"Hallelujah and amen!" she said, and flipped her hair over her head to shake out the excess water. She put on a little makeup and emerged from the bathroom. She didn't feel sober—not by a long shot—but knew that the drug would kick in soon, and she would feel like she could conquer anything.

"You look better," Megan said when she saw Dana scrubbed and confident.

"I *feel* better," Dana said, her back to Megan as she slipped the extra Dexedrine into her purse. She opened the accordion door to her closet. It was a tiny studio apartment, and getting dressed with company was, by necessity, a public affair.

"That navy blue wraparound—" Megan began.

"Too dark."

"Maybe something pseudo-thriftshop-retro-ironic-hipster-mismatch," Megan offered.

Dana shook her head. "Those shopping channels don't go for uptown chic or downtown cool." She pulled a butterscotch-yellow sweater from her closet and held it in front of herself to show Megan. "They want Scarsdale PTA, but with a little edge. This is off-the-shoulder, so it's perfect."

Megan studied the sweater, her lips tight in thought. "Belted?"

"Why not?"

Megan nodded with admiration. "Reminds me of something Kitty Todd would wear."

"Kitty *who*?"

"The Shopping Channel's golden girl," Megan explained. "They call her the Pitch Queen. Outsells everyone. Viewers adore her."

Dana pulled on her sweater and tried to remember the nights she dozed off watching the station's various pitches. "What does she look like?"

Megan squinted, thinking. "Light brown hair, very pretty in an ex-sorority-girl kind of way."

"That narrows it down."

Megan struggled for more detail and shrugged.

"Skinny hips and lots of eyeliner?" Dana asked.

"That's her."

Dana turned and went back into the bathroom.

"What are you doing?" Megan asked.

"Putting on more makeup."

Dana sipped the strong coffee as they walked across town to the audition. By the time they reached the address, the caffeine and the medication had combined to create rocket fuel, and she felt like she could run straight up the building's brick wall. They got in line with the other women who were there for the audition.

"Nervous?" Megan asked.

"Not really. Not at all, actually. I'm feeling fine. Just hyper."

"Your hands are trembling."

"Damn," Dana said, and shook them out. She still had excess energy to burn, so she ran in place and did a little hand dance.

Megan stared, her brow tight. "Oh, no," she said. "You're not…" She paused and looked deep into her friend's face. "Are you coked up or something?"

"Or something," Dana said. "But relax. It's all good. I'll use the nervous energy to my advantage." Even as she said it, she felt the adrenaline coursing through her, and couldn't stop moving. She stepped from side to side to side to side.

"I thought you refused to do any drugs but weed."

"Just this once," Dana said. "I had no choice."

"I made *coffee*. You would have been fine."

"I was so stoned, Megan. And drunk. Anyway, what's done is done. And I'm okay. Really." She started stepping faster, adding more dance moves, burning off energy. "Honest. I can do this. So what if I'm a little hyper? Chatty is good, right? Hyperchatty. Chatty hyper. This line is moving so quickly. They must be throwing these girls out the second they walk in. I guess they have a particular type in mind. I wonder what they're looking for. Blond, maybe? Am I too dark? You think they want younger? Older? Am I wearing enough lipstick? Anything on my teeth? My hair looks cute, right? It would be great if I got this. I wonder what my mother would say. I wonder what my father would say. My father is—"

"You are talking *a mile a minute*," Megan said.

"Am I? But clearly, right? I'm enunciating? That's what's important."

The line advanced and before she knew it they were at the security desk, facing down a uniformed guard with white hair, doughy cheeks and a determined scowl. He wasn't the least bit charmed by the line of pretty women streaming past his desk, and seemed to regard each as a potential terrorist. His name badge said J. Beecham.

"Twenty bucks if you can make that guy smile," Megan whispered to Dana.

It was meant as a joke, but as soon as Dana was confronted by the surly security guard, she knew she had to take the challenge. After he examined her driver's license, looked through her purse and dismissed her, she pointed to the Dunkin' Donuts cup on the table behind him.

"That yours?" she asked.

"What about it?"

Dana rummaged through her handbag and extracted a five-dollar Dunkin' Donuts gift card she'd received for taking a mall survey. "I've been looking for someone to give this to," she said. It wasn't true—she'd been saving it to treat herself to a sugar rush after her next good audition.

The man looked at her. "'Scuse me?"

"I got it as a gift but I never go to Dunkin' Donuts."

He took the card from her and studied it as if suspicious it might be the work of a master forger. Dana tried to imagine such a person as a member of a band of thieves, desperate and sugar-starved, dedicated to defrauding the doughnut industry. The movie version would star George Clooney and Brad Pitt, and be called *Baker's Dozen*.

Beecham's face softened. "You sure, miss?"

"My pleasure," she said, beaming, as if nothing could make her happier.

He slipped the card into his breast pocket and tapped it. "Thanks, Ms.—" he paused to look at her signature in the visitors' log "—Barry. Appreciate it." And then he smiled, revealing small yellowing teeth.

"I can't believe you sacrificed doughnuts for a bet," Megan said when they were out of earshot.

"Who said anything about sacrifice?" Dana said. "I'm up fifteen bucks." She held out her hand and Megan slapped in a twenty.

"If you get the job, will you use it to treat me to a doughnut?"

"In Paris."

They followed the crowd inside and Megan handed Dana's headshot and résumé to a young woman so perky she could only be an intern. They were ushered into a waiting room with a dozen crisply dressed young women, all in black except for one other brunette in a butterscotch, off-the-shoulder sweater. A beauty model, Dana thought. With drop-dead gorgeous curves and a face like Catherine Zeta-Jones.

Dana bit her lip and Megan patted her hand. "As long as you go in before her, you'll be okay."

The intern walked back into the room with a clipboard. "Tammy O'Neill?" she called.

Dana glanced around the room, hoping one of the black-clad women would respond. But they crossed and uncrossed their legs, stared at their cell phones.

"I'm Tammy," said the luscious sweater girl.

Dana's face fell. "What am I going to do?" she whispered.

"Easy," Megan said. "Surprise them."

2

Easy? Dana thought as she looked down at the ugliest piece of jewelry she had ever seen. She had been ushered into a soundstage labeled Studio C and put behind a table with a single malachite ring on display. It was hideous. Like a cheap prop from a play about pirate booty—something that would look ornate even from the rafters. The green-striped stone was round and large, set high inside a brass circle inlaid with spiky dark gems of indistinguishable origin. If that wasn't bad enough, the striated stone and brass setting were based on a shank of rose gold. It clashed so loudly it clanged, and was almost painful to look at.

There was no script, and prospective hosts were expected to ad-lib. Dana knew she could do a passable job of gushing over the elements of the ring as if it were the very thing that would make any woman's life complete. But she also knew that just about every person auditioning could do the same thing. And if voluptuous Catherine Zeta-Jones had been even halfway decent at it, she was toast.

The house lights were still on, so Dana could see the death panel of judges sitting in a row of director's chairs before her. There was a sharp-jawed woman in glasses, wearing a floral print blouse and dark slacks. She had the fierce-eyed look of a casting director, desperately underfed and ready to fight anyone who went against her expert opinion on the talent in question. Next to her was an alert assistant in black, holding a stack of folders and a tablet. A large man in an expensive suit sat on the other end. He was sixty-ish, African American, with a club tie and a small lapel pin. Though she wasn't close enough to smell him, Dana sensed expensive cologne. This guy was senior management. Maybe even the president or CEO. And in the middle was the star herself, Kitty Todd. The woman every suburban housewife aspired to be. Her silky hair was shoulder-length, subtly highlighted and turned adorably out at the edges. She wore a blue dress today, richly hued, with a sculpted neckline that emphasized her collarbones. It fit like it was made for her, which it almost certainly was.

A wiry tattooed guy in a black T-shirt and jeans approached Dana to hook up her mike. She held her head back as he threaded the wire under her sweater—a potentially awkward moment that hadn't fazed her for years.

"Maybe we should be introduced," she said.

He snorted an appreciative laugh as he clipped the tiny mike to the front of her sweater. "I'm Lorenzo," he said in a gravelly voice that suggested a guy who had substituted cigarettes for a less legal substance. He had an intense energy about him.

"What do they call you?" she asked, thinking he seemed like someone who would have a nickname like Mustang or Spike. The kind of name they gave to someone who was wrapped just a little too tight.

"To my face or behind my back?" he asked, and she decided immediately that she liked him.

"I take it this isn't on?" she said, pointing to her mike.

"Not yet."

"I'm Dana," she said. "Can I ask you something?"

He looked at her with eyes as dark and earnest as Lin-Manuel Miranda's. She felt like he was someone she could trust.

"Do you have a comb on you?" she whispered.

"You look fine," he said.

"It's not that." She took a quick glance around the studio, and spotted a stocky man in coveralls pushing a large broom behind the stage. He had shiny black hair combed neatly back.

"What's that guy's name?" she asked, pointing with her chin.

Lorenzo glanced over. "That's Hector."

She smiled a thanks before he turned on her mike and backed away.

"Are you ready, Ms. Barry?" asked the woman in glasses.

"Just a moment," Dana said. "I have to ask Hector a question."

"Who the hell is *Hector*?" said Kitty Todd, pronouncing the name like it had something sticking to it.

Dana turned to the man with the broom and called his name. He was so surprised to be addressed it took a moment to get his attention.

"Can I borrow your comb?" Dana asked.

The woman in glasses sighed, exasperated, and whispered something that sounded like, "Diva." Kitty Todd took the opportunity to answer a call from the cell phone brought to her by a young male assistant with blond hair. *Natural* blond hair. He looked like a grown-up version of a Hanna Andersson catalog model.

Just as Dana expected, Hector had a small black comb in his pocket. "Thank you," she said when he handed it to her. "I'll give it back when I'm done."

Hector shrugged and went back to his post. Dana pushed the offensive ring to the side and set the comb on the display box. Then she waited for the attention of Kitty Todd, who was still on the phone, but now moisturizing her pretty hands while her assistant stood by, holding her rings. Hands, Dana realized, were the most valuable tool for a TV shopping hostess, and she hoped her days-old manicure wouldn't be a problem. At last, Kitty finished her call, slipped her rings back on and turned her attention to Dana, who took a deep breath. *Kill this*, she coached herself. *Just fucking kill it.* And then she launched herself, aiming straight for the moon.

"I'm Dana Barry," she said in a bright voice as she looked directly into the audition camera. "Thank you for joining us for today's special, which is the *one* beauty product *every* woman with *every* hair type must have. The sixty-eight-tooth Hector Comb is virtually *unbreakable* and comes with a lifetime guarantee. Think about that! How many products do you own that will last a lifetime? And I'm talking about a product you'll use every single day! It works on short hair, it works on long hair, it works on blond hair and brown hair and black hair and red hair. It works on thick hair and thin hair. And look at the construction. Can I get a close-up, please? This is one solid piece of tested polycarbonate. The teeth are not glued or fitted together. And that's what makes it indestructible."

Dana paused to pick up the comb, and demonstrate what it took to bend it.

"You'll see that it's engineered to have some give so that it's not brittle." She slammed it against the side of the table and then held it up to the camera to show that it was still in one piece, and gave a small laugh, as if she were taking the viewer right inside her own incredulousness at the wonder of this gift from the heavens. "You can't break it even if you *try*!"

Dana took a breath, encouraged that no one had stopped her yet. She hoped it meant they were impressed.

"Now," she said, using it to comb through a lock of her

hair, "I want you to notice that the tapered ends of the teeth make the Hector Comb glide perfectly through my hair. But it also works as a spiking tool." At that, she used the comb to lift the short hair on top of her head.

"Oh!" she said, looking up as if she were reading live sales numbers from one of the black screens facing her. "We've already sold two thousand units! I'm thrilled so many of you are taking advantage of this incredible value. At $19.99—and available on our Easy-Bucks option for five dollars a month—it's something you'll want to grab before we're sold out. And while you're at it, get one for a friend, because everyone who cares about looking good will love having this remarkable, unbreakable, tapered-tooth marvel of hairstyling engineering. And, ladies…it's *portable*!" Dana punched the word with near-hysteria, and hoped she hadn't gone too far. "That's right. The Hector Comb fits into your pocket, into your purse, into your backpack. If you're like me and you've struggled to fit your beauty essentials into a tiny evening bag, you'll appreciate that this takes up less room than a compact!"

Dana stopped for a breath, ready to ramble for as long as they would let her. She went on to talk about the polished smoothness of the teeth, fudging facts about the molecular structure of polycarbonate plastic, explaining why it didn't create static, no matter how often you combed your hair. She laughed charmingly as she recounted stories of embarrassing flyaways from other products. Since she didn't have a selection of colors to offer, she marveled at the richness of the black plastic, tilting it to demonstrate how it reflected light like a gem. She gushed over the striking concept that it went *with absolutely everything*. She repeated the price, gave a made-up phone number, recounted stories of friends who bought the Hector Comb and didn't know how they had ever lived without it. Dana amazed even herself at all the things she found to say about the comb, and was struck by the utter silence in the studio. Her gut sense was that they were more awed than bored, but she didn't trust her perception. Not with the drugs still having a party with her neurotransmitters.

Intent on keeping her spot lively, she decided to switch things up and start pulling people from offstage so she could demonstrate that it worked for every type of hair, even as a pick for curly and Afro styles that didn't require combing.

"I have some friends in the studio who would—"

"Thank you, Ms. Barry!" called the woman in the glasses, and Dana swallowed hard. They had let her go longer than she expected, but it was such an abrupt interruption it sounded like a curt dismissal.

The stage lights dimmed and Kitty Todd rose from her chair without even glancing Dana's way. Her male assistant came scurrying over, and the two of them headed toward the door.

"Thanks for the opportunity," Dana said. "If you have any questions—"

Kitty held up a hand to silence her, and Dana could do nothing but watch as the pretty young man opened the door for his imperious boss. She paused there, framed and backlit, and turned to the woman in glasses.

"Did you need something, Kitty?" the woman asked.

"This one," Kitty said, pointing to Dana. "Hire this one."

And that was it. The door closed behind her, and all Dana could hear was the swoosh-swoosh-swoosh of Hector's broom.

3

"Are you listening to me?" Megan asked as they walked back from the studio.

It was late afternoon, and the sun had retreated behind low clouds. Dana hunched against a breeze pushing from behind, reminding her that April weather could be capricious in New York. "I'm listening," she said. "You don't want me to get my hopes up."

She knew Megan was trying to manage her expectations, but it was a useless effort. That was just the way it was with auditions. The waiting was always a maddening game of mental Ping-Pong, as she bounced from joyous hope to agonizing despair and back again. And no matter which side of the court she was on when she got the call, the rejection stung like a paddle to the face.

"Kitty Todd may think the world revolves around her," Megan said, "but she isn't the decision-maker here. That's Sherry Zidel."

Dana played back the scene, trying to make sense of what happened after the door shut behind the Shopping Channel's biggest star. Nobody moved, and tension hung in the air like the conspicuous smoke of a fog machine. Then the woman in the glasses broke the spell. She adjusted her frames and thanked Dana for coming in. Her expression had remained stoic, inscrutable.

"Is she the casting director?" Dana asked.

"She's the supervising producer, actually, but your instincts are spot-on—she started in casting. I asked around about her. A tremendous pain in the ass apparently. Takes the bottom line very seriously. Too seriously. Like a dominatrix with a spreadsheet in one hand and a whip in the other."

"What about the guy in the suit?"

"Charles Honeycutt, company president. He has to sign off on hires, but I think he defers to Sherry's judgment."

Dana was impressed. She hadn't taken it that literally when she agreed to let Megan be her manager. But her friend was all in, and definitely doing more than her agent ever had.

"What did she say to you?" Dana asked. "Did she like me? Did she blow you off?"

"She didn't say anything. Just that they'd be in touch."

Dana stopped and grabbed Megan's arm. "That they'd be in touch?"

"Don't read anything into it."

"But that's a good sign!"

"You'll make yourself crazy, Dana. You know how these things go."

She did. Even *sure things* weren't sure things. And this was far from a sure thing. She released her friend's arm and they trudged on, hurrying against the cold until they reached Dana's apartment building. As they got ready to part, Dana thanked Megan for landing her the audition.

Megan waved it away. "Thank me if you get the job."

Dana rubbed her friend's arm, admiring the soft back and forth of the suede.

"I know," Megan said, feeling it herself. "It's a great jacket."

"Even has a place to keep your hands warm." Dana felt one of the pockets, pretending to admire it as she deftly slipped a folded-up twenty-dollar bill from her palm to her fingertips to the silky interior. She couldn't bear to keep her friend's hard-earned money.

Megan was oblivious. "I'll call you the second I hear anything," she said.

Dana fished in her purse for her keys. "If you value your life."

The next day was Dana's sister's birthday, and they had plans for lunch. Dana usually looked forward to spending time with her sister, but she knew Chelsea would ask how things were going on the job, and Dana would have to admit she'd been fired for attitude from a place that *sold* attitude. Talk about a hot topic. It was humiliating.

Dana wondered if she would be able to steer the conversation in a different direction by leading with the story of yesterday's audition. Her sister was a shopping addict, and the very idea would light her up like Nordstrom's in December. If Dana tossed Kitty's pronouncement in the air as if aiming for the wastebasket, Chelsea might snatch it and insist the news was worth examining. *You need to have more confidence,* she might say. *I really think you have a shot.*

Hell, Dana might even believe her.

She got off the train in Roslyn, Long Island, and took a taxi to her sister's home, which Dana had affectionately dubbed the House of Seventeen Gables, due to the abundance of rooflines. Dana had noticed that this style of architecture had been invading suburbia like well-financed dandelions.

She rang the bell and her sister pulled open the door. Instead of saying hello, Chelsea took in Dana's outfit—a concert T-shirt, distressed jeans, combat boots and faded leather jacket—and said, "I thought we were going to Café Rose-mary."

"We are!" Dana said brightly, realizing she shouldn't have tried so hard to look the part of the defiant younger sister. "But thank you for the warm welcome."

Chelsea shook her head and gave Dana an affectionate hug. "Never mind. I can lend you a cardigan, loser."

Dana didn't take offense. In fact, teasing was the way they showed affection. "Fuck you very much," she said, hugging her sister back. "And happy birthday, by the way. I bought you an ugly scarf."

"I'm sure I'll love it," Chelsea said, and led Dana into the house.

Wesley, the three-year-old, was at his afternoon nursery school program, so the house was quiet. Or mostly quiet. Dana could hear the housekeeper upstairs moving a vacuum back and forth. She didn't hear the au pair, but Dana assumed she was around, as well. Her sister had staff.

She also had stuff. A lot of stuff. Chelsea wasn't merely a rich woman who could afford to indulge. She was compulsive. A casual visitor wouldn't know it to look at the house, which was orderly and pristine, but Dana knew the truth. There was a brightly lit underbelly that displayed the naked shame of her sister's hoarding. It was the finished basement—Chelsea's husband's concession to her habit. The walls were lined with massive shelving racks—the kind people put in their garages. But Chelsea's shelves held stacks of sweaters, rows of boots, entire lines of designer purses, winter coats Wesley would eventually grow into and lifetime supplies of anything nonperishable, such as school supplies, laundry detergent, dryer sheets, paper towels, deodorant, toothbrushes, Swiffer refills, bathroom cleaner, toilet paper, disposable razors, toner cartridges, batteries, shampoo, panty liners, tampons and cases of Diet

Coke. She had backup hair dryers and toaster ovens to replace the appliances when they eventually gave out. There were also items she held on to as future gifts, such as pots and pans sets, luggage, baby clothes, jewelry, perfume, scented candles, silver picture frames and even a few musical instruments. There was an entire shelf of gift sets from Bath and Body Works, and another of designer jeans, organized by hue.

Despite all this, Chelsea wasn't hard to shop for. Sure, she was a woman who, almost literally, had everything. But Dana understood that Chelsea simply loved new things. So no matter how much stuff she got, more stuff always made her happy.

Dana handed her sister the slim box containing the silk scarf she had picked out, and Chelsea accepted it with an enthusiastic smile.

They sat at the kitchen island and Chelsea tore into the wrapping paper. She lifted the lid off the box and gasped in delight at the sight of the softly colored scarf. "Oh my God," she said, holding it up to her shirt, because the match was uncanny. The scarf was a blue-on-blue pattern threaded with delicate lines of turquoise that perfectly matched Chelsea's top. "You're like a witch!" She tied it expertly around her neck. "What do you think?"

Chelsea's joy lifted Dana's mood. It wasn't just because she was glad her sister liked the scarf, but because this meant she was less likely to try to make Dana feel like shit for getting fired from a job that required little more than the ability to remain upright.

"Great," Dana said. "I'm glad you like it."

Chelsea looked at the clock on the wall oven and seemed alarmed by the time. "Oh! We have to go."

"What's the hurry?" Dana asked. She knew they didn't have a reservation.

Chelsea bit her lip and sighed. "Dad is meeting us there."

The bottom fell right out of Dana's mood. "Dad?" she asked. "Why? I thought we were just going to—"

"I'm sorry," Chelsea interrupted. "He called this morning to wish me a happy birthday and asked what I was doing for lunch. What could I say? 'I'm meeting Dana but you're not invited because we'd rather have a human conversation'?"

"To start," Dana suggested. She still hadn't adjusted to her father's retirement. Who the hell was this man who suddenly had time for them? Well, time for Chelsea, anyway. Dana didn't count since she was unsuccessful and struggling financially. Kenneth Barry had little tolerance for the unwealthy. He took it as a moral failing.

"Well, I couldn't," Chelsea said.

Dana's shoulders dropped as she frowned in thought. Now she had to rethink her entire strategy. And fast.

"Listen," she said, "before we go, I have to tell you something. I lost my job at Hot Topic, but I don't want Dad to know. So could you please not bring it up at lunch?"

"You got fired?"

"Yes, but—"

"From Hot Topic?"

And here it comes, she thought. "Well, that's where I worked."

"What did you have to do to get fired from that place? Set it on fire? For shit's sake, Dana, how are you going to pay your rent? Your student loans? You know Brandon said I couldn't give you any more—"

"Don't have a fit. I'm not asking for money." It was excruciating—the thought that Brandon and Chelsea had actually had conversations about her loser sister, conversations that probably mirrored her father's philosophy. Handouts were dangerous and would only make her dependent. But of course her father took it a step further. Handouts were okay if you were already successful. In fact, he had always promised to pay back Dana's student loans if she ever got a decent job. As long as she was struggling, she was on her own.

"Don't tell me not to have a fit," Chelsea said. "I'm worried about you."

"I can always get another horrible job."

"Will you be able to make it until then? Do you have anything set aside?"

"Relax. I can always sell crack or prostitute myself."

"This isn't *funny*, Dana." Chelsea looked genuinely distraught. "What happened at the store?"

Dana let out a sigh. "It doesn't matter. It was a ridiculous job for me. And the pay sucked. Besides…" Dana trailed off, wondering if the timing was right to tell Chelsea about the Shopping Channel.

"Besides what?"

"I might have something else. It's not a sure thing, but—"

"An audition? Please don't tell me it's an audition."

Dana sighed. "Thanks for the vote of confidence."

"You know what I mean."

She did. Her booking ratio with auditions was one in twenty. That was about average for actresses in New York. But to her sister, it simply meant that Dana failed ninety-five percent of the time.

"We'd better get going," Dana said, hoping Chelsea's mood would lift when they got to the restaurant. This was simply not the time to go into detail about the Shopping Channel audition.

"Do you want to borrow a cardigan?" Chelsea asked.

Dana shot her sister a look.

Chelsea shrugged and pulled a bottle of Advil from the top shelf in a kitchen cabinet.

"You okay?" Dana asked.

"I have a headache."

Dana opened her palm toward her sister.

"You, too?" Chelsea asked.

"We're meeting Dad, aren't we?"

And so the Barry sisters took painkillers and headed off to meet their father for lunch.

4

By the time they arrived, Kenneth Barry was already seated, a glass of Scotch in front of him. He was wearing a fine-gauge cotton sweater in pale salmon, which Dana thought made him look almost human. His angular cheekbones had softened since retirement, and he looked ruddy and healthy. A testament to all those extra hours on the green.

They kissed him hello, and Dana noticed that he was wearing more aftershave than usual. Her father normally smelled like soap or, if it was after work, like something vaguely sterile and Band-Aid-y.

"What's going on, Dad?" Dana asked. "You smell good."

"Don't be funny," he said.

It was one of his favorite comebacks. The other was *Don't be childish*. As usual, she was tempted to respond by sticking her hand under her arm and making a fart noise.

They took their seats, and Kenneth put a small gift on the table in front of Chelsea. It looked like a jewelry box, and Dana tensed. She didn't like to indulge in petty sibling rivalry, but come on. Jewelry? For Dana's last birthday, Kenneth had made a production of presenting her with a book called *Success and the Single Girl*. It was a life guide on how to get a better job and a better guy. Most of the advice centered on wardrobe choices. She wondered why no one wrote self-help books for retired neurosurgeons who still taught part-time at Columbia and had more intimate relationships with cells on a slide than with human beings, and who couldn't even manage a single date after their wives left them and moved down to Florida and remarried.

"I love it," Chelsea said after discovering a bracelet inside the box. She held it up to show Dana, who was surprised by the taste level. It was a stylish silver charm bracelet, very on trend.

"Beautiful," Dana said, impressed.

"Thank you, Daddy," Chelsea said, and held out her wrist for Dana to help with the clasp.

"I might have had a little help picking it out," Kenneth said, his lips doing something that looked vaguely like a smile.

Dana stared at him. This wasn't the kind of thing her father said. It was self-effacing and almost…charming.

Chelsea seemed unfazed. "Salesladies always liked you," she said.

"Of course they like him," Dana said. "They know money when they smell it."

Chelsea gave her a reprimanding look.

"Not a saleslady," Kenneth said, ignoring the dig. "A friend." He took a sip of his drink. "A *lady* friend."

Dana's and Chelsea's jaws unhinged simultaneously.

"You have a *girlfriend*?" Chelsea said.

Kenneth gently put down his glass. "I do."

Dana sat back in her chair. Now it made sense—the handsome sweater, the aftershave. But the thought of it almost made her dizzy. Her father with a woman? A woman who actually liked him? She couldn't imagine how he had managed it.

"Who is she?" Dana asked. "What does she do?"

"Her name is Jennifer Lafferty."

"Jennifer?" Dana said. "She sounds too young for you."

"She's forty-two."

"Ew, Daddy," Chelsea said. "That's a twenty-two-year difference."

Dana knew that Chelsea was probably getting the same image she was—a collagen-lipped barfly in a low-cut top who had been sifting around for decades and finally hit pay dirt.

"She's a lovely lady," Kenneth said.

"Where did you meet her?" Chelsea asked.

"That's a private matter," he said.

Chelsea gave Dana a look that said, *This is getting weird.*

"What's the big secret?" Dana said. "Is she a stripper or something?"

"She's a cardiothoracic surgeon."

Dana stared at his expression to make sure he wasn't kidding. He was, as usual, as serious as a glioblastoma. And just like that, it all made sense. He had found a fellow automaton. A doctor nerd. She imagined them sitting side by side on a lazy Sunday morning reading peer-reviewed medical journals.

"So what's the big secret about how you met?" Dana asked, assuming they had been set up on a blind date by a colleague.

"Never mind," Kenneth said.

Chelsea grabbed her arm, a smile spreading as something dawned on her. "I bet I know!" she said. "It was a dating site! That's it." She turned to their father. "I'm right, aren't I? You met online. That's why you're embarrassed."

Their father exhaled through his nose and tented his fingers, as if dealing with a subject that required intense concentration. "Many people meet online."

Dana shook her head as she tried to imagine her father with a Match.com profile. What on earth could he have said about himself to make him sound appealing? *I like long walks on the beach, prescribing MRIs and making people feel insignificant.*

"We should order," Kenneth said, picking up the menu. And that was the end of the conversation about Jennifer Lafferty.

When the waitress arrived, she wrote down their order and Kenneth asked her to read it back to him.

"I got it, sir!" she chirped, smiling.

He folded his arms. "Humor me."

"Dad, she's got it," Dana said. "Chill."

"Let's be sure," he said, and looked back at the waitress. "Go on."

The young woman hesitated, as if it might be some kind of a joke. But Kenneth just stared, like he was prepared to grade her performance, and the waitress's smile dissolved. She read back the order, nervous enough to stumble over a few words, and he was oblivious to her discomfort.

After she left, Dana turned to her father. "Why do you have to do that? Why can't you show people a little respect?"

"You want me to respect a *waitress*?"

"Would it kill you?"

He let out a breath. "Tell me what's going on with you at that clothing store. Have they promoted you yet?"

Chelsea kicked her under the table.

"Not quite," Dana said. "But yesterday I auditioned for the Shopping Channel."

"The Shopping Channel?" Chelsea said, her face lighting up, just as Dana had expected. "Why didn't you tell me? Do you think you have a shot?"

"Explain," Kenneth said. "This place hires actresses?"

"On-air hosts," Dana said. "To describe the merchandise and get people to buy it."

Her father was unimpressed. "Like what you do at the store, but on TV."

"Oh, Daddy. It's much better than that," Chelsea said. She turned to Dana. "What was the audition like?"

"They wanted me to describe this big, ugly malachite ring. I guess that was the challenge—to try to make it sound appealing. But I didn't do that. I described a comb."

"A comb?"

"A little black comb. I got it from one of the guys on the set. I figured anybody could do ten minutes on a ring, but I wanted to show that I could take something so ordinary and make it sound exciting."

"Would it have killed you to follow the rules for once?" Kenneth said.

Dana dismissed him with a wave and addressed her sister. "Do you know who Kitty Todd is?"

Chelsea gasped. "I love her!"

"She was there. And after my audition she turned to the company president and said—"

"The president?" Kenneth said, as if it were the only word she spoke worthy of consideration.

Dana almost laughed. He was so predictable. "Yes, the president. She turned to the company president and said, 'Hire her. Hire this one.'"

"She *didn't!*" Chelsea said, her enthusiasm in hyperdrive.

"But I don't want to get my hopes up," Dana said, counting on Chelsea to put up an argument. "You never know with auditions."

"I think you're going to get it," Chelsea said, and turned to their father. "Don't you, Daddy?"

"Does this mean you would give up that...drama club?"

Dana clamped her jaw to keep from exploding. "Theater group," she said through her teeth. "A well-respected theater group. *Not* a drama club." She hated that he was so intentionally obtuse about it. The Sweat City Company had been the most important thing in her life for the past five years. They performed experimental plays in a small theater downtown, and they were the most talented, generous and dedicated group of people she had ever known. "And no," she added. "I would never give it up."

The waitress brought their food, and the conversation went back to the Shopping Channel, with Chelsea sharing her expertise on the difference between the three major players in the field. When the topic was exhausted, the sisters went back to pressing their father on the details of his relationship. They learned that Jennifer Lafferty lived in Manhattan and they saw each other every Saturday night and on occasional Wednesdays, when Jennifer wasn't on call. He went out of his way to mention that, like him, she had invested wisely. It took Dana a moment to process why he had shared that particular information, and then she got it. He wanted to make it clear she was interested in him, not his money.

As they were finishing their meal, Dana's cell phone rang. She glanced at the caller ID. It was Megan, and she broke into a sweat. Could good news come this fast? Could bad news? It certainly had in the past. Then again, maybe Megan just wanted to know if Dana was free to go jeans shopping, which she did more frequently than most people bought milk. A flattering pair of jeans was Megan's Holy Grail.

As her father snapped his fingers at the waitress, indicating that he wanted a cup of coffee, Dana answered her phone.

"You got it," Megan said triumphantly.

"What?" Dana was sure she misheard.

"I said you got it. The Shopping Channel."

"Are you kidding?"

"Just to be clear—they're giving you a chance to go on air

and see how the viewers respond. But you're the only one who got the call, so it's practically a formality. If all goes well, they'll draw up a contract."

It took Dana a moment to find her voice. "When is this happening?" she managed to say.

"Brace yourself," Megan said. "It's tomorrow."

Tomorrow? Dana's heart thudded with excitement. And nerves. So much was riding on this.

After getting the details, she ended the call and sat back in her chair, numb. She could hardly believe it was happening. Not many actresses got a chance like this—a steady gig, regular hours, high pay, national exposure. Talk about a big break. It was almost too good to be true.

"You okay?" Chelsea asked her.

Her father's brow knitted in medical curiosity as he stared at her, as if searching for a diagnosis.

Dana looked at the two of them, considering exactly what to say. She could, of course, tell them nothing. But this opportunity to impress them—okay, *him*—was as golden as a polished malachite ring under a sparkling spotlight.

"I got the Shopping Channel job," she said, and swallowed hard, because it wasn't exactly true—there was still one more hurdle to cross. But if she had qualified the statement, saying, *I think I have it* or *I might have it*, the news would have landed with a thud, and her father would dismiss it as wishful thinking. But this. This would impress him.

He picked up a napkin and wiped his mouth. "Where's that girl with my coffee?"

5

The next day, Dana awoke so nervous she spent the morning going back and forth on whether it was wise to take a few hits off a joint to mellow her out. She knew she shouldn't. She knew she was perfectly capable of performing sober. In fact, she had spent her whole career performing sober. Or most of it. There was that one time she had a gig on a cruise ship playing Louise from *Gypsy* and downed three shots of tequila just to impress a gorgeous, swarthy steward who wound up sleeping with the girl who played Mazeppa. But this was different. This was pressure. Real-life pressure. She had about two months' worth of rent saved up, and once that was gone she was out of luck.

She had the joint in her hand and was staring at her lighter when Megan rang her buzzer. Dana hesitated. It would be so easy to ignite that tiny flame and take one quick toke.

You are not a child, she told herself. *This is a grown-up job and you need to make a grown-up decision.* Megan buzzed again and Dana pressed the intercom button. "I'll be right down," she said, and slipped the joint back into the secret compartment on her key-chain fob, which appeared to be nothing more than a silver charm in the shape of a dachshund. The tiny white Dexedrine pill already rested inside.

It was raining, so they took a cab to the studio—a seven-story brick building on West Fifty-Fifth Street near the Hudson River. After they passed through security—and Dana got another smile from the cantankerous Mr. Beecham—Megan went off to meet with Sherry Zidel, Charles Honeycutt and whoever else was involved in contract negotiations, while Dana was whisked off to the makeup department by a cherub-faced girl named Jessalyn, who then vanished.

Dana tried to slow her breathing as one woman applied her makeup and another rolled over a stool and began inspecting her nails.

"Not too bad," said the manicurist, leveling her eye on a troublesome cuticle. "We can wawkwiddis."

It took Dana a second to process that *wawkwiddis* was *work with this*. She didn't think it was possible for someone to have a thicker Queens accent than Cyndi Lauper, but this woman managed it. Dana listened carefully, in case she ever wanted to appropriate it for a role.

She learned that the manicurist's name was Jo, and the makeup girl was Felicia.

"Would it be okay if I had a French manicure?" Dana said to Jo.

"Sorry," the manicurist said as she removed Dana's old polish with a saturated cotton ball. "I'll give you pale pink. Only Kitty gets French. It's in her contract."

"You've got to be kidding," Dana said, and immediately wished she hadn't. The last thing she needed was a reputation for being hostile toward the star.

"The worst part?" Jo said. "Her nails is so weak, and she won't let me do gel, won't let me wrap them. Nothing."

"And she has her own makeup box," said Felicia. "With her own special false eyelashes. Extralong. No one else gets them."

Dana was starved for gossip—and knew these ladies had the goods—but she had to be cagey in case her comments got back to Kitty. "Success has its privileges, I guess."

"And she grabs 'em like M&M's," muttered Jo.

"And wouldn't share if you was starving," Felicia added as she dabbed concealer under Dana's eyes.

Dana burned with curiosity. This was getting interesting. "I don't know much about her, but she went to bat for me at my audition."

It was shameless fishing. Felicia and Jo shared a look.

"What?" Dana said.

"Do yourself a favor and be careful 'round her," Felicia said.

"And ask yourself why Vanessa Valdes got canned," Jo added.

Canned? As Megan had explained it, Vanessa Valdes was the woman whose Shopping Channel program aired just before Kitty's. Soon, she would be leaving for a coanchor spot on a local news show in San Antonio, and if all went well with Dana's short segment today, the job would be hers.

"I thought she found greener pastures," Dana said. Megan had told her Vanessa had good sales numbers, so she just assumed she was leaving of her own accord.

"Ha!" Felicia said as she brushed a sweep of blush on Dana's cheek. "She's leaving because Kitty wants her out."

Jo nodded. "Her ratings were slipping, and that pissed off Kitty, because her show comes on right after."

Dana looked from one woman to the other. "Why were her ratings slipping?"

"*I* think it was scheduling changes on the networks," Jo said, stretching the word *I* like Coney Island taffy. "*Ellen* was put in a competing time slot in a few markets, so you know, that's pretty tough. But Kitty don't give a shit."

Dana had to suppress a smile. In the entertainment industry, everyone was a marketing expert—from the accountants to the caterers.

The door opened and a slender-necked young man in a white smock appeared. He had spiky, powder-colored hair tipped in pink, incongruous against his dark skin. He looked like a more feminine version of Thandie Newton. Before approaching Dana, he studied her, his arms folded thoughtfully. Then he leaned over Jo and lifted one of the short locks on the top of Dana's head. He had the perfume-y smell of hair products.

"We have to talk about this cut," he said.

"Something wrong with it?" Dana asked.

He made a face. "It looks a little...*schnauzer-y*."

"It does?" Dana couldn't mask the hurt. She thought her short hair was kind of cool.

"Don't worry, love. I'm really good."

"He does Kitty," Felicia said.

The hairdresser put his hand to his heart as if Felicia had made a shocking sexual suggestion. "In her dreams, girl," he said.

"Kitty's not his type," Felicia explained, as if Dana hadn't already figured that out.

"But is he *her* type?" Jo said pointedly. "That's all that counts."

The hairdresser laid a hand on Dana's shoulder. "Kitty tends to get what she wants. I'm Robért by the way. And I have the dubious distinction of being a male employee who *hasn't* slept with her highness."

"I'm Dana," she said. "And this is getting really juicy."

"Girl, you haven't heard the half of it."

★ ★ ★

After hair and makeup, Dana was whisked off to wardrobe, where she was shown the sleeveless Bastina maxidresses that would be sold during her segment.

"They like you should wear one of these," said Irini, the wardrobe lady, in a heavy Greek accent.

It was offered in four very different prints, and had lovely lines. Dana studied each of them, though she knew immediately which would look best on her—the navy multi that was vaguely Moroccan. She slipped it on and the microfiber knit did its magic, conforming immediately to her subtle curves. Irini produced an array of shoe choices, but zeroed in on a jeweled sandal that was just right.

"Bastina will be so happy," Irini said as she took in Dana's full length. "You look beautiful."

Dana thanked her, and Irini added, "Be careful for that Kitty Todd. She's not kind woman."

"I will," Dana said, and wondered if there was anyone at the Shopping Channel who wasn't terrified of Kitty.

When she left wardrobe, Dana saw a familiar face—it was Lorenzo, the sound guy she had met at the audition. He had been sent to bring her to her next stop—an unused set where she would get a crash course on everything a Shopping Channel host needed to know. He asked how it was going.

"So far," she said, "I feel like I'm getting a master's degree in Kitty Todd."

"I'll save you some time on your thesis," he said, leading her down a long hallway toward the lobby. "There's only one thing you need to know about Kitty—she gets what she wants."

"So I heard," she said. "But it sounds like you speak from experience—like you may have a Kitty Todd story of your own."

"Who doesn't?"

"Tell me," she said.

He set his jaw, reticent. She could tell he was someone who didn't share easily.

"You can trust me," she added.

He exhaled. "Okay. One time her mike went out during a broadcast. Bad cable—happens sometimes. We switched it out in about three seconds, but after the show she acted like I'd been trying to sabotage her. She went on a fifteen-minute rant in front of the whole crew." His eyes went tense as he remembered.

"That's kind of...deranged."

"It helps if you know how to handle her."

"Which is?"

"Just let her have her tantrum and move on."

"You sound like a pro."

"I've dealt with people who would eat Kitty Todd for dinner and swallow the bones," he said, trying to sound casual. But Dana sensed that he wasn't kidding. This guy had some dark characters in his past.

He brought Dana to an unused studio where she received a tutorial from Jessalyn Grage, who seemed to take great pride in her efficiency as talent coordinator, and Adam Weintraub, a segment producer whom Dana pegged as a new dad. He smelled like baby food and was a little disheveled, with a sticky patch of something on his shoulder that had trapped one of his wife's long hairs. At least she assumed it was his wife's, as his hair was dark and curly, and a baby's would be short.

Jessalyn struck her as single and ambitious, but not in a ruthless kind of way. Just the kind of hardworking young woman who was willing to go the extra mile to prove herself. Dana suspected her ambition was to be promoted to segment producer.

The two of them led Dana through everything she needed to know. She was taught the importance of looking straight into the camera, even when she was describing the merchandise. For every segment there was either a pitch chart, which was really a giant poster listing the key selling points of whatever product was currently on display, or a color chart, complete with swatches and their corresponding names. These were never simple words like *red*, *white* and *blue*, but marketing terms like *raspberry cream*, *summer linen* and *deep sky*. There were also three monitors she had to keep an eye on. One showed what the viewers were seeing and another showed what the next shot would be. But the most critical monitor was the one that let her know exactly how viewers were reacting to her pitch. She could see, in real time, whether she was moving merchandise. This was life and death on the Shopping Channel.

Still, Adam didn't want her to focus on it. "It'll make you crazy," he said. "Just do your job. I'll be the voice in your earpiece and will let you know if your pitch is working or not."

Her head crammed with information, Dana was taken to the set where Vanessa Valdes was broadcasting live, selling a line of brightly colored spring tops. Bastina, the designer, was at her side. Vanessa was good—natural, friendly, likable. Dana tried to imagine what she could possibly do better than this woman. Vanessa was enthusiastic about the clothes and found something punchy to say to fill every second of airtime. When the camera went to Bastina, who was about seventy, with hair dyed jet-black and a hint of a Slavic accent, Vanessa let her guard down and at last Dana saw it. She was bored. She had no affection for the designer and no patience for sharing the spotlight. When the camera when back to Vanessa, she lit up again, but didn't express any warmth for the woman at her side. That was a fatal mistake. It made it easy for viewers to switch back to see who *Ellen* was interviewing.

At last, the segment on the spring tops wound down and Vanessa announced that after the break (which was really nothing more than a commercial within a commercial), Bastina would introduce her new line of summer maxidresses, with the help of a new Shopping Channel host, Dana Barry.

Dana's pulse shot up, but she didn't have time to process the fear, because she was immediately led onto the set by Jessalyn. As far as Dana could tell, the talent service coordinator's job was to keep track of the hosts' whereabouts.

"Good luck," Vanessa said to her as they passed. "You're going to need it."

Dana was positioned next to a rack of maxidresses, Bastina at her side. Her heart banged in her chest. This wasn't just stage fright. She was accustomed to the nervous jitters of preperformance excitement. This was something more profound. It was her body's recognition of the stakes. Everything was riding on this. She breathed into the dizzying fear.

Use that energy, she told herself. *Dive right into it.*

She looked straight into the camera, waiting, and when the red light came on, she was ready.

"I'm Dana Barry, your lucky host! It's my debut on the Shopping Channel and I get to do it with *Bastina* herself! I've been a fan of hers forever and..." She stopped and turned to the designer. "Is it okay if I hug you? Is that weird? I've just been wanting to meet you for so long. I love your clothes!"

Bastina looked taken aback, but delighted. And her response was so genuine Dana knew that viewers would react.

"Of course, darling!" Bastina said, and threw her arms around Dana.

"Will you tell us about this gorgeous new maxidress?" Dana asked, as if coaxing one BFF to share a secret with another.

"Because the second I saw it, I knew I had to have it. And what a dream to wear!" She took a step back so the camera could take in her full length, and she did a half twirl to show how the dressed moved.

Bastina caught Dana's enthusiasm and beamed with pride over her creation. "You look beautiful in that."

"Well, the lines are so flattering!" Dana said. "And let's talk about these *colors*!"

And they were off, discussing the dresses in minute, gushing detail. Dana occasionally glanced at the monitor with the sales numbers, and noticed that the one she wore was moving fastest. She assumed this was a good sign.

Bastina was so chatty and had such intimate knowledge of the garments she made it easy. But when Dana stepped up to point out details of the patterns—in language that didn't appear on the pitch chart—Adam's voice came through the earpiece. "That's great! Numbers are skyrocketing." Within a few minutes, she had to give viewers a warning about which dresses and sizes were down to limited quantities. Moments later, Adam told her to pull the navy and the pink off the rack because they were sold out. She pushed hard on the remaining patterns and soon she got the signal to wind it down. And then it was over.

As Dana stepped off the set, Adam emerged from the control booth and clapped a hand on her shoulder. "You knocked it out of the park!" he said.

Dana thanked him and glanced around for Megan, who was nowhere to be seen. She signaled Jessalyn, who rushed to her side and gave Dana back her purse.

"Do you know where Megan Silvestri is?" Dana asked, slipping the strap over her shoulder.

"She's still in the meeting. You didn't hear it from me, but

I think they're negotiating an offer, so it could be a while."
She paused to smile. "Congrats!"

Dana held up her crossed fingers and Jessalyn went on.
"They told me to find someone to give you a tour of the building in the meantime. I'm still working on that."

"I'll do it," said Lorenzo, who was only a few feet away,
listening to the conversation.

"Aren't you on break now?" Jessalyn asked.

"I don't mind," he said.

Dana smiled, and tried to keep herself from thinking it all
seemed too good to be true. She didn't want to jinx herself,
but there was no denying it. Megan was upstairs negotiating
a contract for her, and she had already met a hot guy who
seemed interested. And okay, maybe he wasn't exactly handsome, and he probably had a history that would give her father about forty cerebral hemorrhages—but that was part of
the appeal.

As they walked from the sound studio to the hallway, Dana
told Lorenzo that she had seen a lot of the building while
being prepped.

"But you missed the best part," he said, his eyes bright.

"And what's that?"

He gave an almost imperceptible grin and led her to the
elevator, which they took to the top floor. From the moment
the doors opened, it was obvious this was where the executive offices were located. There was an elegant and expansive
reception area, with a lovely woman sitting behind a rounded
desk that was wider than Dana's apartment.

"Brenda," Lorenzo said to the receptionist, "this is Dana
Barry, and it looks like she's going to be our newest host."

Brenda flashed an easy grin with a mouthful of perfect
white teeth. "I just saw your segment," she said, pointing to a
flat-screen TV on the wall. "You rocked it, girl."

Her manner was loquacious and Dana got a theater-person vibe. She could envision Brenda as an actress playing the role of Pretty Receptionist between gigs.

"That's because her sound levels were perfect," Lorenzo said.

He was being funny, but Dana didn't want him to think she was dismissive of his job. "That's no joke," she said. "Hard to sound slick if they can't hear you."

"A performer is only as good as her mike," Brenda added, and Dana wanted to pat herself on the back for getting it right. This was a fellow trouper.

"I'm showing Dana around," Lorenzo said as he led her toward a corridor.

"Break a leg!" Brenda called after them.

They walked through a bustling open office area with partitions separating the desks, then down a hushed hallway, painted in soft beige tones.

"Is this where Megan is meeting with the top brass?" Dana asked.

"Conference room on the other side. I'm taking you to the penthouse."

Dana cocked her head, confused, because they were already on the top floor.

Lorenzo responded with a wink. "You'll see."

As they passed the office doors, most of which were closed, Dana tried to read the names on the plaques. She couldn't help notice that the corner office belonged to Kitty Todd.

"I thought she would have a dressing room, not an office," Dana said.

"Kitty's got *both*," Lorenzo said, rolling his eyes. "Come on." He pushed open the door to a stairwell just beyond Kitty's office, and they walked up a flight of metal steps. When they reached the top, he held open the door. Dana walked through and gasped. It was the rooftop, and the first thing she saw was an expansive view of the Hudson River, glittering in the sunlight.

Dana walked past a jutting structure to get a full view. "My God," she said, taking it all in. Turning south, she could see the spires of the Empire State Building and the Chrysler Building. Turning north she could make out the George Washington Bridge arcing majestically across the water.

"You should see it at night," he said.

"This would make a great place for a party. It's extraordinary."

"There are chairs on the other side of the compressor, but this is my favorite view," he said, and led them to the railing on the west side, facing the river.

Dana took in the rolling movement of the water and tried to relax. Those fifteen minutes on the air had been intense. But it was hard to unwind knowing Megan was one flight down, deciding her future.

Lorenzo pulled a pack of Marlboros from his pocket. "You smoke?" he asked, making a move to offer her a cigarette.

"Not tobacco," she said, and got the most glorious idea. It didn't take more than a second's deliberation. She deserved this. In the past thirty-six hours, she had lost her crappy job, nailed an audition *and* a callback, and even endured a lunch with her father. And then there was this view. It just seemed like a singular opportunity to enjoy a buzz. She reached into her purse and pulled out her dachshund key chain. Lorenzo watched as she unscrewed the hindquarters and tipped out a slender joint.

"Don't put away that lighter," she said.

He cupped the flame to the tip of her joint as she took a long drag. She held the smoke in her lungs as she passed it to him.

He took it and stared at the joint. "You're killing me," he said.

"What's the big deal?"

"I'm *working*."

"Oh, right," Dana said. "Never mind. Give it back."

"Oh, fuck it." He took a staccato succession of pulls and handed it back. "I hope I don't regret that."

As Dana took the joint back from him their hands touched, and she felt a spark of sexual electricity. She looked in his eyes to see if he felt it, too. He held her gaze for so long she thought for sure he was going to kiss her. But he just kept looking at her with those intense eyes.

Finally, she couldn't take it anymore and said, "You look like you want to kiss me."

"Of course I want to kiss you," he said.

"Well?"

He paused, holding her gaze. "Probably not the kind of guy you want to get involved with."

"Baggage?" she asked.

"A truckload."

"And you keep it locked tight," she said.

He gave a small nod and she moved in closer to let him know it was okay with her. Lorenzo put a hand gently on the back of her head, but didn't make a move. He was waiting for her. Dana knew it was stupid to get involved with someone at work, and even stupider to put the moves on someone before you even got the job. But she had just nailed her on-air appearance, there was a velvety breeze on the back of her neck and Lorenzo had a rugged, almost weather-beaten complexion that spoke of a life lived hard. And yes, there was something alluring about that shadowy cargo. Dana loved a good mystery. She moved in and kissed him softly on the mouth, their bodies not quite touching. When they came apart, he looked at her, and then moved in for a second round, this one initiated by him. But before their lips made contact, a loud bang startled them apart. It sounded like it came from right under their feet.

Her heart rate skyrocketed. "Was that a...gunshot?"

Lorenzo's face tightened. "And damned close."

Dana pointed down. "Sounded like it was right underneath us."

They looked at each other for a moment, and without saying another word, Dana crushed the joint under her shoe and they raced to the stairwell. By the time they pushed open the door to the hallway, people were emerging from their offices to see where the sound came from. No one knew what was going on.

Voices carried up and down the hallway.

What was that?

Did someone get shot?

Where did it come from?

Dana glanced to her right and noticed that Kitty Todd's previously closed door was open. She tapped Lorenzo's shoulder and pointed to it. Dana held her breath as he gently pushed the door wide-open.

The blood caught her eye first—a massive red shape on the window behind the desk, still wet and running down the glass. The sight literally knocked Dana off her feet, and she had to hold on to the wall to keep from falling.

Still, she couldn't look away, and her eye traveled to the figure at the desk, slumped over, with the gun still in her hand.

It was Kitty Todd.

6

Time crystallized as Dana stood, immobile, staring into the room while her brain tried to make sense of the scene's incongruity. The violence was gruesome. Shocking. And yet everything else was so mundane. Kitty's well-tended hair—silky and recently brushed—was swept over her slumped head. A faint trace of pinkish lipstick was visible on the rim of a blue-and-white china cup. An ivory cashmere cardigan, now patterned with blood splatter, was draped over the back of the chair. On the desk, within easy reach, was a bottle of the apricot-scented hand lotion so essential to Kitty. Next to it was a tiny dish that held her rings and an animal-headed gold bracelet that seemed to be looking at her. Kitty's wrist still bore an indentation from wearing it. When Dana was finally able to turn her head from the scene, she felt like she had been in that spot forever. And yet the people running toward her had advanced only a few feet. So it had been a microsecond, stretched to an eternity.

"Someone call 911!" she said, finding her voice, as Lorenzo made an effort to keep everyone back.

And then it was chaos, as people descended upon the doorway, with Charles Honeycutt breaking in to restore order amid gasps and shrieks. The second Dana looked away she heard the sound of a woman's scream, and she turned back to see that it was actually Kitty's male assistant, who was shaking so violently it seemed like he might faint.

Dana pushed back her own rising nausea. It was all so over-whelming. But she wanted to be strong. Fierce. The Woman Who Could Handle Anything.

And as one of the first people to view the scene, Dana felt somehow responsible for what came next. But of course, it wasn't her place. She was an outsider. The least appropriate person to take charge. And so she shuffled out of the way.

"Are you okay?" Lorenzo asked her.

"Are *you*?" She hadn't meant to sound snotty, but Dana had a knee-jerk reaction to being treated as a delicate flower. Even when her hands were shaking and her heart thudded in her chest.

If he was offended, he didn't show it. "They need me on the set. I just wanted to know if there was anything you—"

"I'm fine," she said more gently. "Honestly."

And then Megan was upon her, her eyes wide in alarm. "Holy shit. Did you see it?"

Dana nodded.

"And Kitty?" Megan finished her question by making her hand into a gun and pointing at her head.

"Yup." She shuddered. Minutes ago, Kitty was alive. And now… She closed her eyes, trying to block it out.

Megan led Dana away from the crowd and into an empty conference room down the hall. They lowered themselves onto the leather swivel chairs.

"You're really okay?" Megan asked.

"Of course," she lied. The whole thing felt like an out-of-body experience. She touched her own cheeks to ground her-self, remember where she was.

"Kitty Todd," Megan said, leaning back in her chair. "Of all people."

Dana stared off at the view through the window—the Hudson River now just a dull gray giant lumbering southward—as she tried to process the image she had just seen.

Megan continued. "I wonder what they're going to do now."

"I'm sure someone called 911," Dana said.

"I meant with her show."

Dana turned to her. "Megan. For God's sake."

"Don't get all judgy. This is business. There's millions of dollars at stake. Vanessa's segment ends in about thirty minutes, and then Kitty's begins. So they're going to have to do *something*. And fast. You're not technically under contract yet, so—"

"Oh, come on. You're not honestly thinking about using this as an *opportunity*?"

"Why not? That's my job."

"You know what you sound like?"

"An agent? A business manager?"

"I'm just saying we should take a little time. Out of respect." Even as she said it, though, Dana was aware that there would be few tears shed for Kitty Todd among the staff.

Megan crossed herself and put her hands together in prayer. "Dearest Lord, we entrust Kitty Todd to your undying mercy and love. Amen." She turned to Dana. "Okay? Can we move on?"

"Whatever. I didn't even know the woman. But it's still… *traumatic*."

"I get it. But we have to focus. You're at a crossroads here. I had wrapped up negotiations just before the…you know. And I got you a deal that's going to blow your mind."

Dana gave her a look.

"Okay," Megan said, "bad choice of words. But the fact

is, we had shaken hands and the lawyer left to draw up the contract. I was sitting in the room all alone, waiting, when I heard the bang."

"But are they still going to want me? I mean, Kitty was the one who—"

"Are you kidding? They love you. You can move product like a one-woman convoy. And they need you more than ever. At this point, they're going to rush through that contract like their pants are on fire."

Dana sat back in her chair. This was supposed to be one of the greatest moments of her life. All those auditions. All those rejections. She had at last landed something huge. And okay, it wasn't exactly the role of her dreams—a big part in a movie or a new Netflix series or a Broadway show. But it was a real job. A job that fused her acting ambitions with something that would get her massive exposure and a steady income. She thought about paying off her credit cards and her student loans, and being able to breathe for once. She thought about buying a pair of new shoes without feeling like she was mortgaging her future. She thought about how happy her Sweat City friends would be for her. She thought about having her dad's respect at last.

She turned to Megan. "So what are the details?" Despite herself, she strummed with excitement.

Megan smiled. "You mean the money."

Dana made a face, relenting. "Okay, yes, I mean the money."

Megan rubbed her hands together. "Oh, baby."

She began to lay out the specifics of the deal to Dana, who was stunned. It all seemed too good to be true. And Megan— *damn*. She was right on top of every detail.

Minutes into their conversation they heard heavy footsteps in the hall and looked out the door to see police and paramedics filling the space. Office workers were told to get back to their desks but stay around for statements.

"What kind of statements could they want?" Megan asked. "It was a suicide."

Dana closed her eyes and transported herself back to the scene, examining all the details. In her mind, she walked around the room, the minutiae looming large. Suddenly, she felt a tightening in her chest and her eyes snapped open.

"What is it?" Megan asked. "What's wrong?"

Dana was too choked to respond. She took a few deep breaths and then swallowed against a knot in her throat. At last she said, "I think Kitty Todd was murdered."

7

The cop who interviewed Dana introduced himself as Detective Marks. He was one of those too-tall guys, and Dana had to take a step back to make comfortable eye contact. That was when she noticed he was good-looking, with narrow blue eyes and a French nose, like the Statue of Liberty. But of course, it didn't matter—he wasn't Dana's type. Rule-followers weren't sexy. Guys like Lorenzo were sexy.

Besides, she was still getting her trembling under control. This was not the time to think about whether she was attracted to some handsome stranger.

Still, she checked out his left hand—force of habit. There was no ring, but an indentation where one had been. Divorced. That clinched it, then. She had sworn off divorced guys after being involved with two in a row—first Chris and then Benjamin—and discovering they were cheaters. She was done inheriting other women's problems.

After getting the basic details of who she was and why she was in the building, the detective asked her where she had been when she heard the shot.

"I was up on the roof with Lorenzo, the sound guy."

He consulted his notes. "That would be Lorenzo DeSantis?"

"I didn't catch his last name."

"And what were you doing on the roof?"

She paused. "Just enjoying the view. Why does it matter?"

He ignored her question. "That's it?"

"What do you *think* we were doing? Spitting off the ledge?"

"I wasn't there, so I wouldn't know." His expression remained inscrutable.

"Well, you should check it out. It's quite a view."

He paused to scribble in his notebook, and Dana wondered what the hell he could be writing. Somehow she doubted he was reminding himself to check out the dope view.

Then Dana felt a twinge of anxiety, as she couldn't remember what she had done with the joint. Everything had happened so fast. Had she simply crushed it out and left it there? Maybe she shouldn't be so antagonistic with this guy.

But then, it probably didn't matter. Who cared if they were smoking a joint on the roof? It wasn't like they were under suspicion of anything. Hell, this guy probably just thought he was getting all the background so he could sign off on Kitty's suicide. It would likely ruin his day to hear her observations.

"What's your relationship with Lorenzo DeSantis?" he asked.

She bristled. "Relationship? There's no *relationship*. He was just giving me a tour of the building. Why do you even need to know?"

"It's my job to know," he said. "Did Mr. DeSantis leave the roof without you at any time?"

Now that was a hell of a question. She wondered if he was going to ask Lorenzo the same thing about her. This was damned thorough for a suicide investigation. "No."

"Walk me through what happened," the detective said. "What time did you go up to the roof?"

"I don't know exactly. Maybe 4:15? We went up a staircase just past Kitty's office."

"Was anyone in the hallway at that time?"

"It was actually very quiet," she said, shaking her head. "Once we got up there I was blown away by the view. We walked over to the railing overlooking the river and then... bang! It sounded so close—like it was right underneath us. I mean, it was pretty clear that it was a gunshot. So we ran down the stairs and I noticed right away that Kitty's door was open."

"And it hadn't been open when you went up to the roof?"

"It was closed."

"You're sure?"

"Very."

He scribbled in his notepad. "What happened next—after you noticed the open door?"

Dana shrugged. "That was it, really. I pointed it out to Lorenzo and he pushed it open wide and...that's when we saw her." She took a breath, trying to block out the vision. But it was still there, and she couldn't ignore her frightening conclusion.

"Can I ask you something?" she said as he continued to write in his notepad.

He gave a small nod.

"Do you think it's really a suicide?"

He stopped writing and looked at her. "Do you?"

Dana exhaled. Judging from his questions, it seemed like he was already on the same page. But maybe he wasn't. Maybe he was being thorough because Kitty was a star and this story was sure to get a ton of publicity.

"No, I don't," she said firmly. Dana was pretty sure the guy thought she was some kind of bimbo, and she didn't want to falter.

"And why's that?" His tone was even, but he closed his

notebook, making it clear he didn't think she could have anything valuable to offer.

"Her rings were off."

"And that's significant?"

"Listen," she said. "Kitty takes off her rings to moisturize her hands. Why would somebody moisturize their hands before killing themselves? I mean, besides the obvious futility of the act. Who cares how soft your hands are when you're dead, right? But more important, wouldn't that make it harder to grip a gun? Have you ever tried opening a doorknob after using hand lotion?"

"Can't say that I have."

"Well, trust me, it's almost impossible. And that stuff she uses is viscous enough to run your engine. But okay, let's say she wanted to leave a pretty corpse and thought oily hands were essential. It's a stretch, but let's go with it. And let's say she was able to grip the gun, anyway, and put a bullet in her head. How was she still holding the gun when we found her? There's no way it wouldn't have slipped from her hand. So clearly, someone was trying to make it look like a suicide."

She studied his face, waiting for some kind of reaction. He remained stoic, but as she stared, Dana could detect, just beneath the exterior, the tiniest hint of amused condescension in his eyes. It reminded her of her father and she wanted to scream. But she just clenched her jaw.

"What?" she demanded. "Did I say something funny?"

His expression softened. "Not at all."

"So why aren't you taking me seriously? I'm telling you, this wasn't a suicide. I know you think I'm some kind of idiot, but—"

"I don't think you're an idiot, Ms. Barry."

"But you think my theory is stupid."

"You're on the right track, you just took the wrong train."

"What is that supposed to mean?"

"It means," he said, "her skin could have been as dry as a brown leaf. If she shot herself in the head, there's no way the gun would have stayed in her hand. Someone put it there."

"So, you don't think Kitty killed herself?"

He let out a breath. "No, ma'am. We're investigating a homicide."

8

Sherry Zidel's black-clad assistant, Emily Lauren, led Dana and Megan to the executive guest suite, where four copies of the twenty-seven-page contract were stacked neatly on a glass-top coffee table. The space looked more like a beautifully appointed living room than an office, meticulously decorated with a plush love seat and striped armchairs, an oversize mahogany desk in the corner. The walls were painted in a shade of dark beige often called "paper bag brown." Dana knew it was a color decorators loved for its soothing esthetic.

"We thought you might be comfortable reviewing the contracts here," Emily said. "Mr. Honeycutt will check in shortly to see if you have any questions."

She was a slender young woman with a clear complexion, great cheekbones and studied diction. Dana's actor-radar flashed again, and she wondered how many Shopping Channel employees had SAG cards tucked in their wallets. She guessed that Emily was an ambitious trouper who had taken the job to get close to the career-launching Sherry Zidel. Even the name was a giveaway—Emily Lauren. It was the middle name trick, using it to replace a last name that wasn't quite marquee-worthy. Lea Michele and Jon Stewart came to mind.

Her driver's license probably said something like Emily Lauren Leibowitz.

"That's fine," Megan said, taking a seat. "I'm happy to take a look now. But please know Dana won't be signing anything until the papers are reviewed by our attorney." She sat.

Emily smiled broadly, her young teeth perfectly aligned. "Of course. Can I get you anything in the meantime? Coffee? A glass of wine?"

"We're good. Thank you, Emily."

The assistant left, and Dana went to the side table, where a heavy glass pitcher of ice water perspired delicately onto a gilded tray. She poured two glasses, and they settled in to read.

By page four, Dana was lost in the legalese, and getting anxious. She wanted to review it at home, with her shoes off and her favorite cabernet nearby. "Do we really need to do this now?"

"I just want to make sure they included everything we talked about," Megan said.

"Oh, come on. That's why God invented lawyers."

"And managers."

A few minutes later there was a gentle knock on the door, followed by the appearance of Charles Honeycutt. His expensive suit still looked impeccable, but Dana could see that the man was struggling with the trauma of what he saw, and what he now had to deal with. As president, it all fell on him. His face was sweating, and his shirt collar damp. Charles Honeycutt took out a handkerchief, wiped his hand and stuck it out toward Dana.

"I wish this day could have been different for you, Dana, but I'm glad to welcome you aboard."

"Thank you, Mr. Honeycutt."

"Charles, please," he corrected, and handed her a business

card. She put it in her purse next to the one from Detective Ari Marks.

Up close Charles Honeycutt was handsome, if a little beefy, the flash of a gold watch and shiny Ferragamo shoes narrowcasting his success to anyone paying attention. His cologne was familiar—possibly Sauvage—but when he had leaned forward to shake her hand she caught a whiff of something sweeter. It was familiar, but it passed so quickly she couldn't quite place it.

"Charles," she said, "I'm very sorry for your loss. This must be so difficult."

"I can't imagine," Megan added.

"I appreciate that," he said. "And if you have any concerns about—"

"We do," Megan cut in, "and if it's not too early to ask…"

"Please. That's what I'm here for."

She cleared her throat. "Do you know what you're doing about the schedule?"

"We've already spoken to Vanessa about staying on. So the plan is to move her into Kitty's slot, and Dana, as planned, will take Vanessa's."

Dana bit her lip as she took in the timing of Vanessa's sudden change of fortune. The woman went from being forced out of a job to getting the prime-time slot. Dana let out a breath and tried to dial back her paranoia, telling herself she was being melodramatic. Vanessa wouldn't have murdered Kitty Todd to get her job. It was so… *All About Eve*—the kind of thing that only happened in the movies.

And besides, Vanessa had the world's most bulletproof alibi: she was live on air at the time of the murder. About a million viewers could testify to that.

Then it hit her. The familiar scent rising off Charles Honeycutt's overheated neck. It was apricot—just like Kitty's hand lotion.

God, she thought, *I must stop this. I can't take this job wondering if every person I speak to is a murderer.*

When Honeycutt left, Dana told Megan she was getting the willies. "Is it really a good idea to take a job under these circumstances?" she asked.

Her friend reacted with an inscrutable smile.

"What?" Dana demanded.

"I know you," Megan said. "You don't like things to be easy. If this were the perfect job, you'd be bored as hell, and would probably sabotage yourself in the first week. But this. This makes it sexy."

Damn. Megan knew her too well.

"I hate it when you're right," Dana said.

"Come on. Let's go out for a drink. You earned a celebration." Megan started gathering the copies of the contract but Dana held on to hers.

"I just have one question about that noncompete clause," she said.

Megan waved away her concern. "It's nothing."

"But am I reading it right? It seems kind of overreaching."

"It's pretty standard stuff," Megan said, avoiding her eyes. "You can't take any other acting or performance gigs without getting clearance."

"Wait a minute," Dana said. "What about Sweat City?" She was sure there had to be some workaround. No one would expect her to give up her greatest passion.

Megan sighed and tried to pull the contract from Dana's hand. "Well," she said, and nothing else.

"Well, what?"

Megan's lips tightened. "Sometimes we need to make sacrifices."

Dana held on to the contract and took a step back. "You've got to be kidding."

"Sorry, hon. It's nonnegotiable."

"When were you going to tell me?"

"Dana—"

"I'm serious, Megan. Were you going to let me sign this and not find out until it was too late?"

"I'm looking out for you."

Dana's eyes burned as she stared, stung by the betrayal. "So you're my mother now? I thought you were my friend."

"I'm your *manager*."

Dana grabbed the stack of contracts from her. "Not anymore."

Megan grabbed them back. "Don't get all melodramatic on me. This is the opportunity of a lifetime, and I wasn't going to let you shoot yourself in the foot."

"Sweat City is everything to me!"

"It's an experimental theater group that's going nowhere and will get you nothing. In a typical year, how many people see your performances there? A hundred? A hundred and twenty? And most of them are related to the actors. It's a sweet little group of friends, but don't kid yourself. Sweat City is not launching careers, it's holding them back."

"But that's *my* decision, not yours."

"Don't do this, Dana. Don't blow everything for this useless little group."

"Useless?" Dana could hardly believe what she was hearing. She knew her group did good work, knew they were some of the most talented actors she had ever met.

"You know what I mean," Megan said. "I get it. It's fun. It's enriching…"

"It's *art*," Dana said.

"Okay, yes. It's art. And this is…commerce. But you'll make a living. You'll be seen by millions. And who knows? In a few years—"

"Years!" Dana said, and put her head in her hands. It was all too much.

There was a soft knock on the door. Megan quickly pulled out a tissue and handed it to Dana, indicating that she needed to tidy up the mascara that had run. Dana hadn't even been conscious of crying, but the combination of rage and betrayal was potent.

"Come in," Megan called, and Dana was surprised to see Lorenzo standing there.

"Can I talk to you?" he said to her.

"Sure," she said, waving him into the room.

He cocked his head toward the hallway, indicating that he needed a private word. "It'll just take a minute."

Dana followed him out of the room. "What's up?" she asked.

"Did you talk to that detective?" His expression was even, but he shifted his weight from one foot to the other to cover his nervousness.

"A tall guy named Marks," she said.

"What did you say to him?"

"Just that we were up on the roof when we heard the gunshot."

"You didn't tell him about the joint?" Lorenzo asked.

"Of course not."

"Are you sure?" His dark eyes looked even more intense than usual.

"What are you so worried about?"

Just then, Emily Lauren appeared in the hallway carrying a stack of folders. Dana and Lorenzo backed apart as if they were having a more casual conversation. Emily gave them a smile as she passed, and they waited until she disappeared down the hall before continuing.

Lorenzo leaned in, hesitated for a moment and whispered, "I'm on *parole*."

Dana nodded. It wasn't a shocking piece of information. She knew he had been incarcerated at some point in his life, because she had noticed that in addition to the artful ink that trailed down his arm, there was a crude prison tattoo on his hand—a little square created by five unconnected dots. Now she burned to know what crime he'd committed.

"Do you mind if I—"

"Armed robbery," he said.

Her eyebrows went up.

"I was young," he explained. "An idiot. Had a shitty group of friends."

"Do they know? I mean, the people here?"

"Only Bess Haskins, the woman in HR who hired me. She's a friend of my parole officer's—got a kid who's locked up, so she was sympathetic. Otherwise, it's nearly impossible for an ex-con to get a real job. But if I blow parole…"

"For the joint?"

"It's a violation that can send me back to prison faster than you can sell one of those crazy-ass long dresses."

"But you only took one toke."

"That's enough. And, Dana…" He paused, making sure she was looking directly at him. "I can handle a lot of shit, but I can't go back to prison. *I can't*."

His eyes were pained, serious. She swallowed hard. "I promise I won't tell anyone about the joint. You have my word."

He nodded, as if he were trying to convince himself he could trust her.

"Really," she added. "You have nothing to worry about."

"Oh, I have plenty to worry about. Weed or no weed, when that detective runs my name through the system and sees my record, I'll be the prime suspect."

"But you have an alibi," she said, pointing to herself. "They'll believe me."

He gave a dubious shrug.

"Why wouldn't they?" she asked.

"I think someone saw us," he said. "Up on the roof. The detective didn't say it in so many words, but he hinted at it."

Dana hadn't known anyone else was up there, so this surprised her. Still, she couldn't see how it mattered. If anything, it gave more credibility to her statement.

"I don't understand," she said.

"Someone saw us *kissing*."

"Screw them. Who cares?"

"Dana, if the detective thinks we have a romantic relationship, he won't believe your statement. He'll think you're willing to lie to cover for me."

"That's ridiculous," she said, even as the light came on. This was why Marks had asked about her relationship with Lorenzo.

"It's reality. I'm the only ex-con here. And I was the one who discovered the body. I'm going to be in some deep shit."

Dana breathed into the mess she had created for this guy. *She* was the one who instigated the kiss. *She* was the one with the joint that could send him back to prison.

The joint, she thought. Was it still up there on the roof? And what if the detective found it?

"Are you okay?" Lorenzo said. "You look pale."

"I'm fine," she said. "I just… I don't want you to worry. No matter what, I got your back."

He squeezed her shoulder in appreciation and she returned to the paper-bag-brown suite.

"Everything okay?" Megan asked as Dana reached for her purse.

"Fine," she said, and rummaged around until she found her dachshund key chain. She screwed off the hindquarters and looked inside. Nothing there but the white pill. Dana imagined Detective Marks finding the joint on the roof and dropping it into an evidence bag. If he were really after Lorenzo, he might do a DNA test on it, and Lorenzo could wind up back in prison.

Dana thought about hightailing it to the roof to retrieve the joint, but that would be impossible. There was police tape blocking off the end of the hall that led to the staircase. If she wanted to go up there, it would have to wait. And she would have to hope the detective hadn't thought to go up there. Yet.

And of course, she would have to take the job.

If she didn't, well, she'd be leaving Lorenzo vulnerable. It would be too risky for him to retrieve it himself. And besides, Marks would think there was something even more suspicious about Lorenzo's alibi if she suddenly decided to turn down the opportunity of a lifetime.

Dana dropped the key chain back into her purse and retrieved a pen. She reached for the contracts.

"What are you doing?" Megan asked.

"I'm signing this damned thing."

9

Megan, of course, didn't let Dana sign anything before an attorney went over it—several times—with something as least as fine as a sixty-eight-tooth Hector Comb. But after it was tweaked a bit, and new copies generated and hand-delivered, Dana initialed all twenty-seven pages on all four copies and signed on the line.

Meanwhile, Kitty's death was reported on the news as an "apparent suicide." Only *TMZ* revealed that police were investigating it as a homicide. But there were other things going on in the world and, much to the chagrin of her devoted fans, it quickly slipped out of the news cycle.

Before it even hit the airwaves, though, Dana had given her sister a heads-up on the news of Kitty's death, and she'd been horrified. Still, Chelsea told Dana she had to take the job, listing the same reasons Megan had given. The opportunity of a lifetime. Financial freedom. And a shocking tragedy to make it all a little more interesting. So once the contracts were signed, Dana knew who to call for validation.

"It's done," Dana said over the phone to her sister. "Signed, sealed and sent."

Chelsea squealed. "I'm so proud of you! And I understand

you have to settle in and everything, but let me know when I can come and tour the studio and watch you in action. That would be *amazing*."

"Of course," Dana said, laughing. She couldn't remember the last time she had done anything that impressed her sister.

"And will you let me go shopping with you?" Chelsea asked. "I mean, you'll need a whole new wardrobe."

"They dress me, Chelse," she said, reverting to her child-hood nickname for her sister. "I can go to work in sweats."

"You can't! You'll be famous. You need a certain look."

"The hell I do."

"No," Chelsea said, adamant. "I am not letting you walk around in torn jeans and concert T-shirts. What will people think?"

"Who cares?" Dana said, though in truth she thought she looked pretty cool in her concert tees and jeans. A pair of killer boots and a retro choker could elevate an *I don't give a damn* look to *I'm a little bit biker, a little bit rock and roll.*

"Dana, please. You can afford new clothes. You don't have to go around looking like an adolescent."

"Maybe I'll get some new T-shirts."

"You're impossible."

Next she called her mother in Boca Raton, who said, "Oh, sweetheart. I'm so pleased for you! Unlike some people, I always had faith in you. Always. I have to run, darling. We have court time. Love you!"

The "some people," of course, referred to her father. Dana was pretty sure her mother hadn't called him by name since the divorce. But then, once Mom had moved down to Florida and started her new life, she'd barely said the names of her daughters, either.

Dana stared at her phone, wanting and not wanting to call

her father. This news would impress him. And though she didn't like to admit it, she craved his approval like crack.

He doesn't deserve this good news, she thought. *I should just freeze him out*. But then, giving up her Sweat City group was such a huge sacrifice that she felt she had earned the tingle of pride her father's blessing would bestow. And so she scrolled through her contacts to his number, which was listed under *Dr. Barry*. It had been her own private little protest, not that different from her mother's. In Dana's case, she had been simply too chafed by her father to alphabetize him under "Dad."

"I have great news," she said after he answered the phone with his gruff hello.

"Did they promote you to manager?"

"No, Dad. Don't you remember what I was telling you about the Shopping Channel? It's official. I signed the contract. I start tomorrow." Without waiting for his reaction, she launched into the part she knew would impress him most—the money. She explained her base salary and the bonus structure, which could put her above what he had made during his best years as a neurologist.

"And really," she added, "it's the opportunity of a lifetime. I couldn't be—"

"I agree," he said.

"You do?" Despite herself, Dana felt a beautiful warmth breaking through the cloud of her relationship with her father, as if a white-pink sun were finally shining down on her, brilliant and full of joy. She knew she was being ridiculous. She was, after all, a grown woman. There was no reason for her to feel like a teenager filling a page with happy face emoticons. And yet...

"I'm proud of you," he said.

Dana swallowed against a lifetime of disappointment balled up in her throat. "Thanks," she said.

"Now surprise me and don't get fired."

Ice water. Pouring from the sky in buckets and ruining everything. The sad part was that she should have seen it coming, because it always did.

After the briefest pause, she choked out, "Love you, too, Dad," and then disconnected the call without saying goodbye.

Dana's airtime was 1:00 to 5:00 p.m., Monday through Friday. For her first day, though, she was told to come in at eight thirty for orientation, which started with an hour-long meeting with Bess Haskins from HR, who began by asking Dana if she wanted free counseling to help deal with the trauma of Kitty's death.

"I'm fine," Dana said, despite how shaky she felt every time the image of Kitty's blood on the window made an unexpected appearance in her mind. "But thank you."

When pressed, she insisted that yes, she was sure. Because Dana knew she could handle it on her own, the way she handled everything. And besides, she didn't want to start a new job looking like the delicate little ingenue who couldn't take a punch.

Bess went on to explain the benefits package and the company's policies on everything from sexual harassment to security. Next, Dana had an appointment to see Sherry Zidel up on the top floor, and thought it might be her best opportunity to take a quick detour up to the roof to check around for that joint.

She was greeted by Brenda, the pretty receptionist, who welcomed her aboard. Dana thanked her and said she had an appointment with Sherry.

Brenda picked up her phone. "I'll buzz Emily and she'll come get—"

"You know what? I need to learn my way around the place.

Is it okay if I head back on my own?" She showed Brenda the security badge Bess Haskins had given her. "I'm official now."

"Of course," the receptionist said, and gave Dana directions on getting to the hallway that led to Sherry's office.

Dana thanked her and went through the door, intentionally taking a wrong turn to head toward the end of the building where Kitty's office was located. As soon as she turned the corner she saw that the yellow police tape was still there, blocking access. There were people about, so she couldn't simply duck under it. It would have to wait. *Damn.*

She turned back and found her way to Sherry's office, where she had to linger in the anteroom with Emily while Sherry finished a meeting with someone else. When the door finally opened, Sherry emerged with the towheaded young man who had been Kitty Todd's assistant. Emily and Sherry shared a look, and Dana surmised that it had to do with the young man's emotional problems. He looked as if he'd been crying, and Dana hoped he was one of the employees who had accepted the offer of free counseling.

"Dana," Sherry said, "I don't know if you've met Ollie Sikanen, our wonderful intern who joined us on an exchange program from Finland. We've been so lucky to have him."

Sherry was being patronizing, and it didn't come naturally to her. She had the tight smile of someone handing back a baby that had just spit up.

"It's lovely to meet you," Dana said gently to Ollie as she shook his cold, narrow hand.

"Oh!" he replied, as if startled by the news. "It is lovely to meet *you*! I am a fan already."

He spoke with a Finnish accent, enunciating his words carefully. He had a post-hipster style of dressing that said *I'm so fashion-forward I can pull clothes from a Dumpster and make them look cool.* Today he wore skinny red corduroy pants with a burgundy plaid shirt and a white bow tie. It was a ridiculous getup but he managed to make it work. Dana gave him a soft smile before Emily guided him away.

Dana followed Sherry into her office and took a seat across from her wide desk. She glanced around at the decor, and imagined that the interior designer had been instructed to give it a "power-fem" ambiance. The walls and furniture were white, but the side chairs were upholstered in pale pink, and the large window was dressed in heavy, black-and-white striped curtains with a satiny finish. Four large-screen television monitors were mounted on the wall across from the desk, so that Sherry could keep a constant eye on the programming.

"What did you think of Ollie?" Sherry asked, taking a seat in the white leather armchair behind her desk.

It struck Dana as an odd question. "I don't know. He seems fine."

Sherry raised an eyebrow, as if she weren't buying it.

"Okay," Dana admitted. "He seems a little off. But I guess that's to be expected."

"He's a crackerjack assistant. Great attention to detail, utterly doting."

"Kitty seemed pretty attached to him," Dana offered. She couldn't quite figure out where Sherry was going with all this.

"They were thick as thieves. She trusted him implicitly."

"That's important, I suppose."

Sherry adjusted her glasses. "Would you like him?" she asked.

"Excuse me?"

"As your assistant."

At that, it all made sense. Sherry was trying to figure out what to do with this fragile, damaged intern, and figured she'd palm him off on Dana, who was taken aback by the very idea of having an assistant, let alone a broken one. Her first instinct was to say, *No, thanks, make him someone else's problem.* But she stopped herself. Ollie would know more about Kitty than anyone else at the Shopping Channel. If Dana wanted to clear Lorenzo's name by digging for information, Ollie was the place to start.

"Okay," Dana said. "I'll take him."

"You will?"

"He seems like a good kid."

"Great," Sherry said, relieved. "Just great. He'll be thrilled."

"Anything in particular I should know about him?" Dana asked.

"He's very loyal," Sherry said, avoiding eye contact.

"Yeah, I got that. But please, be straight with me. Is he going to be okay?"

Sherry nodded, as if accepting a deal. "Look, I won't lie. He's taking this very hard—seems to think it's his fault—but he'll get over it. And really, he was a terrific assistant to Kitty. I mean, she was pretty demanding, so he'd have to be. But just know that he imprints like a baby duckling. So once he's yours, he's yours."

Dana nodded. "I think I can handle that."

She expected a tiny bit of warmth after that—or at least a perfunctory welcome aboard. Maybe some clucking about the tragedy of losing Kitty. But Sherry launched into a frigid monologue about sales figures, and Dana kept waiting for the ice to break. After a while, it became clear that Sherry's goal was to intimidate her. And she succeeded. Dana felt shrunken by Sherry's descriptions of the mountains she would need to scale on a daily basis to reach her benchmarks.

Sherry went on to explain that unlike their larger competitors, the Shopping Channel sold only beauty and fashion products. She detailed the product lines and how decisions were made regarding which products to market on which shows.

The hosts had no input on any of it. They were told what to sell, when to sell it and how many items they were expected to move. Sherry pulled out a massive binder of Excel spreadsheets that made Dana dizzy. Until that moment, it hadn't occurred to her that she would be dealing with the kind of grown-up job pressures she had never faced before. Dana always thought of herself as a worker, but her entire career history had consisted of acting gigs, ushering jobs, waitressing stints and insulting teenagers at a mall store. There was a lot of crap to deal with—from terrible bosses to internal politics to utter disasters—but this was different.

Sherry said that she would walk Dana through the spreadsheets, but she didn't. She ran. Or rather, she sprinted. It was barely comprehensible, yet Dana kept nodding and hoped that someone else would be willing to review it at a human speed.

The only part she caught was the bit about the column tracking display inventory, because Sherry's tone turned hostile, as if she expected Dana to be a thief.

"People around here have sticky fingers," Sherry warned, "so we keep careful track of the inventory." She pointed for emphasis, and Dana wanted to smack her hand away. Or clamp her teeth on it.

"Are you getting all this?" Sherry asked when Dana didn't respond.

"I think so," Dana said. "I'm pretty sure you'd prefer if I didn't steal anything."

Sherry didn't laugh. "There's more to it than that."

"Of course," Dana said. "I'm sure I'll catch on."

"Tell you what," Sherry said, handing the binder to Dana. "Take this for a few days and study it. We can meet again on Friday."

Dana felt like she was back in high school math class, with a teacher who had just dropped a massive calculus textbook on the desk and announced there was a test on it at the end of the week.

But Dana was a trained actor, and so she smiled brightly as if she had it all under control and thanked Sherry for agreeing to part with the binder. She thought Sherry would dismiss her then, but the producer clasped her hands on her desk and asked if HR had gone over the finer points of her contract.

"We went over quite a bit, but—"

"I just want to make sure you're aware of how important it is to meet your benchmarks." She laid a hand on the binder as if the secret of life were contained within its columns of numbers.

"I think I get it," Dana said.

"Just so you understand. We don't have much wiggle room here. This is a profit center with a lot of overhead and hundreds of salaries to pay. We have to make our numbers or we're out of business. So if you miss your benchmarks…"

"Of course," Dana said. "I'm here to sell. I get it."

"And you understand the noncompete clause in your contract?"

Of course I do, Dana thought. *It means you own me.* "Yes," she said.

"And if you're looking for clearance to do any other projects, I'm the one you come to. But I'm warning you right now, I almost never say yes. I'm not trying to be a bitch. I'm just looking out for the Shopping Channel. There are other people here whose job it is to keep the talent happy. Me? I'm here to keep the lights on."

Sherry stood, indicating that the meeting was over. But when they stepped out of the office, Sherry asked her to wait a moment.

"Get Ollie down here," she said to Emily. "He has a new boss."

When the young man arrived, his eyes wide with joy, he insisted on carrying the heavy binder as he led Dana to her new dressing room. Sherry had described him accurately, though Dana thought he was as much puppy dog as he was duckling, hungry for affection and eager to please.

They took the elevator to the second floor. "I hope you like the dressing room, Miss Dana," he said as they walked down the hall.

Miss Dana? She tried not to laugh, and told him to please just call her Dana.

He lit up. "Okay, Dana," he said. "The dressing room has no windows, Dana, but good walls. Pretty. All new furniture, too."

Dana didn't know what "good walls" were, but when she arrived she understood that Ollie was pleased with the color of the fresh paint. Previously, he explained, it was coral, but it had been repainted in a soft sage green. Like most dressing rooms, it had a bunker-like feel, complete with dropped ceiling, but the long lighted mirror on the wall almost made up for it. In front of that was a white vanity counter and a sink. The rest of the space was set up like a cozy living room, with a beige sofa long enough to nap on, and matching upholstered side chairs. There was also an alcove with a full-length mirror and a portable chrome clothing rack, looking conspicuously naked.

Dana still had time before her scheduled daily briefing on the product lineup she'd be selling, so she asked Ollie if he knew anything about spreadsheets.

"Yes, I do, Dana! I reviewed the paperwork for Miss Kitty every week."

"Could I trouble you to explain it to me? I'm a little confused by it all."

"It would be my pleasure, Dana."

She took a seat next to him on the sofa, and tried to re-sign herself to the idea that he'd be using her name as often as he could. And as he went over what the different columns meant, it began to click.

"I think I'm starting to get it," she said.

"Dana, that's good. But please, I will review for you every page. Once I found for Miss Kitty a big mistake on her spread-sheet, and oh! She was so glad I saw this." His eyes went moist.

Dana took a tissue from the box on the side table and handed it to him. Then she delicately tiptoed through the conversational doorway he had opened.

"I understand that you really liked working for her, Ollie. I just want to say that I'm so sorry for your loss."

"She was a wonderful lady, Dana. Wonderful boss."

"If you ever want to talk, please feel free."

He wiped his nose with the tissue. "Excuse me, Dana," he said. "I don't mean to be sad in front of you."

"It's okay."

"The policemen asked me so many questions, Dana. Do I think anyone would want to hurt Miss Kitty? Do I think she had a boyfriend? Do I think she had a lover here at the company?"

Dana tried to keep her voice even. She knew Kitty was sleeping around, but if she had an actual relationship with someone at work, he would be a more important suspect than Lorenzo. "What did you tell them?"

"The truth, of course, Dana!"

She sighed. "I'm glad you're cooperating with the police. I'm sure you're eager to help them find…the truth." She had wanted to say "killer," but thought better of it. He was so fragile.

"Then they asked if her boyfriend was married."

Married, she thought, and wondered if her suspicions about Charles Honeycutt were right.

"And were you…forthcoming?" she asked.

"I had to tell them the truth, right, Dana? I hope I didn't get him in trouble."

"You did the right thing," she said.

"I know he wouldn't hurt Miss Kitty. He loved her, Dana, and she loved him."

"Did she tell you that?"

"Oh, Miss Kitty trusted me. I had a very important job to keep her secret. But now…" He blew his nose.

There was a soft knock on the door. It was Adam Weintraub, the curly-haired segment producer she had pegged as a new dad, who came to go over the details of what she needed to know for that day's program. Ollie stood, as if waiting for instructions from Dana on whether it was okay for him to stay for the meeting.

"Thank you, Ollie," Dana said, dismissing him. "I'll let you know if I need anything." It was, she decided, important to set boundaries. Otherwise, he would expect to be privy to the minutiae of her life, and she couldn't have that. Not while she was covertly investigating Kitty's murder. And sure, he seemed trustworthy, and willing to do anything for her. But she needed to keep Lorenzo's past a secret, and that meant keeping her interest in the case as quiet as possible.

Ollie gave a small nod and left.

Adam surveyed the room. "They remodeled for you. Nice."

"Good walls," she said.

"Excuse me?"

"That's how Ollie described it."

"Oh!" He gave a small laugh. "You okay with him? He's half puppy, half pitbull. At least that's how he was with Kitty— very protective."

Adam was midthirties with a boyish, trustworthy face, and struck Dana as the kind of guy who warmed bottles in the middle of the night and tried to influence his baby to appreciate guitar solos. Dana wondered how much he knew about Kitty's love life, and if her affair was sort of an open secret in the company.

"I think we'll be fine," she said. "I just have to acclimate to the idea of having an assistant. This is all new to me."

"Culture shock?"

"It's nothing compared to spreadsheet shock," she said, pointing to the binder. "And I have no idea when I'll get time to study all this."

Adam opened the cover and glanced down. "Where did you get this?" He seemed surprised.

"From Sherry. She wanted me to study it."

"Why?"

"I guess I need remedial spreadsheet training."

He blinked, confused. "Dana, you don't need to know all this stuff."

"I don't?"

"Our other hosts have probably never even *seen* an Excel spreadsheet."

"Sherry made it sound like it was my job to be well-versed in all this."

"That's *my* job," he said. "I'll always keep you apprised of how you're doing and what benchmarks you need to meet."

Dana rubbed her forehead and wondered why Sherry had been so compelled to intimidate her. Maybe it was just her way of making sure Dana understood how important it was to meet her numbers. But maybe it was something else.

"She also made a fuss about missing display inventory."

Adam looked surprised. "She did?"

"As if she expected me to be a criminal."

Adam's brow furrowed as if he, too, were trying to unravel the mystery of Sherry's vexation. Finally, he seemed to give up, waving away any concern. "Don't worry about Sherry's bluster," he said. "I want you to trust that you're in very good hands. If you have any questions, I'm here. And of course, Ollie will do anything for you."

"He told me he went over Kitty's spreadsheets every week."

"That's what I'm talking about. He was the only assistant who did that. Most of them don't know Excel from Expedia."

"I'm just hoping he gets over Kitty's death," Dana said.

"It'll be interesting to see what he posts on the In Memoriam page."

Dana nodded. She had been told the company was setting up a special webpage for Kitty's distraught fans. It was a living memorial—a place for them to pour their hearts out about their beloved host. Employees were expected to submit their own memories of Kitty through the PR department, which would screen them before the web department set the quotes to tender, heartbreaking music. Vanessa Valdes would be expected to write the most emotional tribute of all so that fans would accept her as Kitty's replacement. By the time it was all over, Kitty Todd would be immortalized as a cross between Princess Diana and Shawn Killinger.

Dana turned back to Adam. "Did you ever work with her?" she asked, hoping for more lowdown on Kitty. She needed all the information she could get.

"I was her first segment producer here."

"What was that like?" Dana asked.

He let out a breath. "You don't want to know."

The hell I don't, she thought. But Adam shifted uncomfortably in his seat and slammed the subject closed.

"Let's talk about today's show," he said.

10

Felicia, Jo and Robért—these were the folks with the juicy gossip, the ones she could probe for information on Kitty's affair. But Ollie had trotted along with her to hair and makeup, and so she couldn't get any information. By the time she was on set and getting miked by Lorenzo, there wasn't much she could tell him.

"Everything okay?" she whispered.

"That detective was here again yesterday and cornered me," he said.

"About what?"

"Just asking the same questions over and over. He thinks I'll trip up and contradict myself."

Dana huffed. It was infuriating. "He knows damned well there's someone else he should be talking to," she said.

Lorenzo's eyebrows shot up, and she continued. "According to Ollie, Kitty was in the middle of a torrid love affair with someone here at the company."

Lorenzo nodded, taking it in, but he didn't look surprised. "Do you know who it was?"

"I have a suspicion."

"Thirty seconds!" the tech director announced.

"I'll talk to you later," Lorenzo said, then he turned on her microphone and backed away.

Dana adjusted her earpiece, straightened herself behind the display table of earrings, and stared into the camera like she was looking into the face of a friend. Not just any friend, but a beloved. The kind of friend a woman relies on. Adores. The kind of friend who reflects the feeling right back. It's more than mutual admiration. It's an infinity of mirrors reflecting nothing but love.

The camera's red light blinked on, and at that moment everything else ceased to exist. Kitty's murder, Lorenzo's trouble, her Sweat City group, her father's approval and even the patent leather shoes pinching her feet. It all turned to vapor, and Dana's focus was complete. She talked straight to the viewer at home, tracking her reactions with occasional glances at the sales numbers scrolling through the tracking monitor like an EKG. She got into a rhythm that felt as natural as breathing. She took calls. She gushed. On Adam's instruction, she beckoned for close-ups on the products. She described design and color and clasps and light refraction. She shared her feelings. She gushed some more. When told the earrings were nearly sold out, she switched to the matching bracelets. Then she moved on to a line of freshwater pearl necklaces. Her fourth segment switched from jewelry to fashion, and she had a moment of panic because she distinctly remembered that Adam told her it would be the midpoint of her programming and it felt like only minutes had passed. Nervous, she glanced at the time on the monitor, and was stunned to discover she had been on the air for two hours. She had been in such a zone it had felt like no time at all. And that was when she realized that Megan had been right. She was born for this job. All of her skills and talents—including her ease in front of a camera and the hyperawareness of details she had always taken for granted—coalesced to make her shine.

At last, Adam told Dana to wrap it up, and she smiled brightly at the camera. "Thank you for staying with us, and now here's Vanessa Valdes with today's special on gemstone jewelry. You won't want to miss it!"

And then she was done. Dana unclipped her mike, took out her earpiece and walked off the set.

Adam approached and went over the numbers with her, explaining the benchmarks that were met and surpassed. Apparently, she had done quite well. During the conversation she looked up and saw Sherry Zidel at the back of the soundstage. Dana waved, hoping for a word of encouragement from the prickly supervising producer. But either Sherry didn't see her, or pretended she didn't, as she slipped out the back door without returning the gesture.

Dana walked back to her dressing room with Ollie hurrying alongside. Her plan was to dismiss him and go upstairs to see if she could sneak onto the roof without being seen. It was after business hours, and so she presumed those hallways would be mostly empty.

However, when she turned the corner toward her dressing room, there, in the hallway, was Megan, in her cinnamon-colored Saks Fifth Avenue suede bomber jacket, holding a bouquet of purple irises.

"I watched about half of it from home," she called, "and couldn't resist coming by."

"I let her come up," Ollie said. "I hope this is okay, Dana."

Technically, Dana had already forgiven Megan for withholding critical information on the noncompete clause of her contract. Emotionally, though, it was hard to release the feeling of betrayal. She wanted to, wanted to forgive her friend fully and completely. They shared so much history, and had been close since the day they met in an acting class at NYU Tisch, when they were both freshman theater majors.

"Are those for me?" she asked, pointing to the flowers.

"No, they're for the key grip," Megan said, deadpan. "I never show up on set without a bouquet for the key grip." She handed the flowers to Dana, who accepted them with a smile.

"Come in and see my new digs," she said, opening the door to her dressing room.

Megan surveyed the room and gave a long, low whistle. "Not bad for a kid who got chewed out by Santucci for sitting on an imaginary cat."

It was true. They had been in the middle of an improv class when Dana forgot that one of the other student actors had been petting his beloved Min-Min on the sofa. Dana was playing a despondent teenager, and had let herself drop heavily right onto the spot where the imaginary tabby had been happily purring.

Nice work, Barry, the acting coach had boomed, *you just killed the fucking cat.*

Her nickname for the rest of the semester was Scar, after the murderous character in *The Lion King*.

"I will find a vase for your flowers, Dana," Ollie said.

"Don't worry about it," Dana said. "Why don't you go home for the day? I'll take care of it."

"Are you certain?" he asked.

"It's fine. I'll see you tomorrow."

After he left, Megan acted as if she was checking for cats before taking a seat on the sofa. Dana let herself fall into one of the upholstered chairs, and Megan howled like a wounded feline. It wasn't the first, second or even third time she had made that exact joke. It had reached a point where the very stupidity of repeating it so often had usurped all the humor.

"So it went well," Megan said, as more of a statement than a question.

"Apparently."

"Any problems I should know about?"

Dana shrugged. "I don't think Sherry likes me."

"Why? What happened?"

"Nothing huge. Maybe I'm reading too much into it, but I think she was trying to intimidate me."

"She's pretty intense," Megan said.

"I know. It's probably nothing." Dana got up and went to the dressing alcove. She took off the pearl gray sheath she had borrowed from wardrobe, hung it up on the rack and got back into her own clothes—jeans and a V-neck top she had picked up from the clearance shelf at Hot Topic, using her employee discount. It appeared to be a black-and-white houndstooth pattern, but when you looked closely, the white part of the pattern was actually skulls.

"What the hell is that?" Megan said, pointing to her top.

"This?" Dana said, pulling on it.

"Alas, poor Yorick," Megan said.

"I thought it was subtle."

Megan sighed and slipped out of her jacket. "Put this on," she said, handing it to Dana.

"Why?"

"Because you need to look like a professional now."

"You sound like my sister," Dana said.

"I sound like anyone who's lived on Planet Grown-up for more than five minutes."

Dana stroked the suede. "This is silly," she said. "The day is over. Hardly anyone will even see me on the way out."

"Humor me," Megan said.

Dana slipped on the jacket in front of the full-length mirror and felt instantly transformed.

"Sweet Jesus," Megan said as she stood behind Dana and peered at her reflection. "That looks amazing on you."

Dana hugged herself and stroked the sleeve. "It's a gorgeous piece."

"You know what?" Megan said. "Keep it."

"Don't be ridiculous!" Dana said. "Absolutely not."

Megan folded her arms. "Don't insult me," she said. "It's a gift. To make up for my massive fuckup."

"No," Dana said. "I can't accept it. Next you'll want to give me a pound of flesh."

"There won't be a next time. I'm done being a jerk. Besides," she said, grabbing the meaty part of her thighs, "if I knew how to give you a pound of flesh I'd have done it years ago."

Dana surveyed her reflection. It really was a hell of a jacket.

"You're keeping it," Megan said. "Resistance is futile."

At last, Dana relented. She threw her arms around Megan. "Thank you," she said. "I'll treasure it." She knew then that she would. And that she had, in fact, forgiven her friend.

"Want to go out for a bite?" Megan asked.

Dana hesitated. She still wanted to search the roof as soon as possible, and for a moment, she considered telling Megan the truth—about the joint and about Lorenzo—but she knew that her friend would go ballistic at the idea that Dana had risked the job by getting high on the premises. And now that Dana considered it from Megan's sensible perspective, she saw how juvenile her judgment had been. If she wanted to keep this job, she would need to start thinking more like someone who lived on Planet You-Have-to-Stop-Acting-Like-a-Snotty-Teenager.

For now, though, she would tell a little white lie to backtrack over her stupid mistake.

"I'd love to," she said. "But the segment producer asked me to see him after the program. Rain check?"

11

After Megan left, Dana lingered awhile in her dressing room, just to be sure the executive floor would be deserted. Her patience was rewarded, because by the time she got up there, the receptionist was gone and there wasn't a soul around. All she had to do was swipe her ID card by the sensor to let herself in, and slip down the hallway.

The yellow police tape was still there, marking off the end of the corridor that led to Kitty's office and the stairway to the roof, but all was still and quiet. The police had packed up and left for the day. And the overnight Shopping Channel crew had no reason to be on this floor after business hours. Still, Dana took an extra sweeping glance to make sure there was no one around who could see her, then she ducked under the tape and went up the stairs. She pushed open the metal door, and was out on the roof, where a pink-and-gold sunset had settled over the Hudson River. The colors were slashed with blades of silver clouds that edged the bright white setting sun. It was so beautiful her hand automatically went to her heart, as if it took extra effort to keep it inside.

But Dana didn't want to take too much time for her rapture. She was up there with a mission, and would lose light soon. And so she retraced her steps from the door to the west side of the building, scanning the ground for any sign of the joint. She realized it could have blown into a corner, or even off the roof. But she needed to check the entire surface. And so she took out her cell phone and, using the flashlight app, began scanning every inch of the roof, walking from one end to the other. The ground was dirtier than she realized, and every light-colored splinter of debris caused her to stop and crouch for a closer look. At last she saw something that seemed to be joint-like in dimensions, but when she kneeled to get a better view, she saw that it was just a sliver of paper.

"Looking for this?" came a male voice behind her, and Dana jumped, her heart nearly flipping in her chest. She whirled around to see Detective Marks looming over her, holding a baggie.

"What the hell?" she said.

He shook the plastic bag at her and Dana could see that there was a familiar joint inside.

"This yours, by any chance?"

"What are you doing up here?" she asked, taking a step back to look him in the eye.

"My job. You?"

"I, uh…" Dana knew she needed to admit she was looking for something, but what? "I'm missing a ring and I thought maybe it had fallen off."

"A ring *fell* off your finger?"

Damn, she thought. *I should have said bracelet.* "It was pretty loose."

"You didn't answer my question," he said.

"What question?"

"The weed. Is it yours?"

"No!"

"Then you won't mind giving me a DNA sample."

The question felt as sharp as a needle. "What?" she said as she struggled to understand his reasoning.

"DNA. That way we can rule you out as the owner of the joint."

"I'm not giving you my DNA."

"I can get a warrant, you know. Up to you."

"Why would you even care whose joint it is? Do New York City homicide detectives bust people for having marijuana now?"

"I'm trying to connect the dots in a murder investigation," he said.

You mean you're trying to connect the dots to Lorenzo, she thought. "Am I a suspect? You want to check my fingerprints against the murder weapon?"

"Interesting that you're willing to give me your fingerprints but not your DNA."

Clearly, he knew it was her joint. Worse, if he tested for DNA it would come up positive for both hers and Lorenzo's. She'd lose her job and Lorenzo would lose his freedom. Dana weighed her options, trying to figure out what an inhabitant of Planet Nip-This-Thing-in-the-Tightly-Rolled-Bud would do. There had to be a way out of this, and it didn't seem like lying was working.

"Okay," she said, "it's my joint. You got me. Can I have it back, please?"

"Why would I give it back to you?"

"Because you're a human being and you don't want to see me get fired from a job before I even have a chance to fuck it up in the usual way."

The corner of his mouth went up. "Is that what you normally do—fuck things up?"

"In general, yes. But I was hoping that for once I could be

an adult and have a real job and maybe not get axed before I have a chance to pay off my credit cards."

She thought he looked at her differently then—like his opinion of her had just gone up a notch. Or maybe he just found it amusing that she wasn't your average, well-behaved TV hostess who liked to get high once in a while.

"When was the last time you were fired?" he asked.

"Is this part of your investigation?"

"I'm just curious."

She shrugged. "About two weeks ago. From a mall store where teenagers buy stuff they think is rebellious, using their parents' money."

"Two weeks ago you worked in a mall store?"

"You see what I mean?" she said. "This is my big break. If I blow this, it's all over."

He folded his arms. "Tell me again what happened just before you heard the gunshot."

"I had just had an audition and was waiting to hear if I got the job. Lorenzo offered to give me a tour of the building and he thought the roof was pretty cool. So we came up here. That's really the whole story. Except for the part about the joint. I was stressed and thought it would chill me out a little. That's it. Then we heard the shot and went running downstairs."

"And your relationship with Mr. DeSantis?"

"There *is* no relationship. That was only the second time I met him."

"And yet you felt comfortable enough with him to take out a joint?"

"You've seen Lorenzo. Does he look like the judgmental type to you?"

The detective ignored her question. "And he never left your sight during that time?"

"Never. Now can I have my joint back, please? Pretty please? I'd really like to keep this job."

He went silent as he considered that, and Dana stared at him. As the seconds ticked by, she became aware of her own breathing. *Say yes*, she thought. *Say yes. Just reach into your pocket and pull out the plastic bag.*

"I'll make you a deal," he finally said. "Tell me what happened at the mall store to get you fired and I'll give you back the joint."

"Seriously?" she asked.

"Seriously."

Dana squinted at him. "Why do you want to know?"

"Does it matter?"

She let out a long breath. It didn't. And clearly, this guy was prone to asking questions, but not answering them. Her only conclusion was that he found her wayward behavior entertaining.

"Okay, okay," she said, considering where to begin. "So I was having a bad day and I let it get the better of me. I made a snide comment to a boy who came in looking for black lipstick."

Detective Marks's smirk widened into a smile. She actually saw teeth. And they were nice, too. This hardboiled detective had worn braces.

"And that was a firing offense?" he asked.

"Well, he dragged his mom back into the store and in the midst of her screaming at the manager to fire me, I may have suggested that she buy the black lipstick for herself to improve her looks."

The detective got his face back under control, though she could still sense a smile under the surface. He pulled the baggie out of his pocket. "You earned this back, Ms. Barry," he said, holding it just out of her reach.

"Call me Dana," she said, opening her palm.

Detective Ari Marks placed the baggie in her hand, then turned and walked toward the door to the building.

"Wait a second, Detective," she called out. "Are you investigating the married man Kitty Todd was having an affair with?"

He stopped and faced her. "Where did you hear that?"

"From Ollie, sort of. He's my assistant now and he let it slip."

He gave a small nod. "Good night, Ms. Barry."

So much for her request to be on a first-name basis. Clearly, he was set on keeping this relationship professional, despite breaking protocol to return the weed. It was probably for the best. The guy was too good-looking. Too tall. Too divorced. She didn't need to be tempted.

"Good night, Detective."

He opened the door to the building and went through it. Just before it closed she heard him say, "Nice jacket."

12

Dana bristled. If this guy thought he could charm her, he was dead wrong. Even if he did have nice teeth and eyes the color of the sky on a winter morning.

After making a quick stop at home, she took the subway downtown to the small theater where the Sweat City Company was meeting. She had already told them she would have to quit, but she wanted to say goodbye in person.

She found the troupe in the backstage area they referred to as their green room. It was really a dark alcove separated from the rest of the area by a musty red velvet curtain Dana assumed was a leftover prop from some period piece performed long ago. The walls were painted black, and the furnishings consisted of two mismatched sofas, several worn chairs and a wooden crate they used as a coffee table. When Dana arrived, the group was sitting around trying to rework their summer schedule. They had been planning to do a production of *Mrs. Woodbridge*, with Dana as the lead. Now, though, they were discussing whether they could still manage it, as the next most likely member to play the title role was Carolyn Beattie, who was having neck surgery in a few weeks.

"Sit next to me, traitor," said her friend Tyrel when she entered. He patted a spot on the sofa, unselfconscious about the tremor in his hand. When he first joined the group, he had explained to everyone that it was from a medication he took to control his borderline personality disorder. Dana thought the world would be a better place if everyone were as open about their issues as theater people.

"Don't joke," she said, lowering herself onto the sofa. "I'm feeling too guilty to take it kindly."

"Oh, come on," he said, giving her a hug. "Don't you dare. We're thrilled for you."

"Seriously, Dana," said one of her actress friends. "You're not allowed to feel guilty. That's grounds for having your SAG card revoked."

"I don't want you to have to give up on this play," Dana said.

"I don't know that we have a choice," said Nathan, the director. "I'm looking at a couple of other scripts."

Dana glanced at Raj Mahajan, an actor with paraplegia who had been cast as Mrs. Woodbridge's wise and irascible husband, an ex-athlete who used a wheelchair. The role was a show-stealer, and a tremendous opportunity for a talented actor with limited options. Despite the warnings, guilt gurgled in her gut like acid.

"What about Rachel?" she asked, nodding at the willowy blonde who could, at the very least, pull off the role visually, given the right wig. Even as she said it, though, Dana understood that it would be a struggle for this newest member of their troupe. Mrs. Woodbridge was a monster role. Dana was heartsick over giving it up.

"I just don't think I'm ready," Rachel said.

No one argued with her.

"Don't even think about it," Sylvia said. "I'd get laughed off the stage."

Her leading man sat in the corner, staring down at his hands, and Dana almost started crying. "I'm so sorry, Raj," she said, and turned to Nathan. "Can you put it on the schedule for the fall, when Carolyn is recovered?"

"I don't think we'll be able to get the rights," he said.

"I guess an audition is out of the question?" Dana asked, though she already knew the answer. The Sweat City players were committed to their ensemble's bylaws, which included the rule that new members played supporting roles for their first year with the troupe. Bringing in a new actor was a big deal, and there was almost no chance they would make an exception and agree to thrust her into a lead.

Nathan shook his head. "We voted on it."

"This is a nightmare," Dana said.

"Hey, it's showbiz," Tyrel responded, doing jazz hands.

He meant to make her laugh, but Dana had a lump in her throat the size of a large rat. "I hope you guys know I would have fought the noncompete clause if I—"

"Of course we know," Sylvia said.

Nathan walked over to Dana and put a hand on her shoulder. "We'll work something out."

She trusted Nathan, and knew what he meant. He'd find a script that wouldn't shortchange a single member of the troupe. Still, it would be a massive pain in the ass, and it was all her fault.

Dana rubbed her forehead and imagined staying with the group, consequences be damned. She'd get caught, of course, and would have no excuse, no way to play dumb after the conversations she'd had with Megan and Sherry. Then she'd lose her contract and possibly even get sued. And despite herself, Dana discovered that she actually liked the damned job—was, in fact, still high off her triumphant first day—and was hoping to keep it long after the murder investigation was wrapped up and Lorenzo was exonerated.

If only Sweat City didn't promote so aggressively, with the names of its members on every poster and on the cover of every program. There was simply no way to keep her commitment to the group while flying under the radar. And then… an idea. Dana turned it one way and then the other, examining it for flaws. It was so simple. A little dangerous, sure, but she could mitigate all that. "My God," she murmured, barely realizing she had said it out loud.

"What is it?" Cyndi asked.

"I think… I think I may have a solution." Her heart thudded in her chest, which she knew was probably a warning to leave the idea alone and stick to the game plan. But damn, it could work. It could!

Raj picked his head up. "Seriously?"

Dana swallowed hard. "Kayla Bean," she said.

"Who's Kayla Bean?" Nathan asked.

Dana held out her arms to indicate that he was, in fact, resting his eyes upon the very woman.

"You?" Raj asked.

"Why not? It's a cool stage name, isn't it?"

"Is that a loophole in your Shopping Channel contract or something?" Tyrel asked.

"Hell, no," she said. "That thing is airtight. But if I perform under a stage name, how would they ever find out?"

"Someone could see you," Nathan said. "In the play. Those squeaky things out front are seats. People sit in them, watch the performances."

"But there are only eighty of them," she said. "What are the chances someone from the Shopping Channel would see me?"

"Your face will be known, honey," Tyrel said. "Someone could spot you and then word would get out."

"I'll wear a wig, maybe a prosthetic nose."

"That could actually work," said Rachel.

Nathan shook his head. "I can't let you put yourself in that kind of jeopardy."

"Nathan is right," Cyndi said. "It's too chancy. If you got in trouble—"

"We can't let you risk so much," Raj added.

"Shouldn't that be up to me?" Dana asked.

Nathan paced around the room, thinking, and everyone followed him with their eyes, waiting for some kind of definitive opinion—something that would put everyone on the same page. He walked the perimeter of the room twice, and finally stopped behind Raj.

"Well?" asked Dana. "What are you thinking?"

"I'm thinking," he said, massaging the muscles on the back of Raj's neck, "that we should take a vote."

13

The biggest problem, as far as Dana could see, would be keeping her secret from Megan, who would want to know where Dana was on those evenings she was busy rehearsing with Sweat City. She hated lying to her friend, but she had no choice. The challenge would be inventing a story that would hold up. Maybe she would tell her she was taking French lessons. No, cooking classes. Maybe French cooking classes. That would work.

Meanwhile, the danger of her double life gave Dana an electric charge. She even discovered there was something liberating about performing under a pseudonym. Free from the worry of people judging the talent of Dana Barry, she let herself go into the role in a way that felt new to her. The rehearsal that followed the vote had been a revelation.

"Damn, girl," Tyrel had said. "If you don't watch it we'll wind up on Broadway, and then you'll be hip-deep in the shit."

"But happy shit," Dana said, as it was hard to imagine such a thing being bad news, even if it meant getting fired from the Shopping Channel. Okay, so she could get sued. But still. Broadway!

It was ridiculous, of course—utterly farfetched. But as an actor, such dreams kept her going.

At work the next day, after Adam Weintraub briefed her on the products she would be selling in her show, Dana asked if Sherry had been impressed with her sales the day before.

"She doesn't impress easily," Adam said.

"But she was pleased?"

"She wasn't *displeased*. That's about as good as it gets with her."

It was time then for hair and makeup. Dana hoped to pump Felicia and Jo for dirt on Kitty's affair with Charles Honeycutt, but Ollie insisted on accompanying her, and again, she couldn't think of an excuse to leave him behind. She was starting to wonder if it might have been a mistake to take this guy as her assistant.

Afterward, as she walked with Ollie to the elevator, he filled her in on the Bastina shifts Irini would be bringing by.

"I saw photos, Dana," Ollie said. "Very pretty dresses. Short. I think you'll like these."

He pushed the down button for the elevator, and when the doors slid open, there stood Charles Honeycutt with a very attractive forty-ish black woman in a purple knit dress and a diamond ring that seemed to need its own circuit breaker. She was fit, with ten-mile legs highlighted by a pair of tan suede pumps.

"Ah, there's Dana," Charles said, as if he'd been talking about her. He introduced her to his wife, Victoria, and said they were going out to lunch for her birthday.

"Happy birthday!" Dana said, and studied the woman's face for any signs she might know she was married to a cheater. But she was as cool as a frozen margarita made with top-shelf tequila, and twice as fancy. She exuded confidence, and Dana

sensed that she was a successful professional in her own right—
a lawyer, perhaps. Or maybe an executive like her husband.

Then Dana glanced at Charles Honeycutt's face to see if
there was anything in his eyes to indicate that he might be
a murderer. But there was nothing in his countenance that
telegraphed a sinister beast lurking beneath the surface. If
anything, he seemed relaxed—like a man who just returned
from vacation.

When they got off the elevator, Dana turned to Ollie, determined to use this opportunity to squeeze him for information. But when she saw his face she paused. There was a
whole story in his expression, though she couldn't quite tell
what it was. He looked pleased but uncertain, his eyes moist.

"What is it?" she asked. "Is something wrong?"

"No, no. They are a fine couple. Happy."

"Yes, that's how they seem."

He cleared his throat. "Miss Irini is meeting us at your
dressing room. We must get there now."

Not exactly a slippery dodge. This guy moved out of the
line of fire like there was gum on his shoes. "Ollie," she said,
"tell me what's upsetting you."

"I am not upset, Dana. I am very glad to think that Mr.
Honeycutt will not leave his wife. This is good."

"Was there trouble in the marriage, as far as you know?"

He shrugged.

"You can tell me," she said, leaning in. "Is Mr. Honeycutt
the man who was in love with Kitty?"

His eyes filled with fear. "I can't tell you that, Dana."

She laid a gentle hand on his arm. "I know you want to
protect her. That's noble, but—"

"But she is gone," he said, nodding. "Yes, Dana. I understand. But I don't wish to get Mr. Honeycutt in trouble."

If he murdered Kitty, she thought, *the last thing he deserves is your protection.* "You didn't tell the detective about him?"

"No, I...I told him I didn't know who Miss Kitty's boy-friend was, only that he was married."

"Why would you say such a thing, Ollie? The detective needs to investigate."

"He wouldn't hurt her! I know this! They were so much in love. But if the police know it was Mr. Honeycutt, they will think the worst. You must not tell them, Dana. Please. Miss Kitty trusted me with this very big secret."

"Ollie, even if you're right about their romance—"

"I *am* right, Dana! You should see what he bought for her. A necklace with a heart of diamonds! A watch. A special bed for her house—big and with memory foam. So expensive! And the flowers. All the times, the flowers!"

"And he was going to leave his wife for Kitty? You're sure of this?"

"Yes, they wanted to be together forever. She was so happy in love with this man, Dana. And he was with her, too."

"Does Mr. Honeycutt have kids?" she asked.

"Two girls," Ollie said. "Very sad. But he was going to make new family with Miss Kitty."

Dana supposed it was possible, but she doubted it. From what she saw, Charles Honeycutt had it all—a drop-dead gorgeous successful wife, a great career, a couple of kids. To Dana, it seemed highly unlikely he was ready to walk away from all that.

They rounded the corner of the hallway and saw Irini pushing a rack of colorful frocks toward Dana's dressing room.

"I will leave you with Miss Irini now," Ollie said, holding open the door. "Please tell me when you are finished."

After getting into wardrobe, Dana sent Ollie to the lobby to wait for her sister, who would be coming to the studio that day as Dana's guest. She knew Chelsea wouldn't be arriving for at least another half hour, but she wanted Ollie out of her hair so she could get a few minutes alone with Lorenzo.

Dana rushed off to the set and poked her head into the sound booth, where Lorenzo was seated next to a coworker. He looked up and nodded.

"Be right back," he mumbled, taking off his headphones.

"I have some news," she said when he joined her in the hallway. "It's *Charles Honeycutt*."

She had hoped her enthusiasm would be contagious, but Lorenzo was anxious and distracted. "What about him?" he asked. His eyes were tense.

"He's the one Kitty was having an affair with," she whispered. "According to Ollie, Kitty believed he was getting ready to leave his wife for her."

"Honeycutt," he repeated, his voice even.

"You don't sound surprised."

"Just…disappointed," he said.

"Why disappointed?"

"I guess I hoped she was carrying on with someone less… impeccable."

"No one's impeccable," she said.

"Maybe not impeccable, but the kind of guy more capable of white-collar crime than homicide."

"That kind of guy has a lot to lose," she said. "I mean, what if Kitty was threatening to go to his wife or something?"

Lorenzo rubbed the stubble on his cheek. He needed a shave. A haircut, too. But there was something appealing about the scruffiness. In the theater world, it was hard to find a man so lacking in vanity.

"Well, I'm going to call Marks and tell him," she said.

"Won't fight you on that," he said. "Not when the guy is so itchy to slap me in cuffs."

"Did he question you again?"

"He spoke to my parole officer. Now I'm being watched like a lab rat."

Dana wanted to comfort him in some way. But she knew that a hug would feel more risky than soothing. They couldn't afford to look like a couple right now. Dana reached out and grazed his wrist with her fingertips. He grabbed hold of her hand and closed his eyes, as if making a wish. When he opened them, his look was smoldering. His eyes went from her lips to her throat and his desire tugged at her.

Dana looked up and down the hallway. No one was around. She stood on her toes and kissed him on the lips, holding on to his shoulders. He hesitated for a moment, and then kissed back. His stubble scratched her face and she wanted more, wanted to press her body against his, to feel the warmth of him. But he quickly pushed her away.

"We can't," he said.

She was about to respond when two prop guys pushing a display table rounded the corner. Lorenzo took a step back and put his hands in the pockets of his denim jacket. Then he gave her a small nod, and slipped back into the engineering booth.

Dana stood there for several minutes, waiting for her pulse to slow. She was just about to go inside when the studio door opened and Jessalyn stepped out.

"There you are," she said. "Ready?"

Dana exhaled and took a moment to focus. "Ready," she said, and followed Jessalyn inside, determined to make today even better than yesterday. She would impress Sherry Zidel if it killed her.

14

"Not bad for a loser," Chelsea said, giving her sister a hug.

The show had gone well. At least, that's how it seemed to Dana. She had transported into that zone again, and the four hours whizzed by as she gushed about the products and kept an eye on the monitor to see the sales numbers clicking ever upward.

"Was I okay?" she asked.

"Are you kidding? You're a rock star."

"If you mean like Nickelback, I'll—"

"Dana, seriously. I was so blown away I texted Dad and told him to turn on his television."

Her father. She knew she would have to see him again soon, as her nephew's birthday was coming up, but she managed to block him from her mind on most days.

"Dad was watching? I'm surprised he didn't call in to ask when I'd be fired."

"To hell with him," Chelsea said. "*I'm* proud of you. You were amazing. So focused, so...*natural*. You looked like you've been doing this your whole life!"

Sherry Zidel and her assistant, Emily, were a few feet away from them, chatting with Adam Weintraub as they scrolled through some data on a tablet. But if Sherry heard the praise, she gave no indication.

Adam looked up. "We were just going over the numbers," he said, waving Dana over. "You did great on the skirts, even better on the dresses."

"I'm so glad," Dana said, and introduced Sherry, Emily and Adam to her sister.

"Did you see the whole segment?" Adam asked Chelsea.

"Most of it," she said. "I wanted to buy everything she was selling...in every color!"

Adam grinned. "Our kind of customer."

"No kidding," Dana said. "If Chelsea stopped shopping the economy would collapse." She turned to Sherry and tried to make her laugh. "Hey, maybe you should hire Chelsea as a buyer here. She's got experience purchasing in bulk."

Adam and Chelsea laughed, but Emily looked down and Sherry's expression got even tighter. "That would be nepotism."

"I was kidding," Dana said.

"It's kind of an issue around here," Adam explained. "There was a scandal a few years back with a VP installing his nephew into a no-show job. So now we don't hire relatives of employees except in the rarest circumstances."

Sherry coughed and brought the conversation back to Dana's performance. "You didn't sell out the bracelets," she said.

Adam's forehead tightened and he swiped through some pages on the tablet. "Two percent over projections."

"Two percent isn't much," Sherry said. She turned to Dana. "Why didn't you put it on?"

"I draped it over my wrist for the camera," Dana said. "I thought that would do it."

"Viewers couldn't see the toggle. If you had just slipped

the T-bar through the loop we might have sold a few hundred more units."

Adam gave Dana a reassuring look to let her know Sherry was being unreasonable.

"Thanks for the heads-up," Dana said to Sherry. "I'll do better next time."

"Toggles are easy to manage with one hand," Sherry said, as if Dana were fighting with her. "That's the whole point."

So's a karate chop to the throat, Dana thought. "Yes, of course."

And that was it. Sherry told Adam that she'd see him tomorrow, and walked away.

"She doesn't seem pleased," Dana said to Adam.

"Don't take it too hard," he said. "If there were any problems with your sales, I'd be the first to let you know."

"If it's not my sales, I guess she just hates me in general."

"No, no," Adam said. "It's nothing like that. I think Kitty's death really threw her."

"Were they close?" Chelsea asked.

"Hell, no," Adam said. "Half the time I expected one of them to spontaneously combust."

Dana folded her arms. It made no sense. If they didn't get along, why would Sherry be so broken up over her death? As an actor, Dana was accustomed to digging deep into characters to understand their motivations. But Sherry's eluded her.

Adam patted Dana's shoulder. "Keep up the good work. Your sales are averaging eight percent above projections, which is astounding, especially for a new host. Just keep doing what you're doing. Let me handle Sherry."

"I think I know what the problem is," Chelsea said as she walked down the hall with Dana. "I've seen it on the tennis courts more times than I can count."

"A weak serve?" Dana asked.

Chelsea ignored the joke. "Sherry needs an adversary. With Kitty gone, you're it."

Dana considered that, and realized her sister might be right. Some people were just so tribalistic at their core that they needed an enemy. "You know, you're not as blond as you look," she said.

"And you clean up okay," Chelsea responded, indicating Dana's head-to-toe appearance with a sweep.

"Don't get too excited," Dana said. "I have to give all this stuff back."

She held open the door of her dressing room and Chelsea stepped inside.

"This all yours?" she asked, looking around.

"All mine."

Chelsea walked to the clothing rack where Dana's jeans and T-shirt hung. "And you still wear this shit to work?"

"But look at my jacket!" Dana said, not bothering to explain that it had been Megan's.

Chelsea felt the suede. "Calfskin," she cooed, as if falling in love.

Dana pulled the dress off over her head and put it on a hanger. "So what did you think of Lorenzo?" She grabbed her jeans and started wriggling into them.

"Who's Lorenzo?"

Dana reached for her shirt. "The sound guy."

"Are you kidding?" Chelsea said. "With the tattoos and the stubble?"

"Cute, right?"

"No!" Chelsea sounded horrified. "He looks like a felon."

Dana grimaced. "He kind of…is."

"Dana!"

"I know… I know. But he's reformed."

"You're not involved with him, are you?"

"I've only been working here two days." It was a hedge. She stole a furtive glance at her sister's expression. She wasn't buying it.

"Answer the question," Chelsea said.

Dana sighed, relenting. "Come here," she said, leading her sister to the couch. "I have to tell you something."

Chelsea clucked and settled in next to her. "Do I want to hear this?"

"Maybe not," Dana said, "but you're going to." And then she unloaded, as it had been simply too much to hold in. She told her sister everything—the kiss on the roof, what it was like to see all that blood in Kitty's office, the terrible realization that she had left the joint behind, getting caught by the detective and even her suspicions about Charles Honeycutt.

"And since Lorenzo has a record…" Dana trailed off.

"He's a suspect?" Chelsea offered.

"*Prime* suspect."

"And this Honeycutt guy?" Chelsea asked.

"I don't know. That's the tough part. He doesn't strike me as a killer."

"They never do. That's why we have police departments. You can't keep this to yourself, Dana. You have to tell the detective."

"I *know*." Her tone was petulant, but Chelsea's directive was exactly what she needed to hear. It was the right thing to do.

"So what are you waiting for?" Chelsea picked up Dana's phone from the coffee table and handed it to her.

Dana stared at the screen for a moment, hesitant. If Honeycutt was innocent, she could be ruining his life for nothing. Even if he was exonerated, an investigation would reveal his affair to everyone, including his wife. That would be a hell of a thing. But of course, he might be guilty. And Kitty—as difficult as she was—deserved justice.

And then there was Lorenzo.

She dialed the number on the detective's card, and he picked up on the first ring.

"It's Dana Barry," she said, and then added, "from the Shopping Channel."

"I know who you are," he said, his tone even. "What can I do for you?"

"I have some information—something I think you should know. About Kitty."

"Where are you?"

"Now? I'm...in my dressing room." She paused, worried that it sounded suggestive. "At work."

"I'm in the area," he said. "I can be there in fifteen minutes."

She thought about Ollie, who was still in the building, running interference for her on a paperwork issue with the payroll department.

"Wait a minute," she said. "I'm not sure that's a good idea. I'm kind of betraying a confidence to tell you this and I don't want to—"

"Got it," he said. "You know Forks, on Fifty-Third?"

"The diner?" she asked.

"Five thirty," he said, and hung up.

Dana put down her phone and looked at her sister. "You up for a walk in those things?" she asked, pointing to Chelsea's spike-heeled boots.

"Pretty sure I can keep up," Chelsea said.

But she couldn't. Dana had to slow her stride in order to match the pace of the tight *click-click-click* of Chelsea's heels. Still, they beat Detective Marks to the diner and slid into a booth, sitting across one another as they watched the door, waiting for him.

"There he is," Dana said, pointing out the window, where the detective was getting out of a dark SUV. He wore a slate-gray suit and white shirt, open at the collar. The last time Dana had seen him he'd been wearing a tie. She thought sunglasses would have made him look more like a cop, which she presumed was the reason he didn't wear them. He hesitated and glanced around. In that quick moment, he might have been pegged as the kind of guy that got featured in slick magazine articles with titles like "New York's Hottest Real Estate Brokers" or "Entrepreneurs to Watch." But those guys strutted with self-conscious bravado. Once Marks started moving, it was clear his focus was outward—not on himself and his place in the world, but on just about everything else.

"Are you kidding me?" Chelsea said. "What a tall drink of gorgeous! Is he single?"

"Divorced."

Chelsea raised an eyebrow. "You'd make a cute couple."

"Not a chance."

"Really? You're not attracted to that guy?"

Dana studied him, wishing he weren't so damned handsome. "I don't date divorced men."

"But ex-cons are fair game?"

Dana shrugged.

"You're a mental case," Chelsea said.

"Twice burned," Dana whispered as Marks entered the diner.

Chelsea stood. "Scoot over," she said, "I'll sit with you."

"No, let me sit on your side."

"Why?"

"Because he's a cop," Dana said. "He won't want to sit with his back to the door."

"Hello, ladies," Marks said when he approached.

The women stood, and Dana introduced him to her sister.

"Which side do you want to sit on?" Chelsea asked.

Marks pointed to the seat facing the door.

Dana tried to shoot her sister a subtle *told-you-so* look, but Chelsea pounced on it. Out loud.

"You were right!" she squealed. "He's like a movie detective."

Marks let out a small breath that could have been a snicker, and signaled the waitress for coffee. He slid into the booth, and she came right over to pour coffee for all three of them.

"Hey, Ari," the waitress said.

"How's the diner biz?" he asked.

"A three-Advil headache," she said. "How's the murder biz?"

"Ran out of Advil a long time ago."

When the waitress was out of earshot, Marks leaned forward. "Tell me what you learned," he said.

"It was from Ollie," Dana said.

Marks squinted, remembering. "Oliver Sikanen—you said he's your assistant now."

She paused to wait for a roll of the eyes—something to indicate that he knew Ollie was a piece of work—but Ari Marks didn't offer opinions so generously. "Here's the thing," she continued, "he told me that Kitty was having an affair with our company president, Charles Honeycutt."

"Anything else?"

"Apparently, it was serious. Kitty thought he would leave his wife for her."

"And you got all this from Oliver Sikanen?"

Dana hesitated, wondering if he doubted Ollie's veracity. Or maybe hers.

"He didn't want to tell me," she said, "but he couldn't

help himself. He was utterly devoted to Kitty and has been a wreck. In any case, I don't know if Honeycutt really planned to leave, but apparently Kitty believed it and so does Ollie."

"But you don't?"

Dana shrugged. "It's possible, I guess. But it seems unlikely."

Marks took a sip of his coffee. "Do you have any proof of this affair?"

"Kind of," Dana said. "The day of Kitty's murder I got close enough to Honeycutt to smell him."

"Smell him?" Chelsea asked.

"And guess what he smelled like?" Dana asked, looking from Chelsea to Marks.

"I can't imagine," the detective said, his voice flat.

"Apricots!" Dana said. "He smelled like *apricots*. You know what else smells like apricots? Dr. Lydia's California Dreams Skin Repair Lotion."

Chelsea gasped. "It does!" she said. "I bought it once."

Dana laughed. *"Once?"*

"A few times," Chelsea admitted.

"By the case?"

"Can we get back on topic here?" Marks asked.

"The point is," Dana said to him, "Kitty was addicted to California Dreams. She rubbed it on her hands all day long. It was even on her desk when she died."

Marks took his notepad from his pocket and quickly flipped through several pages. "Right."

Dana looked closely at his face, and thought she saw a flicker of admiration. But maybe not. This guy was hard to read.

"Dana notices *everything*," Chelsea gushed.

"Clearly," Marks said, and turned to Dana. "Have you spoken with anyone else about this?"

"Not yet," Dana said. "But I can ask the girls in makeup if

they know about the affair. And Robért, the hairstylist. They know everything about everyone."

Marks shook his head. "Leave that to me. Don't talk to anyone else about this."

"I wouldn't say anything stupid," Dana said.

"I'm sure you wouldn't."

"Dana can be an asset to you, Detective," Chelsea said.

"I appreciate that. But you need to let the police handle the investigation."

"She's also single," Chelsea said.

Dana kicked her sister under the table.

The detective put down his coffee and reached for his wallet. "I'm well aware of Ms. Barry's marital status," he said, and signaled the waitress for the bill.

Well aware, Dana repeated silently to herself. If she was interested in him, it was just the kind of remark she would want to dissect. She wasn't, of course, but thanks to Chelsea, he'd be leaving with the wrong impression entirely. She had to try to set the record straight.

"I'm sorry about my sister," Dana said to him. "You'll have to excuse her. Sometimes she's…an idiot."

"I doubt that very much," he said, and Chelsea kicked Dana under the table.

He smoothed his collar. "Is there anything else?"

Dana wanted to ask about Lorenzo—to find out if this meant he was off the hook. But she knew that the more interest she showed, the worse it would be for him.

"Are you going to pursue this?" she asked.

"We pursue everything that's appropriate," he said, standing.

"What about Charles Honeycutt?" Chelsea asked. "Is he a suspect now?"

The waitress put the check on the table. Marks grabbed it

and thanked her. "That's not something I can discuss with you," he said.

"I think he means that everyone's a suspect," Chelsea said. "Is that right, Detective?"

"Have a good night, ladies," he said.

As they watched him walk away, Dana thought about Charles Honeycutt and swallowed against a knot in her throat. She hoped she had done the right thing.

"What do you think?" she asked her sister.

"I think he likes you."

15

"I forgot to ask," Megan said. "How did your Sweat City friends take the news?"

It was the next day, and they were at the Shopping Channel, sitting in Dana's dressing room. Megan had insisted it was her job to run interference with Sherry, so when Dana called to explain how tense things were, she insisted on coming in.

"They were...supportive. Of course. Everyone was happy for me."

"What are they doing about that play? The one where you were the horrible grand dame."

There was no way she could tell Megan the truth—that she was still playing the role, albeit under a stage name. "Uh, not sure. Recasting, I suppose."

"I hope you're not too upset," Megan said, her eyes soft with sympathy. It was clear she wanted to help Dana work through her grief over leaving her beloved group.

Dana dismissed it with a wave. "I'm dealing with it," she said, and made a quick pivot. "So how are things at the restaurant?"

"You don't have to change the subject."

"I'm fine with it, really."

"And you don't blame me?"

Dana shook her head emphatically. "I've moved on."

Megan gave her a dubious look, and Dana went mute. It was a tough moment. She knew she could convince Megan she was bereft at having left Sweat City behind—she was an actor, after all. But that would mean digging deeper into the lie, and guilt tugged at her.

"You used to be honest with me about *everything*," Megan said. "I don't want that to change just because I'm your manager."

Dana sighed and committed to pushing the fiction just as far as she had to, and not an inch more. "Okay. Look, I'm still upset. I'd just rather not dwell on it. Don't take it personally."

"But you forgive me?" Megan said.

"Yes, I promise. I forgive you."

There was a soft knock on the door. It was Ollie.

"Miss Felicia is ready for you, Dana," he said.

"Come in, Ollie," she said. "I want you to meet Megan Silvestri, my manager."

"If I can be of service, I hope you will let me know," he said, shaking her hand.

"Kind of you," Megan replied, smiling, and Dana could tell she was amused by Ollie's odd formality.

"You like Dana's dressing room, yes?" he asked. "It was painted just for her. Nice green walls."

"Lovely," she said. "What color was it before?"

"First white, then Miss Kitty says no, she likes coral."

Dana's breath caught in her throat. This was news to her. "Are you saying this room was Kitty's?"

"You didn't know?" Megan asked.

"I thought it was Vanessa's."

Ollie shook his head. "Miss Vanessa has same dressing room as before."

A wave of nausea pressed on Dana as she pictured the gruesome murder scene. The blood on the window. Bits of Kitty's brain. She had no idea she'd made herself comfortable in a murdered woman's private space. "I think I'm going to be sick," she said.

Megan put a hand on her shoulder. "It's okay."

Ollie looked stricken. "Dana, I am so sorry. I thought that you knew. Please. Don't be sad for this. Everything is new. The police took away all of Miss Kitty's things in boxes, and then everything is replaced. Everything but counter and drawers and mirrors."

"Oh, God," she said, imagining the police storming the room in rubber gloves, placing evidence in baggies and boxes. She glanced up at Ollie, who looked worse than she felt.

"Are you okay?" she asked. He had gone as white as copy paper.

"I… I am just remembering that bad day," he said.

Me, too, she thought. But of course, she had barely known Kitty. And certainly hadn't worshipped her. "Sit down, Ollie."

He did as she said, and Megan got him a glass of water.

"I am very sorry," he said. "I try not to think about Miss Kitty but sometimes I am too weak." He rubbed his sweaty hands on his mauve skinny jeans.

"You're allowed to be upset about this," Dana said.

"She would have been so angry to see the police take her things. But what can I do? I cannot protect her."

"There was nothing you could do," Megan said. "And I'm sure the police will return her things to her family after the investigation."

"I do not know what they got," he mumbled.

Dana studied him as he stared down at his bitten nails, and realized what he was talking about. The gifts. The ones Kitty got from Charles Honeycutt. If Marks had them, he could trace them to the source.

"Ollie," she said gently, "those gifts Kitty got from…from her lover—did she keep them here at the office?"

He gave a sideways glance toward Megan.

"It's okay," Dana said. "You can trust her."

"I don't know. I think she had them somewhere hid. She did not tell me where they were. But she was so careful."

If they had been hidden in this room, the police surely found them, as everything had been emptied and cleaned. And given how carefully the detectives had combed Kitty's office, Dana doubted there was anything unfound there, either. She hoped Marks was taking a close look at Kitty's possessions.

After calming Ollie down, Dana went to the hair and makeup department, while Megan went up to see Sherry.

"I'm going to give you a French," Jo said to Dana as she removed her pale pink nail polish with a saturated cotton ball that felt cold on her skin.

"I thought that was off-limits," Dana said.

"Not anymore," she said. "You've heard the expression, 'You can't take it with you'? That applies to manicures, too. Kitty's dead. I can give a French to whomever I want."

Whomever. Dana smiled at the proper grammar usage, even though Jo had pronounced it *whomevah*. The woman sounded like a character from *Guys and Dolls*.

"It's hard to find anyone who's broken up over her death," Dana said. "Other than Ollie, I mean." Regardless of Marks's warning, she was determined to find out as much as she could.

"She was a witch," Felicia said.

Jo clucked. "I was thinking of a different word entirely."

"What about the men?" Dana asked. "You had said she was sleeping around."

"Are you kidding?" Jo said. "They hated her the most."

"She held it over their heads," Felicia added.

Dana looked at her. "Over their heads?"

"She used them," Jo said. "You know, like give-me-what-I-want-or-I'll-tell-everybody."

Felicia dabbed blush onto Dana's cheeks. "That's why she went after the married ones."

"She was one twisted lady," Jo added with a nod. "They say she had at least a couple of breakdowns."

"While she worked here?" Dana asked.

Jo turned to Felicia. "Remember that time she went to Paris? For a whole month?"

"I heard she was committed," Felicia said.

"What brought it on?" Dana asked.

"Love," Jo said. "What else? Most of us just bawls our eyes out for a few days when our hearts is broken. But Kitty? When she don't get what she wants, she falls apart."

"Goes completely crazy," Felicia added.

"So these guys she sleeps with—you don't think any of them were in love with her?" Dana asked.

Felicia made a face. "How could *anybody* love Kitty?"

"Was that a constant thing for her?" Dana asked. "Falling in love?"

Felicia and Jo shared a look.

"What?" Dana asked.

Felicia leaned forward. "Honeycutt," she whispered.

Dana's heart sped up. "What about him?"

"You really want to know?"

"Of course!"

"Well," Felicia said, "there's this girl, Micaela. You probably met her—she's Robért's assistant?"

"Does his blowouts sometimes," Jo added.

"She's best friends with Brooke, Honeycutt's assistant."

"Like sisters," Jo said, pushing at Dana's cuticles.

Felicia fished around for something in her makeup kit. "Brooke told Micaela that she heard the two of them fighting in his office. Kitty and Honeycutt, going at it. Said she was *hysterical*. Screaming and everything."

"What was she saying?" Dana asked.

"Something like, 'You said you loved me, you bastard.'"

"I think it was 'prick,'" Jo corrected. "'You said you loved me, you prick.'"

"Right," Felicia said. *"Prick."*

"So, like, a week later she's got this massive gold bracelet," Jo said. "An alligator bangle."

"Alligator?" Dana asked, searching her memory for where she had seen it.

"You know—a bracelet shaped like an alligator that wraps around your wrist. Frigging thing was huge. With emeralds for eyes and diamonds down the tail. Like supershowy, you know?"

At that, Dana remembered exactly where she had seen it. It was in the dish with Kitty's rings on the day she was killed.

"And you think Honeycutt gave it to her?"

"I *know* he did," Jo said.

"How?"

Jo held up the white ceramic bowl she kept on her manicure table. "She put it right here when I was doing her nails. Took it off with her rings. And there was an inscription inside—*Love, Charles.*"

"Hey, relax your forehead," Felicia said, rubbing the spot between Dana's brows.

"Sorry," Dana said, and tried to smooth out her confusion. "Why would a married guy want that kind of proof lying around? It doesn't make sense. I mean, if he was trying to keep the affair a secret..."

"Personally," Jo said, "I think she *made* him do it."

"That's what Brooke told Micaela," Felicia said. "That she thought it was a...what do you call that?"

"An ultimatum," Jo said.

'Yeah, a ultimatum. Kitty said something like, 'Prove you love me or I'll go to your wife.'"

Dana leaned back in the chair and closed her eyes as Felicia feathered on some eyeliner. She felt herself unwinding. Going to Marks about Honeycutt had been the right thing to do. The guy had a perfect motive for murdering Kitty Todd.

"Next week I want to put in a few highlights," Robért said as he shook a can of hairspray. "Just in the tips. It'll look *gorge*. Close your eyes, honey."

He encircled her in a cloud of suffocating mist. She waited until it settled before speaking. "Just in the tips? Won't that look a little weird?"

"You'd be surprised. You know Emily up in Sherry's office?"

"Emily Lauren," she said, nodding.

"I did it for her just before she auditioned."

"Auditioned? For what?"

"For Vanessa's spot—just like you."

Dana paused, trying to process the news. "Emily auditioned? Are you sure?"

"Of course I'm sure. I did her *hair*. Felicia gave her to-die-for boyfriend eyebrows. She looked like a *Vogue* model."

Dana let out a long breath as it sunk in. Sherry's beloved assistant had auditioned—with her boss's blessing, no doubt. If Sherry had lobbied for Emily to get the job that went to Dana, it would explain her animosity.

"How did she do?"

"Not as good as you, obviously."

"But Sherry thought she was better?"

Robért shrugged. "I can't get inside that bitch's head. All I know is, those two go at it like sisters but are twice as loyal. So if Sherry wanted Emily to have the job, I promise you she fought for it."

"I didn't think anyone could overrule her on casting."

"Only one person, love. Honeycutt."

16

It was almost 9:00 p.m. Dana had showered, changed and straightened up her apartment. Lorenzo would be there any minute.

They had been unable to get any time to talk at work that day, and she wanted to tell him what she learned, especially since he looked even more strained than usual. So she texted him her address and told him to come by "around nine." She tried to sound casual, like it wasn't a date. Or a booty call. But in truth, she wanted him in her bed. She liked Lorenzo—liked him more than Marks. And yes, sure. Marks was good-looking. And okay, he had a certain enigmatic appeal, especially since he looked at her so intensely while she spoke. But no, he was not her type. Divorced. And a cop. A suit-wearing rule-follower. No, thank you. She wanted to wipe him from her thoughts.

Meanwhile, Lorenzo was late. Dana looked out the window to check the weather. The delicate spring rain had morphed into an uncompromising downpour, and was pounding First Avenue with furious force. She pushed open her window and inhaled. The spring rain in New York was one of her favorite smells—like metal and brine and hope.

She tried to imagine Lorenzo on his way to her apartment in this weather. Maybe he was standing under an awning somewhere, waiting for it to let up. Then again, Lorenzo didn't seem like the kind of guy who cared about getting wet.

At twenty after nine, her cell phone buzzed with a text.

On my way.

That was it—no apology. No explanation. She tapped her foot, wondering if she should be irked, and decided no, it was fine. Twenty minutes wasn't such a big deal. He probably thought she meant any time after nine. In his mind, he was just stopping by to talk. And anyway, she didn't want to be the kind of woman who whined over such things.

At nine-thirty, Dana blew out the candles on her tiny bistro table. Then she lit them again. Then blew them out again. At 9:45, he finally rang from downstairs.

Lorenzo entered her apartment in the same clothes he had worn to work that day—a denim jacket, gray T-shirt and black Levi's—but they were soaked. His only concession to the weather was a baseball cap, which dripped when he moved his head.

"Sorry," he said, watching the water trickle onto the mat in front of her door.

"It's okay," she said. "Do you want to borrow a sweatshirt or something?"

He shook his head, unaware that doing so sprayed her with droplets. "I'll just sit on a towel."

She sighed. This did not seem like a man who planned on taking off his clothes anytime soon.

"At least let me take your jacket," she said.

He shook it off and handed it to her, along with his hat. Dana liked the way he looked in his T-shirt—lean and ropey.

She laid his wet things on a chair, then smoothed a long towel onto the sofa and handed him a smaller one to dry himself. He wiped his face, patted the back of his neck and sat.

"Can I get you something?" she asked.

"I'm fine."

"How about a glass of wine?"

"No, thanks. I can't really stay long."

"Oh?" So much for romance. A guy who came late and left early had other things on his mind. Maybe other women. She thought about that truckload of baggage he mentioned.

"Things are a little tense for me right now," he said.

"I have weed," she offered.

He held up his hands. "That's the *last* thing I need."

Dana glanced at his face. Usually, when she was alone in her apartment with a man, he was looking at her, thinking about when to make a move. But Lorenzo was so engrossed in his stress it was as if he didn't even see her. She poured herself a glass of wine. "What's going on?"

"I'm in some deep shit."

She sat next to him on the sofa and waited for him to continue.

"They gave me a urine test," he said.

"Who? The Shopping Channel?"

"My parole officer. Thanks to whatever Marks told him, he tested me for drugs."

That bastard, she thought. He may have been generous enough to give her back the joint, but he went ahead and fucked Lorenzo over. She was working up a full steam of hate for the guy.

"Have you done any drugs besides that one toke on the roof?" she asked. She tried to picture him in his own place, sitting in a haze of smoke, a giant bong by his side. Or maybe a handful of pills. Or worse—a needle and bent spoon. She hoped that wasn't true.

He let out a breath. "Nope."

She studied his face, which looked sincere. Those Lin-Manuel Miranda eyes. She exhaled, relieved. "So what are you worried about?"

"It could show up."

"One toke? Seriously?"

"It's fifty-fifty, Dana. And if it comes back positive, I'm fucked."

"They would send you back to jail for that? For just—"

"In a heartbeat."

Dana felt so sick she had to lower her head to keep from getting dizzy. This was a nightmare. "Is there something I can do?"

He shook his head. "Not your fault."

"Of course it's my fault."

"Dana, I'm an adult. I could have said no."

"But—"

"But nothing. I knew I was subject to random drug tests. I took a chance. My parole officer likes me, so I figured he'd never test me. Dumb assumption. I knew better."

"You couldn't have anticipated you'd get wrapped up in a murder investigation."

"But shit happens. All the time. I've seen it." He paused. "I've lived it."

Dana leaned back and closed her eyes. She was done blaming herself. This was Marks's fault. She finished her wine and poured another glass.

"You know the worst part?" he said. "I've got one month left on parole. That's it. Thirty days and I'm like any ordinary citizen. I don't even have to stay in New York. I can move to Wyoming. Or China."

"Is that what you want?" she asked. "To travel?"

He shook his head. "I just want to be *free*. That's the point. But if I get busted…" He trailed off, and she could tell he was playing the worst-case scenario in his head.

Dana held the wine bottle toward him. "You sure you don't want some?" she asked.

He looked tempted, then shook his head. "I have to leave soon."

"You have something to get home for?"

It was the kind of question she hoped he would shrug off with a light response. *Not at all, I'm just tired.* Or *I forgot to DVR the Mets game.* But the silence that followed was as heavy as a falling tree. He turned the face towel over on his lap and stared at it, as if he might find an answer there.

"Yes," he finally said. "I do."

And here it comes, she thought, sitting back down on the couch. "What's the big mystery?"

He stood. "You know what?" he said. "I *will* have a glass of wine. Unless you have beer?"

"Sorry," she said, and pointed at the bottle to indicate that he should help himself to the wine, which he did.

Lorenzo took a few sips before turning back to her. He let out a long breath.

"Sophia," he said.

Sophia?

He had pronounced it clearly, to be sure she heard, and the word rang like a song—the melody to his harmony. Sophia. A symphony in syllables. Not like *Dana*, which was two beats on a toy drum. She pictured a raven-haired beauty with soft curves and full lips.

"You could have told me," she said. "I wouldn't have—"

"She's my kid."

"What?"

"She's four."

Stunned, Dana put down her wineglass. Lorenzo had a *kid*?

"And her mom?" She swallowed hard, wondering if there was a happy little family he had neglected to mention.

"Evelyn," he said. "Not in the picture. Never was, really."

"I see," Dana said, wondering if it was about a thousand times more complicated than "not in the picture."

He shook his head, as if she didn't see. "Evie's in the joint," he said.

"She's in *jail*?"

"That's what I wanted to tell you. Sophia lives with me." He paused. "Right now, a neighbor is watching her. A nice lady who lives upstairs. But Sophia—she's my whole world, Dana."

A chill prickled her flesh. Lorenzo was a single father. It touched the depth of her heart. He was caring for a tiny girl. Brushing her hair in the morning. Pouring cereal into a bowl. Holding her small warm hand while they walked on the street. Shopping for clothes and toys. Scheduling doctor appointments and playdates and making sure she was cared for while he was at work.

And now, he could be going to jail. Dana shook off the terrible thought that her own recklessness was partly to blame. No, it wasn't her fault. It was Marks who had done this.

Dana unclenched her fists and picked up her wine. She took a long sip, trying to put out the fire of rage that was burning inside, but it was no use. She stood and paced the apartment.

"Hey," he said. "You all right?"

"That fucking Marks," she said.

Lorenzo approached and wrapped her in a hug. "It's okay," he said.

"It's not okay." She wanted to cry.

He backed up just enough to look at her face. "I'll deal with it," he said, and moved a lock of hair from her eyes. Something in her stirred. It was such a tender gesture.

"You shouldn't be comforting *me*," she said. "You have enough to worry about."

He pulled her tighter. "How about if we comfort each other?" he whispered in her ear.

His warm breath sent a shiver down her neck and throughout her body. He moved his hips forward. Or maybe she did. She couldn't tell anymore. All she knew was that he kissed her deeply and she didn't want it to end.

"I thought you had to leave," she said.

"Not right away."

"Are you sure?"

His dark eyes grew even blacker as they traveled down her body and back to her face. And of course, he didn't need to say anything, because his answer was in that look, and in the way his hand ran all the way down her back to pull her toward him.

He was sure.

17

The next day, Dana's producer had some good news for her: they had hired three models for her segment, which would focus on a new line of Bastina cap-sleeve mixed-lace tunics and ballet flats. That was a big deal. Unlike its larger competitors, the Shopping Channel didn't often hire models for shows outside prime time. But the station was investing money in her program. Dana loved the idea of gushing over the models as they sashayed out in the tunics, accessorized to illustrate versatility. It gave her so much to work with.

When Adam finally wrapped up, she thanked him and he started for the door. Then he stopped and turned to her. "By the way, Sherry wants to see you after the show today."

"She does?" As far as Dana knew, Megan had spoken to Sherry and smoothed everything over. She was even given a pass on the spreadsheets.

"She asked me to tell you."

"But why?"

He shrugged. "I'm sure it's no big deal."

Easy for him to say, she thought after he left. Sherry hadn't targeted him as nemesis number one. And he didn't have a secret rehearsal to rush to right after airtime.

She called Megan.

"He could be right," she said. "It might be no big deal. Still, I want to come with you. What time are you going to see her?"

"Right after airtime."

Megan let out a breath and told Dana she had a dentist appointment at four, but would try to get there on time.

"If I'm not," she said, "see if you can stall."

But by the time her segment ended, Megan still hadn't arrived and wasn't answering texts. Dana changed to her street clothes and paced her dressing room, imagining Megan in the dentist chair, suffering. Still, at that moment, Dana would have gladly changed places.

She checked the time again, and felt the weight of her schedule bearing down on her. Rehearsals were about to start, and there wasn't much the rest of the cast could do if she wasn't there.

After stalling another fifteen minutes, Dana knew she couldn't wait any longer. She took a deep, fortifying breath and went up to see Sherry on her own.

When she arrived, Emily was standing behind her desk tidying up, as if she were getting ready to leave. Jessalyn, Dana's talent coordinator, stood nearby waiting. Emily was decked out in a sage green raw-silk sheath and a crisp white denim jacket with the sleeves carefully rolled up. She wore a pair of Bastina ballet flats and dangly gold earrings. At first, Dana wondered if Emily and Jessalyn were heading out together for some hot double date. But then she realized Emily didn't look date-ready; she looked camera-ready. Dana burned with curiosity. What kind of gig did this girl have?

"Sherry's expecting you," Emily said, nodding toward the door to indicate that she should go right in.

Dana thanked her and paused. She didn't know if Emily

would consider a compliment an intrusion, but she went for it. "You look good enough for a catwalk," she said.

Emily beamed. "You think?" she said earnestly. "One of Vanessa's models didn't show up and they asked me to stand in."

"I'm bringing her right to set," Jessalyn added.

So the gig was right here. That made sense. Dana nodded and smiled back at the two of them, wondering if Sherry had engineered the whole thing to get Emily on the air. Not that the girl couldn't pull it off—except for her height, she really did look as good as any model. But clearly, Sherry was using her position to throw her assistant a bone. After all, the company had a contract with a modeling agency. One call and Sherry could have summoned another professional model. Dana almost wanted to ask Emily what her secret was. How had she managed to get on Sherry's good side? Hell, how did she even *find* a good side?

Dana sighed and told Emily to break a leg, then knocked on the open door to Sherry's office.

"You're here," Sherry said, glancing at her watch.

Dana smiled, pretending she missed the subtle dig about her tardiness.

"Have a seat," Sherry said.

Dana lowered herself into one of the chairs across from Sherry's desk. "Emily looks terrific. She's rocking that cotton bomber jacket."

She hoped the comment would soften Sherry's demeanor, but after the briefest flicker of appreciation, her countenance turned serious. She squinted at the monitors mounted on the wall. "We have eight thousand units to move. She'd *better* rock it. Vanessa, too." She looked back at her desk and rearranged some papers.

"Adam said you wanted to see me." Dana studied Sherry,

trying to get a read on her expression. "Is everything okay? I understand my numbers were pretty strong today."

"There's no problem with your numbers."

"Oh, good!" Dana gushed, pretending the conversation was a dream come true, as if there was no place in the world she would rather be than right here in Sherry's office. But it was like trying to charm a Rubik's cube. She just sat there, obstinately unsolvable.

Sherry laced her fingers and stared Dana down. "Tell me what's going on with you."

"What do you mean?" Dana asked.

"I've been hearing certain rumors."

"Rumors about what?" Dana was perplexed. Her encounter with Lorenzo was still fresh in her mind, so she wondered if somehow people in the office were gossiping about it. But that seemed impossible. Lorenzo wouldn't have told anyone. She was sure of that. And she had certainly not spoken about it, except for a whispered cell phone conversation with Chelsea as she walked to work.

"You tell me," Sherry said.

Dana shrugged. "I have no idea."

Sherry took her glasses off and laid them on the desk. "Dana, are you in breach of contract?"

"What? No!" Even as she said it, her heart rate skittered and her mouth went dry. Had Sherry found out about Sweat City? "I don't know what you're talking about."

"Are you performing somewhere without permission?"

"No! Of course not. Why would you think that?"

"You telling me the truth?"

"Yes," Dana lied.

"Because if you're involved in anything, now is the time to ask permission."

Dana didn't hesitate, as she knew there was no way in hell

Sherry would give her permission to perform with her Sweat City group. "I'm not," she said. "I promise."

Sherry stared at her, and Dana felt like it was a test. If she blinked, she was dead. So she played the wide-eyed innocent, staring back in bewilderment. If all Sherry had was some uncertain gossip, she could win this.

At last, Sherry put her glasses back on. "Okay," she said. "I guess it was just a rumor, then."

Dana exhaled. "So we're good?"

Sherry had already checked out of the conversation, and was staring past her at the monitors. "Just keep your numbers up," she warned.

"Will do!" Dana chirped. She stood and rushed out the door still shaken, but determined to make good time getting downtown to rehearsal. She almost ran smack into Megan, who was dashing down the hall toward Sherry's office. Her blouse was wrinkled, as if she'd been sitting in it for hours, and her lips were swollen.

"I'm shorry!" Megan said, her pronunciation slurred. "I came as fasht as I could."

"Are you all right?" Dana asked.

"Jusht a little Novocain. I'll be fine as shoon as it wearsh off. Tell me what happened."

"I think we're okay," Dana said. "But she asked if I was in breach of contract."

"What?"

"She said there's some kind of rumor going around that I was performing somewhere."

There was a pause as Megan studied her face. "But you're not, right?"

"Of course not," Dana said, her expression even.

"Hang on a shecond," Megan said. She pulled some cotton

wads from her mouth and balled them into a tissue. She looked at Dana dubiously. "And there's no truth to the rumors?"

"No! No truth at all. I quit Sweat City. Told them I was done." That part, at least, was true. She *had* told them she was done. But of course, that all changed once she became Kayla Bean.

"Where would the rumor have come from?" Megan asked.

"Maybe from someone who wants my job?" Even as she said it, Dana realized it might be true. The office was swimming with aspiring actors. Anyone could have a connection to a member of Sweat City. They had all sworn secrecy, of course, but people talked. And maybe someone here had got wind of it and decided to use it against her.

"Do I need to talk to Sherry?" Megan asked.

"I put it to rest," Dana said. "We're fine.

"Good," Megan said, though she remained pensive, maybe a little troubled. It was hard for Dana to gauge whether it was concern or pain.

"You sure you're okay?" Dana asked.

"I could use a drink, for sure," Megan said. "Maybe that pub on Ninth?"

"Drinks?" Dana said. She was already late, and couldn't possibly spare the time. "I… Is it okay if I take a rain check?"

"Again?" Megan said. "You have someplace to be?"

Dana paused, fumbling. She considered blurting out something about French lessons or cooking classes, but there would be too many questions to answer, lies she hadn't yet invented.

"I…just have this major stress headache coming on."

Megan squinted at her. "A stress headache?"

"Sherry makes me crazy," Dana said. "And you didn't show up and I knew I had to go see her and, well, it just came on, like a vise. Like a pounding vise."

Megan stared as if she were trying to decide whether to believe her, and Dana regretted her metaphor. A pounding vise?

"I'm really sorry," Dana continued. "I know you ran here from the dentist in pain and everything. I feel awful."

"It's okay," Megan said, her expression softening. "Come on, let's go downstairs. I'll put you in a cab."

"I can take the subway," Dana said.

"No, I insist. My treat. In fact, I'll ride with you."

"You don't have to do that," Dana said.

"I want to. I'll stop at Pete's for a FroYo." Icy Pete's was an ice cream parlor two doors down from Dana's apartment. She couldn't very well fight her suffering friend on the idea of getting a soothing frozen dessert, and so, even though Dana had planned on taking the subway directly downtown to the theater, they headed off to catch a cab to the East Side.

When the taxi reached Dana's apartment building, the two women argued over who would pay and Dana won, swiping her credit card faster than Megan could scrounge through her cavernous purse for her wallet. It did little to soothe her guilt over the lie.

"You're a pain in the ass," Megan mumbled.

"I love you, too," Dana said.

The two women parted. Megan headed for Icy Pete's and Dana entered her apartment building. She didn't go upstairs, though. She waited in the small lobby for several anxious beats and then glanced out the door to be sure Megan wasn't loitering in the street. When she was confident the coast was clear, Dana dashed to the subway and went downtown to the Sweat City theater.

18

It wasn't that she didn't love her nephew. She did—with all her heart. But Dana had a hard time imagining any place she would less rather be on a beautiful Sunday afternoon in early May than a birthday party filled with screaming four-year-olds, judgmental suburban moms and a certain retired neurosurgeon she shared DNA with. And so she succumbed to an impulse to make the day less disagreeable. She invited Lorenzo and his daughter. To her delight, he said yes.

Lorenzo had a car—a ten-year-old Honda—so the three of them headed out to Long Island, with the grown-ups in the front and Sophia strapped into her car seat in the back. As they crossed the Fifty-Ninth Street Bridge, the skyline behind them, Dana opened her window to the breeze off the East River. It came in valiant puffs, as if fighting to scrub the air of car exhaust. She tried to relax, settling into the notion that the party might not be so bad.

When she called, Lorenzo had insisted he wasn't thinking about the urine test. "Whatever happens, happens," he had said, as if he was at peace with it. She knew that couldn't be true. He had to be roiling with turmoil over the possibility that he could wind up back in jail. But he seemed to be someone who could cram all his anxiety into a neat little compartment while he went about his life in brisk, tense motions. It seemed to work for him, so she wasn't going to rock his precarious lifeboat. She would simply follow his lead.

Sophia was a darling child, with a head full of frizzy caramel curls and a pair of pink eyeglasses bridged on a wide little nose. Lorenzo's competence with the mechanics of fatherhood touched Dana, and her heart ached as she watched him help his tiny girl into the car seat, patient but firm, securing the straps with expertise. He handed her a juice box from a navy canvas shoulder bag, then gave her sneakered foot an affectionate squeeze before shutting the car door.

Dana blinked against her burning eyes. The drug test simply had to come back negative. This man needed to be with his daughter.

"You okay back there?" Dana asked the little girl.

"I'm hungry," she said.

Dana looked at Lorenzo. "Cheerios," he said, nodding toward the bag at Dana's feet. "In a green container."

Dana took off the lid and passed it to Sophia, trading it for the half-empty juice box. The girl grasped it happily and went to work picking up the tiny circles with practiced dexterity.

"Mind if I get the Mets score?" Lorenzo asked, reaching for the radio.

She didn't, and so they rode for a while listening to the game. When the team was down by three runs, he shut it off.

"You don't have to do that," she said.

"No mood for a bloodbath."

She took a breath. "I guess this would be a bad time to tell you my father's going to be at the party."

"Does he have a mean fast ball?"

"He has a mean everything."

Lorenzo glanced in his rearview mirror and changed lanes. "As long as he's unarmed, I'm good."

Dana turned to look into the back seat and saw that Sophia was fast asleep, her little fingers still inside the Cheerios container.

Relaxing into a slump, Dana pushed her knees up against the dashboard. "You can tell him to go fuck himself, for all I care," she said, softly enough to keep her voice from traveling to the back seat.

He laughed. "I think you'd like that."

"I'd pay cash money for it." She looked out the window, imagining her father's chagrin at the sight of her with a tattooed ex-con and his out-of-wedlock child. And with his new girlfriend there, he'd be especially dismayed. It warmed Dana—this thought of bedeviling her father and his narrow-minded expectations.

She gave Lorenzo directions to the house, and when they turned the last corner it was clear the party was already under way, as a line of luxury SUVs beaded the length of the winding block. Lorenzo parked behind a Lincoln Navigator just as a stylishly dressed couple emerged with a squirmy boy in tow. While the wife held on to the child, the husband pulled a massive, professionally wrapped gift from the trunk—complete with a cellophane overlay on which someone had expertly painted Wesley's name in circus-y capital letters. Yes, it was going to be one of *those* parties.

Lorenzo turned off the ignition and the three of them exited the Honda with their own small gift—a set of puzzles Dana thought Wesley would love—and headed for the backyard. Dana opened the gate on the white PVC fence and was barely three steps inside the plush green yard when she was nearly tackled by a small child who wrapped her legs in a hug.

Dana laughed and knelt down until her face was on eye level with Wesley's. She gave him a kiss.

"It's my birthday," he said.

"Yes," she responded, "it's all over CNN."

"But my *real* birthday's tomorrow."

"And you're turning what? Twenty-seven? Twenty-eight?"

"Four." He focused hard on the fingers he held up.

She introduced him to Lorenzo and Sophia. The girl responded by pulling on her father's pants leg and pointing to an inflated bouncy castle in the far corner of the lawn. "Can I go there?" she asked.

"Sure," he said, and Wesley and Sophia ran off together.

Dana surveyed the backyard. The lush landscape had been divided into sections—grown-ups on the right, kids on the left. In addition to the bouncy castle, the children's area had face-painting, a minicarousel and a guy on stilts making balloon animals. A woman in some kind of action hero costume led a group of earnest kids in the chicken dance. The children's tables had blue covers and in the center of each was a large plastic action figure that served as the anchor for a bouquet of red, green and yellow helium balloons.

The other side of the yard was more sophisticated, but almost as colorful. Mexican serapes served as table runners, and cacti in varying shapes and sizes served as centerpieces. Dana realized, with a heart-heavy feeling, that the theme for the adult side of this very white suburban party was Cinco de Mayo.

She spotted a table for the gifts, and deposited Wesley's present before taking Lorenzo's hand and scanning the crowd for her sister or brother-in-law.

"Just to be clear," Lorenzo said, ogling the scene, "this is a four-year-old's birthday party?"

"Welcome to Long Island," she said.

He gave her hand a squeeze. *"Olé."*

She heard her name called and turned to see her father sitting under an umbrella at one of the serape tables. Next to him was a thin, fortysomething woman with thick, chemically straightened brown hair and a nose job. She could have been one of Chelsea's friends or neighbors, but Dana decided it had to be Dr. Jennifer Lafferty. They had drinks in front of them. Margaritas, Dana surmised.

"I saw you walk in with the little girl," Dana's father said as she bent to give him a half embrace. "You looked like part of the crowd."

She stared at him a moment until his expression registered. It was…approving. She glanced around at the other partygoers and understood. She had dressed up for the occasion in black skinny jeans and a stylish spring top, while Lorenzo had sacrificed his denim jacket for a loose plaid shirt, rolled up at the sleeves. Dana hadn't realized it, but they actually blended in. Even the tattoos didn't make Lorenzo stand out. She could see at least two other men with inked forearms, and one well-toned woman with a barbed wire tatt around her biceps. Entering the backyard, her trio looked like just another suburban family trying not to look like just another suburban family.

Here she was, trying to piss off her father, and she had done the exact opposite—showed up looking like the perfect daughter he had always wanted her to be. She hated that this actually made him happy. If he couldn't love her for who she really was, he could take his approval and stick it where the perfectly manicured grass didn't grow.

"Dad, this is Lorenzo," Dana said. "Lorenzo, this is my father, Kenneth."

Her father hated being introduced by his first name, and gave her a reproving look. "This is Dr. Lafferty," he said, putting a hand on his girlfriend's back.

"Jennifer, please," the woman corrected, extending her hand. "I've heard such nice things about you, Dana."

"You must be confusing me with my sister," Dana said with enough of a smile to show she was, more or less, kidding.

"She met Chelsea earlier," her father said.

Dana sighed. He never got her jokes. Ever.

"Congrats on the new job," Jennifer said. "I hear you're a star on the Shopping Channel."

Dana looked from Jennifer to her father, and wondered if he had actually used that word—*star*. Not possible, she decided. Still, if he had told this woman about Dana's new job with any kind of pride...well, that was something.

"I've only been there a week," Dana said, smiling graciously, "so certainly not a star. But thank you."

"And what a way to start, right?" Jennifer said, her face concerned. "I saw that murder covered on the news. Must have been shocking."

Dana and Lorenzo shared a look.

Jennifer leaned forward. "Were you there?"

Lorenzo cleared his throat. "Unfortunately," he said.

"Kind of a front row seat," Dana added. "We...discovered the body."

Jennifer's mouth opened. "Did you know this?" she said to Kenneth.

"She never told me," he said.

"Yeah, well. It must have slipped my mind during one of our lengthy heart-to-hearts," Dana said.

Jennifer seemed to register the sarcasm, but she kept the conversation on track. "You poor things," she said. "That must have been traumatic."

Dana wasn't eager to open up about the horror of what they had witnessed, and was saved from the necessity of responding by her sister, who approached with a squeal.

"There you are!" she said, wrapping Dana in a hug.

"Just got here," Dana said.

"What do you think?" Chelsea asked, indicating the entirety of the party with a flourish.

Dana focused on the adult tables. "When does the mariachi band arrive?"

"Too much?" Chelsea said. "Is it the serapes?"

"It might be the upside down sombreros as cactus planters," Dana said.

"I was going for festive. You think it's culturally insensitive?"

"I don't know," Dana said. "Why don't you ask one of your Mexican friends, like, um…" She pretended to look around.

"Don't be funny."

"Sorry. I know you hate it when I'm *sarcástico*."

"And to think I was just bragging to Jennifer about my wonderful baby sister the superstar."

Of course, Dana thought. It had been Chelsea and not her father who had been talking her up. That made more sense.

She introduced her sister to Lorenzo and they shook hands.

"Where's Brandon?" Dana asked, referring to Chelsea's husband.

"He's back there," she said, pointing. "Supervising that bouncy thing."

Dana turned to Lorenzo. "Come on," she said. "I'll introduce you."

Kenneth stopped them. "Not so fast," he said to Dana. "I didn't even get a chance to talk to you and your young man."

"You want to *talk* to us?" Dana asked, wondering if this was his way of convincing his girlfriend that he actually did have heart-to-hearts with his youngest daughter. Dana wanted to tell him she was pretty sure Jennifer was too smart to buy it.

Kenneth folded his arms. "I'm sure he'd like to tell me what he does for a living."

Oh God, Dana thought. Here it comes. The Kenneth Barry scrutiny.

"I'm an audio engineer," Lorenzo replied, and Dana almost wished he had said "sound guy," which would have rankled her father enough to show his true colors.

"That's what my nephew does," Jennifer said, smiling. She turned to Kenneth. "I understand it's a very competitive field."

"Is that right?" Kenneth said, as if he didn't quite believe it.

"Highly skilled," Jennifer explained, and he took it in with a nod as they shared a look. To Dana, it was clear he respected his girlfriend's opinion, and now that Lorenzo's profession had Dr. Lafferty's seal of approval, Dr. Barry could accept it.

Dana studied Jennifer. The woman wasn't as awkward as she had expected. In fact, she was socially adept, and Dana wondered what she saw in her father.

"I'd like to check on Sophia," Lorenzo said.

Dana nodded at him and turned back to the table. "See you later."

"Can't you sit down for a minute?" Kenneth asked. "There's something I want to talk to you about." He paused. "It's important."

Dana wished she could dismiss the request, but something about her father's expression told her he was serious. She sighed and turned to Lorenzo. "Okay if I catch up with you in a bit?"

He gave her arm an encouraging squeeze and set off. Dana pulled out a chair and sat.

"I made a decision about something," her father began. "And I think you'll be glad to hear it."

"Decision?" She wondered if it was something major. Was he getting married? Moving to Arizona? Getting Dr. Jennifer Lafferty to transplant a real human heart into his chest?

"I'm going to pay off your college loans."

"Huh?"

"I did it for Chelsea and now I'm going to do it for you."

He sat back, beneficent and satisfied, and Dana felt the heat rising in her face. She thought of all those months when she was so strapped for cash she sweated when she swiped her ATM card at the bodega, worried her balance had run too low for groceries. Normally, she didn't resent the sacrifices. After all, it was her choice to pursue such an unstable career. Except when she thought about the fact that her father was trying to teach her a lesson by paying back her wealthy sister's student loans and not hers. Then she resented it like hell.

"I'm making good money now, Dad," she said through her teeth.

"Yes, I know. I want to reward you for that."

"Do you have any idea how hard it was for me to make those payments every month?"

"I think so."

"And you enjoyed the fact that I was suffering for my choices."

"It was good for you. It built character."

"Newsflash," she said. "My character didn't need that much building." She thought back to the humiliation of telling a cashier at the supermarket that she didn't want the tampons when she realized that her coupon had been for a different brand. The weird look she got from a casting director when he noticed that the scuff marks on her shoes had been colored over with marker. The embarrassment of getting caught stuffing rolls into her purse on a date. She also thought about the time she had been so desperate she almost stole a hundred dollars from an old man on Forty-Seventh Street.

"Didn't do you any harm," he said. "Look where you are now."

"Seriously? You're taking credit for my success?"

"You might want to keep the attitude in check. I'm offering you thousands of dollars."

Dana considered that for a moment. "Let me ask you something," she said. "What if Lorenzo wasn't an audio engineer? What if he was the guy who swept the floors?"

Kenneth tented his fingers. "I'm pleased that he's not."

"But if he was," she pressed, "would you still be offering me the money?"

Kenneth and Jennifer shared another look. "Moot point," he said.

"It isn't to me."

"Dana, don't be a child."

"And what if I was dating an ex-con?" she asked.

"But you're not," he said.

She let out a breath. There was no sense in telling her father the truth. For all she cared, he could believe whatever he wanted. "Just to be crystal clear," she said. "You're agreeing to pay off my student loans because I'm involved with a man you approve of?"

"That's only part of it," he said.

She stood up. "Thanks, anyway, Dad."

"You're not seriously turning down my offer."

"Why don't you give the money to charity? That is, if you can find one that benefits privileged children." She pushed in her chair. "I'm going to find Lorenzo."

"You know," her father said, "when I saw you walk in with him, I thought maybe you were growing up. I guess that was wishful thinking."

"Lorenzo will be thrilled he has your approval."

"Don't be so dismissive. The man seems like a solid citizen. That's important, Dana. You should make a real effort this time."

Like you did with Mom? she wanted to ask, but held back for Jennifer's sake. The woman didn't deserve to get caught in their hail of old grievances.

But her father deserved that and more for insinuating that all Dana's failed relationships were her fault. She took some comfort that her father had called Lorenzo a "solid citizen," because if he knew the truth it would shatter him. She glared at her father, deciding whether to tell him about Lorenzo's past.

"Can't change my stripes, Dad," she said. "But thanks for the relationship advice."

She turned to walk away, and Kenneth called after her, "What will you do when he leaves you?"

Dana stopped. She knew she could let it go, keep moving. So what if her father believed Lorenzo was a good catch and that she barely deserved him?

But she could feel his judgmental eyes burning into her, and couldn't take it. She turned back to him. "Don't worry, Dad, Lorenzo can't go that far." Dana paused for effect. "At least, not without reporting to his parole officer."

19

"I have a message from Lorenzo DeSantis," Ollie said to Dana on Monday morning.

"Oh?" Dana was surprised. She and Lorenzo were keeping their relationship a secret from their coworkers, so if he was passing a message through Ollie, it had to be important.

"He asked you to please come to see him before your show. He has a new microphone for you. He needs to test this."

Dana nodded as if the request were no big deal, and pretended to reread the notes for her show one last time before hurrying downstairs. Lorenzo was busy in the sound booth when she arrived, but when he saw Dana through the window, he nodded toward the hallway and met her out there.

"Marks is here," he said, his face tight.

"In the building?"

"He's upstairs with some uniforms, nosing around Kitty's office again."

"That could be good news," she said, "if they're on the trail of something solid."

Lorenzo let out a breath before looking up and down the hallway to be sure they were still alone. "He cornered me again," he said quietly. "Made me go through everything that happened that day."

Dana shook her head. It was infuriating that Marks still didn't believe Lorenzo...or her.

"How many times is he going to question you? It's ridiculous. There are other leads he should be following."

"We just have to be really careful," Lorenzo said. "About us."

"Trust me," she said. "I haven't told anyone here."

He nodded absently, his mind on something else. "And I thought this was going to be a good day."

She searched his face, looking for any trace of hopefulness. Dana didn't want to get ahead of herself, but she thought she saw something in his eyes, some tiny spark. "Any particular reason?" she asked.

He gave her an enigmatic grin. "Can you handle some good news?"

"Always."

He waited a beat, licking his lips. "I'm in the clear," he finally said.

"The drug test?" she asked, just to make sure she was understanding. Because this was glorious news, a huge weight lifted. She had been envisioning his parole officer showing up with handcuffs to drag him off, leaving poor little Sophia without her daddy.

He nodded. "It came back clean."

"Oh, thank God!" she said. Dana was just about to hug him when she saw an alarmed look on his face. He took a step back.

Dana turned to look over her shoulder and saw Ari Marks. He hadn't actually witnessed anything other than two people talking, but she sensed he had picked up on a feeling of intimacy.

"Can I speak to you for a few minutes?" he asked her.

"I'm on the air soon."

"It won't take long."

She glanced quickly at Lorenzo and then walked off with Marks, who led her to the unused studio across the lobby. The room was dark and cavernous, its high black ceiling dotted with dim emergency lights. Officially, it was Studio E, but staff members had nicknamed it the planetarium. She could just about make out Marks's shadowy features.

"Anything you care to tell me?" he asked.

"About what?"

"About you and Mr. DeSantis."

"We've been through this," she said. "There's nothing to tell."

"Nothing?"

She took a steadying breath. This zealous cop had very nearly cost Lorenzo his freedom—and Sophia her childhood— for one drag on a joint. And he was still stuck on breaking Lorenzo's alibi.

"Come to think of it, there *is* something," she said, her tone icy. "He's a single father. Did you know that when you got him in trouble with his parole officer?"

"You seem to care a lot about someone who's just a co-worker."

"I'm a human being, Detective. I don't have to be romantically involved with someone to care if their child is left orphaned. But I guess you're cut from a different cloth." Even as she said it, Dana realized she sounded like someone's prissy aunt. Or more precisely, like Mrs. Woodbridge, as she had borrowed the phrase directly from her script. Still, it was accurate, and she waited through the silence for his response.

For several seconds she heard nothing except hard breath coming from his face in the darkness. At last he said, in measured calm, "I have a job to do."

"I understand that," she said. "You're trying to find out who murdered Kitty Todd. But you *have* to know it wasn't Lorenzo."

He didn't say anything, and she wanted to shake him.

"He has an alibi," she said through gritted teeth. "I was with him."

"So you've said."

"Why the hell don't you believe me?"

"Because you don't always tell the truth."

"Yes, I do."

"You want me to believe that a man entered your apartment alone at 9:45 on Thursday night and left sometime after midnight, but you're nothing more than coworkers?"

She took a step back, a breath catching in her throat. "*What the fuck?* Are you staking out my apartment?"

"Take it easy," he said. "I'm not."

Take it easy? Was he kidding? She wanted to kick his shin. "So what—you're following Lorenzo? Jesus!"

"You didn't answer my question."

"Answer *my* question," she said.

"What question is that?"

"Did you know that he had a little girl, and that her mother is in prison and Lorenzo is all she's got?"

"I know a lot of things."

"And that means nothing to you?"

"I didn't say that."

"Lorenzo's been clean since the day he was arrested, and you damned well know it. Plus, there are plenty of people around here who had the motive to murder Kitty, and Lorenzo isn't one of them."

"Are you finished?"

"Hell, no, I'm not finished. Here's another question. Why aren't you investigating Charles Honeycutt? Unless you've re-

ally screwed up, by now you've seen the inscription on Kitty's bracelet."

"What bracelet?"

"The gold alligator bracelet. It was on her desk—in the
dish with her rings."

Marks paused. "There was no bracelet."

"Of course there was. I saw it."

"Describe it."

"It's gold—about an inch thick—and looks like a curved
alligator, with emerald eyes and a diamond tail. And it has an
inscription inside—*Love, Charles.*"

He looked dubious. "You were able to see a bracelet inscription from the doorway of the room?"

"I didn't see the inscription. The manicurist told me about
it."

"Manicurist?"

"Jo—she works here."

"Last name?"

Dana shrugged.

"What does she look like?"

"Petite," she said, concentrating. "Blue-black hair—an un-
dercut on the left side. She wears smudgy black eyeliner under
her lower lashes and has four studs in each ear."

"Anything else?"

"She has a reedy neck and likes bright pink lipstick."

"What else?"

She paused, realizing he was teasing her. "I *could* go on,"
she said.

"Oh, please do. I'm curious to see where this ends."

She thought for a moment, still indignant, but eager to
prove he could trust her powers of perception. "She has an un-
derbite. Her nails look like hell, but that's true of most mani-
curists. She wears a citrusy perfume. Skinny ankles. And she's

a Capricorn—or at least I think she is. She wears a pendant with a symbol for that sign."

"Is that all?"

"She sounds like Cyndi Lauper. Usually wears sleeveless shirts. You want more?"

"I think I'm good."

"Are you serious about the bracelet?" she asked. "You didn't see it?"

"I've been over the evidence several thousand times. There was no bracelet in that dish with the rings. No bracelet like the one you described anywhere in her office or her dressing room."

Dana closed her eyes. She could envision what she saw on that day. The blood on the window, Kitty's body and a hundred other details, including a gold bracelet in the shape of an alligator. That meant someone had taken it before the police arrived.

She remembered Charles Honeycutt rushing through the crowd and taking charge. She imagined him panicked about leaving behind any evidence, and grabbing the bracelet before anyone saw it.

"You have to believe me," she said. "The bracelet was there, in the room, when she died. Someone took it—someone who didn't want you to see it."

"Okay."

"Okay? That's it?"

"It's an interesting story."

No wonder this guy was divorced. He was infuriating. "Listen to me," she seethed. "Find that bracelet and you've found your killer."

"I'd be more inclined to trust you if you were honest about your relationship with Lorenzo DeSantis."

Dana tried to steady her breathing. If he had someone

watching Lorenzo, then he probably knew they had gone out to Long Island together. Still, she was going to stick to her story.

"I know why you're targeting Lorenzo," she said. "But you've got the wrong guy in your crosshairs."

"Exactly how much do you know about Lorenzo DeSantis?"

"Enough."

"Are you sure?"

"What is that supposed to mean?"

Marks rubbed the stubble on his cheek, as if contemplating what he could divulge. "There may be something your boyfriend isn't telling you."

"He's not my boyfriend."

"Have it your way. Just don't make any assumptions about him."

She squinted, trying to read his face in the dark. She didn't know if he was playing her, or if this was a real warning.

"He's not my boyfriend," she repeated, "but he's a good man."

"Sometimes good men keep secrets, too."

20

On air, Dana faltered. She was edgy thinking about whatever secret Lorenzo was keeping from her. Why did Marks have to drop that bomb right before she went on? Again and again, Dana told herself to focus, keep her head in the game. But her mind wandered and she mixed up the iced vanilla and warm cream-colored handbags, kept referring to the green one as "sage" instead of "avocado" and, most egregious of all, referred to the "summer sky" selection as simply "light blue." She pictured Adam in the control booth holding his head to prevent a blood pressure explosion.

Dana glanced at the sales figures with mild panic. She wasn't meeting her projections. With an hour to go, Dana closed her eyes right there on camera. She had to go deep inside to find her ebullient sales persona—the one who had gushed about the Hector Comb at the audition. The one who spoke to the viewer as if she were her best friend. And then…she found her. Dana opened her eyes and she was back, right there in the zone, gushing effusively about the large-size version of the handbags she had been selling. And just like that her numbers started to climb. By the end of her segment, she raised her figures enough to reach her minimum. It was a squeaker—and Sherry wouldn't be pleased—but she hadn't failed.

"Everything okay?" Adam asked.

She thought of a million excuses. The lighting was bad. The displays were crooked. The color chart was confusing.

"I'll do better tomorrow," she said.

In her dressing room, she texted Lorenzo. They had to talk. Soon. She didn't want to do it at work, with everyone around, and he said he had to go straight to pick up Sophia from day care. He suggested she come to his place after Sophia's bedtime, and since she didn't have a Sweat City rehearsal that night, she agreed.

He lived uptown in Washington Heights, in the semisubterranean apartment of an attractive brownstone with an ornate cornice and wrought-iron handrails lining the stoop. When she arrived, he opened the private entry door to let her in and she understood why he had moved so far uptown. In addition to a modern kitchen with a granite counter, the place had ample charm and space, including a long living room with overhead windows facing the street. There was an ashtray perched on one of the windowsills, and Dana imagined Lorenzo standing and smoking after Sophia went to bed, carefully exhaling out the window. Behind the sofa there was an oak wall unit. Toys lined the lower shelves, and an assortment of old radios was perched on the upper shelves. A few of them were just the naked interiors, as if Lorenzo had been working on restoring them. Dana realized she knew so little about this guy.

In the middle of the room there was a big square wooden coffee table with rounded corners, and she imagined Sophia sitting in front of it on her tiny painted chair, playing games and coloring while her dad watched the game on TV. At present, it was the folding station for laundry, with clothes stacked in neat piles. Lorenzo began putting the clothing into a plastic basket.

"Sorry," he said. "It's hard to keep up."

He had a lot on his plate as a single father, and she almost felt guilty for being so suspicious…but not quite.

"Nice apartment," she said.

"I guess. We're a little cramped with only one bedroom."

"Where do *you* sleep?" she asked, surmising that Sophie had the bedroom.

"Right here," Lorenzo said, pointing to the couch. He shrugged, as if it weren't a big deal. "Can I get you something to drink?"

She shook her head. "Sophia's asleep?"

"Should be."

"Can she hear us talking?"

"Not unless we shout."

Dana paced the apartment, studied the radios, tried to figure out where to begin.

"Why don't you sit?" he asked.

"I'm okay."

"Is something wrong?"

Dana inspected the colorful Bakelite radios, which looked like they were from the thirties and forties. Another had a burled wood cabinet with rounded edges and the distinctive cutouts of art deco design. It had to be about ninety years old. "Do these work?"

"Most of them." He put the laundry basket on the floor. "You sure you don't want a drink?"

She shook her head and faced him. "Marks said there's something you're not telling me."

He stared at her for a moment, alarmed. His expression went somber and he turned to open a locked liquor cabinet. He pulled out a rarefied bottle of Scotch with a gold painted label. It looked like something her father might drink. She knew, then, that she had struck a nerve. Lorenzo was a Heineken kind of guy. If he was going for the Scotch, there had to be a reason.

"On second thought, pour me one of those," she said. Dana didn't much like Scotch—the burn was too intense. But now that he looked so guilty she wanted to cost him a little of his precious nectar. He poured the drinks and handed her one.

"Well?" she demanded.

"What did he say exactly?"

"Does it matter?" she asked.

"I'd like to know what he knows."

She put down her drink. "How many secrets do you *have*?"

He took one gulp and then another, swallowing audibly. "There is something," Lorenzo finally said, his back to her. "About another woman."

The back of her neck went icy cold. She glanced around the apartment looking for evidence that someone else lived there, but could see nothing but a man and his daughter. "Lorenzo—"

"Maybe I should have told you."

"Of course you should have told me! Who is she?"

"Was," he corrected,

"Was? You mean Evelyn? Sophia's mom?" She was confused. This wasn't even close to being a secret.

Lorenzo shook his head. "I mean Kitty."

For a quick second, her brain couldn't process it, and she tried to imagine a different Kitty. "I don't—"

"That had to be what Marks was talking about. I slept with her. With Kitty Todd."

"You?" she said, her tone sharp.

He shrugged, as if to say he had nothing more to add.

"I thought she hated you. And that the feeling was mutual."

"It's a little more complicated," he said.

Her face burned. "I can't believe you didn't tell me this," she said, trying to contain her anger. Here she was, doing everything possible to exonerate him, and he had withheld this critical piece of information.

"What difference would it make?" he asked.

"For one thing, it helps me understand why Marks thinks you're a suspect."

"And for another thing?"

"How many things do there need to be?" she said, seething. This wasn't an innocent omission. It was a lie. "What did you think would happen if you told me? Did you think I'd fly into a rage because you had a past?"

"I don't know," he said. "But it's not the kind of thing women like to hear."

As if she had to be *handled*. "Did you think I wouldn't go out with you because you'd slept with Kitty?"

"That was part of it."

"What was the other part?" she asked, and then got it. He needed her as his alibi and didn't want to take any chances. "Oh my God. You thought I'd turn on you…with the police. Is that it?"

"I didn't know *how* you'd react."

How little he thought of her! White-hot rage rose up in her, and before she knew it, Dana held the glass of Scotch over her head. She wanted nothing more than to smash it against the wall, but the knowledge that Sophia was sleeping in the next room constrained her fury, and with no other outlet she flung the liquid at Lorenzo. It splashed into the middle of his T-shirt, darkening the area over his heart.

"Take it easy," he said.

"I won't take it easy. How could you think so little of me?"

"It's not you, okay? It's me. I've had some bad experiences."

"With crazy women," she said, seething that he lumped her in with them.

"With crazy women," he confirmed, and pulled the wet shirt from his chest as if it were proof.

She put the empty glass on the coffee table and sat, ashamed that she'd lost control. "I'm sorry," she said. "I guess that was a little excessive. I just hate to think that you were afraid I would turn on you."

He sat down next to her and took her hand. "I should have told you. I should have trusted you."

"Yes. You should have."

"Can you forgive me?" he asked.

"I'm trying." She stared down at his strong hand holding hers.

"How can I make it up to you?"

She looked at his face. "Can I throw another glass of Scotch at you?"

"Some J&B, maybe. Not the Glenmorangie."

"But why Kitty?" she said. "I'm not asking in a jealous way. It's just a…strange match."

"I told you," he said. "Kitty got whatever she wanted."

"And she wanted you?"

He raised an eyebrow.

"You know what I mean. Kitty didn't seem that egalitarian in her choices. You don't fit the rich and powerful profile."

He shook his head. "I was wondering the same thing. But I think she just wanted to get someone else jealous, and I was handy. So she made me an offer I couldn't refuse. Threatened my job."

"Seriously? Like, 'sleep with me or I'll get you fired'?"

"It was more subtle than that. She told me she didn't *want* to get me in trouble again. Said it was the last thing she wanted."

"So your choice was, either sleep with a gorgeous woman or get fired."

"That's about it."

"And how did you know it was about getting someone else jealous?"

"I didn't at first. The weird thing was that when I left her dressing room, I couldn't find one of my socks. It didn't make sense. I mean, I looked everywhere. And then, like a week later, I spoke to another guy who had a similar experience."

"Honeycutt?"

"God, no. Could you see me having this kind of conversation with Honeycutt?"

"Then who?"

"Don't ask me that," he said.

"What's the big deal?"

"He's married. It's a huge secret. I can't break that confidence."

"Fair enough," she said, but her mind riffled through a list of other married guys in the company. It could, she realized, be anyone.

"So," Lorenzo continued, "this guy said she pulled a similar thing with him—threatened his job or promised a promotion or something. And then when he left he couldn't find his tie. We came to the conclusion that she hid these items so she could leave them around for some other guy to find."

"And that's where Honeycutt comes in," she said.

"That's my guess. I mean, I didn't know at the time it was him. But now…"

"Do the police know about your friend who left the tie behind?"

Lorenzo shook his head. "He's got too much at stake."

"But his story could help you. It connects the dots to Honeycutt."

"I can't do that to this guy, Dana. He's a family man, and scared enough as it is. He just got in over his head with Kitty."

Dana put her face in her hands. "The more I learn about this woman…"

"She was seriously fucked up."

"I almost feel sorry for Honeycutt," she said, "even if he did kill her." She picked up Lorenzo's glass of Scotch and took a small sip.

"You still want to throw something at me?" he asked.

His warm hand was on her knee, and the heat radiated up her leg. She looked at his eyes and felt herself melting into sympathy. Kitty had manipulated him. And Dana could understand that confessing it felt…tawdry.

"Maybe," she said. "How soundly does Sophia sleep?"

She moved his hand higher on her thigh. The memory of him in her bed was fresh enough to raise her temperature. She leaned in for a kiss, and that was all it took. The flame of her anger had been doused, but the heat of her desire could ignite the night sky.

"Pretty soundly," he said. "Should I get you a glass of J&B?"

Dana knew exactly what she wanted to throw at him then, and it wasn't Scotch. She helped him out of his wet shirt, then hesitated, wondering if this was a good idea. But he moved in for a long, deep kiss.

"You sure this is okay?" she asked as his mouth found her neck. But the question floated into the atmosphere as if evaporating from heat. It was more than okay.

21

"How are your teeth?" Dana said to Megan on the phone the next day.

"Recovered, why? You need me to bite someone?"

"Sherry Zidel."

There was a pause. "Is she still insisting you're in breach of contract?" Megan sounded genuinely worried.

"It's not that. I had an off day yesterday, and Ollie said she wants to talk to me after my show today."

"How off was it?"

"I met my numbers, but barely. Have to admit I'm scared she's looking for an excuse to boot me."

"That's why God invented contracts."

"I know, but—"

"Don't sweat it. I'll come with you. What time do you need me?"

Dana sighed, relieved. She was so grateful to Megan, and so glad she'd had the sense to accept her friend's offer to become her manager all those months ago. Looking back, Dana found it hard to believe she'd had any hesitation. Megan was so loyal, and such a pit bull. Plus, she believed in Dana's talents with her whole heart.

"Can you make it by five?" Dana asked.

"With sharpened fangs."

After she got off the phone, Dana texted her Sweat City director and told him she would be late for rehearsal that night, because she knew there was simply no way she would be able to blow off Megan again without arousing suspicion. She hated doing it—getting to rehearsal on time was sacrosanct—but she didn't have a choice.

A few minutes later, Adam Weintraub came to see Dana for their daily briefing. It was day two of the handbag sale, and he wanted to make sure she had a firm handle on the colors and styles. She did. In fact, Dana was determined to make it her highest sales day ever, despite the sleepy cobwebs she was still trying to shake. She was going to break records if it sucked her of her very soul.

"I don't want to put too much pressure on you," he said, "but—"

"But I need to kill it today or Sherry will kill *me*."

"Something like that."

Dana nodded. She was prepared today, ready to do battle. "I've got this," she said, but Adam didn't look assured. In fact, he looked as tired and stressed as she felt.

"Are you okay?" she asked. "Is Sherry putting her sharpened stiletto to your throat?"

He waved it away. "I'm used to it. I'm just beat. I barely slept."

Me, too, she thought, but probably for a different reason. "Kids keep you up?" she said.

"I can't wait for that baby to start sleeping through the night."

"You know, you never showed me pictures," she said, hoping to distract him from his misery.

Adam found his smile again. "You don't have to ask twice."

He took out his phone, scrolled to a picture and handed it to her.

She noticed a crack running across his screen. "Did you drop this?"

He shrugged. "Three months ago, but it's hard to justify buying a new phone when you have kids."

Or a Manhattan rent on a mall store paycheck, she thought, nodding sympathetically. She remembered how distressed she had been when her old Samsung broke. Fortunately, Chelsea got a new phone every year, whether she needed it or not, and was able to give Dana her old one. Dana decided that once her student loans were paid off, she would get herself a brand-new phone and give Adam the old one. Or maybe she'd stick with Chelsea's hand-me-down for another year or so and buy him the new phone. This was sweet—being in a position to pay it forward. It had been so long since she felt flush.

She looked down at Adam's family photo. Despite the crack, she could see that they were all in coordinated white T-shirts. His wife was an exotic beauty, with dark curls and a silver lariat choker pointing downward to her impressive décolletage. The baby was as bald as a peeled potato, but the toddler had a massive head of dark curls, like his daddy.

And his mommy.

It took Dana only a second to remember why she had assumed Adam's wife had straight light hair. And once she did, her stomach fell. He seemed like such a good family man, the last guy in the world who would cheat on his wife. Dana stared harder, hoping she was wrong. But no, the pieces all fit.

"Gorgeous family," Dana choked out. "And Ethan's got your hair. Or…is that from your wife?"

He tilted his head toward the screen. "Hard to say. I've got the Jewish coils and Francesca's got the Italian crimp, but it's one big curly family. My sister says we look like the before picture for a hair straightening product."

Dana smiled tightly and handed back his phone. "Your boys are darling."

She didn't want to believe what she was thinking, but there was no way around it. On the day she met Adam, the long hair sticking to a patch of dried baby food on his shoulder had been neither dark nor curly. What was more, she now realized that the smell she had mistaken for strained peaches was actually the scent of apricots.

There was still a chance she was wrong, and that Adam wasn't the married man Lorenzo had mentioned. But she had to find out, because if she was right, he might be the one person who could help prove Lorenzo's innocence.

She studied his face. "You and Lorenzo are pretty good friends?" she asked, trying to sound light.

"He's a nice guy. Trustworthy. Why do you ask?"

Dana pointed to the sofa. "Let's sit down."

When they were both comfortable she leaned forward. "I guess you know that Lorenzo is under suspicion for Kitty's murder."

He went quiet for a long moment. "It's so insane. There's no way he—"

"Of course not," she said. "I was right there with him when it happened. We were on the roof together."

Adam nodded. "He told me."

Dana sighed. "The problem is that the detective doesn't trust me. He thinks I might be lying to protect Lorenzo."

"The truth is going to come out, Dana." He tried to smile, but looked ready to cry, and it broke her heart. Still, she knew they needed to have this conversation.

"As long as everyone is honest with them," she said.

Adam rubbed his forehead. "I'm really tired."

"I know this is hard," she said. "But, Adam...you have to go to the police and tell them you slept with Kitty."

He jumped up. "What? Who told you that?"

"No one," she said. "I promise."

"Then how do you know?"

She shrugged. "I tend to notice small details."

His eyes looked terrified. "What small details?"

"Kitty's hair on your jacket, her smell on your skin. I wasn't one hundred percent sure I was right until, well..."

"Until I confirmed it," he said, collapsing back into the couch. He cradled his head in his hands. "Oh, God. My life is over."

"It isn't. I promise. I won't tell the police. But if things really get hot for Lorenzo, I want you to think about going to them yourself. You could be saving his life...and Sophia's."

"Of course, of course," he said, rocking. "But Francesca. She would never forgive me."

"You don't know that."

He looked up at her, his eyes red. "I never cheated on her before. But Kitty. She promised she would talk to Honeycutt about getting me a raise. And money is so tight. We're over our heads with our condo. It was stupid. We could barely afford it when Francesca was working. But now that she's on leave for the baby, it's a nightmare. I thought if I got a raise it would solve everything."

"You're dealing with so much," she said gently. She really didn't want to hurt him, but in the end, there might be no choice.

"And I knew Kitty was using me. After a while, she didn't even try to pretend it was about sex. Or even power. It was like, you do this favor for me, and I'll do this favor for you."

"What did she want from you?" Dana asked, curious for his perspective.

"She was trying to make someone jealous."

"Did she say who?"

He shrugged. "I never told anyone this, but I always assumed it was Honeycutt. She seemed obsessed with him. She had a picture of the two of them on her phone's home screen."

Dana took in the news. "This is what I don't get," she said. "With evidence like that, why aren't the police all over Honeycutt?"

"Because he couldn't have done it. There's no way."

"How do you know?"

"He was in a meeting with HR and legal when it happened."

"Are you sure?" Dana's pulse raced. If this was true, it changed everything.

"I heard it from a couple of people."

She felt nauseated. No wonder Marks was all over Lorenzo. Compared to Honeycutt, his alibi *was* shaky.

"I swear to God, Adam, I'm going to figure this out if it kills me."

"I believe you." He stood to leave.

"What about the raise?" she asked. "Did that ever come through?"

Adam shook his head. "On the day she was killed, Kitty promised she was getting ready to approach Honeycutt about it."

Dana clucked in sympathy. He sighed and moved toward the door.

"I guess it could have been worse," Adam said. "At least she didn't get me fired." He pulled on the doorknob and there was Ollie, practically standing at attention.

"I beg your pardon very much," he said. "Dana, your sister has come. She is in the lobby."

★ ★ ★

"Surprise!" Chelsea said after Ollie led her to Dana's dressing room.

Dana gave her a hug. "What are you doing here?"

"I had an appointment in the city so I thought I'd say hello."

Dana backed up to look at her sister. "Oh, your hair," she said, noting that it looked especially shiny and freshly colored.

Chelsea shook her locks for effect. "What do you think?"

"I think it looks the same as it always does, only more perfect."

Ollie was still standing in the doorway, so Dana politely dismissed him and shut the door. She was getting used to the fact that if she didn't specifically ask him to scram, he'd never be more than a foot away from her.

"Am I intruding?" Chelsea asked. "If you're busy—"

"I'm glad you're here," Dana said.

Chelsea took in her sister's wardrobe, an intentionally sedate light blue shift and dark blue cardigan. "Is that what you're wearing on the air?"

"On second thought," Dana said, "I'm really busy."

"Not that you don't look perfectly lovely," Chelsea said. "I can barely see the dark circles under your eyes."

"I think I look pretty good for someone on three hours' sleep. And my clothes are *supposed to* fade into the background today. I'm doing handbags again. And they're gorgeous."

Chelsea gasped. "Can I get a preview?"

"You know, I was just thinking, 'What my sister needs is more handbags.'"

"You sound like Brandon."

"Must be that star I wished on last night," Dana said, bringing her hands together in mock delight. "Come sit down. I need to talk."

They settled themselves into the sofa, and Dana explained

how concerned she was about the state of the murder investigation.

"I was so sure it was Honeycutt, but now... I don't know."

"What changed your mind?"

"I had a conversation with Adam, my segment producer, and he told me Honeycutt has a rock-solid alibi. It seems to rule him out entirely."

"So what does this guy Adam think?" Chelsea asked. "Does he have any ideas?"

"He's kind of wrapped up in the whole thing himself. Between us, he's another of Kitty's victims." Dana was glad she had Chelsea to confide in, especially since her sister didn't know anyone she could share the gossip with.

"Victims?"

"He slept with her," Dana said. "And he's *married*. He's wrecked over the whole thing."

"Maybe he should have thought of that before he dropped his pants."

"Kitty didn't leave him a choice."

"Oh, come on," Chelsea said.

"I'm serious. You have no idea how toxic this woman was. She was using Lorenzo and Adam to get Honeycutt jealous."

"Lorenzo slept with her, too?"

"Don't," Dana said.

"What are you *doing* with this guy?" Chelsea asked. "He's trouble."

"I like him."

"And I like cherry cheesecake. But you don't see me eating it."

Dana pictured all the hoarded merchandise in Chelsea's basement, and gave her a judgmental glare. "My sister, the model of restraint."

"I mean it, Dana. Don't throw everything away on this man. He's not worth it."

"He's a good guy, Chelse."

"And I suppose Adam's a good guy, too, even though he cheated on his wife?"

"He *is* a good guy," Dana insisted.

Chelsea folded her arms. "Please."

"He was under a lot of financial pressure, and Kitty promised him a raise. He didn't know what else to do."

"He could have said no."

"He was desperate."

Chelsea stuck out her chin. "And how do you know *he* didn't murder Kitty?"

"Adam?" She laughed. "I just know. He's a really decent guy. A lamb. He has two kids and a wife he loves. His family is everything to him."

Chelsea licked her lips. "You're not seeing the whole picture, Sherlock."

"Of course I am."

Chelsea tucked her golden hair behind her ears. "What if Kitty threatened to go to Adam's wife?"

"Why would she?"

"I don't know. Maybe she wanted something from him."

"Doesn't add up," Dana said. "Kitty was about to get Adam a promotion. If he wanted to murder her, he would have waited."

"I'm just saying, Dana, you have no idea if you can trust *anyone* here, including Lorenzo."

"Lorenzo's the one person I know I can trust."

"Why? Because you have the hots for him?"

"Because I was with him when Kitty was shot," Dana said. "And because he's honest."

"How do you know he's honest?"

"He's got the most earnest brown eyes I've ever seen. They're like dark chocolate. The kind that's eighty-six percent cacao. Eyes like that can't hide anything."

Even as she said it, though, Dana knew it wasn't true. He had hidden Sophia. And Kitty. How could she really be sure he wasn't hiding anything else?

22

"Can I get you something, Dana?" Ollie asked after Chelsea left.

"A cup of coffee would be great," she said. "Thanks, Ollie."

Dana needed all the energy she could muster. She was still dragging her feet after being up half the night with Lorenzo. At the time she thought it was worth it, but now that she was faced with a single show her whole career could turn on, she wasn't so sure.

With the right energy level, she knew she could knock this one out of the studio and clear across the Hudson River, maybe clear across the country, propelled by the thumbs of eager shoppers and their remote controls. After all, she really did love the handbags. They were ruggedly constructed in pebble leather, styled in sumptuous summer colors with coordinating trims. And the hardware was… What was the word? It was something simple but evocative. Damn. She could not afford to lose vocabulary today.

Dana thought about the extra Dexedrine pill she had slipped into her purse the day of her audition, just in case. As it turned out, that one dose was more than enough. But the tiny white tablet was still there, tucked inside the secret compartment of her key chain.

It would be so easy to take it. And God knows it would give her the boost she needed. She would be awake, alert, focused.

Then again, she didn't want to make a habit of this. It was dangerous. Doing it once was bad enough. But doing it a second time? That was a step toward addiction.

I should just flush the damned pill down the toilet, she thought. *That way I won't be tempted.* She took it from her purse and went into the bathroom.

As Dana held her palm over the toilet—the tiny pill in the center of it—she thought about how tired she was. So very tired. Coffee might help a little, but would it be enough?

Dana tried to refocus on the handbag hardware. She could picture the heavy chrome rings and the fasteners, but couldn't remember the adjective she'd had in mind. What was it?

She imagined herself struggling for words on the air. She could envision the monitor as the numbers slipped more and more while she struggled to find the perfect language. And then what? She would be beyond saving. There would be nothing Megan could do for her.

She heard Ollie knock on the outer door and enter the dressing room.

"Dana?" he called. "I have your coffee."

"In the bathroom!" she yelled, still staring at the pill. "Be right out."

She heard Ollie move toward the bathroom door, his voice closer. "I just saw Miss Sherry again," he said. "She asks me to please remind you about meeting her after your show today."

"Did she really say 'please'?" Dana asked.

There was no response.

"Ollie?" she prodded.

"Perhaps I am the one who said 'please.' I asked her please not to worry."

"And what did she say?"

"Miss Sherry says it is her job to worry, and… I think she says some American idiom I'm not understanding. Something like, you should not be across her."

"I shouldn't cross her?" Dana suggested.

"Oh, yes, Dana. This is what she said. You should not cross her."

Okay, then, she thought, bringing her hand toward her mouth, maybe just this once. And in twenty minutes or so, she'd be good as gold. Better. As good as shiny chrome handbag hardware that complemented any style. And from now on, she would be sure to get enough sleep. Always. Never mind sex. Well, okay, maybe not entirely. But sleep was nonnegotiable from this point on.

She tossed the pill toward the back of her throat, turned on the tap and put her face under it to slurp in a single gulp.

She relaxed in her dressing room with Ollie, and by the time Jessalyn knocked on her door to say they were ready for her on set, the medication had worked its magic.

"Great!" Dana chirped. "Let's make this our best show yet!"

Ollie smiled, clearly thrilled to see Dana so positive. The three of them walked together to the set, Dana leading like a majorette. If she'd had a baton she would have thrown it in the air. And caught it.

The first display was ready for her when she got there, and it was magnificent. The table was draped with a gold cloth, and the colorful tote handbags were arranged upon it, a rainbow in hand-dyed leather. It was like a Fisher-Price playground of joy for grown women. Dana was thrilled.

She hit her mark and managed to hold still while Lorenzo clipped on her mike. When Jessalyn rushed over to straighten her cardigan and pull a lock of hair to the side, Dana had to restrain herself from slapping the woman's hand away. She could no longer keep still. She was a racehorse who needed to run. And win.

Then the red light flashed and she took off. "Thank you for joining me for this hour!" she gushed to the best friend sitting at home in front of the television. "I'm so excited about this new line of Barlow and Ricci handbags. We're starting with the shopper's tote, which is just a must-have for summer. And the prices! I never expected to see them so low. Never!" She laughed to show her delight and stepped to the side of the display table. "I want to go through the colors first, because they are just absolutely gorgeous." Dana glanced at the names on the color chart as she went through the selections one by one.

She cooed over the product, explaining the wonder of owning something so incredibly practical yet so beautiful, stylish and luxurious. She marveled at the price and reminded viewers how to order as she ran her hand lovingly over the leather. She talked about the construction and design.

"I have to show you the inside, because you won't believe what it holds. But first, I just want to point out how on-trend this tote is, with bold, chunky, statement hardware." *Chunky.* That was the word she'd been groping for. Dana smiled and stole a quick glance at the monitor. Orders were pouring in.

After just a few minutes she heard Adam's voice in her earpiece, telling her which bags to remove from the table because the colors were sold out. It was sooner than expected, which was a great sign. Now the sales would move even faster, because once colors started to deplete, viewers panicked and rushed to the phones.

Her next step was to run through the colors that were remaining, giving shoppers the chance to pick whichever one they coveted most before it was too late. Dana glanced up at the color chart, but it was missing. What the hell? That was supposed to stay in place for her reference.

She took a steadying breath. She had studied the colors carefully, but they were confusing, because she would be selling four different styles that day, and there was a slight variation in color names for each one.

"Well, I don't have my color chart," she said cheerily, "but that's okay. Here's what we've got for you. And please, we're running out and I don't want you to miss this. So lock in your order as soon as you can."

It was a little bit of a stall, a cry for help to her producer and the crew. But the lights prevented her from seeing if they were even on set, as they usually watched from the control booth. Either way, she hoped they were scrambling to get her information back.

Well, to hell with it. She could do this. She had just gone through the colors and they were fresh in her mind. She started with the key lime. Nailed it. Moved on to the pink, and caught herself. No, it was blush. The gray was silver. The yellow was dandelion. But the beige. Was it sand? No, desert! The white was gone, but the warm cream was still there. No, that was yesterday. Same color, but a different name. French vanilla!

Dana glanced up at the monitor. She was doing it! They were selling at a million miles an hour. It supercharged her. She went through the colors again, made love to the handbag's leather with her fingertips, showed the roomy compartments, gushed over the coordinated linings, slung it over her shoulder to demonstrate size and comfort.

The dandelion sold out, then the blush. Then the French vanilla. Adam told her to wrap it up and move on to the next style. God, she had done it.

The viewers saw a price screen followed by website instructions as Dana gave an energetic voice-over, and the shopper's tote display was rolled away and replaced by a table with the pebble leather hobo. When the camera came back to her, she was ready with her ebullient chatter about the styling, and was relieved to see that the color chart had been replaced. Thank God.

But then. Oh, no. The gray was listed as silver, and she distinctly remembered that in this style it was called dove. Her eyes made a sweep of the chart. It was the wrong one! Dana swallowed hard. Someone was sabotaging her! Or maybe it was just a simple mistake, and the medication was making her paranoid. For the life of her, she couldn't tell.

Either way, she had to do this. She had to get through this. No, not *get* through it, *sail* through it. *Soar* through it. She was not going to let this derail her.

She made a decision. Every color had a name, and if she got it wrong, that was okay. The sales associates would deal with it. They'd know that a caller asking for the hobo in cream was actually requesting the French vanilla. Or vice versa. It didn't matter. It wasn't going to hurt sales. Not as long as she sounded confident, and kept gushing and chatting and cooing and delighting.

That zone, she told herself. That zone. You *love* these handbags! They are everything. They are the sun and the moon and the stars. They are joy. They are holy. They are the culmination of everything humankind is capable of. Go!

And she did. Even with the wrong color charts for the pebble leather hobo as well as the satchel and crossbody foldover styles that followed, Dana was a sales goddess. She was unstoppable.

And then, at last, the final signal. It was over. She had done it. And her sales were so high Adam actually applauded.

Dana was tempted to go all Kitty Todd on the crew and scream for heads to roll over the screwup, but she caught herself. She didn't need to bring out the guillotine. That was what she had Megan for. Besides, she wasn't entirely sure she trusted her own judgment. A simple mistake was one thing, treachery was another. But which was it?

Ollie trailed after Dana as she stormed back to her dressing room.

"You are not happy, Dana," he said. "Please, what can I do? I will help. Okay, Dana? Tell me what is making you troubled."

"Nothing!" she blurted. "I just need to talk to my manager."

"She is in your dressing room."

"Fine. You can go home now."

"Are you sure, Dana? Maybe there is something I can help you with?"

"I'm sure!" she spit out. "Just go home."

Ollie practically bowed, his eyes scared, and it occurred to Dana he had never seen her angry before. Still, she couldn't worry about it. There was simply too much to deal with. If there was anything to smooth over tomorrow, she would take care of it then. For now, he would simply have to cope.

Dana threw open her dressing room door. "Did you see what happened?" she said to Megan.

"You killed it."

"Megan," she said, containing her fury, "I think they tried to *sabotage* me."

"What are you talking about?"

"Someone took away the color chart during the first segment, and then screwed up the charts in the rest of the segments."

"And you think this was intentional?"

Dana could barely catch her breath. "Of course it was intentional! And even if it wasn't, someone should get fired. This is not acceptable! I was hanging on by a thread out there."

"Okay, calm down."

"Do you know how lucky it is that I was able to remember all that? It could have been a disaster! I'd be out on my ass."

"Dana, listen to me. You need to settle down. I don't want Sherry to see you like this."

"Why not? My rage is justified!" She opened one of the drawers and slammed it, just for emphasis, but it bounced open again, as if in defiance. She gave it an angry hip-check to let it know she meant business.

"Okay," Megan said. "It is. Absolutely. But—"

"Are you *handling* me?"

"It's part of my job description, sweetie—act as sycophant, nursemaid and patronizing sounding board, as needed."

Dana didn't laugh. She paced her dressing room, thinking. She was so furious she wanted to turn over the table or put her fist through a wall. And her indignation was righteous! She knew this. It was not a drug-fueled rage. She was left dangling out there for four straight hours and no one came to her aid.

Okay, so maybe it wasn't sabotage. Maybe someone had just royally screwed up. She still couldn't tell if the medication was making her paranoid. But damn it, the whole thing was a clusterfuck and there was no excuse. She explained the particulars to Megan, leaving out the part about the Dexedrine.

"The good news," Megan said, "is that you handled it like a pro. You didn't get flustered. You didn't doubt yourself. You just plowed on. And you nailed it. And now, instead of being on the defensive with Sherry, we can turn the tables."

Dana let out a breath, trying to release her anger. Megan was right. "It better not happen again," she said.

"Of course not. We'll make sure of that. In the meantime, trust me. I can make this work in your favor. Just let me do the talking."

Megan brought her a glass of water and made her drink the

whole thing before they went up to see Sherry. Even though Dana understood that it was just Megan's clever way of shifting her focus and calming her down, it worked. By the time they reached Sherry's office, she had her game face back. Also, the medication was starting to wear off.

"I wasn't expecting the two of you," Sherry said.

"Buy one, get one," Megan said. "Today's special."

Sherry didn't smile. "Look, I don't have much to say." She folded her arms. "Yesterday's numbers were terrible, today's were markedly better. Just remember that we don't have the luxury of accommodating even occasional bad days."

"Oh, please," Megan said. "Dana met her numbers yesterday."

"Barely," Sherry said.

"Point is, her numbers weren't 'terrible.' It's just that she's been such a superstar your expectations have gone haywire. You expect her to break a record every day, which isn't fair or reasonable, and you damned well know it."

"If you expect me to coddle her—"

"Oh, knock it off. Dana's not a diva, so don't even go there. Do you even *know* what happened today?"

"Happened?"

"Someone screwed up the color charts. The first one was pulled while she was still on the air. And the rest were *wrong*. But she didn't panic. She didn't mess up. She just plowed on and sold, sold, sold. You should be kissing her ass right now for saving the show when someone else wasn't doing their job."

Sherry turned to Dana. "Is this true? Did you get the wrong charts?"

"It's true," Dana said.

Sherry pressed the button on her intercom and spoke. "Get Adam Weintraub up here immediately."

Dana's heart sank. Not Adam. He was the last person she

wanted to get in trouble. And besides, it wasn't his fault. The color charts were handled by the interns, Topher and Becky, and sometimes Jessalyn, when she was on set. Dana assumed the problem was that the charts had been mislabeled. But she had no idea who was responsible for that…or if it had been done on purpose.

Adam bounded into Sherry's office, grinning. Clearly, he thought he was there to celebrate Dana's success.

"Almost twelve percent over projections!" he said, waving his tablet.

Sherry's brow tightened. "What the fuck happened with the color charts?"

"You mean in the first segment?"

"In the whole show," Sherry said. "She got the wrong charts and had to wing it."

Adam looked at Dana. "Is this true?"

She shrugged. "Unfortunately."

"I had no idea," Adam said.

"Well, that's just great," Sherry seethed. "My segment producer had no idea what the hell was going on with his own show."

He looked at Dana. "I'm sorry. Everything seemed to be going so smoothly."

"And where was Jessalyn?" Sherry asked, referring to the talent coordinator. "Did she spend the show with her thumb up her ass?"

Adam shrugged. "I'll get to the bottom of it. I promise."

"You'd better," Sherry said. "Because if it happens again, *someone's* getting fired."

Sherry dismissed them. As they filed out of her office and walked toward the elevator, Dana turned to Adam.

"I didn't mean to get you in trouble," she said.

"It's not your fault," Megan interjected.

"Don't sweat it," Adam said. "If Sherry didn't chew me out at least once a day, I'd call the paramedics."

"Do you have any idea how it could have happened?" Dana asked.

They reached the elevator bank, and Adam pushed the down button. "I'll figure it out."

Dana watched the lights as the elevator car made its way up to them. "Do you think it could have been intentional?"

He looked at her. "Intentional?"

"I know it sounds crazy, but I feel like... I don't know."

"You think someone has it out for you?" he asked.

Dana hesitated. She liked to think she was good at reading people, and Sherry seemed genuinely furious at the screwup. So it was hard to believe she was the culprit...even if deep down she'd enjoy sabotaging Dana and replacing her with Emily.

Maybe Emily herself had done it. Or perhaps she put her friend Jessalyn up to it. But no. Even as Dana reminded herself that people rarely telegraphed their guilt, she couldn't picture them capable of such duplicity.

When Dana and Megan reached her dressing room, Ollie was standing outside the door, waiting for them.

"Is everything fine, Dana?" he asked. "Any trouble with Miss Sherry?" His eyes were filled with concern.

"I thought you were going home."

"I just wanted to make certain that everything is okay. You were having troubles before, I think."

Dana shook her head. The kid's loyalty was pathological. She had practically bitten his head off, and he stuck around to make sure she was all right. She put a hand on his shoulder. "I'm fine," she said. "Nothing to worry about."

"I leave now?" he said.

"Yes, Ollie, you can go home." She dismissed him with a kind smile and went into her dressing room with Megan.

After shutting the door, Dana slipped out of her on-air wardrobe. "I have time for a drink," she said.

"It's Tuesday," Megan said, as if it were she, and not Dana, who had a rehearsal schedule.

"You have someplace to be?" Dana asked as she hung up her dress. She knew that Megan still worked as a waitress to supplement her income, but that was only weekends and Thursday nights.

Megan picked up an unused eye shadow palette and examined it. "Do *you*?"

"I'm good," she said. "Why don't we go to that place on Ninth?"

Megan considered it for a moment as she studied the shades of browns and nudes in the palette. "I think I'll get going."

"You sure?" Dana asked.

Megan waved away the question. "I haven't had a second to myself for a week. If I don't get home and do some laundry, I'll be running errands tomorrow in a sports bra and Chanel No. 5."

"I'm glad you rushed over here," Dana said. "I probably would have fucked up that conversation with Sherry."

"You did seem ready to punch someone in the throat. Just promise me you'll call if you ever get that urge again."

Dana promised and noticed Megan was still holding the eye shadow set. "You want that?" she asked. "The makeup girl gave it to me. She gets a ton of freebies and insisted I take it."

"I don't need it," Megan said. "Thanks, anyway." She opened the undercounter drawer to put it away. "Hey, what's this?"

Dana looked up to see Megan peering into the drawer she knew was empty. "What's what?" she asked.

"This gold bracelet."

"Bracelet?" It was the same drawer that had flown open when she slammed it in anger, so Dana knew it was empty before they went up to see Sherry. Still in her underwear, she crossed the room to see. And there, in the middle of the barren drawer, was a gold bracelet in the shape of an alligator, its two emerald eyes staring up at her.

23

"And you have no idea how it got here?" Detective Marks said as he peered into the drawer.

Dana had called him in a panic right after Megan found the bracelet. If someone was trying to set her up for Kitty's murder, she needed to be as careful as possible. Dana guessed she had caught him off duty, because he wasn't wearing his suit. He was in jeans and a white Athletic Club T-shirt. Since his hair was wet, she figured he had been at the gym working out. Also, he looked pumped, his veined biceps straining against his sleeves. If she knew him better, she'd lay her cool fingers on the smooth mound, admiring its firmness.

Stop this, she told herself. *You're seeing Lorenzo. And even if you weren't, this guy would be a mistake.*

"The only thing I know is that the drawer was empty before I went up to see Sherry a short while ago," she said.

"Who has access to this room?" he asked.

She shrugged. "I didn't lock it, so anyone, really."

The detective opened the door and poked his head out into the hallway, looking up. "No security cameras," he said.

"I asked a few people if they saw anyone come in here," she said, "but everyone was busy."

"Did you notice anything before you left your dressing room? Anyone hanging around?"

"No," she said, though she knew her usual powers of perception might have been skewed, due to her fury and the Dexedrine. "I was in here with Megan, having a little bit of a meltdown about something that happened on air today. I was in such a state I slammed the drawer shut, and it bounced open. That's how I know it was empty at that point." Dana shrugged, and the strap of her tank top slipped off her shoulder. She quickly fixed it in place, but not before noticing that his eyes darted there and then away.

"What happened on air?" he asked, now fixed on her face. His expression was inscrutable, but she thought she saw a bit of pink rising up his cheeks. Was this gritty detective blushing?

"I'm sure it's not relevant," she said.

"Tell me, anyway."

Dana sat on the sofa, hoping he would take the chair opposite her so they could be eye-to-eye, but Marks stood by the drawer as if guarding it.

She launched into the story of what had happened with the Barlow and Ricci color charts, and he showed more interest in the details than she expected. He pressed for information on who was responsible for the charts, and who had access to them on and off set.

"Of course, it might have been an honest mistake," she said. "A random screwup."

"But you don't really believe that."

Dana stood, as it was too hard to have a conversation with her head craned back. "Honestly, I think someone might be trying to sabotage me," she said, and hoped he didn't think she was being paranoid.

"And why would that be?"

"It's a pretty plum gig," she said. "A lot of people would like a shot at it."

He folded his arms, thinking, and the pressure on his biceps made them enormous. She swallowed.

"Tell me about your amateur sleuthing?" he asked.

"Sleuthing?"

"Have you been poking around," he clarified, "asking questions about Kitty Todd?"

Dana bit her lip. "Not really."

He gave her a look that said he didn't buy it.

She let out a breath. "You didn't leave me any choice," she said. "You're hounding Lorenzo like a dog and I *know* he's innocent."

"You need to have faith in the process."

"I'd have a lot more faith if you believed what I told you."

"Tell me who you spoke to about the investigation," he said.

Dana squinted at him. "You think what happened on the air today is connected to the murder?" she asked.

"That's what I'd like to find out."

Dana considered that, trying to understand if it really made sense. She hadn't thought the bracelet and the color charts screwup were related, but now she wasn't so sure. If the murderer knew she was probing, and worried she was getting close to the truth, it might make sense for him—or her—to try to get Dana fired.

"I'm struggling to understand why someone who wants to get me in trouble would leave the bracelet in my dressing room for me to find. Doesn't it make more sense that they were leaving me a clue to the murderer's identity?"

"That's one possibility," he said.

"What's another?" she asked.

"I'm sure you'll figure it out."

"Oh, come on," she said. "Don't do that. I'm deep in this shit. I deserve to know."

Marks sighed and glanced at the door, as if he were waiting for someone. He looked back at her and his expression softened into something like sympathy, as if he really did regret that she was so embroiled in the mess.

Finally he said, "Okay. It could be a false lead."

"Like…someone trying to steer me in the wrong direction?"

He nodded. "Or…"

"Or what?"

There was a knock on the door and a calm male voice said, "Police."

Marks opened the door and greeted two uniformed officers by name. It was obvious to Dana that he had asked them to come. One of the cops took a few photographs of the bracelet in the drawer, and the other snapped on a pair of blue plastic gloves before picking it up by its tail and dropping it into a baggie.

"Thank you for your help, Ms. Barry," Marks said, and moved toward the door.

She wanted to stall so they could finish their conversation. "What about the alligator?" she asked. "What will you do with it?"

"What would you like me to do—release it to the wild?"

The other officers snickered.

"I just want to make sure it doesn't wind up in the sewers," she quipped back. It was ancient urban legend every New Yorker knew—the myth of abandoned baby alligators growing to enormous lengths and sloshing around the dank dark corridors of Manhattan's underbelly.

Marks shook his head. "Then it might find its way down to Wall Street," he said, "and we can't have that."

"Why not?"

He shrugged. "Might get eaten alive."

24

As the E train rattled downtown toward the Sweat City theater, Dana thought about rehearsals. She loved the show and was grateful for the opportunity to play the role of the horrible Mrs. Woodbridge, despite that she would never get career credit for it. She still grappled with that. Because even though she recognized that releasing herself from the shackles of judgment had enabled her to fully immerse in a role as she had never done before, it was hard to erase all traces of ego. Dana knew who she was, knew that beneath the dedicated artist beat the heart of a ham. She couldn't get away from it. She was an actor, after all, and that meant she came alive in the limelight. So it was hard to reconcile that she would be giving the performance of her career and no one would know it was her. She wouldn't be able to call family and friends and tell them to come see the show. She wouldn't even get to grasp Megan's arm with two hands after the play and ask, in needy desperation, if she liked—*really* liked—her performance.

Art for art's sake, she told herself over and over.

When the train stopped at Fourteenth Street, a crowd pushed in and Dana got jostled deeper into the subway car. She tried to escape the proximity of strangers by disappearing inside her head, replaying the conversation with Marks to figure out where it had been leading. But there were too many distractions. In particular, two young women nearby—high school girls, she surmised—were having an animated conversation about a teacher they thought had been egregiously unjust. The taller girl, with a backpack slung carelessly over one shoulder, complained that the teacher refused to accept a paper handed in late, and yet wouldn't let her do an extra credit assignment to make up for it. She was indignant, and the other girl agreed again and again that "Martins is, like, a total dick."

Dana noticed a man seated by the door who was peering furtively toward the girls. She followed the line of his vision and saw that he was looking at what appeared to be a pink leather wallet peeking out from the vocal girl's backpack. The man stood and edged closer to the teens, and Dana had a pretty good idea of what was going on. She tapped the girl on the shoulder.

"Excuse me, I think your wallet is sticking out," she said.

"Ugh. Again?" The girl swung the backpack around and moved her wallet to a zippered section deep in the interior. "If I lost my wallet again my mother would kill me." She thanked Dana over her shoulder and went back to her important conversation with her friend.

Dana wanted to tell the girl she had to look out for herself. She couldn't expect her teachers to cut her a special shortcut to success. And she couldn't rely on strangers like Dana to warn her when she was in trouble. *There are thieves everywhere*, Dana wanted to say. Not just professional pickpockets, but regular people pushed to desperation.

Dana had almost been that person, just a year ago. Her checking account had been in overdraft due to an unexpected visit to the doctor for strep throat, and she was on a spending freeze until her next check came in. She was hungry, and couldn't even duck into a deli to fill up a small salad bar tray. She would have to make do with whatever unappetizing scraps she could find in her pantry and fridge.

And then it happened. She was walking down Forty-Seventh Street when an elderly man in front of her reached into the pocket of his cashmere overcoat to pull something out, and a folded hundred-dollar bill floated to the ground behind him. Dana knelt to pick it up and paused as she considered slipping it into her pocket. She even glanced around, and knew that no one had seen her. It would be so easy. She thought about filling up a big salad tray, topping it with one of those pickled hot peppers she liked so much. Maybe throw in a handful of pine nuts for good measure.

She tried to justify it by telling herself the man wore an expensive coat and almost certainly had a cushy bank account. The hundred dollars probably meant nothing to him. And anyway, he should have been more careful with his cash. She would be teaching him a lesson.

But of course, it was wrong, and she knew it. The pressure in her throat told her so. She croaked out, "Sir!" and when he turned and saw her holding the folded up bill, the terrible tightness released. She had done the right thing.

Dana thought back to the gold alligator bracelet, and wondered if it was possible someone had stolen it simply for the money. If that were true, then the theft of the bracelet had nothing to do with the murder. And maybe that was where Marks was headed with his theory.

Of course, that left the question of why the bracelet wound up in her dressing room. Was it possible the thief's conscience got the better of him, just as Dana's had on Forty-Seventh Street? And was it a *him*? Better to think in non–gender-specific pronouns, she reasoned. So maybe the sticky-fingered perpetrator's conscience got the better of *them*. Maybe they were worried that if they tried to sell it they would come under suspicion for the murder. In either case, the thief might have assumed that slipping it into the drawer of Kitty's old dressing room was the most inconspicuous way to return it. They might have figured it would take a while to be noticed, and by then it would be assumed it had somehow been overlooked when the room was cleaned out.

But of course, it still meant that the bracelet was stolen by someone who had access to Kitty's office between the time Dana viewed the murder and the police arrived. She tried to remember who she saw running down the hallway toward Kitty's office on that day. Dana had been in such a state it was hard to remember. She knew Honeycutt was there, and possibly his secretary. She was pretty sure Brenda the receptionist had been in the crowd, and possibly Adam Weintraub and Sherry Zidel. There were people she didn't know, faces she couldn't recall.

Dana was still searching her memory when she reached the theater. She felt a pang of guilt for being late, and for not quite being off-book. She had the first half of the script down cold, but she still had a lot of work to do on act two. She promised herself she would go straight home after rehearsal and work on her lines. No booty call with Lorenzo.

"Sorry I'm late," she said to Tyrel when she arrived backstage. She put her suede jacket on a hook.

"Don't worry about it," he said. "Nathan is working on some blocking with Raj and Sylvia. Tough day at the office, dear?"

"You could say that."

"I've been watching, you know. Don't think it was easy for me to resist that big pink handbag."

"I beg your pardon," she said. "It's *blush*."

"Of course. And I forgot to tell you—I think I know one of those models who was on the other day."

"Which one?" she asked. "Natasha, Chloe or Amy?"

"No, someone else. Emily, I think. She was on the show after yours. White denim jacket."

"Emily Lauren," Dana said. "You know her?"

"We took an acting class together a couple of years ago. Only her last name wasn't Lauren."

Dana laughed. "I figured that was a stage name. What was she back then?"

He squinted, thinking. "Can't remember. It wasn't something terrible, though. Not something you'd need to change."

"If you think of it, let me know. I'd love to look her up."

The rehearsal was rougher than most, because they were doing the second act and Dana was frustrated with herself for still needing her script. She had some good moments, though. No, some great moments, where she found a previously hidden truth inside her character. But she couldn't forgive herself for being a slacker, and silently vowed she would be caught up by the next rehearsal.

On her way home, she texted Lorenzo to say she wouldn't be coming over. By the time she got into bed, he still hadn't responded, which she thought was odd. Odder still: he wasn't at work the next day, and didn't reach out.

Early in the afternoon she texted, Hey, everything okay?

Later in the afternoon she wrote, Worried about you. Just wanted to check in.

In the evening, Are you sick? Is Sophia? Let me know if you need anything.

Before she went to bed that night, she called and got his voice mail. By this point, Dana felt sure that if something was truly wrong he would have reached out. This was something else. Lorenzo was avoiding her. Still, she left a message saying she was concerned, and would he please just let her know if he was alive or dead. Nothing.

25

He wasn't dead. But Dana wanted to make him wish he was, because he showed up at work on Thursday acting as if nothing was wrong.

"What happened to you yesterday?" she whispered as he clipped on her microphone. "Why didn't you answer my texts?" She took a furtive glance around to see if anyone was looking at them, and of course they were. Dana was onstage. The cameras were moving into place.

"We'll talk later," he said, his voice low and his expression even.

She snorted. Would it have killed him to shoot back a message? She felt like she had been ghosted and wanted to throttle him.

"Is Sophia okay?" she asked, catching herself. Maybe there was an innocent explanation, after all, and she was being perverse. Part of her hoped there *was* something wrong. At least it would be a reasonable excuse.

"She's fine."

So much for that.

"Can you come over later?" Dana asked. Better her place than his, she thought. She knew they were headed toward an argument and didn't want to have to do it in furious whispers as Sophia slept. Once was enough for that kind of scene.

"I'll try," he said.

You'd better, she thought.

The show started out fine. But an hour into it, Dana's microphone cut out. Within seconds, the tech director instructed the engineers to break to a promo, and Lorenzo rushed to replace the malfunctioning lavalier.

"What happened?" Dana asked.

"One of the cables got severed," he said. "No big deal."

"*Severed?*" she said, horrified. She pictured guillotines and machetes.

"Don't get excited. It happens. Probably wasn't taped down well and a jib ran over it."

She knew that the crane cameras they called jibs were operated robotically by guys in the control room, and she reasoned that it was entirely possible the heavy machinery could have clipped a cable.

"So you don't think—"

"No, I don't. It was just an accident."

The tech director called for places, Lorenzo stepped away and Dana was back on the air, selling her heart out. Accident or not, she wasn't going to let an audio cable derail her success.

The rest of the show was trouble free. Afterward, Dana returned to her dressing room to find Ollie facedown on the sofa, his body shaking in sobs, an odd, high-pitched siren-whine emanating from within. He didn't just sound like a wounded animal. He sounded like a wounded animal from another planet. Something strange and alien, with the body of a giraffe and the head of a Kardashian.

"Ollie!" she said. "What's wrong?"

He sat up quickly, looking terrible. His cheeks were drained of color, but his eyes were puffy and pink, his nose swollen and red. Even his lips—wet and engorged—seemed to protest the assault of his blubbering meltdown. Ollie wiped his nose with his sleeve, and held up a limp white silk scarf in both hands as if it were a dead child.

"Oh, Dana. I am sorry for crying, but Miss Binky has sent this to me," he said.

"Who?"

"Miss Binky," he repeated. "She is a good, loyal person who took care of Miss Kitty after she had a big depression. She is Miss Kitty's aunt."

Of course she is, Dana thought. Those people always have names like Binky and Bitsy and Bunny. She could picture her. A golfer, ropey and tan. Like a sun-damaged Mary Tyler Moore with blond hair and an athletic neck.

Ollie continued. "She has cleaned out her home and said maybe I would like a memento since I meaned so much to her niece. So she sent me this. It was Miss Kitty's favorite scarf!"

He set the precious object aside and collapsed in on himself in sobs. Dana retrieved a box of tissues from the counter and sat next to him, wondering what she would do if she couldn't calm him down. The man seemed ready for hospitalization. She rubbed his back.

"It's a terrible loss," she said gently, and wondered if he had a personal history that intensified the pain in moments like this. "Do you want to talk about it?"

"My heart is broken," he said, and then mumbled something incoherent.

"Was that Finnish?" she asked.

"I guess I was thinking about Mummo—my grandmother. She cared for me after my mother died. But then Mummo passed when I was ten."

"So you lost your mother *and* your grandmother?"

"But Mummo died of natural causes," he said.

"And your mother?"

"She had the depression disease. I was six when she killed herself with a…a…*hirttosilmukka*. I forget the English word." He mimed tying a knot around his neck and yanking it.

"A noose?" she asked. "Your mother hanged herself?"

"Yes, that is correct, Dana."

She was almost afraid to ask if he was the one who had found her, because the look on his face said it all. No wonder he had such pathological attachment issues.

"That must have been hard," she said gently.

"Then my father remarried and I had the most lovely stepmother. But they got divorced so then it was only Isä and me. My father, I mean."

Dana had to cough to keep from choking on the tragedies of his life. She took a deep breath and centered herself. "You've suffered so much loss."

Ollie pulled a tissue from the box and wiped his wet face. "Kitty was the most wonderful person," he said, taking a jagged breath.

"Of course she was."

"I know that many people here think she was a hard woman. But they did not understand her, Dana. She had a very human heart. I know this."

"Tell me," Dana said. "Tell me about her heart."

"She loved very deeply, you know. Very, very deeply."

"I understand," she said.

"Oh, Dana!" he cried. "They must catch the man who did this terrible thing to her. They must!"

She paused. "Do you know for sure that it was a man who killed her?"

"I think… I think a woman wouldn't do this kind of thing, yes?"

"I don't know," Dana said, deciding it was the wrong time for a lecture on feminism. "It's hard to imagine *any* human who could do this kind of thing."

"This is true, Dana. It is a horrible thing. A horrible thing for any human to do. This is why they must find the person and punish him."

"I agree with you, Ollie."

"I am bereft," he said. "Is this the right word, *bereft*?"

"It's the perfect word," she said. "Do you want to talk about her? About her heart? It might make you feel better."

He nodded. "Her love for Mr. Honeycutt, it was very beautiful. She wanted only him."

Oh, sure, Dana thought. That was why she'd slept with Lorenzo and Adam and God knows who else.

"Love is a powerful emotion," she said, groping for something innocuous to say.

"Yes, powerful! You are so wise, Dana. Miss Kitty's love for Mr. Honeycutt had big power. And he had powerful love for her, too. But as a man, he was not so strong, you understand? He loved Miss Kitty with his full heart, but not with courage."

"Because he wouldn't leave his wife, you mean?"

"Yes. And Miss Kitty, she did everything to make him understand that they should be together always. She wants him to understand that love is all. Love is everything."

Dana shifted in her seat. It sounded like Ollie was saying Kitty had threatened Honeycutt. "What kind of things did Kitty do to...convince him?"

"Some things not so nice, I am afraid. But this is how strong is Miss Kitty's love."

"What kind of things?"

"She had proof, you see, of their love. She tells Mr. Honeycutt she will make this public so the whole world will know.

Then his wife will leave him. So even if Mr. Honeycutt is not strong enough, they can still be together."

"What kind of proof?" Dana asked.

He looked down, embarrassed. "She keeps camera in her bedroom, Dana."

"A video camera?"

Ollie nodded.

"You mean, she secretly taped them...making love?"

"It was for his good, you understand? For both of them. Miss Kitty's love was strong. They must be together no matter what. This is what she knows. This is her heart, her wonderful heart."

A sex tape! And she was threatening him with it! This was huge. Possibly even huge enough for Charles Honeycutt to have hired a hit man.

"Can I share with you a secret, Dana?"

"Of course."

"Miss Kitty was so certain Mr. Honeycutt and she will get married that she bought a wedding dress. It was beautiful!"

"A wedding dress? Are you serious?"

"Oh, yes, Dana. Very serious. She took me with her to shop for it. It was my best day in America!"

"That's...lovely," she said, and changed the subject. "I need to ask you—where is the...video? Is it on Kitty's computer? On a flash drive?"

"I do not know."

"But you said Miss Binky cleaned out her apartment. Do you know if she found anything?"

"This kind of thing I do not ask." He smoothed his shirt, as if getting ready to leave. His crying had ceased, but his face was still a mess.

Dana laid a hand on his shoulder. "Do you have a friend I

can call to take you home? You still seem a little shaky. You mentioned a roommate?"

"Kimmo," he said. "But he is not at home now." Ollie blew his nose and stood. "I am fine, Dana. You are so kind to me."

"Are you sure you're okay?"

"Crying is good for me. It cleans my grief." He straightened his shoulders, showing how much better he was. And he did look recovered.

"Okay, then," she said. "I'll see you tomorrow."

After he left, Dana changed into her street clothes, replaying the conversation. When she got into the elevator, she pressed the button for the lobby and her head was so filled with revelations about the secret sex tape that she barely registered that Emily stood behind her.

"Great show today," Emily said.

It was the reflexively polite response she often got from her coworkers. And while it was indeed a good show—despite the microphone problem—Dana took it as courteous small talk. "Thank you," she said. "I heard you were a smash on Vanessa's fashion segment."

Emily smiled warmly. "I think it went well."

"You know, a friend of mine saw you. He said he knows you."

Emily's smile vanished. "Really?"

"Tyrel Goodson. He said you took an acting class together."

"That wasn't me."

"Are you sure?" Dana asked.

Emily's brow tightened. "Of course I'm sure."

Dana opened her mouth to respond, but the elevator reached the lobby and the doors parted. Before she could say a word, Emily scurried off.

Weird, Dana thought, and wondered if Emily had a secret in her past she wanted to keep hidden. Maybe she had a sex tape of her own—some porn movie she foolishly did under her own name. Or maybe it was something as innocuous as an embarrassingly bad performance she wanted to distance herself from. In any case, Dana would be pressing Tyrel to remember that last name.

26

Later, Dana got a text from Lorenzo saying he couldn't get a sitter. She texted back, Then I'll come to you.

She waited for a reply. Five minutes went by. Then ten. Then fifteen. She wondered if she should just get on the subway and head up there, but at last her phone pinged.

Wait, found a sitter. Be there in a little while.

This time, she wasn't lighting romantic candles or setting out a bottle of wine. In fact, Dana wasn't even going to take a hit off a joint. She didn't want to do anything to mellow her anger. Unless Lorenzo had one hell of an excuse, he deserved it. And damn it, she resented the hell out of him for making her feel like a high-maintenance woman. She wasn't high-maintenance. She just didn't deserve to be ghosted by a guy she was sleeping with.

An hour went by, and she wondered what he had meant by "a little while." She texted, On your way?

After a few minutes, he responded.

Sitter canceled. Can we do tomorrow night?

Dana gritted her teeth. This was starting to look like a terrible pattern. She wrote back, Busy tomorrow.

She knew it seemed like a lie, because she probably would have said it even if it weren't true. But it was. Jennifer Lafferty had extended a dinner invitation. Dana, Chelsea, Brandon and Wesley would be joining Dad and his girlfriend at her East Side apartment. And at this point, she certainly wasn't going to invite Lorenzo to come along.

When he didn't respond right away, Dana decided to ignore her phone. She silenced it and went about her evening. By bedtime, she guessed he had texted her a few more times, suggesting when they could meet. Still, she would wait until the morning to respond. He could just stew in it.

After she had gone through her nightly ritual of washing, exfoliating and moisturizing, Dana slipped under the covers of her bed and at last picked up the cell phone on her nightstand. Her mood was softening, and she decided that if he had texted at least three times, she would answer him tonight. Less than that and he could wait until the morning.

She swiped her phoned to life and stared at the screen. Since her last text saying she was busy tomorrow night, the number of times he responded was exactly zero.

Zero.

That was three less than the number of times she pounded her pillow before eventually falling asleep.

She awoke the next morning feeling even less generously toward him than she had when she'd drifted off. And despite herself, she checked her cell phone again before she even got out of bed. He had texted her a little after 1:00 a.m.

Fell asleep reading to Sophia. You up?

She exhaled, releasing about ten percent of her tension.

All was not forgiven, but she could at least put her fury on hold until they made plans to talk.

Jennifer Lafferty's apartment was a boxy two-bedroom on East Fifty-Seventh Street, with pale cream walls and lots of right angles. Dana was the last to arrive, or so she thought. Passing the dining room, which was really just a rectangular area off the sunken living room, she noticed one extra place setting. She had made it perfectly clear she was not bringing Lorenzo, and wondered who the extra guest might be.

Chelsea and Brandon were side by side on a trim plaid sofa. Her father was in a shabby chic brown leather easy chair, reading a picture book to Wesley, who sat on his lap. Dana stopped and stared. Her father. Kenneth G. Barry, MD. Reading to a wriggly little boy. She had never imagined such a thing, and it was a surprisingly sweet sight. That was, until Wesley's thumb went into his mouth as he burrowed deeper into his grandfather's chest, and Kenneth pushed on his hand and said, "Stop that. You're not a baby."

"Oh, goody," Dana said. "It's Mr. Rogers."

"Don't be funny," her father said.

"Can't help it." She winked at Wesley as she flicked her pinky from the inside of her cheek and made an impressive *pop.* Wesley laughed.

Dana greeted her sister and brother-in-law, who were nicely dressed in complementary blues and beiges. Dana wore the same snug V-neck T-shirt and tight jeans she had on the day they went to Café Rosemary for her sister's birthday—a fact that didn't escape Chelsea's notice.

"Seriously?" Chelsea said, looking Dana up and down.

Dana shrugged, sheepish. "I'm behind on laundry."

"Liar."

There was nothing for Dana to say. Her sister knew her too

well. If she hadn't been in such a dark mood over Lorenzo, she might have dressed up. But she was brimming with resentment over the whole situation, and decided that if Jennifer and her father wanted to judge her for her clothing, they could go to hell.

Besides, she had dressed up the outfit with sexy, over-the-knee boots and thought the effect was pretty rocking.

"With that figure," Jennifer offered with a smile, "Dana looks great no matter what she puts on."

"See?" Chelsea said. "You're not pissing anybody off, so what's the point?"

"The night is young," Dana said.

Jennifer offered Dana a glass of wine and urged her to help herself to the appetizers. Dana settled herself into the other leather side chair as her father finished reading Dr. Seuss's *Oh, the Thinks You Can Think!* to his grandson.

He closed the book, and Wesley climbed off his lap. Dana insisted on a hug from the child, but made no move toward her father.

"At least you didn't bring your convict," Kenneth said.

"Lorenzo," she said. "Even felons get to keep their names."

"You're still seeing him?"

"What's a felons?" Wesley asked.

"It's a bad man," Kenneth said. "A criminal."

Dana tsked. "It's a man who made a mistake." This was a hell of a time to be sticking up for Lorenzo, but she refused to give her father a free pass on his tiresome bullshit.

Confused, Wesley looked from one parent to the other.

"A felony is a type of crime," Brandon explained, "and a felon is a person who commits it."

"So he *is* a bad man," Wesley said to Dana.

"It's a little more complicated than that, sweetie," Dana said.

"I liked him actually," Brandon said.

Wesley wedged in between his parents on the couch. "You liked a bad man?"

"Why don't we change the subject?" Chelsea suggested.

"Great," Dana said. "I was going to ask you what I should wear for the elopement this weekend."

"She's kidding," Chelsea said to the group, and then turned to her sister. "You are kidding, right?"

Dana exhaled. "It's not even a serious relationship." She could have added that, at this point, she wasn't sure if there was any relationship at all. But she wasn't going to give her father the satisfaction.

"Thank God for that," Kenneth said. "Maybe the young man we in—"

"Hang on a second, Ken," Jennifer cut in. "I need to apologize to Dana first."

"Apologize?" Dana asked.

Jennifer let out a sympathetic breath. "I set up this dinner party before I met Lorenzo. Your father had told me you weren't seeing anyone, and so I suggested he invite a colleague. I'm sorry. I hope this isn't too awkward."

A colleague of her father's? For her? It was unbearable to even contemplate. She pictured a pasty-faced neurologist. Or maybe some overtanned anesthesiologist he played tennis with. A guy with dyed black hair and capped teeth. A gold neck chain.

"It'll be fine," she said to Jennifer, trying to tamp down her resentment. It could be a long night. "As long as he's not expecting a love match."

"He's a *doctor*," her father pronounced, as if that was all she needed to know.

"So?"

"So maybe you should give him a chance."

The doorbell rang, and Jennifer went to answer it. At first,

Dana assumed the guy standing in the doorway with a bouquet of lilies had the wrong apartment. This couldn't possibly be a colleague of her father's. He was young. Very young.
A boy. Twenty, maybe? No, not twenty. Maybe twenty-four,
with one of those doughy faces that stubbornly refused to ma-
ture. His protruding cheeks were smooth, like they couldn't
yet grow a beard. Even so, he wore enough aftershave to smell
clear across the room. He was small and round, with thinning
hair and a low center of gravity—the kind of guy it would be
hard to knock over.

"Good to see you again," Jennifer said, giving him a kiss on
the cheek and accepting the flowers. She turned to the group.
"Everyone, this is Rusty Lindemuth."

As they were introduced, Rusty's eyes lit on Dana and his
entire face changed. It was rapture, like he had just seen the
Lord. His eyes went wide and wet as he disappeared into his
own stunned reverie. Oh, no, Dana thought. Not this. Please,
anything but this. A lot of men skimmed over her lanky body
without a pause. For them, she was not the kind of girl who
made the rocking world go 'round. But there were others—
often with arrested development—who projected onto her
their thwarted teenage desires. Her gamine silhouette, combined with her womanly sexuality, made her an object of intense desire. She could spot these guys a mile away, and Rusty
was only a few feet from her. Dana wished she had made a
different wardrobe choice. At the very least, the dominatrix
boots were a mistake.

"Nice to meet you," she said.

There was a pause, and then he said, "Oh!" as if awaken-
ing. "Hello. Hello, Dana. Nice to meet you, too. Very nice."
He grabbed her hand in his soft, damp palm and shook it
vigorously.

Jennifer steered Rusty into the kitchen to get him a drink,

and Dana whirled toward her father as she wiped the kid's hand sweat on her jeans.

"What the hell, Dad?"

"Excuse me?" He seemed utterly perplexed.

"You seriously thought this guy was a match for me?"

"He's a nice young man."

"He's *twelve*."

"Don't be ridiculous. He's a student of mine. Must be in his midtwenties."

"He does look pretty young," Brandon agreed.

"I was thinking he might enjoy the Dr. Seuss book," Chelsea added, smirking.

"*My* book?" Wesley said, delighted to be a part of the conversation. His mother patted his head.

Dana stared at her father. "I thought you said he was a doctor."

"Close enough," Kenneth said. "Top of his class at Columbia. His internship starts in the fall."

"Dad, I'm twenty-nine years old."

"You're making a big deal out of a few years."

"They're important years," Chelsea said.

"Isn't this what you gals call a double standard?" Kenneth asked. "If the age difference were reversed—"

"He's got a point," Brandon said.

"He's just saying that to justify his age difference with Jennifer," Dana said.

The conversation abruptly ended when Jennifer and Rusty emerged from the kitchen. Dana picked up a deviled egg and sank deep into the chair, hoping to avoid a conversation with Rusty. She worked assiduously on the canapé, taking tiny, careful bites.

"Dinner will be ready in a few minutes," Jennifer announced as she began setting out plates of salad on the table just a few feet away.

Chelsea asked if she could help and Dana was sorry she hadn't thought of it first—an excuse to be occupied. But Jennifer waved it off. She had everything under control.

Rusty took the straight-back chair next to Dana's. She avoided his eye as she nibbled away, and he pressed his damp fingers on her leg to get her attention.

"You like eggs?" he said.

"Who doesn't like eggs?" she snapped. She hadn't meant to be rude. But for heaven's sake, he'd have to be a little less of an idiot if he wanted to have an actual conversation.

"I like eggs," Wesley said. "But not these eggs. These are devil eggs."

"Deviled," Brandon corrected, with an emphasis on the final *D.*

"What's that stuff on them?" the boy asked, a small pointed finger hovering close to the food.

"That's paprika," Chelsea said. "It's a spice. You'd like it."

"I'd vomit."

"That's not nice, honey," Chelsea said. "And you wouldn't vomit."

Wesley stood in front of Rusty, his arms straight down at his sides, his little belly protruding. "My friend Ahmed is allergic to eggs. They could kill him dead." Abruptly, he put his hands on his throat and let his head fall forward as if he'd been murdered.

"That's called anaphylactic shock," Rusty said.

Wesley looked at him and then back at his parents. "What is this guy talking about?"

"It's a medical term," Brandon said.

Wesley contemplated that and turned back to Rusty. "Are you a doctor?"

Rusty sat up straighter and stole a glance at Dana. "I will be."

"You give people shots?" the boy asked.

"Sometimes."

"I'm four," Wesley pronounced.

"Oh." Rusty looked deflated, and Dana could tell he'd hoped to get more traction on the doctor topic.

"Are you twelve?" Wesley asked him.

The mood in the room shifted as Brandon, Chelsea and Dana traded looks. Chelsea opened her mouth to intercede but Rusty responded earnestly before she could get anything out.

"I'm twenty-five."

"That's more than twelve, right?"

"Quite a bit."

Wesley turned to Dana. "Aunt Dana, he's not twelve."

"You know," she said quickly, "all this talk about vomiting and anaphylaxis has gotten me hungry." She stood and turned to Jennifer. "Would you like us to move to the table?"

They were only seated a few minutes when Dana felt her cell phone buzz in the pocket of her jeans. She surreptitiously pulled it out and placed it on her thigh, glancing down at the screen. It was a text from Lorenzo.

You free later? Sophia is sleeping at a friend's.

Dana mixed her salad around as she decided how to respond.

"Let me know if you find anything good," Rusty said, pointing to her salad bowl. It was meant to be a joke, but it made her want to stomp on his foot. She didn't appreciate having her eating habits scrutinized with a running commentary. Dana ignored the remark, but he was unperturbed.

"Are you a model?" he asked, and she could see how thrilled he was at the thought of it. His eyes danced with joy.

"I'm an actor," she said.

"Don't you mean actress?"

"Would you call Jennifer a doctress?" she asked him.

"Not if he values his life," Jennifer said.

Everyone laughed, and Dana managed a smile. "I rest my case," she said.

Jennifer began to tell a story about sexism she had encountered at medical school, and Dana stealthily tapped out a reply to Lorenzo.

Probably not.

She went back to her salad and her phone buzzed again.

Why?

She typed, At dinner party sitting next to a young doctor who wants to fuck me.

Let him simmer in that, she thought as she went back to trying to pierce a grape tomato with her fork. Her phone buzzed again, which surprised her. She thought he'd go quiet after that.

I don't blame you for being mad.

She responded quickly and sarcastically.

Big of you.

Dana was pretty sure everyone at the table knew she was secretly looking at her cell phone, but they were all too polite to say anything. Except Rusty, that is.

"I guess you have a lot of boyfriends," he said.

She landed her fork into the tomato. "Just one."

Rusty Lindemuth blinked painfully, as if he were the one being pierced. Dana knew she had hurt him, but damn it, he left her no choice. Her father had undoubtedly led him to believe she was available, and clearly Jennifer hadn't set him straight when she pulled him into the kitchen. So what was she supposed to do—let him go on believing he had found his soul mate? And anyway, what kind of guy got so instantly besotted? He didn't know a thing about her.

"Is it serious?" he asked, his eyes pleading.

She let out a breath. "I don't know."

The glint returned to his eyes and Dana sank. She hadn't meant to give him hope. Her phone vibrated again and she glanced down.

There was a reason I couldn't tell you what was going on.

She typed back, Why? Were you robbing a bank?

She put the phone on her chair and stood to help Jennifer clear the salad dishes.

"Sit, please," Jennifer said. "Kenneth will help me."

And then, to her complete shock, Dana's father rose and began clearing the table. In her entire life, she had never seen her father lift a finger to help her mother. Not once. She wanted to break something.

Dana sat back down and typed out another message to Lorenzo.

Well?

Her father came back into the room carrying a platter of lemon chicken, which he set ceremoniously in the middle of the table.

Another message from Lorenzo came through.

No, but I was in violation of parole.

She responded, WTF?

As Jennifer laid out the side dishes, Dana noticed something that had managed to escape her attention earlier. A brilliant square-cut diamond engagement ring. It caught the light with such dramatic sparkle it was practically alive. Dana looked up to see if anyone else had noticed, but they were all engaged in conversation. When she looked back, Jennifer was seated, her hand hidden beneath the table. Dana looked at her face, and she quickly looked away. She knew Dana had seen it.

"Dad?" Dana said. "Do you have something to tell us?"

Chelsea put down her fork. "What? What's going on?"

"We were going to wait until after dinner," Jennifer said. "But I guess the cat's out of the bag."

"Did I miss something?" Chelsea asked.

Dana conveyed the story to Chelsea with some very simple sign language. She pointed to the place on her own finger where an engagement ring would be and then cocked her head toward Jennifer.

"Seriously?" Chelsea asked.

"Is there some sort of secret female communication going on here?" Brandon said.

"Where's the cat?" Wesley asked, looking under the table.

"There's no cat, honey," Chelsea told him. "It's an expression."

Dana's phone buzzed. She glanced down.

Was in PA overnight. Not supposed to leave the state.

She wrote back, What were you doing in PA?

Kenneth reached over and took Jennifer's hand. "We invited you here tonight for a reason. We have some news. Jennifer and I are getting married."

"I couldn't be happier," Jennifer said. She and Kenneth shared a look of pure love before she turned back to the group. "Your father is the dearest man I ever met, and I can't wait to spend the rest of my life with him."

Her father? A dear man? Dana was tempted to ask Dr. Lafferty if she'd been dipping into the propofol. Another text from Lorenzo buzzed in.

Interviewing for a job at QVC.

Chelsea and Brandon rose to offer hugs and congratulations to the happy couple, but Dana remained stuck to her seat. Lorenzo was planning to move to Pennsylvania and hadn't bothered to tell her. She wondered how long he had been pursuing it and keeping it a secret from her. Hadn't he said something about being free to move away once his parole ended next month? She felt like an idiot. He'd been planning on leaving all along.

It was just like his deception about Kitty. He'd kept it from her because he didn't trust her to do right by him. Dana felt like she'd been played.

And now this. Her father—who was barely civil to his wife and daughters for their entire lives—had become a tender soul, making a new life with a woman who, Dana had to admit, seemed pretty damned terrific. But where was this man when his mother needed him? Where was he when *she* needed him?

Dana stood, choking back a lifetime of hurt, and congratulated the happy couple. Then she picked up her phone and, using her facile thumbs, told Lorenzo to go fuck himself.

27

She spent the rest of the weekend ignoring Lorenzo's texts and studying the second act of *Mrs. Woodbridge* until she had every line memorized. It was important, because they were blocking the final scenes this week, and she wanted to be sure she was ready. *I shouldn't be involved with someone, anyway*, she told herself. *I should be concentrating on my work. The job and the play are enough.*

At work on Monday, Dana was with Irini getting into wardrobe when Ollie knocked on her dressing room door and said the sound engineers asked if she could get down to the studio a few minutes early.

"You need I should leave now?" Irini asked her.

"Don't worry about it," Dana said, because she knew the request had come straight from Lorenzo, who was trying to get some time alone with her. She still had no desire to hear his excuses.

"I'll take care of it, Ollie!" she called, but didn't go down to the studio until the very last minute.

"I wanted to talk to you," Lorenzo whispered as he clipped on her mike.

"I know."

"Maybe after the show?" he asked.

"I'm busy."

"Dana—"

"Sixty seconds!" the tech director called.

Lorenzo huffed, and Dana ignored him. He turned on her mike and backed away. She hit her mark, looked straight into the camera and waited, trying to remain focused. Adam was out that day, and Dana was concerned about what might happen without him on set making sure everything was okay. But Sherry had assigned a substitute producer, and Jessalyn had assured her everything was in order. So Dana psyched herself up. It was going to be a great show. The best! It was a Bastina day, after all, which meant the time would fly by, and before she knew it, she would be all finished and on her way to rehearsals.

And then Dana heard a familiar female voice in her earpiece. It was Emily. At first, Dana thought there must have been some sort of last-minute emergency with the substitute segment producer. But no, Sherry had actually assigned her assistant to the task. What the hell? Producers needed to supervise the entire operation. What did Emily Lauren know about inventory tracking and camera angles and the pressures of live broadcasting? At the very least, if she was going to turn the job over to a rookie, it should have been Jessalyn, who was on set every day and made it quite clear what her ambitions were.

"Relax," Emily said. "I have Sherry here, walking me through this. We'll take good care of you."

Great, Dana thought. *Just what I need. A neophyte and a fire-breathing dragon.*

But after a couple of awkward moments, the show went smoothly. Bastina made the four hours pass quickly as the two of them chatted and gushed and sold, sold, sold. At last the

time ran down, and Dana could hardly wait to take off. She
got ready to introduce Vanessa's show, and glanced at the set
to her right, where she expected to see the other host standing by the display. But there was no one there. Dana tapped
her earpiece, a signal to Emily that she needed guidance—
and she replied that she needed to stretch. Apparently, Vanessa
was held up somewhere.

Dana went back to the Bastina shirts she was selling. There
wasn't much stock left, but she pushed hard to move the remaining sizes and colors. After five minutes, Vanessa still
hadn't arrived, and so Dana was told she had to stay on the air
and cover for her. This presented a special challenge. Kitty's
fans were just starting to settle in and accept Vanessa. They
would not be thrilled to see yet another host in her place.

Dana had no choice but to make the best of it. While the
camera was focused on the display, she strode across the set to
take the other host's place as she got a message in her earpiece
from another voice—Vanessa's segment producer. He assured
Dana he would feed her the details she needed on the jewelry
she knew nothing about.

She managed to pull it off, digging deep into her acting
skills to convince the audience that she was thrilled to have
the opportunity to tell them about the white, yellow and rose
gold bangles they were offering as today's special. In reality,
she was furious that she would be so tardy for rehearsals.

At last, Vanessa showed up almost thirty minutes late. "I
owe you one," she mouthed to Dana as they passed on the set.

Lorenzo rushed up to take off Dana's mike. Sherry walked
out of the control booth to Dana, with Emily and Jessalyn
following closely behind.

"Good work," Jessalyn said to her as Lorenzo fished the
wire out of Dana's clothes. "That was seamless."

"What happened?" she asked. Being late was simply not an

option for broadcasters. People like Dana and Vanessa had to get to work on time even if it meant leaping over tall buildings and doing flips over hot coals.

"Accident on the L.I.E.," Sherry said.

"The Long Island Expressway?" Dana said. "I thought she lived in the city."

"She weekends in the Hamptons," Sherry said. "Apparently, a tractor trailer turned over and they shut down the whole highway."

"You're a trouper, Dana," Emily said.

Dana looked to Sherry, to see if she might have some similar words of gratitude, but she was staring at the monitors. Dana was tempted to say, *If I were late, you'd fire me in a second.* But she bit her tongue, because there was no reason to get Vanessa in more trouble—she'd probably get a lashing from Sherry as it was. And anyway, it was a handy card for Dana to keep in her pocket.

When Sherry looked back at her, Dana smiled broadly. "Anytime," she said. "Glad I could help."

She rushed to her dressing room to get back into her street clothes so she could hurry off to the Sweat City theater, but Ollie was there, pacing nervously as if he wanted to talk to her. He seemed to be staring down at something small in his hand.

"Everything okay?" she asked, moving brusquely.

"You look like you are in a hurry, Dana," he said.

"I am," she said. "I got held up on set and now I'm late for an appointment."

"Miss Vanessa was delayed, yes. I heard that spoken of."

"Is there a problem?" she asked, feeling more motherly toward him now that she understood all the tragedies of his young childhood. "You need something?"

"I can wait until tomorrow, Dana. It is not an emergency."

"You look upset," she said, and immediately regretted it.

She needed to leave. This was no time for a drawn-out counseling session with her damaged assistant, no matter how tenderly she felt toward him.

"There is something I told you that was not honest," he said. "I feel bad about this."

"I don't want you to feel bad," she said, putting a hand on his shoulder. "But can it wait until tomorrow? I'm running so late."

"Yes. Yes, of course, Dana. It can wait for tomorrow."

28

The next day, Dana arrived at work early enough to talk to Ollie before she had to meet with Adam for her daily briefing. When she rounded the corner toward her dressing room, she saw her assistant's slim form in the hallway. He was talking on his cell phone, and she heard the tail end of a conversation in Finnish, which she assumed were plans for dinner as he said something to the effect of *"Haluatko tavata Gramercy Parkissa Farmer and the Fish."* Dana was tempted to tell him it was a good restaurant and he should order the lobster roll, but she didn't want to intrude, so she just gave him a small smile and slipped into her dressing room.

Ollie got off the phone immediately and followed in after her.

"I am so sorry, Dana," he said. "I know I should not make personal calls, but it is my friend Kimmo's birthday."

"It's okay, Ollie," she said gently. "You're allowed to have a personal life. You look nice, by the way."

And it was true. He looked even more Dumpster chic than usual, wearing a restyled flannel print pajama top that depicted black-and-white cows on an aqua background. It had been tapered to fit his slender body, with the sleeves cut short and rolled. He wore it tucked into a pair of wide black bell-bottoms, accessorized with a red leather belt.

"Oh, thank you, Dana," he said. His eyes looked appreciative but nervous.

"Is everything okay?" she asked. "You seemed so edgy yesterday."

"Yes. Everything is okay. Only I need to make a confession to you." His face looked tight with worry. "I am so sorry. I should not lie to you. It is not a loyal thing."

"You lied to me?"

"I hope that you can forgive me, Dana. It is hard to sleep with this on my heart."

She sat on the couch and indicated that he should do the same. "What did you lie about, Ollie?"

He lowered himself carefully, looked down at his hands and swallowed. "Remember when I said to you that Miss Kitty has a camera in her bedroom?"

"The sex tape," she said. "Of course I remember. Did you make that up?"

"No! I did not make that up, Dana. Miss Kitty made recordings of their love. But I told you that I did not know where the tape was."

"And you do?"

"Please. You must understand. Mr. Honeycutt is innocent. This is why I did not want to tell you that I know where the tape can be found. He must not go to prison, Dana. That would be tragic. Miss Kitty would not wish this to happen."

So Ollie knew where the tape was. She studied his expression and understood why he was so tense. He wasn't there to tell her where to find it, only that he had the information. He was still intent on protecting Kitty…and Charles.

Her knee-jerk reaction was to do whatever was necessary to pull information from him so she could hand the tape over to the police and get them off Lorenzo's back. But then she thought about his betrayal and stopped herself. Lorenzo had lied to her. And she had trusted him. She had looked into those dark earnest eyes and bought whatever he was selling. It made her heart ache.

Dana stood up and crossed the room. *Lorenzo can just go to hell*, she told herself. *This isn't my problem.*

But the anguish still tugged at her, and it gave her a terrible headache. She rubbed the spot between her eyes to relieve the dull pressure. Lorenzo was a dog. And he didn't deserve her kindness. Not that she thought he deserved to go to jail for a murder he didn't commit. But exonerating him simply wasn't her business. She should throw her hands up and walk away. It wasn't her problem. And yet the thought of it made her sick, and she knew why.

Sophia.

Dana had to face it: she couldn't turn her back on Lorenzo now.

And of course, her curiosity burned and popped and smoked. Kitty was an even more interesting character than Mrs. Woodbridge. Dana was dying to know what kind of fuel ignited Kitty's motivations.

She pivoted toward Ollie. "But you don't really know Honeycutt is innocent," she said.

Ollie looked stricken. His eyes glistened and his mouth opened, but she cut him off before he could protest.

"I know it seems impossible to you, because you believed he loved her," she said. "And maybe he really did. But sometimes, when people feel threatened, they get aggressive. If Mr. Honeycutt was afraid that Kitty would show the tape to his wife, he might have done something rash."

"He would never, Dana!"

"Ollie," she said, "you don't know that for sure."

"But their love."

God, this poor kid was so romantically invested in this relationship. It was painful to burst his bubble. But really, he needed to know.

"Love can be tragic, Ollie. I'm sure you know that."

"Romeo and Juliet," he said.

"Yes, like Romeo and Juliet."

He stared into the distance, thinking. Dana waited, hoping he would understand.

"Yes, this might be," he said under his breath.

"What might be?" she asked.

"Do you think maybe Mr. Honeycutt wanted to go to heaven with Miss Kitty, Dana? Perhaps he thought he will kill his love and then himself so they could be together always. This is a possibility, yes? Maybe this was his plan but then he cannot finish his act."

Dana let out a long breath. If this ridiculous scenario was what he needed to believe, then fine. She'd go with it.

"It's possible," she said. "Entirely possible."

"Only Mr. Honeycutt was not in Miss Kitty's office when she was killed," Ollie said. "So it must be someone else, yes?"

"Perhaps he was smart enough to hire someone," she offered.

"I have heard of such a thing," he said thoughtfully. "What do you call this? A hit man?"

"That's right," Dana said. "He might have hired someone to do it for him."

Ollie shook his head doubtfully. "This, I do not know, Dana. Such an act, it has no passion. Mr. Honeycutt could not be so cold for Miss Kitty."

He was resolute, and she could tell she was losing him. Her head pulsed with pain.

"Ollie," she said, "where is the sex tape?"

He stood and walked toward the door. "I did not wish to lie to you, Dana. So now I feel lighter in my heart. But I cannot tell you where this is, for I know that Miss Kitty would not want me to. She would not wish for Mr. Honeycutt to be in trouble."

"But we have to turn it over to the police," she pleaded. "So they can investigate. And if he's innocent…well, he'll be cleared."

"He will be so embarrassed, Dana. I cannot do this."

"But if he's guilty…"

"I do not believe he is."

"What if I can prove that it's *possible*?"

"Possible that he was so cold to hire someone to kill his love?"

"Yes," Dana pleaded. "If I can prove that's possible…"

"Then of course. I will give you the video recording. But how can you prove such a thing?"

"*Give me* the video?" she repeated. "You mean you have it?"

Ollie put his hand in his pants pocket. "I keep it here with me, Dana. On a flash drive."

Dana's heart raced. She could hardly believe the evidence was so close, yet beyond her grasp. Now more than ever she felt like she had to have it.

Dana paced the dressing room, thinking about providing Ollie with the proof he needed. She considered how difficult it would have been for a hit man to get into the building. He would have to get past security at the front desk, and then past Brenda on the executive floor. Only an invited visitor would be able to get in. She turned back to Ollie.

"The visitors' log," she said. "At the security desk."

He cocked his head. "What about this?"

"If Honeycutt hired a hit man, he would have had to sign in."

Ollie nodded. "Yes. I understand. Maybe this is why the police have taken the book from the security desk."

Her heart sank. "They took the visitors' log?"

"Oh, yes, Dana. On the day of the murder they took it away."

She sat heavily at her vanity table and rested her pained head in her palms. "I wish I could get my hands on that," she said.

"I am sorry, Dana," he said. "It is unfortunate we have only photocopies."

"Photocopies?"

"Yes, from the Ricoh photocopier machine."

"You mean there are photocopies of those pages from the visitors' log?"

Ollie nodded. "Mr. Beecham asked Abigail to make copies before he hands it on to the police. Do you know Abigail?"

She didn't, but she knew Beecham, the head of security, and could imagine him barking orders at an underling. "And she did as he asked? She made photocopies? Are you sure?"

"Oh, yes. Of every page, Dana. She was in the copy room for such a very long time that night."

"Do you know where those pages are kept?"

"I think they are in the file room. But I am not certain."

"Is there any way we can check?"

"I don't know this, Dana. I cannot have clearance to go into this room, nor you."

"Who does have clearance?" she asked.

He began to tick off a list on his fingers. "Mr. Beecham… and the accounting department…and HR…"

"Anyone else?"

"The producers, of course."

"The segment producers?" she asked.

"Yes, all the records are in this room. Personnel records, financial records, sales records."

"Those damned spreadsheets?" Dana asked.

"Yes, those damned spreadsheets, Dana. The producers may see them if they wish."

Now that was a bit of good news. Her headache started to lift.

"If it is okay, Dana, I will go to the set now to prepare for you."

"That's fine, Ollie. But can you do me one small favor?"

"Yes, Dana. Anything."

"Tell Adam Weintraub I'm ready to see him."

29

Dana listened as Adam went through the beach-themed items she would be selling on that day's show: a cotton cover-up available in mini and maxi lengths and in seven different colors, two styles of bejeweled sandals and a beach blanket that came in three prints—rainbow stripes, Hawaiian floral and a pink flamingo pattern—each with its own matching nylon tote.

"Ready for a great show?" he asked as he was getting ready to leave.

"Hang on, Adam," she said. "I have a question."

He turned to her.

"Can you get me into the file room?" she asked.

"The file room?" He looked perplexed.

"It's important."

He shook his head and moved toward the door, as if he couldn't wait to get out. "Can't. It's not allowed." He avoided her eyes.

"Wait a second," she said, surprised that he shut her down before even asking what she was after. "I want to talk to you about this."

"Sorry, Dana. I can't let you in there."

"Are there dead bodies or something? I just want to look for some records."

"I could get fired," he said. "I can't take chances like this."

Poor Adam, she thought. Sherry had him living in constant fear that his job was on the line.

"I know you have a lot of pressure," she said, "but in the scheme of things, it's not that risky." She told him about the conversation she had with Ollie, explaining how much more was at stake for Lorenzo and Sophia. He softened, but only a little.

"It's a big room," he said. "It won't be easy to find those pages."

"Isn't there some kind of a system?" she asked.

"Each department has their own."

"I'd like to give it a shot," she said. "It's important. Please. We won't get caught."

"Tell you what," he said. "I can't let you in, but I'll look for them."

Dana was dubious. "When?" she asked.

"I don't know. When I have time."

"Will you go now?" She knew if she wasn't aggressive he would try pushing it off until she forgot about it.

"I have things to do, Dana."

"Please," she said, imploring him with her most intense stare. "At least do this much for Lorenzo…if you're not going to tell the police the truth about you and—"

"Okay, okay," he said, shaking his head. "I'll do it."

Later, after Dana finished with hair and makeup and arrived on set for her show, she pulled him aside.

"Well?" she asked. "Did you find it?"

"Sorry," he said.

"Oh, Adam. Did you really try?"

"It's a massive room," he said. "The shelves aren't labeled. I didn't even know where to look."

"It's like you don't want to help," she said.

"Of *course* I want to help," he said. "Lorenzo is my friend. But this is ridiculous. There are thousands of files. If I spend too much time snooping in areas I shouldn't, I could get caught."

Dana bit her lip. She was confident she could figure out a way to find those pages if she could get into the room, and Adam was her only resource. She wondered what she could do to change his mind. She knew that his paranoia about getting fired was a direct result of his financial stress, and that he would probably be more willing to take the risk if there was economic incentive. She could offer to pay him, but Dana was pretty sure he'd find that offensive. Then she got an idea.

"Your wife likes necklaces, right?"

He looked alarmed. "How do you know that?"

Dana laughed. "Most women do. And anyway, I noticed the lariat necklace she was wearing in that family photo."

"What about it?" he said, staring at her with a mixture of wonder and alarm. Dana was used to that look—people were often surprised by the things she noticed. Still, the poor guy seemed awfully skittish. He was clearly breaking under the stress of exhaustion and job pressure.

"Adam," she said gently, "I'd like her to have this." She unhooked the chain around her neck and put it into his hand. She didn't mind the sacrifice as she never really liked it very much. In fact, it had been a present from her cheating ex, Benjamin, and she had considered hocking it at least a dozen times. She only wore it today because she thought it might complement the pale pink polo dress she got from wardrobe. "People think it's silver but it's actually white gold," she said.

"White gold?" he repeated, staring down at the puddle of

precious metal in his hand. She was pretty sure he was calculating the gold's value in baby formula.

"It's brighter than silver. See?" She angled his hand toward the light.

Adam went silent as he assessed the necklace. Finally he nodded, dropping the chain into his pocket, and they made plans to meet at the file room after the show.

A short time later, Dana was onstage, staring at the ceiling as Lorenzo affixed the microphone bodypack to the back of her bra strap under her dress and threaded the wire through to the front. He clipped the mike to her collar. They were in front of the display of sandals she would be selling in her first segment.

"Are you ever going to talk to me again?" he whispered.

"Can you move this a little to the right?" she said, pointing to the tiny mike on her collar. "It's hitting my chin."

He unclipped it and found a better spot. "I said I was sorry."

"And I said, 'Good luck—I hope you get the job and that you live happily ever after in Pennsylvania.'"

Lorenzo glanced around to make sure no one had heard. "I just want what's best for Sophia."

"And lying to me was best for Sophia? That's the part I don't quite get."

He pointed to her microphone. "This better?"

Dana moved her head side to side. "I think so," she said, and then rocked her head up and down, to be sure. When her chin was lowered, she thought she noticed something strange about the display table.

"Does this thing look a little crooked to you?" she asked.

He turned around and assessed it, cocking his head. "Maybe a little." He lifted the skirt of the table. "Whoa."

She bent down to see what he was looking at. One of the table legs was missing and replaced by a cracked-off yardstick.

Ordinarily, Dana would have assumed a prop guy was simply being resourceful. But when she thought about the misplaced charts and the severed microphone cable, her pulse raced.

"Is that stable?" she asked.

"I don't think so," he said. "Looks like the whole thing could come crashing down." Lorenzo poked his head farther under the table. "And there doesn't seem to be anything wrong with the actual table leg. Someone just folded it up and replaced it."

Dana fought a wave of nausea. She couldn't chalk this up to drug-fueled paranoia or a freak accident. Someone was trying to sabotage her. She waved frantically at Adam, who came running over.

"What's wrong?" he asked.

"The display table," Dana said. "It's been…compromised."

"Compromised?"

"Look!"

Adam poked his head under the table skirt. "What the hell?" he said. "I checked this ten minutes ago." He turned toward the crew. "Someone get another table!"

"We're on in sixty seconds," the tech director said over the PA, and dispatched a crew in an instant. Two guys carefully lifted the table straight up while another crawled underneath to remove the yardstick and unfold the table leg. They tested it for stability. There was nothing wrong with the table leg.

With five seconds to go, the crew moved out of the shot, Dana hit her mark and took a slow, steadying breath. She could not afford to let this rattle her. Whoever was trying to sabotage her could go to hell. She was going to make this her best show yet.

The green light when on, and she looked straight through the camera lens into her best friend's eyes and made her believe all she needed for her life to be complete was a pair of strappy bejeweled sandal flats that could go from the beach to a romantic dinner. She was all in. And the show was fun, fast and fabulous.

When it was over, she unclipped her microphone and threw it down. She knew she had done well, but once she broke character, the contained fury had nowhere to go.

"We never sold so many beach blankets," Adam said as he rushed over with his tablet. "You broke a Shopping Channel record."

"Yeah, and I almost broke an entire display, live on the air."

"I'm going to find out who did this, Dana."

"You'd better."

When she went back to her dressing room, Dana called Megan to tell her what had happened.

Her manager friend listened very quietly. When she finally responded, she was all business.

"This is unacceptable. I'll set up a meeting with Sherry as soon as possible. In the meantime—"

Dana cut her off, because she knew what Megan was going to say. "In the meantime, I shouldn't worry about it."

"Oh, hon," Megan said, "I was going to tell you, in the meantime, watch your ass."

After changing into her street clothes, Dana went down to the basement to meet Adam at the file room, but he wasn't there. She waited a couple of minutes and texted him. I'm here. Where are you?

He wrote back almost immediately. Was there earlier. Unlocked door.

Coward, she thought, though she couldn't work up too much anger. The guy had so much more at stake than she did. With a family and a mortgage, the idea of getting fired was just terrifying to him. Dana wasn't exactly calm about it herself, but was pretty sure that if she were careful enough, she could pull it off without getting caught.

She took a long look up and down the deserted hallway to make sure no one was coming, and then checked the door. Sure enough, it opened. She slipped inside and flicked on one light switch and then another. The room was awash in green-hued fluorescents.

When she saw what she was up against, Dana understood why Adam said it was a daunting search. The room was huge—about fifty feet across—and filled with thick metal walls of putty-colored file shelving units. They were labeled only with numbers, so it was impossible to know which one belonged to the security department. Dana let out a breath and clicked off one of the light switches to dim the room, just in case. Otherwise, she'd feel like a spider crawling across a white tile.

She walked across the concrete floor to the far end of the room. There was nothing to do but start at the beginning.

She entered the first corridor between the tall shelves and eyed the rows and rows of blue folders. She pulled out a random file and saw that it was from the payroll department. She pulled out a few more from the same section to satisfy herself that the files were organized by department. She was tempted to sneak a peek at what her coworkers were earning, but it was too risky to linger. She had a job to do.

The next corridor of files appeared to belong to the accounting department, as it was filled with pale green folders containing tax returns. That department seemed to generate more paper than a printing press, because the next three shelving units were taxes and more taxes.

After that came the quality assurance files, in no-nonsense manila. Then marketing, which used bright, lots-of-nonsense yellow folders. She was about to walk to the next aisle when she noticed that the files on the opposite shelf were red. She pulled out a random folder, and it contained a visitors' log. At last—she was in the right section.

Dana began pulling out files to determine how they were arranged, and was glad to see it was chronological. She thought she heard the door to the room open and stopped, her heart thudding. She held perfectly still. Nothing but silence. It had been her imagination. Or maybe someone had poked their head in and left. She hurried down the rows of files to find the folder from the week of Kitty's murder. She pulled out the file and there it was—photocopied pages instead of a spiral logbook. Before she could scan the pages, though, Dana heard footsteps. She tucked the folder under her arm and moved toward the wall, hoping to hide in the shadows in case the person walked past. They were heavy footsteps. A man. They got closer, and Dana didn't breathe, holding perfectly still as a bead of sweat ran down her forehead and dripped into her eye. At last, she saw a figure move into her line of vision.

Dana blinked. She couldn't see the face, but she knew the jingle of keys and the bulky silhouette. It was Beecham! She froze, hoping he couldn't see her, but he stopped, backlit and broad. For several moments he remained perfectly still.

"Who's there?" he said, his deep voice cracking the silence as his hand reached for something on his belt.

On his belt?

Sweet fancy Moses, did he have a gun? Time became a wall of molasses, and it seemed to take forever for Dana to open her mouth and respond. Before she could, the thing in his hand pointed at her and then…a bright white beam shone in her face.

It wasn't a gun. It was a flashlight.

"It's me, Dana," she choked out.

"Ms. Barry?" His tone was gruff, almost angry.

"Hi, Mr. Beecham!" she chirped in the same cheerful voice she used when she passed by his desk.

"What are you doing here?" he said. "You don't have clearance."

"Um…"

"Who let you in?" he demanded.

"No one!" Dana protested. She wasn't going to rat out Adam.

"That door locks automatically," he said.

She shrugged. "I guess it's broken or something?"

"You sure no one let you in?"

"Positive," she said.

He shone the flashlight onto the folder. "What's in your hand? And why were you hiding from me?"

"I, uh…"

"Don't…lie," he said, pronouncing the words with slow, weighty, intimidating precision.

Dana swallowed hard. Lying had been her first instinct. She ran through her options, but faced with a man who clearly had lie-detecting superpowers, she understood she had no other choice. And so she did what he asked. She told him the truth. Not all the details, of course, but enough for him to understand that Marks was breathing down Lorenzo's neck, and that Ollie had access to an incriminating sex tape that might clear him, but wouldn't turn it over until he could be convinced Honeycutt might be guilty.

"That's why I wanted to see these visitors' logs," she said. "If someone unidentified came into the building to see Honeycutt…"

"No one comes into my building unidentified," Beecham said.

"Maybe with a false identity?" she offered.

Beecham went quiet. He wasn't a man who felt the need to fill uncomfortable silences with chatter.

"You should have come to me," he said, his tone starting to soften.

"Yes, of course," she said. "I'm sorry."

In the silence that followed, she hoped he was remembering the Dunkin' Donuts card, and thinking about her charitably.

At last he said, "Follow me."

Dana blotted her damp forehead with her sleeve. "Where to?" she asked, wondering if he was going to take her to some secret room in the bowels of the Shopping Channel where errant on-air hosts were fingerprinted and read their version of the Miranda: *You have the right to remain talking. Constantly. Live, on the air. Everything you say can and will be used to get you fired.*

He didn't respond, and she trotted behind as he marched to the other end of the room and turned right after the last row of shelves.

"There," he said, pointing to a wooden table against the wall.

"There?" she asked, her throat dry.

"We'll look at the logs, find out who came in to see Honeycutt."

And so they did, sitting side by side at the table. Dana's stomach unclenched as Beecham turned the pages in the folder with his meaty fingers until he reached the day of Kitty's murder. He ran his pointer down one page and then the next until he paused at the name *Jason White*. The column next to it listed the person he was visiting: *C. Honeycutt*. The time was 3:55 p.m.—just minutes before Kitty's murder.

At that, her perspiration evaporated, replaced by goose bumps.

"That could be it, right?" she asked. "Honeycutt's hit man?"

He ran his finger horizontally across the page, stopping at

the column on the far right. It was the space filled in by the security guard, and had the letter *O* in it. Or possibly a zero. Most of the other rows had a *D* in that box.

"What is that column?" she asked.

"It's where the guard fills in the type of photo ID the individual provides. *D* for driver's license, *P* for passport, *SI* for state-issued ID, *O* for other."

"Other?"

He let out a breath. "Our guards are told to use their discretion when the individual does not have valid ID."

"So Jason White was let into the building without a valid ID?"

"That's what I need to find out," he said, staring at the page. He turned to her and held out his hand. "Give me your phone."

She had no idea why he wanted it, but he was so imperious she did as he asked.

To her surprise, he deftly swiped it on, found the camera and took a picture of the page that bore Jason White's name. He handed it back to her. "Show that to Ollie," he said, "and get that tape. The police will want to see it."

She gave him a kiss on the cheek and got the distinct whiff of something familiar. Doughnuts.

30

By the time she got back to her dressing room, Ollie was gone for the day. Dana was disappointed, because she had already decided she would take her new evidence straight to Detective Marks on her way to rehearsals. Now it would have to wait another day.

Not that she was looking for an excuse to see Marks. At least, that was what she tried to tell herself. It was all about the case.

Then, while she was on the subway, Dana got an idea—why not pop into Farmer and the Fish on her way to rehearsals and see if she could track Ollie down? It was just around the corner from Marks's office, anyway.

She got off the subway at Twenty-Third Street and walked down Park Avenue South until she got to the restaurant. But once she reached the door, Dana hesitated. Ollie might not mind the intrusion, but was it fair for her to barge in? She wasn't Ollie's friend, she was his boss. Sure, he was so devoted he wouldn't put up a fuss, but he deserved to have a personal life. And his friend Kimmo deserved a birthday celebration free from a visit from a stranger. She hesitated for a few moments, thinking about Marks. But at last she decided no. This wasn't right. She had been acting like a desperate teenager with a crush. That wasn't her. Or at least, it wasn't who she aspired to be.

Dana turned to go, and hadn't taken two steps when she practically ran into Ollie and his friend.

"Dana!" Ollie said, surprised.

"Hi!" she said a little too effusively. She felt suddenly embarrassed and defensive. Because the truth about her clouded judgment was hard to face. She was ashamed of herself. "I'm sorry, I—"

"Why are you here, Dana?"

He looked so alarmed she felt bad for frightening him. "Everything is fine, don't worry," she said, and noticed that he took a step away from Kimmo. That was when she realized she had misinterpreted his expression. He wasn't afraid that some disaster had occurred at work. Ollie didn't want Dana to know that he and Kimmo were a couple.

She wanted to reassure him that he had nothing to worry about. She didn't care that he was gay. She had already made the assumption, anyway. But of course, it would be entirely inappropriate to even broach the subject, and so she stammered an explanation about her presence.

"It's just that I was in the neighborhood and I remembered you were coming here and...well, I hope I'm not intruding."

His expression was so guarded he almost looked like a different person. Dana wished she had thought this through a little more. This out-of-the-office surprise confrontation was so unfair.

"It is okay, Dana," he said, collecting himself. "Is there something you need?"

"Yes, actually, there is, but..." She hesitated and turned to his friend. He was a little taller than Ollie, with strawberry blond hair and a square face. She thought they looked cute together, these boyish Finns in the middle of Gramercy Park. "I'm sorry. I didn't mean to impose on your dinner. You must be Kimmo. Happy birthday!" She held out her hand and he shook it.

"Yes, I am Kimmo. Thank you for the birthday wishes."

She turned to Ollie. "I shouldn't bother you here. This can wait until tomorrow."

"Please, Dana," Ollie said, his face still tight. "Tell me what it is you wish to say."

She sighed, grateful, and took out her cell phone to show him the photo that Beecham had snapped.

"This is proof that Honeycutt might have…hired someone." She didn't know how much she could say in front of Kimmo.

Ollie took her phone and stared down at it. He turned to Kimmo and said something in Finnish, peppered with the words *Jason White*.

He handed back her phone. Then Ollie looked down and took a deep breath. When he glanced up again, his expression had returned to its normal state of obsequious attention. "This is distressing, Dana. I do not wish to think that Mr. Honeycutt could—"

"Yes, I know," she said. "And it might turn out to be a misunderstanding. But I think you have to agree that it's possible. That Honeycutt might have hired this man to kill Kitty."

Ollie went quiet for a moment, his eyes sad, and then Kimmo rambled something in Finnish. *"Anna hänelle mitä hän haluaa. Anna hänelle flash-asema."*

Ollie turned to Dana. "Kimmo says that I should give to you the flash drive."

"I agree with him, Ollie." She put out her open hand. "Please. It's the right thing to do."

Ollie nodded. "My heart is so heavy," he said.

"I understand."

He reached into the pocket of his bell-bottoms and extracted a silver flash drive. He looked at it for a moment, and then pressed it into Dana's palm.

"You're doing the right thing," she said, wrapping her fist around it. "And I don't want you to worry. Everything is going to work out for the best...the way Kitty would want it to."

"Yes, Dana," he said. "I believe this is true."

As she walked away, Dana convinced herself that going straight to Marks's office was the right thing to do. After all, waiting until tomorrow wouldn't do her any good. It wasn't like she could plug the thing into a computer to make sure it really held the file Ollie promised. Her laptop had broken months ago, when she didn't have the cash to fix it. Now that she was bringing home a paycheck it was on her to-do list, but not at the top. And she didn't want to try to watch it at work, though for half a second she toyed with the idea of sneaking into someone's office and popping it into their computer. But even the *chance* of getting caught was too much to bear.

So yes, it made perfect sense to simply drop it off with Detective Marks. She could leave it with him and then go straight to her rehearsals.

"Is Detective Marks here?" she asked the uniformed police officer at the security desk. Visitors were confined to a square caged entry area, and so she had to shout across a space of fifteen feet to communicate with him.

Except for his shaved head and weary expression, the officer looked pubescent. Or at least young enough for her to picture him at home on his sofa, bent toward the television with a game controller in his hands. She could even imagine his mother in the kitchen making dinner. Dana squinted at the stand on his desk, and could make out that his name was Officer Shane McBride.

"Name?" he said in a tone bordering on exasperation, as if he couldn't believe another idiot had the audacity to bother him.

"Dana Barry," she said. "It's about the Kitty Todd case."

He picked up the phone on his desk and pushed in a number.

"Marks there?" he asked and paused. "Dana Barry... Uh-huh. Something about Kitty Todd... I don't know." He looked up at Dana. "Marks ain't here. You want to talk to Detective Lee?"

She exhaled, deflated. "No, thanks, I'll... It's fine. I'll call him tomorrow."

He got off the phone, and Dana turned to leave. "Hang on a second," he said to her, and pressed something under his desk that opened the gate to her cage. He signaled her to approach his desk and she hesitated.

"Just c'mere," he said, exasperated, and she did as he asked.

Officer McBride pushed an old-fashioned pink message pad to her. It had While You Were Out printed across the top.

"Leave him a message," he said.

"It's okay. I don't need—"

"Just write something, okay? Otherwise, *I* got to do it."

Officer Sunshine. She matched his scowl before staring down at the pad. Then she picked up the skittering ballpoint pen he had handed her and wrote, *Found something you will def want to see.*

Dana signed her name, wrote her phone number under it and pushed the pad back to the officer without waiting for his sulky approval. She hurried out and walked briskly downtown to Sweat City's theater.

The troupe ran through the entire second act, which was emotionally exhausting for Dana. Her goal was to scoop herself inside out even if that meant she would have to crawl home. Afterward, she and Raj remained onstage while Nathan gave them notes from his seat in the audience. He had a lot of praise, but a few points about blocking nuances that could be stronger. Since the spots were off, she could just about make out Nathan's face, even though the houselights weren't on. She could also discern the shadowy silhouette of a suited man in the back row, and wondered if someone in the cast had a new boyfriend.

Nathan dismissed them and called for some of the other cast members. Before Dana left the stage, she asked him if she could borrow his laptop for a couple of minutes and he agreed.

She went through the velvet curtain into the dark alcove that served as their green room—grateful that no one was around. As long as she had the opportunity, she just wanted to make sure the file in question was actually on the drive Ollie had given her. Dana approached Nathan's computer on the wooden crate that served as their coffee table. She woke it up with a tap to the tracking pad, and sat cross-legged on a large pillow on the floor. She plugged in the flash drive and promised herself she wouldn't watch more than a few seconds. Anything beyond that was prurient. And gross. It wasn't that she was a prude about porn, but these weren't actors—and one of them didn't even know he was being filmed. She put a hand on her stomach to quell the nausea.

Dana clicked the arrow on the video. A few seconds of static were followed by an image of an empty bedroom. After some moments, she could hear murmured voices from outside the room, and then there they were—Kitty and Charles, in their underwear. Kitty, of course, was in a matching set—baby pink, as if she were an innocent little girl. They were panting and rushed, but Kitty put a hand on Charles's bare chest when he tried to move her toward the bed. She stripped naked as he watched, and led him to a spot right in front of the camera. The crazy witch, Dana thought. She wanted to be sure whoever saw this video got a full image of Charles Honeycutt's cock. Kitty got down on her knees, pulled off his boxers, and there was his erection, front, center and close up. She ran her hand up his thigh and opened her lipsticked mouth as her head moved toward him.

Dana had enough. But before she could shut it off, a male voice from behind made her jump.

"Am I disturbing you?"

Dana fell off the cushion as she turned to see who was behind her. It was Ari Marks! He just stood there, holding back the heavy red curtain to the room.

"What the hell are you doing here?" she asked, her heart pounding like a dryer full of bricks as she scrambled to stand.

He let the curtain fall behind him. "I got a message that you wanted to see me. What the hell *is* that?" he said, nodding toward the computer.

"I…uh…" She heard grunts coming from the video and lost her train of thought. "I… How did you know where to find me?"

He shrugged. "Lucky guess."

Dana knew that wasn't true, but she was too startled to focus. The grunts from the computer got louder and Marks stepped closer to it. "What kind of porn is that, Ms. Barry?"

She felt a flush rise up in her face. "It's not porn!" she said.

"Could have fooled me."

"It's evidence," she insisted.

Marks raised a dubious eyebrow. She turned toward the computer and saw Kitty's face moving up and down on Charles Honeycutt's slick erection. Until that moment, Dana didn't think it was possible to die from embarrassment, but now she was so burning hot she thought she'd spontaneously combust.

Marks glanced at the screen and let out a breath. He shifted uncomfortably. "If that's not porn, then—"

"Please," she said. "You can't think that I was just sitting here *watching* this."

"But you *were* just sitting here watching this. Not that I'm judging..."

"No," she said. "No, no, no. I just wanted to make sure it was there. The sex. Before I gave you the flash drive." The groaning increased as Charles Honeycutt called out indecipherable syllables. *Kih sta...kih sta.*

"Okay..." Marks said slowly, as if he were trying to process what Dana was talking about.

She glanced back at the screen and realized Honeycutt was trying to say, *Kitty, stop.*

"Don't you know who that *is*?" she said, pointing toward the action.

He looked back at the screen as the groaning increased. "The lady seems to be Kitty Todd. I'm not sure I recognize the gentleman from this angle."

"It's Charles Honeycutt!"

Just then, the president of the Shopping Channel cried, "Kitty, Kitty! I'm coming!"

Dana practically tackled the laptop, slamming it shut. She yanked the flash drive out of the USB port and handed it to Marks.

He stared down at the small item in his hand. "It's not even my birthday."

"You're making this worse," she whimpered.

"I'm not sure that's possible."

"Well, then...say something to make this less embarrassing."

"Like what?"

"I don't know." She paced the room, turned back to him. "Do you have your service revolver?"

He looked at her quizzically.

Dana pointed to her head. "Because a bullet right here would feel really good right now."

"A mercy killing?"

"I'm begging you."

"Maybe after you answer my questions," he said, still holding the flash drive in his open palm. "Where did you get this?"

"From Ollie. Kitty was threatening to show it to Honeycutt's wife."

He paused, thinking. "I see."

"I didn't want to watch it," Dana said. "I just wanted to make sure it was actually on the flash drive before I gave it to you."

"Who else has seen this?"

"No one, as far as I know. About that bullet…"

He looked at her as if he were actually considering her request. "How about I take you out for a drink instead? I think you could use one."

"Is that…allowed?"

He shrugged. "Do you care?"

Dana stared at him, surprised to discover he wasn't the rule-follower she had assumed. It didn't take her more than a second to agree. And so she gathered her things and walked into the velvety Manhattan night with the tall detective. Despite herself, she began wondering what might happen after a drink or two.

"How did you know where I'd be?" she asked, glancing at him. Again, he wore a suit without a tie. But tonight it struck her as the sexiest thing a man could wear.

"I followed you," he said.

Dana stopped and looked at him, wondering if he was serious. There was amusement in his eyes, but he wasn't joking—

only gratified that he could get a reaction from her. "That's a little creepy," she said.

He shrugged. "Truth is, when McBride told me I had just missed you, I rushed outside, but you were all the way down the block already. I could have caught up with you, but you seemed so determined that I decided to hang back and see if you stopped somewhere. Then, when I saw you turn into the theater, I figured I'd slip in and see what was going on."

Okay, so maybe it was a tiny bit stalkerish. But he was a detective. Nosiness was an occupational hazard. Besides, the image of him rushing out of the precinct to find her was too delicious to release. She was pretty sure it meant he liked her. A lot. Chelsea had been right.

"You watched the rehearsal?" she asked.

"The whole thing."

Do not ask him what he thought, she coached herself. *It's vain. And childish.*

"What did you think?" she said. *Damn it.*

"I think…" He stopped to rub his face, weighing his words carefully.

Oh God, she thought. He hated it.

"I think," he repeated, "that this is what you're meant to be doing."

"Acting, you mean?"

"Watching you transform like that. It was… I never saw anything like it. I almost didn't believe it was you up there."

Yes, she thought. That's exactly how it felt to lose herself in the role. It was a transformation. She was so grateful he understood that she didn't want to cheapen the moment with false modesty. Dana knew she was doing the best work of her life.

"Actually," she said, "no one is going to know it's me up there. Aside from the cast and crew, I mean. And now you.

I have to keep the whole thing a secret." Saying it out loud choked her up.

"Why?" he asked.

Dana took a ragged breath and exhaled slowly before responding. "My contract with the Shopping Channel. I'm prohibited from performing. So I'm doing it secretly, under a stage name."

He cocked his head, his eyes warm with concern. "You okay?" he asked.

"Don't I sound okay?"

"Not really."

"So much for my acting skills."

He steered her into a bar called The Hollow, and they slid into a dark booth, where she ordered a vodka martini and he got a bottle of Sam Adams.

He straightened his hair with one hand—a self-conscious gesture she found endearing. Dana touched her throat and his eyes went there, then traveled to her face. She wondered what it would be like to kiss him.

"What would happen if your boss found out about your show?" he asked.

"She'd fire me. On the spot."

"So why did you do it?"

"I felt like I didn't have a choice," Dana said with a shrug, and went on to explain about Raj and what it would have meant to him and the rest of the troupe if she backed out of her commitment.

"That all *sounds* very noble," he said, emphasizing the word *sounds* to imply that it was not, in fact, noble at all.

"Meaning?" she asked.

He tossed it back to her with a gesture of his hands.

She sighed, exasperated. "I had no ulterior motive, if that's what you're implying. It's not like this is going to make me a star."

"But you have to admit you get a certain charge out of the risk. Right?"

Dana took a sip of her drink and folded her arms. "You think I'm some kind of maniac?"

"I didn't say that."

"You make it sound like I'm an adrenaline junkie, jumping out of airplanes and crossing against the light."

"Some people run with scissors," he said. "Others hand the scissors to their boss."

So it was back to this again—her habit of self-sabotage. She wanted to be mad at him, to resent the hell out of him for not tripping over himself to compliment her on her sacrifice. But of course he was right.

"You're not an easy guy to get along with," she observed.

"I've heard that."

"From your ex-wife?"

He took a pull on his beer and sat back. "Nice detective work, Ms. Barry."

"Dana," she corrected.

"Okay... *Dana*. How did you know I was divorced?"

She reached across the table, took his left hand and pulled it toward her. She ran her finger gently, seductively, over the spot where his wedding ring had been. "You bear the mark," she said.

"So I do," he said, and turned his hand over.

She laid hers in his, and he curled his fingers over ever so slightly, stopping just short of holding her hand. The tease of it was almost too much to bear.

"Ari..." she said, testing it out.

"Dana," he responded.

"You can make all the obnoxious psychological observations you like, but I'm still going to get you to kiss me good-night."

"And how will Lorenzo feel about that?"

"I'm not seeing Lorenzo anymore."

He moved his head toward hers to study her face. "You're serious."

"I am."

His hand tightened around hers. Dana wanted to play it cool, but the warmth that rivered through her forced a grin. He smiled back, and that did something wonderfully terrible to her heart.

They left the bar and walked back to the precinct where his car was parked. He didn't hold her hand in public, which she supposed was a cop thing. He was on a case, after all, and she was involved in it.

He drove uptown to her apartment and pulled into an illegal spot in front of her building, big enough for his oversize SUV.

"I just realized why you became a cop," she said.

"For the parking privileges?"

"It's like getting a key to the city."

He cut the engine, and there was an awkward pause. She wondered if he was going to make a move, or if the ball was in her court. It wasn't that she minded being the aggressor, but she had already said the thing about the good-night kiss. It was his turn. If he wanted her, that is.

He brushed a lock of hair from her forehead and touched her cheek with the whole of his warm hand. She was tempted to move her face against it like a cat. The smell of him was more intoxicating than her martini.

"Ari…" she whispered. She was getting breathless.

"You meant what you said about a good-night kiss?" he said softly.

She wanted to tell him she had already moved on to thinking about a good-morning kiss. Instead, she said, "Not here."

They got out of the car and went into her building. When
they got off the elevator on her floor, she was surprised to see
a huge bouquet of flowers on the floor in front of her door.
She knew they could only be from Lorenzo, which was the
worst possible timing. A small white card was forked into the
middle of the arrangement, and without even bending down
she could make out the words. *I hope we can work things out.*

Ari saw it, too.

"I guess things aren't entirely over with Lorenzo," he said.

"No, they are. Trust me."

"It seems he doesn't think so."

Dana was determined. She was not going to let Lorenzo
ruin this for her. With her back to the wall, she pulled Ari by
the shirt until they were pelvis-to-pelvis. He kissed her, and
it was everything. Crazy and wonderful and so loaded with
feeling she would have been scared if she wasn't so roused and
ready, breathless and off balance.

He pulled away and looked at her hard. Then he held her
by her shoulders and took half a step back.

"What is it?" she asked.

"I'm not going to come in," he said.

"You're not?"

He opened his mouth to speak and hesitated, as if waiting to
make sure she was really tuned in. When he finally spoke, his
voice drifted over her like vapor. "I don't want to share you."

Her breath caught. At that moment, it felt like the most seductive line she had ever heard.

"You're not sharing me," she said. "Lorenzo and I are finished."

He nodded toward the flowers. "Talk to him."

"There's nothing to say."

He kissed her on the forehead. "Call me when you're ready," he said, and turned to walk away.

She wanted to call after him, *I'm ready now!* But she knew how desperate it sounded. And so she watched him step into the elevator and disappear.

Dana picked up the bouquet, wondering what to do with it. She'd never hated flowers so much in her life. Damn you, Lorenzo, she thought, and wondered why he decided to do something so uncharacteristic all of a sudden. And it was such a garish, oversize arrangement. As a father on a limited budget, he had no business spending that kind of money on her.

She picked up the card to get a closer look at what he wrote, and that was when she saw it. The flowers weren't from Lorenzo. They were from Rusty Lindemuth.

31

The next day, Dana used her cell phone to take a picture of the card, and sent it to Ari with the text message, I told you it was over with Lorenzo.

She hurried to work before hearing back from him, excited and nervous about her show. A jewelry designer named Quentin Daye was being featured, which was a big deal, because the gemstone products were usually sold only on prime time. It was a lot of pressure on Dana, but she was eager for the chance to show what she could do with some sparkly merch. As long as she wasn't sabotaged again, she could shine.

When Adam came to brief her on the products, he had photographs on his tablet, and explained that if she wanted to see the actual jewelry before the show, she had to go down to the set where it was under the careful watch of the designer's staff.

Dana nodded, remembering Sherry's admonitions about the theft of display merchandise. "I guess this is the kind of stuff that's gone missing in the past," she said.

"We've had…issues," he confirmed. "But we've tightened security."

"Have to admit I'm grateful for the extra protection right now."

"Dana, I promise you, I spoke to the crew about being extravigilant. And I'm going to check and double-check every single thing personally—the color charts, the display tables, the audio cables. You're not going to have a problem today."

Dana wasn't usually superstitious, but a life in theater had made her wary of certain phrases. You don't say "good luck" before a performance. You don't say "Macbeth" backstage. She hoped "You're not going to have a problem today" wouldn't be added to that list.

When Adam left, she picked up her cell phone, glad to see a reply from Ari. Who is Rusty Lindemuth?

She texted back. Inappropriate friend of my dad's.

After a minute his reply came through. Disturbing age difference?

She laughed and wrote back. Might be even worse than you think.

Dana went to hair and makeup, getting a little more glammed-up than usual for the jewelry show. Irini brought her three outfits to choose from, and she picked a solid plum body-hugging cocktail dress with a V-neck. It was elegant and a little sexy—tight to the hips with a flirty flair at the hem—but plain enough to let the jewelry be the star of the show. She paired it with high-heeled gray pumps that made her legs look seven or eight miles long.

The dress might have been a little sexier than she bargained for, because when she got down to the set, she noticed elbow-jabs among the male members of the crew. And then she found Lorenzo waiting for her at the jewelry display.

"I'm not ready to be miked yet," she insisted.

"I know," he said, and stared at her expectantly. She didn't soften. "You look beautiful," he added.

Dana folded her arms. "What do you want?"

"You *know* what I want," he said, lowering his voice to a

whisper because Quentin Daye's assistant stood just feet away. "We really need to talk."

Dana hesitated. Though her fury was no longer white-hot, it had solidified into stubbornness. She didn't want to let him off the hook. He had treated her badly, and she didn't deserve it. Still, there was something about her new connection with Ari Marks that altered her mood. She felt…redirected. And brimming with a bubbly anticipation she hadn't experienced in a long time. It was hard to stay closed with all that effervescence coursing through her. She considered the possibility that maybe it wouldn't kill her to hear what he had to say.

"I'm not your enemy," he said. "I just want to explain what happened. Can we find someplace to talk?"

"Now?" she asked.

"After the show," he said. "Just give me five minutes."

She let out a breath. "Okay, five minutes. But not here."

"The planetarium?" he asked, referring to the empty studio across the lobby.

She agreed and went to take her place on the set, where the crew was arranging the first display table of jewelry, under the watchful eye of Quentin Daye himself. Beneath the lights, the gems seemed to come alive, and she knew how dynamic that would look on the air. She could hardly wait to get started.

Dana introduced herself to the designer and told him how she felt. "Your pieces are…dazzling," she said. "I'd love to own any one of them. Hell, I'd love to own all of them!"

Quentin smiled, his broad face growing even rounder. "Those earrings look sublime on you, darling. And that dress!" He took her hand and twirled her around. "It's almost enough to turn me straight."

She laughed and gave his arm a squeeze. "I think we're going to get along just fine." Dana pointed to the camera. "And she is going to *love* your jewelry."

He beamed, getting her point. "It's going to be a fabulous show," he said, his rumbling theatrical baritone nearly shaking the set.

They got miked, and Dana fit in her earpiece. She hit her mark and looked at the camera as Adam gave the final count. At last, the green light went on and she took off, letting her friends at home know exactly how thrilled she was to be introducing them to this new Quentin Daye Gem Drop collection, starting with three-tiered dangling earrings that were available in two color stories. The Midnight version had stones of blue topaz and amethyst, surrounded by tiny cubic zirconia. The Multi had those gems plus yellow topaz and Burmese rubies. Dana had a hard time deciding which one she liked better—they were really so lovely.

With their connection established, Dana and Quentin chatted like old friends as she gushed about the sparkle and the cut, and he explained the origin of the designs and the value of the gems. He was a good talker—impassioned and articulate—making it easy for Dana to sell his wares. Her occasional glances at the sales monitor told her that when the camera came in for a close-up on the earrings in her own lobes, the viewers reacted. And so she made sure she went from the display to cooing about how much she loved the way they dangled and moved and caught the light. Before long, Adam alerted her that the Multi was almost sold out, and so she gave her friends at home warning to act quickly if they wanted these beautiful earrings.

The rest of the show went just as well, as Dana gushed about bracelets and necklaces and even more earrings. At last they got to the final and most expensive item in the collection—a solid gold bracelet watch with a dial encircled in tiny diamonds and gemstones. The price was listed as $4,975, lowered from $9,995, and available on their Easy-Bucks option that divided it into five payments. This was the tough one—she had to be on her game to convince viewers to part with that much money. She would live and die by the sales monitor.

But about a minute into the presentation the screen went dark. Dana could hardly believe it. At the very moment the numbers were more important than ever, she was driving blind, with no idea what the viewers were reacting to. She swallowed against her fear. Whoever was sabotaging her had picked the right time to do it.

"It's okay," Adam whispered through her earpiece. "Your monitor is out, but I can see the numbers on the master computer and I'll walk you through it."

It worked. He narrated the rise and fall of the sales numbers, so Dana could tell exactly what the viewers were responding to. Very soon, it became clear that it wasn't just the details of the watch that excited the buyer to action, but the idea that she deserved to treat herself to an heirloom piece. The word *gift* tended to backfire, as it was too much of a budget-breaker. But letting the viewer feel justified in treating herself to something this beautiful and expensive without guilt (after all, she could pass it on!) was the magic dust.

Finally, Adam told Dana it was time to wrap up and introduce Vanessa. "And your numbers are spectacular," he added.

Spectacular! It was such a relief Dana almost clapped. Instead, she bid a cheerful goodbye to her viewers and barely had time to unclip her mike before Quentin Daye wrapped her in a bear hug. "That was brilliant," he said, his face glistening with sweat. "When that monitor went down I almost threw myself onto the floor!"

She pictured this mountainous man, in his two-thousand-dollar Italian suit, collapsing in a tantrum, and laughed. "Don't say that too loud," she managed. "There are people who would pay money to see it."

"I think you outshine even the Pitch Queen herself," he gushed.

Now she knew he was truly carried away, referencing Kitty. Dana didn't know how to react to that, but before she could decide, he clapped her on the shoulder. "Relax," he said. "Somebody's got to pick up the scepter. May as well be you, my dear."

Two of his staff members walked over and carefully wheeled the display off the set. Adam emerged from the control booth and approached the table, apparently taking careful inventory of the pieces. He signaled to Dana, who walked over with Quentin.

"You want the good news or the great news?" Adam said, and proceeded to go over the sales figures with the two of them. They had exceeded expectations, and had even broken the record for selling jewelry off-season in a non-primetime slot.

Quentin put his hands on Dana's shoulders. "When I come back with my holiday collection," he said, "I want to work with this wonderful lady. She's a superstar."

Dana beamed. With such a success, Sherry simply had to back off now.

Quentin excused himself to talk to his staff, and Adam got called into the control booth. "I'll be right back," he said to Dana. "Stay here."

She did as he asked, eager to hear what he had to say about the problem with the monitor, but he was gone for several minutes and she figured he got caught up with something. And so she waited another minute or two, and then walked across the lobby to meet Lorenzo in the planetarium. She figured she could catch up with Adam later.

"Congratulations," Lorenzo said when she entered.

"You caught a break," she said. "I'm in a good mood."

He laughed. "Lucky me."

"Doesn't mean I'm going to let you off the hook," she said.

"I know. I was an asshole. I'm sorry."

"So you said."

"You're still not going to make this easy?" he asked.

"That's not my job. But I'll listen to what you have to say."

"Okay," he said, and looked down to gather his thoughts. When he looked back up at her, his dark eyes shone in the narrow beam of light filtering down from one of the starry points in the black ceiling. "It's the parole thing. It makes me paranoid. I felt like I had to keep my travels a secret or I'd be screwed. Can you understand that? The whole thing felt very cloak-and-dagger—like I was taking this huge risk to build a better future for Sophia."

Dana shook her head. "But that's the part I don't get. Why would you take such a crazy risk? If you got caught—"

"I knew I *wouldn't* get caught," he said. "Not if I was supercareful. You have to understand, this job is an incredible opportunity for me. When I saw the listing, I almost couldn't contain myself. I knew it was something I could do, and that the timing was almost perfect. I would be able to start right after my parole ends. The only problem was getting to the interview."

"And you couldn't just go to your parole officer? I would think he'd make an exception."

"Normally he might have. But there was so much shit going down with this murder investigation. I just don't think he would have cut me any slack here."

Dana thought back to the days before he left for the interview—all those opportunities he had to open up to her. "I still don't understand why you didn't trust me. I wouldn't have told anyone."

He gave a defeated shrug. "Secrecy becomes a habit. Or

maybe a superstition. Like if I could just keep it to myself, I could pull it off." He put his hand to the middle of his chest. "I'm a single dad, Dana. My job is to do whatever it takes. And you have to understand—the QVC job is almost twice the salary."

That stopped her cold. "Twice?" she said.

"And you should see the way we'd be able to live there. In a house. A normal house, in a safe neighborhood. With a backyard and good schools. It's everything I could want for Sophia."

Dana looked away. She understood. And now that she admitted that to herself, she had to face another truth: on some level, she had always understood, but was too insulted to accept it. It was easier to think he was a dick than to face the fact that she couldn't handle coming second to his kid. And it wasn't even that she was pining for him, or had any illusions about a future together. She had simply been selfish enough to want to be his everything. The shame of it pressed down on her.

"I think maybe I've been a little unfair to you," she said.

"No," he said. "It was my fault. I should have told you."

She nodded. "You should have trusted me. You should have known I would keep your secret." He started to talk, to offer another mea culpa, but she cut him off. "On the other hand, you were making decisions based on what you thought was best for Sophia…exactly what you were supposed to do."

"So you forgive me?" he said.

She looked into his eyes. "I do."

"Thank you," he said, and reached for her hand.

She pulled it away. "No, Lorenzo."

"No?" He looked wounded.

She shook her head. "This isn't going to work."

"I thought we had something."

"It doesn't matter," Dana said. "Even if the QVC thing

doesn't work out, you're planning to leave New York the second you get the chance."

He nodded, taking that in, and went quiet for a long moment. "Actually," he said, "it *is* going to work out."

"What do you mean?"

His expression softened. "I heard from them this morning," he said quietly.

"And?" she asked, almost bursting.

"And...I got it! I'll be giving notice next week, and moving in a month."

"Oh, Lorenzo. That's wonderful!" She was overcome with joy for him, and for what this would mean for Sophia. Without even thinking, she threw her arms around him. He hugged her back and spun her around in a dance of joy. She squealed and laughed, forgetting that they were just feet away from their coworkers.

Apparently, her voice carried outside the door, because almost immediately she heard someone outside call, "Dana?"

"Put me down!" she whispered, and he did, but not before the door burst open, flooding them with light.

As her feet hit the ground, she looked up to see who had witnessed this spontaneous burst of affection.

It was Ari Marks.

32

It might have taken only a nanosecond for Dana to understand what Ari saw, but it played out like taffy stretched to its brittlest breaking point. Dana, in her flirty purple dress, twirling in joy with the man she had sworn she wasn't seeing. The way her smile gave way to distress and then panic when she met Ari's eyes. The fall of his expression. The hurt.

She tried to speak, to find the language to explain what had happened. But before Dana could utter a single word of explanation, Adam rushed up behind Ari, breathless and alarmed.

"There you are!" he said to Dana. "I've been looking all over for you."

"What's the matter?"

"Please tell me you know what happened to the watches," he said.

"The watches?" She was so flustered she was having trouble making sense of Adam's panic.

"The two watches that were on the display table. I left you there guarding them."

"I…I wasn't guarding them. I was waiting for you and you didn't show up." Her heart thudded. The watches had been stolen and they were blaming her.

Adam put his head in his hands. "So they're really missing. Both of them."

Lorenzo sucked air. "This is bad."

Dana heard the jangle of keys and then Beecham appeared at the doorway. "You called?" he said to Adam.

Adam nodded, his face tense. "Ten thousand dollars' worth of merchandise just disappeared."

Beecham's hard expression went even harder...and then harder still when he noticed the detective. "What is he doing here?"

"I was just leaving," Marks said, holding up his hands.

"Ari, wait!" Dana called. But he ignored her and kept walking.

Her stomach did a flip. How would she ever get him to believe her? "This is a disaster," she said.

Adam let out a breath. "No kidding."

She didn't want to deal with this work crisis. She wanted to run after Ari, to replay every word of her conversation with Lorenzo and make him understand. *I didn't lie to you!* she wanted to cry. But then Quentin Daye showed up, and his pained expression broke her heart. He was altered—not even the same man she had seen just minutes ago. It took her a moment to understand why he looked at her the way he did, and then she understood. He, too, was disappointed in her. Did he think she stole the watches? It was eviscerating.

A few minutes later, Dana, Adam and Quentin Daye were squeezed into Adam's small office as Beecham peppered them with questions. Dana tried to focus on the conversation, but her mind kept going back to Ari and what he was thinking. She wanted to clarify everything immediately, to tell him that she was merely congratulating Lorenzo on his new job. She thought about typing it in a text, but realized it wasn't wise to put it in writing—not while Lorenzo was still on parole.

At last, she took out her phone and tapped out a quick message. I hope you'll let me explain.

"Put that away," Beecham said, angry.

She put it down on her lap, trying not to look like a guilty child.

As the questions and answers continued, Sherry Zidel showed up and stood in the doorway, her arms folded across her bony frame, her jaw twitching. After listening awhile, she interjected. "Here's what I don't understand. Adam leaves Dana guarding the merch, and Dana just walks away, leaving it alone for anyone to pilfer."

Her tone was so accusatory Dana wanted to spit. "That's not fair," she said. "I was never told to guard anything. I was just waiting for Adam to come back and tell me what happened with the monitor."

"And you thought it was okay to leave two diamond watches out in the open?"

"Don't blame Dana," Adam said. "It was my fault. I should have been more specific."

"To be clear," Sherry said through her teeth, "I'm blaming both of you."

Beecham turned to Quentin Daye. "Wasn't your staff supposed to be keeping an eye on your products?"

"They were putting away the rest of the pieces," he said. "I thought the producer was looking after the watches."

"Aren't we forgetting the most important question?" Dana asked before Quentin could turn his accusatory expression back to her. "Who took them?"

"I was in the booth," Adam said. "I didn't see who was around."

"I was busy with my staff," Quentin added.

Dana thought about the last time an expensive piece went missing, and how it ended up in her dressing room. Now she wondered if this was part of a pattern. Whoever was sabotaging her might have taken the watches just to pin the blame on her. Her heart thudded in panic. She had to protect herself.

"I'm going to question everyone in the crew," Beecham said. "Someone had to see something." He rose, and Dana stopped him.

"Wait," she said. "I'd like you to search my dressing room." Everyone turned to her.

"'Scuse me?" Beecham said.

"Someone here has been trying to sabotage me," she explained. "And I think it's possible that whoever took the watches did it just to get me in trouble. So… I'd like someone to check my dressing room before I go back, just in case someone planted the evidence there."

"I think you're getting a little paranoid," Adam said.

"Maybe," Dana admitted. "But humor me."

"All right," Beecham said, and headed toward the door. They all followed him down the hall and up one flight of stairs. They found Ollie standing outside Dana's dressing room.

"Did you see anyone go in or out of this room in the past half hour?" Beecham asked him.

"I see no one, but I have been here only one or two minutes. I was on the set seeking Dana." He looked at the group assembled and his eyes went wide. "Is there a problem?"

"Some valuable merchandise is missing," Sherry said, and pushed open the door to Dana's dressing room.

"Stay here," Beecham said. "All of you." And they stood crowded in the doorway as he began opening and closing drawers, picking up items and looking beneath them.

"This is ridiculous," Sherry said to Dana. "I don't know what kind of show you're putting on."

She exhaled and said nothing, but when Beecham reached the last section of the room, Dana asked if she could come in.

"Just you," Beecham said, "and don't touch anything."

She walked around, looking for anything that seemed out of place. She went to the dressing area that wasn't visible from the doorway, and pointed to the cabinet that held her purse.

"Was this door open or closed when you came in?" she asked.

"Open."

She felt a chill. It had been closed when she left. She was sure of it. "Did you look in my purse?"

He shook his head.

"Mr. Beecham," she said, "I left this cabinet closed. Also, I hung up my purse with the zipper facing in. Now it's facing out." She took a step back and held up her hands to show that she wasn't touching it.

Beecham took the purse from the hook, opened it up and dumped the contents on the counter. There, amid her wallet, makeup case, dachshund key chain, hand sanitizer, tampons, tissue pack, breath mints, MetroCard, pens and loose change, was the diamond watch. He picked it up for the group to see.

"I'll be damned," said Sherry.

"I'm sorry I called you paranoid," Adam added.

Dana hung her head, vindicated, but roiling. Her saboteur was still out there. But even that didn't compare to her despair over Ari. He would never trust her again.

Now, all she wanted was for these people to disappear and leave her alone.

But Beecham went back to searching the room to see if he could find the other missing watch. It wasn't there, and the conclusion was that the thief had probably kept it for personal gain.

At last the group dispersed and Dana changed into her street clothes. Although she wanted nothing more than to go home and pour herself a tall glass of the pinot grigio chilling in her fridge, she dragged herself to rehearsals. It was a commitment she simply wouldn't break, no matter how terrible she felt. And besides, the first performance of the show was only a week away, and every rehearsal was critical.

Still, she assumed she would just walk through the scenes. But once she started saying her lines, something happened. Her sadness over losing Ari found its way into Mrs. Woodbridge's icy resolve, creating a layer that hadn't been there before. When the scene ended, Nathan literally bowed at her feet.

She choked out a thank-you, and then rushed home, where she kept her date with a crisp Napa Valley white that carried her away.

33

"You drunk-dialed a *cop*?" Chelsea asked, incredulous.

It was the next night—Friday—a planned dinner in midtown with Chelsea and Megan. They were in a seafood restaurant, darkly paneled, and Dana was on her second vodka martini.

"That's not what I said," Dana insisted. "I didn't call, I *texted*. So my humiliation is digitally etched into eternity."

"It can't be that bad," Megan said.

"Girlfriend," Dana said, slapping her phone into Megan's palm, "see for yourself."

Megan scrolled to the top of the long line of texts Dana had sent to Ari, and went quiet for a few seconds. "Shit," she whispered.

"What does it say?" Chelsea asked.

Megan looked at Dana, as if asking for permission to read it out loud.

"Go ahead," Dana said. "You may as well. Just let me order another drink first."

"Don't you think you've had enough?" Chelsea asked.

Megan looked up from Dana's phone. "Trust me, she needs another drink. Maybe two."

"Maybe ten," Dana added.

"It can't be that bad," Chelsea said.

"Like Hurricane Katrina wasn't that bad," Megan said, and began reading out loud.

9:08. Hello, are you there?

9:10. It's me, Dana. Can we talk?

9:35. I can't believe you're not assering me.

"Is that what it says?" Chelsea interrupted. "Assering?"

"I was starting to get a little fucked up," Dana said.

Megan went on.

9:37. I promise you I am not datting Lorenzo.

9:38. I meant dating. I don't know what datting is.

9:39. But I'm not datting him, either. Lol.

Megan stopped and looked at her.

"It seemed hilarious at the time," Dana said.

Megan continued.

9:42. The only one I want to dat is you.

9:50. I'm getting a little fucked up here. I wish you would answer.

10:16. I shunt tell u this but Lorzenzo is moving after his payroll ends. So even if I was fucking him, which I am not, I would not be anymore.

10:17. Parole. Not payroll. Fucking autocorrect.

11:27. I fell asleep but you still did not ersoon.

11:28. Respond. You still did not respooon.

11:29. I cannot type respond! Lololol!

11:32. I like you so much. Why want you answer?

11:40. I just spilled wine all over my shits.

11:42. Lol. Sheets.

Megan stopped and looked up. "The next text is a series of emojis. There doesn't seem to be any pattern or meaning."

"I don't even think I was looking," Dana said. "Just randomly tapping. It was some kind of game."

Megan read on.

12:01. In case you dint no, that means I want you in my bed.

"Oh, God," Chelsea said.

Dana exhaled and put her head in her hands. Megan kept scrolling.

12:12. Did I tell you I love the way you smell?

She looked up. "You typed that perfectly."

Dana shrugged. "A moment of clarity. I *do* love the way he smells." She pointed to the phone. "You're almost at the end."

Megan read.

12:15. Falling asleep.

12:31. I drank some water and went pee-pee.

12:33. Will you call me before I go to seep?

12:35. Yoy are not calling me. Why?

12:36. Good night, Ari.

12:37. You are too tall, anyways.

1:11. I want to suck yr fingers.

Megan looked up. "That's it." She passed the phone back to Dana.

Chelsea's face looked pained. "I want to suck your fingers?"

"I have no recollection of writing that," Dana said. "I think I was sleep-texting at that point."

"You look miserable," Chelsea said.

"Miserable would be an improvement."

"It's not really that—"

"Oh, come on," Dana said. "It's exactly that bad."

"Okay," Chelsea conceded. "It's pathetic."

"What are you going to do?" Megan asked.

Dana shrugged. "What are my options? Change my name? Apply for the witness protection program?"

"Look on the bright side," Megan said.

"There's a bright side?"

"He wouldn't be so hurt if he wasn't invested. He cares about you."

"Cared," Dana corrected. "Past tense. Pretty sure he hates me now."

"Are you sure?" Chelsea asked.

"It doesn't matter," Dana said. "I'm done. And I'm not going to pine over some guy I didn't even have a relationship with, just because his hands smell good and he has a nose like the Statue of Liberty and he's brave and smart and has a moral core made of titanium."

"He *does* have a nose like the Statue of Liberty," Chelsea said, surprised by her own agreement. "You need to try to talk to him."

"Pointless," Dana said.

"But when you explain—"

"He'd never believe me. And besides, I sent him twenty-six texts. *Twenty-six.* In four hours. My humiliation is complete."

"I think you just need to give it some time," Chelsea said. "And then reach out to him again, sober."

"Great idea. If I'm still single when I'm eighty-five, I'll see if he's interested in hooking up."

"What if *I* spoke to him?" Megan said. "Tried to smooth things over."

"You're my manager," Dana said, "not my consigliere."

Megan reached out and took Dana's hand. "I'm also your friend."

The kindness touched the softest spot in Dana's heart. Megan was so good to her. Such a loyal and devoted friend. She felt a dagger of guilt over lying to her about the Sweat City show, and dreaded to think what would happen if Megan ever found out. It might be the end of the friendship. She folded and unfolded her damp cocktail napkin, understanding that Megan would have every right to feel betrayed. Now, Dana wondered if telling her was worth the risk of telling her. It was the right thing to do, wasn't it? Just come clean and confess? As long as she was feeling this shitty, she reasoned, she might as well go all the way. She signaled the waiter for another drink, and wondered if this was just another instance of her addiction to self-sabotage. She decided to think about it some more. After all, she had just blown up her chances with Ari. She didn't need to throw a lighted stick of dynamite into this friendship. She rolled the napkin into a ball.

"Should we order?" Chelsea asked. "Get some food behind all that alcohol?" She looked down at her menu, unconsciously fingering the silver lariat choker at her neck.

"Is that new?" Dana asked, pointing at it.

"Not really, but I never wear it."

"I wonder why it looks familiar," Dana said, trying to remember where she'd seen it.

Chelsea shrugged. "I bought it from the Shopping Channel a few months ago—before you worked there."

Dana moved in for a closer look. "Are those real diamonds?"

"Don't judge me," Chelsea said. "Kitty Todd talked me into buying it."

"I'm not judging, I'm just asking."

"In that case, yes. They're real diamonds. But I think it's quite tasteful."

"Oh God," Dana said, a memory pulsing into view. "I know where I saw it before. On Adam's wife—in a picture he showed me." A sickening idea took hold, and she didn't want to believe it was true.

"So?" Megan asked.

"How much did it cost?" Dana asked. "Tell me the truth. Was it more than five hundred dollars?"

"It was more than seven hundred."

"Damn it," Dana said. "He would never have spent that money." She knew she was right. Adam was strapped. Struggling to pay the mortgage and afford diapers. He wouldn't have bought his wife a delicate lariat choker with two small diamonds at the tips. Even with his employee discount, it would have crushed him.

"What are you saying?" Megan asked.

Dana took a breath. "I think Adam stole it." As soon as she said it out loud, it felt true.

Chelsea looked dubious. "That's a pretty big leap."

"But it makes sense." Dana remembered what Sherry had said about display merchandise going missing in the past... and recalled how defensive Adam was when she mentioned his wife's necklace. She could picture his expression. At the time, she'd been confused by how alarmed he was. But now that she played it back, his expression looked like something very specific. It looked like guilt.

"Isn't it possible he just wanted to buy his wife a nice present?"

Dana shook her head. "Sometimes people legitimately can't afford things, Chelsea."

"Thank you. Because I'm not just a spoiled brat, I'm also an idiot."

"Take it easy," Dana said. "The point is, Adam is broke. He wouldn't have bought it. And he would have had easy access to the display merchandise. He might be the one who's been taking things all along."

"He seems like such a decent guy," Megan said.

Chelsea snorted. "Those are always the ones."

"I can't believe I'm saying this," Dana choked out. "But I think he's the one who stole those watches."

"And put one of them in your purse?" Megan asked.

Dana paused. "That's the part that doesn't make sense."

"What about Kitty's alligator bracelet that wound up in your dressing room?" Chelsea asked. "You think he took that?"

"I do."

Megan downed the last of her mojito and practically dropped the glass. "You don't think he murdered Kitty, do you?"

"No! I mean… I don't know. It doesn't really make sense, does it?"

"I think it makes perfect sense," Chelsea said. "He was sleeping with her, right? Maybe Kitty threatened him like she threatened Charles Honeycutt."

"But why would she do that?" Dana asked.

"Because she was a fucked-up crazy-ass bitch," Megan said.

Dana shook her head. "Motivation is everything. Kitty was in love with Charles Honeycutt. She threatened to go to his wife in desperation. She was trying to force him to leave her. But she didn't love Adam. She was using him."

"But if he stole the alligator bracelet…" Megan said.

Dana closed her eyes and thought back to the day of Kitty's murder, to the crowd of people rushing toward her office. Had Adam been at the front of the pack? If he had sticky fingers, it might have been too tempting to resist—such an expensive piece out in the open like that. He might have simply slipped it into his pocket when no one was looking.

"He had the opportunity," Dana said.

"Thieves can be very opportunistic," Chelsea said, clearly excited by her own observation.

"Thank you, Dr. Phil," Dana said.

"You know what I mean. Sometimes they don't plan their thefts. They see an opportunity and, well…it's like leaving a pile of Hershey's Kisses in front of a five-year-old. They just can't resist."

"Who are you calling a five-year-old?" Megan asked.

Dana thought about the man on the subway—the one who spotted the girl's wallet sticking out of her backpack—and agreed.

"Dana," Chelsea said, "what are you going to do?"

Dana grunted. "I can't believe I'm saying this, but I think there's only one thing I *can* do." She stopped to take a big gulp of her drink. "I have to call Ari Marks."

34

The first tech rehearsal for *Mrs. Woodbridge* was scheduled for Sunday, which meant Dana would be occupied for an entire day, running through all the technical details of the performance. It was a chance to find any mistakes that could screw up the show. Inevitably, someone threw a fit during these dry runs. Either the set designer thought the lighting ruined everything, the costumer was horrified by something that didn't work from the back row, the sound effects were completely out of sync or the microphones decided to screech every time two of the actors approached one another. Tech rehearsals were almost always a clusterfuck that sent the cast and crew into a terrified panic that they would not be ready in time for the first performance, and this one was no exception.

They stayed at the theater until 11:00 p.m., when everyone was so tired, dusty-throated and worn out they had no choice but to go home, and try to fix the problems the next day.

Despite her anxiety about what she faced at work, Dana fell into a dead-black sleep. There was little in life more exhausting than the stress and tedium of tech rehearsals.

She slept so late she was woken up by a text from Megan saying that she had called Sherry and demanded a meeting for that morning. Dana had an hour to grab a cup of coffee, shower and get to the studio. But she made it in time to meet up with Megan in the lobby before heading up to Sherry's office.

"What's the game plan?" Dana asked.

"I need to raise hell about your working conditions. The diamond watch thing was the last straw."

When they were alone in the elevator, Megan asked Dana what had happened with Marks.

"I didn't even call him yet," Dana said.

"Why not?"

"Haven't had a chance. I was sound asleep when you texted and I rushed over here."

"You could have left him a message over the weekend."

"Saturday I was hungover and Sunday I was in..." Dana caught herself. "Sunday I just needed to chill."

"Well, I'm putting the pressure on, Dana. The cops need to know about this. Frankly, I think Sherry should be told immediately. But I understand if you want to wait until you have more solid proof."

"I'd like to at least talk it through with Ari first to make sure I'm on solid ground with this. It's a massive accusation. If I'm right—and I think I am—it will ruin Adam's life. If I'm wrong, it will ruin mine."

Megan nodded and they continued on to Sherry's office.

"Adam's already here," Emily Lauren said when they arrived. "Go right in."

Adam? Dana hadn't anticipated he would be in this meeting, though she supposed it made sense. She took a deep breath, understanding that she would need to fortify herself to face him.

Dana stopped before going into Sherry's office, and closed her eyes.

"What are you doing?" Megan whispered.

"Getting into character."

"What character?"

"The character of Dana-before-she-knew-Adam-was-a-thief-who-was-probably-sabotaging-her-career."

"Cool," Megan said. "I'm going to play a character too—pissed-off-manager-capable-of-tearing-off-someone's-balls."

"Typecasting," Dana said, and gave her friend's arm a squeeze as they walked in.

"Let me just say," Sherry began when Dana and Megan took their seats, "that I understand your concern."

"I'm not sure you do," Megan said. "Whatever the hell is going on here is unacceptable. It was supposed to stop, and it's only escalating. I don't know what's next, but I can tell you that if anything happens to my client, I'm holding the company liable."

"Now let's just take it easy," Sherry said. She looked uncomfortable, and Dana suppressed a smile. She loved that Megan was able to put this imperious woman on the defensive.

"I need to know what steps you're taking to assure her safety," Megan said.

Sherry knitted her fingers. "I promise you, Adam has been over every detail."

Dana glanced over to check out Adam's expression, which looked pained but sincere. She had to hand it to the guy—he didn't break character.

Megan gave an exasperated grunt. "That's what he said before someone stole a diamond watch from the set and planted it in Dana's purse."

Adam looked from Megan to Sherry to Dana. "I'm really sorry that happened," he said.

Dana studied him, trying to gauge his sincerity. He looked so tired it was hard to get a good read on him. Either he had been up with the baby again, or nervous guilt had been keeping him awake.

"And don't think you're off the hook," Megan said to him. "You tried to blame Dana for not guarding over them."

He put his hand to his heart. "I was in shock to find the watches missing. And I really thought Dana had been guarding them."

Dana clenched her teeth and fought the urge to bring a heel down on his foot.

Megan wagged her finger at Sherry. "I want to know what measures you're taking to protect my client."

"I promise I'm going to be even more vigilant," Adam said.

"Clearly, that's not enough," Megan added, more to Sherry than Adam.

"Tell you what," Sherry said. "Today, I'll have someone from security on set. And I'll be there, too."

"All week," Megan said. "I want this kind of insurance all week."

"Okay," Sherry agreed. "All week."

Dana swallowed hard. This was more than she had bargained for. She needed this to be an easy week at work so that she could slip out quickly to rehearsals. It was what theater people called "hell week"—the days leading up to the show. Tech rehearsals would continue late into the night for the next three days, followed by a dress rehearsal on Thursday. Friday was opening night. If Sherry demanded her attention after airtime on any of these nights, it would be a disaster.

After thanking Megan and saying goodbye, Dana went to her dressing room. Ollie wasn't in yet, so it was a good time to put in that call to Ari. But she hesitated. Her embarrassment felt like a muck she couldn't wash off. Or rather, like a pain she deserved. She scrolled to his name and placed the call.

It rang once, twice, three times. On the fourth ring it went to voice mail, and Dana wasn't surprised. No one wants to talk to someone who sent them twenty-six unhinged text messages. She was about to hang up, but thought better of it.

She took a deep breath and left a message.

"Ari, it's Dana. I don't blame you for not wanting to talk to me, but this is related to Kitty's murder. At least, I think it is. But first… I just want to apologize…for the crazy texts… for what you thought you saw between me and Lorenzo. I won't even bother trying to explain that now, but…whatever. It doesn't matter. The thing is, I think Adam Weintraub is the one who stole the diamond watches and Kitty's bracelet. I think he's also the one who's been sabotaging my show. Can you call me? We don't even have to talk about the Lorenzo stuff. I just… I want to explain to you about Adam and get your take. It's important. Okay. That's it."

She hung up, stared at her phone and shook her head, doubting he would call back. She sounded like a crazy woman making up an excuse to talk to a guy she was obsessing over.

When Ollie arrived, he was in a state. Apparently, news of the diamond watch theft had spread through the company, and there were all sorts of rumors about one of the watches being found in Dana's purse.

"I tell everyone this is not true, Dana! I tell them you are not a thief!"

"You're right, Ollie," she said. "I'm not a thief. But someone did take those things, and put one of them in my purse to try to pin it on me."

Ollie gasped and his eyes began to water. "Oh, no, Dana! Oh, no!"

"It's okay," she said. "I promise. I was with Mr. Beecham when he found it. He knows someone tried to frame me."

"Oh, Dana," he said, grasping his chest. "My heart! I was so worried."

"Everything is going to be okay," she said.

"But who does such a thing to you? Do you know?"

Dana hesitated. She didn't want to tell him about Adam. She couldn't risk it getting back to him before she went to the authorities. Besides, she didn't think Ollie could handle the information without having a small stroke. He seemed so distraught.

"I'm confident they'll find out soon enough," she said. "In the meantime, Sherry is going to be on set for my show to make sure nothing happens."

Her assurances couldn't penetrate Ollie's dark mood. "My fault," he mumbled. "I should have protected you."

He looked so bereft that Dana suspected he wasn't really talking about her, but about Kitty. She laid a gentle hand on his arm. "There was nothing you could have done."

Ollie seemed to disappear into his own sorrow for several long seconds, and Dana imagined that he was thinking about what he could have done differently to save Kitty. Or his mother or grandma.

"You okay?" she asked.

He looked as if he had forgotten where he was. Then he took a fortifying breath. "Miss Sherry is very smart and very strict. Nothing bad will happen if she is watching."

"Exactly," Dana said, and hoped he was right.

A few minutes later, Adam came to brief her on the upcoming show. Normally, she made Ollie find something else to do during these sessions, but she asked him to stick around. She thought it was best if she weren't alone with Adam. This way, the conversation would stay focused and professional, and Adam wouldn't pick up on her suspicions.

While he spoke she heard her phone vibrate, and sneaked a look. It was from the Thirteenth Precinct. So Ari had called her back, after all. She felt a lightening in her chest as she let it go to voice mail. She would call him back as soon as she got a chance.

When Adam left, Dana was eager to play back the message, but time was too tight. She had to go to hair, makeup and wardrobe and then hurry down to the set. Ari would have to wait. She told herself it was just as well. She didn't want to look desperate or needy.

Having Sherry on set was disconcerting, as she made everyone nervous. It was as if every member of the crew was suddenly rushing from one task to the next like they were putting out fires.

Sherry stood in the middle of the floor, her arms folded like Mussolini, as she scrutinized the entire production.

"Keller," she yelled at one of the guys as she pointed at the floor. "What is this?" She sounded angry enough to side with the Axis powers in a major world war.

He came rushing over to see what she was pointing at. "Um…it's a cable. Taped down so no one bothers it."

"What the hell kind of tape is that?"

Keller shrugged. "It's what we use."

"It's what we *use*?" she repeated, as if it were the most offensive answer he could have given. "It stuck to my shoe and I almost tripped."

"I'll…I'll fix it right away," he said, his face pale.

Lorenzo approached Dana and clipped on her mike. "Fun. Is she going to stay for the whole show?" he whispered.

"The whole *week*."

He crossed himself. "At least you'll be safe. Wish I could say the same for the rest of us."

It was handbag week again, and Dana was grateful. They were just so damned easy to sell. As long as the color charts were there, she could talk and talk and talk and talk about the various features. In fact, by the time the selections ran out, there was usually a lot more she had to say. So despite Sherry's presence, she was focused and on point, and the hours went quickly by.

When the show ended, Adam gave Dana the cue to introduce Vanessa, which she did with her biggest smile. Then she unclipped her mike and tried to avoid eye contact with Sherry and Adam as she hurried for the exit so she could get to rehearsal on time.

"Hang on a second," Sherry said. "Let's go over your numbers."

"Great!" Dana chirped, as if there was nothing she would rather be doing. She followed Sherry into the control booth, where Adam went over the sales figures in painstaking detail, instead of just giving Dana the highlights, as he usually did.

Sherry, of course, had feedback on what Dana could have done better, and what was wrong with each display and camera angle. The ten-minute conversation had stretched to thirty minutes by the time Sherry was done and Dana was dismissed. She bolted out of the studio without even changing into her street clothes, and made it to the theater only five minutes late, wondering how the hell she was going to survive the week.

It wasn't until Dana got home that night, physically and emotionally exhausted, that she played back the message. To her disappointment, it wasn't Ari's voice.

"Detective Lee here. I understand you left a message for Detective Marks about the Todd case. He's tied up today and asked me to return your call. Please phone me back when you get a chance."

It left Dana slightly nauseated. No doubt Marks didn't even want to hear her voice. He probably didn't even believe she had any real information to share. Maybe he even showed Lee her texts and said something like, "Do me a favor and deal with this crazy bitch."

Dana drank a tall glass of water—no booze this week—and went to sleep.

The next day, Dana called Detective Lee as she walked across town to work. She didn't want to speak to him. She wanted to talk to Ari, who knew the people involved and would be able to offer perspective. But she felt compelled to return his partner's call. If she didn't, Ari would think the message was nothing but a ruse to get him to talk to her.

She tried to sound as factual and sane as possible. But his questions frustrated her. He kept asking what facts she had, what she had actually witnessed. And the more he probed, the more she realized that all her conclusions were based on conjecture and speculation.

"What do you think I should do?" she asked. "Should I report it to management at the Shopping Channel?"

"Maybe not just yet," he said. "Let us look into it, and we'll get back to you."

"Okay," she said, not entirely convinced it wasn't his way of blowing her off. "But can I ask—have there been any other breaks in the case?"

"That's not something I can discuss with you."

"I know," she said. "But Detective Marks mentioned something about expecting the forensics report any day. Has that come in?"

There was a pause. "I promise you," he said, "we're working as quickly as we can. We'll make an arrest when we have all the facts."

35

Beecham, Dana thought. He was the one she needed to go to. He wasn't at the security desk when she arrived, so she asked the young guy on duty—Zack Higashi—where she could find him.

"He should be in his office. Is there anything I can do for you, Ms. Barry?"

She waved him off, and hurried to the security office at the far end of the first floor. She found him on the phone at his desk behind a wall of monitors showing live feeds of the front and rear doors to the building from different angles. He got off the phone and waved her in.

"Everything okay?" he asked.

"Mr. Beecham," she said, "I think I know who the thief is."

He told her to take a seat, then rose to shut the door.

"Talk to me," he said, pulling out the chair behind his desk.

She explained everything—Adam's financial situation, the necklace his wife wore, his reaction when she brought it up and how he had more access to the display merchandise than just about anyone else.

"And then there's Kitty's gold alligator bracelet," she said. "I know it was stolen between the time I saw Kitty's body and when the police arrived. And Adam was one of the people who went into her office."

Beecham rubbed his chin, taking it all in.

"I know it's not proof," she said, remembering the reaction she got from Detective Lee. "But I can't help thinking about his guilty expression when I brought up his wife's necklace and—"

"It's compelling," he said.

"It is?" Dana was so relieved to be taken seriously she didn't know how to react. "I told one of the detectives on the case and he was so…dubious."

"That's his job," Beecham said. "But if it's true, I think we might be able to find some corroborating evidence."

After discussing it a few more minutes, Dana agreed to come back to see him the next day so they could get exactly what they needed.

She arrived the following morning with a bag from Dunkin' Donuts—her way of thanking Beecham for his help. She thought they might spend a few minutes chatting more about her suspicions while bonding over caffeine and sugar. But Beecham had been waiting for her and wanted to get right to work. He stood and told her to follow him.

"Where are we going?" she asked.

"Back to the file room," he said. "I need your help looking for evidence. Do you know how to read a spreadsheet?"

Dana almost laughed. "In fact I do," she said, grateful that Ollie had taken the time to teach her.

Once inside, Beecham steered her to the shelves containing the computer printouts that Sherry had intimidated her with.

"What we're looking for," he said, "are any segments with reported diminution of display merchandise. Then we want to see who the segment producer was for those shows. If my suspicions are correct, we'll see a pretty strong pattern."

Diminution. She remembered that word—a fancy way to say that stuff went missing.

"I don't suppose you have access to the computer files?" she asked. "Then we could find it with a few clicks."

"The police could probably get it with a summons," he said. "But I'm afraid we're stuck following an old-fashioned paper trail."

And so they began to pull the binders off the shelves and pile up the ones that showed anything other than a zero in the "dim" column. After an hour, they had found seventeen instances of display merchandise that had disappeared without explanation.

"I think that's enough for now," Beecham said.

The two of them carried the binders to the table in the back and scanned the pages to see who the segment producer was on those shows. When they were done, the evidence was overwhelming. Adam Weintraub was the producer for fourteen out of the seventeen.

"I'm amazed Sherry never made the connection before," she said.

"Sometimes even the smartest people only see what they want to see. Besides, he was probably pretty clever about covering his tracks."

"So what do I do now?" she asked.

"You do nothing," he said. "I'm going to gather more evidence—build a really solid case—and then go to management."

"What about the police?" she asked. "I mean, if he stole Kitty's bracelet, they'll want to know."

"One step at a time," he said.

Dana tried to be patient. But her tension was off the charts.

She had to sit through her briefing with Adam and pretend everything was okay. And then there was the show itself, with his voice whispering in her earpiece.

Afterward, she had to stay steady while Sherry and Adam went over the sales figures. Every part of her wanted to explode. When at last she was able to leave, she felt like she had pulled a noose off her neck. Again, she was late for rehearsals. Nathan was understanding, but told her that he really needed her to be on time tomorrow. It was their dress rehearsal, and it was critical.

When she came to work the next day, Dana didn't know what to expect. It could be the day the shit hit the fan. If Beecham went to management, Adam could already be fired or suspended. But everything was quiet. Normal. Except for the drumbeat in Dana's chest, which made her feel like she needed to nail shutters to the windows and hunker down in the basement for the impending storm. There was nothing to do but wait.

When Adam came to see her for her daily briefing, she did everything she could to pretend it was just another normal day. Except that she had to be sure she could get out in time for rehearsal.

"You okay?" he asked as he wrapped up his briefing. "You seem a little tense today."

Despite herself, she had been thinking about the dress rehearsal instead of focusing on acting chipper and relaxed.

"I'm fine, but I have a doctor's appointment this evening and have to leave right after the show. I hope that's okay."

"Of course," he said. "I'll tell Sherry. Everything all right?"

She looked at him, feeling her throat tighten as she thought of his wife and children.

"I hope so," she said.

36

Once she got into costume for dress rehearsal, Dana's tension about work disappeared, supplanted by preperformance butterflies. It wasn't stage fright that made her belly feel squirmy, but a kind of nervous excitement. It was her drive. An intense desire to stay focused, to perform from the deepest place in her soul, to connect with her fellow actors, to communicate with the audience. She felt it almost as intensely for dress rehearsal as she did for the real thing, and that was intentional—a way of assuring that she was all in.

Nathan called for places and they began.

When they were done he praised them lavishly, though not without some consternation over the mistakes. Sylvia's nerves seemed to rattle her focus in the first scene. At one point, Raj skipped over a chunk of dialogue and Dana had to ad-lib to get them back on track. The sound guy missed one of his cues for the doorbell. Despite all that, Dana felt confident. She trusted her cast and crew. They were ready for opening night.

When she went to work on Friday, she was less concerned with Adam than with her Sweat City performance. She just wanted to get through the day and make it to the theater for opening night. In fact, she hoped that Beecham was still gathering evidence to take to management, and that nothing would happen until Monday at the earliest. She needed this to be a mellow day at work.

But that wasn't the way it went down.

First, she saw Ari, his face grim and serious as he walked down the corridor toward the exit. But he wasn't alone—he was with Detective Lee, and they were leading Adam out of the building. There were no handcuffs, yet Adam's face was so washed of color it was clear he was in trouble. She tried to be angry with him. After all, he had been stealing for years. And sabotaging Dana to keep himself safe. But she felt only disappointment and pity. Here was someone who didn't think of himself as a bad guy, but as someone who worked hard, loved his family and did what he had to do.

Because she had made her own share of mistakes, Dana felt uniquely qualified to judge his. She thought back to the time she was hostess at a midtown restaurant. She had become friends with one of the waitresses, Londra, whose ex was a deadbeat. Since Londra had a kid and was struggling to keep up, Dana steered the more affluent-looking diners to her tables so she'd take home more in tips. Helping a friend made Dana feel good. Also, she took a bit of perverse pleasure in pissing off one of the other servers—Big Mike—who was always getting in everyone's way in the kitchen and was an all-around pain in the ass. But he wasn't the only one who noticed Dana's behavior, and the management gave Dana a warning. She should have stopped at that point. After all, her interference didn't make a life-changing difference in Londra's tips. But Dana kept on, feigning innocence, until she was fired.

So yes, she understood Adam's compulsion. But stealing? And trying to cover it up by getting Dana fired...or worse?

Oh, Adam, she wanted to say. *There were so many different decisions you could have made. How could you have been so stupid?*

She looked into his face, trying to see if there was something darker there—the kind of heart that could commit murder. But all she saw was a weak and broken man. It made her feel cold and alone.

She glanced at Ari, hoping for a connection, but he gave her only the smallest nod, as if they barely knew each other. Beecham stood at the security desk behind Zack, watching as the three men disappeared out the front door.

"What happened?" Dana asked him, and Beecham nodded toward his office. She followed him there and he shut the door.

"I found nine more instances he was probably involved in—mostly jewelry. I went to management first thing this morning. They weren't sure they wanted to press charges without doing an internal investigation first, but due to the murder they agreed that I had to contact the detectives."

"Is he under arrest?" Dana asked.

Beecham shook his head. "They just want to bring him in for questioning."

"What will happen?"

"I don't know, Dana. He might be involved in the murder, so brace yourself."

She pulled a tissue from her purse and blotted the sweat forming on her upper lip. This was a lot to take in.

"What about Jason White?" she asked, picturing the neat signature in the visitors' log. "Did you ever figure out who he was? Does he have any connection to Adam?"

"That's for the detectives to figure out. I shared a copy of the security tape with them, so I assume they'll try to identify him."

"There's a security tape?" Dana asked.

"Of course."

"It shows his face?"

"Pretty clearly," Beecham said.

Dana considered this. She doubted he would look familiar, but she burned with curiosity. This was the mystery man. Their connection to the murderer. "Can I take a look?" she asked.

"I don't see why not," Beecham said, and started to tap at the computer keyboard on his desk. After several moments, he told Dana to turn toward monitor five on his wall, which was now playing a video of the front desk with a time stamp showing the date of Kitty's death. Zack was at the front desk.

After a few moments a man in a dark coat and baseball cap approached the desk and spoke to Zack. Beecham clicked something on his keyboard, and a different camera angle appeared on the screen, showing the back of Zack's head, and the front of the man in the baseball cap signing the visitors' log as Jason White.

The man looked up just as Dana leaned forward, and she gasped as goose bumps rippled up her arms. She opened her mouth to speak, and couldn't get anything out.

"Freeze it!" she finally said, and he did.

"You know who that man is?" he asked.

"Oh my God," she said, gripping the arms of her chair as if she needed to pin herself to earth. "Oh hell. Oh fuck."

"What's wrong?" Beecham asked. He looked from the screen to Dana.

She stared at the monitor, trying to make sense of the constellation of facts struggling to connect into a coherent picture. There was no doubt who the man was—the square face, the strawberry blond hair peeking out from under his cap. It was Kimmo.

She didn't want to believe what it meant. She *couldn't* believe what it meant.

"Are you okay?" Beecham asked.

She was cold as stone, and understood that her face had

probably gone ashen. But she found her voice and looked Beecham in the eye.

"That's Ollie's boyfriend," she said. "That's Kimmo. He's the one pretending to be Jason White."

She sat back and hugged herself as the scenario played out. If Ollie's friend Kimmo was posing as Jason White, who had signed in saying he had an appointment with Honeycutt, it meant Ollie was the one setting up the company president for Kitty's murder. Now that she thought about it, Dana understood that Ollie had carefully manipulated her to dig for the evidence in the logbook. Even the sex tape was part of the setup. Despite his protestations, Ollie had meant all along for Dana to conclude that Honeycutt was the murderer.

The one thing Ollie hadn't counted on was her sudden appearance at Kimmo's birthday dinner. That was why Ollie had looked so tense when she showed up. It wasn't because he was self-conscious about his relationship. It was because he didn't want her to be able to identify Kimmo.

She couldn't breathe. Because it all added up to a truth she couldn't accept: that Ollie had murdered Kitty Todd.

All the evidence was there and yet Dana felt sure, deep in her gut, that it was impossible. Ollie loved Kitty. He worshipped her. His devotion was pathological. It simply didn't fit. There was no reason for him to kill her.

Dana closed her eyes, trying to picture the murder scene again. There was something she was missing.

Beecham picked up the phone and dialed a number.

"Who are you calling?" she asked. She wanted to slow him down and listen to her before he took it any further.

But Beecham held up a hand to quiet her and spoke into the receiver. "Ms. Zidel? It's Beecham." He paused. "You'd better get down here."

37

Sherry took it all in so stoically Dana thought the woman's teeth would crack. When Beecham finally finished explaining the facts, she simply pushed her glasses up on her nose and said, "I see."

"What do you see?" Dana asked.

"It's obvious," Sherry said. "Ollie is guilty. He's the one who murdered Kitty."

"I don't think so," Dana said.

Sherry rolled her eyes. "Don't be ridiculous. He did everything possible to frame Charles Honeycutt. There's no other conclusion."

"There might be," Dana said, wondering how to explain the feeling deep in her gut that countered every piece of evidence.

"Such as?"

"I'm still working on it," she admitted.

Sherry waved away her comment. "Don't be so naive. Just because he seems innocent doesn't mean he is."

"What will you do now?" Dana asked. "Are you going to call the police? Do we just stay down here waiting for them to come for Ollie? Will we—"

Sherry held up her hands to slow Dana down. "First of all,

no one's taking Ollie out of here in handcuffs. At least not today. He called in sick this morning."

Dana's eyes went wide. She knew this was yet another piece of damning evidence against Ollie, and it gave her pause. If Ollie had stayed home because he was feeling the heat, it was a troubling sign. "Do you think he knew that we might—"

"I have no idea," Sherry said. "I just hope he's not already on a plane back to Finland. Right now, the most important thing we can do is go through our day and pretend everything is fine. Because people around here gossip. A lot. And if Ollie learns he's a suspect before the police can find him, he'll flee for sure."

"So you want me to pretend it's just an ordinary day?" Dana asked her.

"You'd *better*."

Dana shook her head, wondering what on earth could get this woman to give it a rest. "Don't forget my segment producer was taken by the police for questioning," she said. "Not exactly a run-of-the-mill morning for me."

Sherry rubbed her head as if massaging a problem. "I have to find a last-minute substitute producer for you," she said. "And Emily is in a meeting with the buyers."

Now Emily was meeting with buyers? Sherry seemed to think the girl was some kind of Shopping Channel prodigy.

"Guess I'll have to do it myself," Sherry said.

Herself? *Shit.* Despite everything going on, this felt like the single thing that could push Dana over the edge. She tried to think of anything to say that might convince Sherry it was a terrible idea, but there wasn't an excuse in sight.

"Don't look so excited," Sherry said.

Dana exhaled, trying to cover for her miserable expression. "It's just a lot to take in."

"I know you think I'm a witch," Sherry said with a wave, as if it didn't matter.

Dana opened her mouth to protest, groping for a quasi-sincere rebuttal, but Sherry cut her off. "Don't even bother."

Dana offered a weak smile in agreement—not her most convincing performance. Then she and Sherry lingered in Beecham's office as he called Detective Marks to report what had happened.

"Yes," Beecham said after several minutes. "She's positive about the identification... Uh-huh. She's right here. Hold on." He handed the phone to Dana. "He wants to talk to you."

Dana didn't feel prepared to face his icy hostility. Not now, in the middle of all this. She cleared her throat, and hoped for even a hint of kindness in his voice—something to indicate he might be willing to forgive her.

"Hello?" she said, trying not to sound as needy as she felt. She wanted to come across as strong, smart and in command. The kind of person who would never dream of sending twenty-six desperate texts.

His voice was cold. "I'm going to keep this businesslike, Dana."

"Good," she said, as if it was exactly what she had hoped to hear.

"Beecham tells me you identified the man on the security tape."

"I did," she said.

"Tell me," he said. "In your own words."

"It was Kimmo, Ollie's roommate."

"Are you certain?"

"One hundred percent. I met him on the same day..." She paused and looked from Beecham to Sherry. "I mean, it was only last week. Tuesday."

There was a pause, and she could tell he was connecting the

dots and recalling that it was the night they had been together. But all he said was, "Okay. Thank you. We'll be in touch."

When Dana showed up at the makeup department, Felicia and Jo were twirled in breathless gossip about Adam.

"Did they really take him out in handcuffs?" Felicia asked as she stroked contour onto the hollows of Dana's cheeks.

"I heard he took a swing at the detective," Jo said, running a buffer across Dana's fingernails.

"The handsome one?" Felicia asked.

"It was nothing like that," Dana insisted. "There were no handcuffs. No arrest. They just brought him in for questioning."

"You sure?" Jo said.

"Saw it with my own eyes."

"I think he might've done it," Felicia said.

"He *was* sleeping with Kitty," Jo observed. "Maybe he got jealous over the whole Honeycutt thing."

Dana sighed. She was certain the evidence had already ruled out Adam as a suspect. But she understood that there was no force on earth more powerful than a rumor mill, and there wasn't a damned thing she could do to stop the giant wheel from churning out chaff.

Even Lorenzo wasn't immune from participating. When she got to the set and he clipped on her microphone, he leaned in and whispered, "I'm hearing a lot of shit about Adam."

"Most of it untrue," she said.

"Sounds like you have inside information."

She shrugged, understanding the seriousness of Sherry's admonition against gossip. "Guess I'm the one keeping secrets now."

Dana put in her earpiece and waited for Sherry's signal as she closed her eyes, meditating herself into a place of peace and focus. She couldn't afford to think about Adam or Ollie or Kitty or even Mrs. Woodbridge. She had to be in the moment. *Nothing exists but your sublime love for these handbags*, she told herself. But it didn't work as well as it usually did. Today, they weren't the panacea for every problem in the human race. They were just handbags.

When the red light came on, she was more hyper than usual, compensating for her trouble focusing. "It's the final day of our handbag extravaganza!" she gushed. She thought she sounded a little too ebullient. Maybe even crazy. But viewers responded, and the show took off like a rocket. Thank God for her training. She could fake it like a pro.

Today, the monitor was working and she could track the spikes in sales. She oozed and gasped over the expensive satchel bags in nine different colors, the trim, triple-zip crossbody and even the new team spirit medium shopper's tote, which was available with patterned imprints of major league baseball team logos. That one was the toughest sell, but somehow they were moving.

The show seemed to drag on and on and on. An endless parade of adjectives becoming superlatives and morphing into sales figures.

At last, she glanced at the clock and saw that her time was winding down. Dana was elated. She had done it. She had gotten through the show. In another minute, she would pull out her earpiece, unclip her mike and run out the door. It was opening night, and she could barely wait.

"Vanessa's not here yet," she heard Sherry whisper. "You need to stretch."

Oh, no, Dana thought. Not again. Not tonight.

But she had no choice. And so she continued jabbering about the team spirit handbags. So fun! So different! Such a perfect way to show your team pride! Meanwhile, her heart was thudding to the beat of *Get out, get out, get out.*

"Small problem," Sherry said after several minutes. "Vanessa's stuck on the Long Island Expressway again. You'll have to fill in."

What? No! This was not supposed to happen. Vanessa couldn't be stuck in Long Island traffic on a Friday. She lived in the city during the week...didn't she?

"Don't worry," Sherry said. "Won't happen again. I'll tell Vanessa she can't keep commuting from the Hamptons."

A lot of good that did Dana now. She had to get off the air this minute. But how? She was broadcasting live. She couldn't very well just unclip her mike and walk off the air. At least, not without getting fired.

No, she had to think of something to say. Some way to introduce a promo clip so she could appeal to Sherry off the air.

But she knew that Sherry would never let her go. She would say that Dana had to stay on the air. There was no one else around to cover for Vanessa.

That was when she got an idea.

"I have some exciting news!" she said through the camera lens to the friend sitting on her sofa, remote in hand. "Filling in for Vanessa Valdes tonight is a brand-new Shopping Channel host, Emily Lauren. She'll be here in just a few minutes, and I can't wait for you to meet her!"

"No!" Sherry whispered, furious. "You can't do that. Emily's not prepped. She's not in hair or makeup. She's just out of a meeting. You have to stay on the air."

Dana continued smiling into the camera. "We're going to break for a promo right now, and when we come back, you'll be in for a treat. Have a lovely night!"

"Damn you!" Sherry said, but she scrambled to get a promotional clip on the air as Dana ripped off her mike.

Sherry came huffing out of the control booth, looking murderous.

"What the hell was that?" she seethed. Dana noticed that her eyebrows were pulled so close together it looked like they could change places.

"I have to go, Sherry," Dana said. "I'm sorry. It's not open for negotiation."

"Are you going to try to tell me you have another *doctor's appointment*?" She made it sound like there were quotes around the words.

"I just…have someplace to be. That's all. I'm sure you can get Emily on the air in five minutes. She'll be thrilled."

"If you walk out that door, don't bother coming back."

"Are you kidding?" Dana said. She had expected anger, but not this.

"You heard me," Sherry said. "You leave and you're fired."

"No, she's not," came a voice from behind. It was Megan, stepping out of the darkness.

Sherry turned to her. "What are you doing here?"

Megan shrugged. "I had a sense my client needed me."

Sherry folded her arms. "How very…*supportive*." Her tone was sharp enough to draw blood. "But I have a business to run, and I can't have a host who's not willing to go the distance when I need her. If she leaves, you'll never see—"

"You can be as pissed off as you like," Megan said. "But we have a contract, and she's not in breach." She turned to Dana. "Come on. Let's get you out of here."

Dana scurried after Megan to her dressing room, so grateful to her friend that her eyes watered. At the same time, guilt pelted her like a sudden storm. She wished she hadn't lied to Megan about Sweat City. She deserved the truth. Dana decided she couldn't keep the secret a second longer.

"There's something I need to tell you," she said.

Megan glanced down at her phone, as if she were barely paying attention. "I'm listening."

Dana considered her words as she pulled off the cream dress she had worn on the air. She put it on a hanger, and then grabbed her jeans, which she wriggled into with a jump and a tug. "There's a reason I'm in such a hurry to get out of here tonight," Dana said.

Megan glanced up from her phone. "I'm listening."

"It's the show," Dana said. "I never really quit Sweat City. I'm playing Mrs. Woodbridge. It's opening night."

There was a moment of silence as Megan took it in, and Dana braced herself for the recriminations. She was ready to apologize. To beg forgiveness. To take full responsibility. She pulled on her T-shirt.

"I know," Megan finally said.

Dana stared at her. "Huh?"

"I've known for weeks. Why do you think I came here today? I wanted to make sure that witch didn't try to keep you a minute late tonight."

"I..." Dana said, trying to catch up. "How did you find out?"

"I know you too well, Dana. You should have realized you couldn't keep such a big secret from me."

"But you seemed so—"

"It took me a little while, I admit. I didn't want to believe you would lie to me. So when you moved on and didn't wallow in grief and anger over leaving Sweat City, I told myself you were just evolving into the kind of person who could let go, and that it was a good thing. But that night after I rushed over from the dentist..."

"And I pretended to have a headache," Dana offered.

Megan nodded. "Even then, I bought it. But when I woke up the next day and replayed the scene, I realized you didn't have a headache until I brought up the idea of going out to-gether. It made me suspicious enough to sneak into the Sweat City rehearsals the next time I was downtown, and there you were."

"But why didn't you say anything?"

"Because I knew it was torturing you and you deserved it, you little shit. Why didn't you think you could trust me?"

Dana threw her arms around her friend. "I'm so sorry!"

"I would hope so."

"I should have told you."

"Of course you should have. You should never lie to your manager."

"Or your best friend," Dana added. "How can I make it up to you?"

Megan said she would think about it, then walked Dana outside and hailed a cab for her. She opened the door.

"Wait a second," Dana said before getting in. She reached into her purse and pulled out a comp ticket for that night's performance. "Will you come?" she asked, holding it toward her friend.

Megan snatched it from her. "Of course, you idiot. I wouldn't miss opening night."

"Do you want to share the cab?"

Megan shook her head. "I'll stay behind and smooth things over with Sherry. Now go break a leg. I'll catch up with you after the show."

An hour later, Dana was in makeup and costume, sitting in the green room with the rest of the cast as Nathan reviewed his notes from last night's dress rehearsal.

"How's the crowd?" Raj asked when Nathan wrapped up.

"It's early, but I think we'll have a full house," Nathan said.

Some of the cast members ambled out so they could get a peek at the auditorium as it filled, but Dana stayed put, her head down as she focused on clearing out the stress of escaping Sherry's stinging tentacles so she could get to the theater, as well as the shock of discovering that her quivering assistant had been framing Charles Honeycutt. There was no room in her head for any of that. She had to concentrate on getting into character. Tyrel, who sat across from her, did the same thing, folding his trembling hands into his lap.

After a few minutes, she heard Nathan say, "Can I help you?"

Dana looked up and had a moment of déjà vu. Ari Marks stood in the doorway beside the red velvet curtain. Only this time, she wasn't in the middle of watching a sex tape.

"What are you doing here?" she asked.

Tyrel came to attention and gave Ari Marks the once-over. "Ooh! Now this one's a keeper," he stage-whispered to Dana.

The detective's face remained serious. "I have some news," he said to Dana. "I thought you'd want to know right away."

She stared at him, hoping it was about Kitty Todd's real killer, and grateful that he still cared enough to deliver important news in person.

"What is it?" she said, but before he could answer, another person appeared behind him. It was Megan, looking alarmed.

"Everything okay?" Dana asked her.

"Yes and no," Megan said, a little breathless. "Vanessa showed up on set, so that's the good news."

"And the bad news?"

"Sherry's here, with Emily."

"What?" Dana felt dizzy with shock. This was a disaster.

"I just wanted to let you know so you have time to process the information. I thought it might throw off your game if you spotted her in the audience during the performance."

"But...what are they doing here?"

"Sherry found out about the show. Someone tipped her off."

Betrayal. The thought of it made Dana sick. "Who could have told her?" she asked, glancing at Ari. Would he have done such a thing out of spite?

"Not me!" he said.

"No, no," Megan said. "It was that efficient Shopping Channel rumor mill. Apparently, some receptionist from the executive suite has a friend in the Sweat City Company and she found out. She whispered it to a coworker who whispered it to someone else, and the next thing you know it got back to Sherry. She thought it was some idle rumor, and since you denied it and she couldn't trace it back to the source, she let it go. But not completely. And then, after you ran out tonight, she wrung a few necks until someone pointed at the receptionist, who admitted it was true."

The assistant director poked her head into the room and gave the ten-minute warning.

"Wrap this up," Nathan said to Dana. "I'll be calling places soon."

He left, and Dana looked back at Megan. "So I'm fired?" she asked. "Right after the performance?"

"Maybe sooner," someone said, and then Sherry appeared in the doorway with Emily Lauren.

Dana put her head in her hands. "And I thought learning that Ollie was being arrested for murder would be today's big news."

"I'm not arresting Oliver Sikanen for murder," Ari said. "That's what I came here to tell you."

Sherry turned her glare from Dana to Ari. "But he's *guilty*," she seethed. "And he tried to frame my boss."

Ari shook his head. "Ollie isn't the killer."

"Then it was his friend," Sherry said. "That Kimmo. Ollie must have hired him to—"

"It wasn't Kimmo, either," Ari said.

"I knew it!" Dana said. "I *knew* Ollie couldn't be guilty. Kimmo, either. I just couldn't put the pieces together."

"This might help," Ari said. "The forensics report just came in and it led us to the truth, though we still have more questions than answers."

"What did it reveal?" Dana asked.

Ari cleared his throat. "The trajectory of the bullet plus the powder marks on Kitty's hand tell the story. It wasn't a murder staged to look like a suicide." He paused. "It was a suicide staged to look like a murder."

Tyrel, who had been listening to the whole conversation, said, "I'm confused as hell."

"You're in good company," Megan added.

But in a chill of understanding, Dana got it. The whole picture.

"Kitty Todd's murderer was Kitty herself!" Dana said. "She pulled the trigger. She committed suicide, but not before enlisting Ollie's help. He put the gun back in her hand after she killed herself, and did everything else she had asked him to do."

"Why would he help her like that?" Sherry asked. "And why would Kitty stage her own murder?"

"We're still working on that," Ari said.

"I knew she was twisted," Megan offered. "But it still doesn't make sense."

It does if you go deep inside character motivation, Dana thought. It was all a matter of getting in someone else's head and thinking like them.

"I think I can help," Dana said to Ari. "In her own disturbed way, Kitty loved Honeycutt. Loved him obsessively. She felt like they were meant to be together, and was willing to do anything to get him to see that. And to get him to leave his wife for her. She believed, deep in her core, that this was the right thing to do. Kitty felt like she understood the depth of their love, and was fulfilling some mission by getting Honeycutt to see that. And so she slept with other men to get him jealous. When that didn't work, she tried blackmailing him with a sex tape. She convinced herself that each of these things would work. But when it became clear at last that there were no other doors open for her, she snapped. It wasn't even the first time she had a breakdown." Dana paused to look at Sherry, who nodded.

"We had to hospitalize her once after she tried to kill herself. But I thought she was better."

Dana continued. "I'm taking a leap here, but playing a character like Mrs. Woodbridge helps me understand the mind of a person whose rage short-circuits their reason. Once Kitty knew that Charles really didn't love her, she became consumed by irrational anger. His rejection shook the foundation of her beliefs, and she decided that if he didn't love her, he must be... I don't know. Evil. Or something like that. In any case, she felt justified in wanting to hurt him as much as possible. She was so irrational it was worth dying over. So she came up with this elaborate plot to kill herself and frame him as the murderer. Sending him to prison for murder."

"You know, I can buy all that," Megan said. "But how did she convince Ollie to help her?"

"It was a perfect storm of two damaged souls," Dana said. "Ollie worshipped Kitty. She was a substitute mother for him. And he had so much death in his young life that it must have seemed natural to him that yet another mother figure would be taken from him. I mean, he probably objected at first— even begged and pleaded. I can imagine his terrible desperation at losing her. But Kitty knew how to manipulate him. She had the power to convince Ollie that by helping her do this thing, he was somehow saving her in a way he had been unable to save his own mother."

"This is some sick Freudian shit," Tyrel said.

"Like Shakespeare meets Quentin Tarantino," Megan added.

For the first time, Emily spoke up. "So Kitty staged her suicide to look like a murder that had been staged to look like a suicide."

Tyrel stared at Emily then, and didn't look away. He was trying to catch her eye, but she wouldn't glance up. Dana was more interested in Ari's reaction to her revelations than in any drama between these two, and studied his face.

He looked at her, and she noted the wave of emotions that flickered across his eyes, like a whole movie in a single second. She thought she saw admiration, and maybe even longing. But it was quickly crowded out by hurt, then washed clean with stoicism. He set his jaw back to its inscrutable position and locked it in place.

"And I thought *you* were a twisted bitch," Megan said to Sherry.

Sherry ignored the insult as she tried to process the news. "So Ollie's *not* a killer," she said, like she was thinking out loud and trying to decide if the news was a relief.

"An accessory," Ari said. "And then there are the obstruction of justice charges."

Sherry grunted. "If I'd known she was this psychotic, I never would have let her back on the air."

Dana glanced at Tyrel, who'd spent a lifetime dealing with mental illness. If he was hurt by Sherry's remark, he didn't show it.

"Was she medicated?" he asked.

Sherry threw her arms up. "That wasn't any of my business."

"Nah," Dana said to Tyrel. "I doubt she would take medication."

Ari folded his arms. "And how do you know that?"

"Because hand tremors are a possible side effect. I just don't think Kitty would have taken that risk. Her hands were her livelihood."

The assistant director called into the room, "Places in five!"

"I'm sorry," Dana said to the assembled group. "You have to go now."

"This doesn't mean you're not fired," Sherry said to Dana.

"I know," Dana said, frowning. She turned to Emily. "I guess this means you're getting my job. Congratulations."

Tyrel looked up. "I just remembered your name!" he said to Emily.

She turned her face away. "I think you have me confused with someone."

"No, I don't," he said. "We took a class together."

"That wasn't me," she insisted.

"Sure it was," Tyrel said. "Only you weren't Emily Lauren back then. You were Emily Zidel."

"Zidel?" Dana said.

The oxygen seemed to drain from the room, as Emily looked horrified and Sherry's hands went to her head.

"Your daughter?" Megan asked.

Sherry sighed, defeated. "My niece."

"Doesn't the Shopping Channel have a policy against nepotism?" Dana asked.

"It sure does," Megan said. "That's why she hired her niece under a different name."

Sherry folded her arms. "This is confidential information. You'd better keep it to yourself."

Megan wedged her body between Sherry and Emily, and put an arm around each of them. "I can be persuaded," she said, and Dana knew that her friend would manage to broker an agreement that would let her keep her job.

Sherry snorted, catching Megan's meaning. "Fine," she said through her teeth. "But I'll need you both to agree to keep quiet."

Dana was about to weigh in when the AD called, "Places!"

The crowd shuffled out of the room, engaged in a conversation Dana consciously blocked out. She needed to remove herself from everything that had just happened. She needed to become Mrs. Woodbridge. This time, she couldn't fake it. She had to be all in.

"Break a leg," Megan said. "You got this."

Dana lingered in the green room as the cast took their places. Then she heard Nathan's sonorous voice over the speakers. He thanked the crowd for coming, asked them to please silence their cell phones.

And then the play began. Everything else faded away as Dana inhabited Jeanette Woodbridge for the next two and a half hours. She wasn't Dana again until it was time for the curtain call, and the houselights came on. It was only then that she looked out into the audience. She saw Megan, Sherry and Emily. Her eyes continued roaming, as there were two people she hoped she might see. One was Ari, who would be easy to spot. But apparently he hadn't stayed for the performance. Of course not, she told herself. He was in the middle of a huge break in a murder case. Or rather, a suicide case with some nefarious elements. Either way, he couldn't take the time to stop for a show, whether he wanted to or not.

Her disappointment didn't last more than a second, because Dana spotted the other person she was looking for. Chelsea. Her sister had said she couldn't promise anything, because she didn't know if she could get a sitter for opening night, but there she was, in the second row, with Brandon by her side.

And then Dana noticed who was sitting next to them. Her father and Jennifer Lafferty. They were on their feet, like the rest of the audience, giving Dana a standing ovation.

38

On Sunday morning, Dana was grateful Megan brought bagels, lox and coffee over for breakfast, but even more grateful she had brought a copy of *Theatrix*, a weekly trade publication, folded open to a review page. She slapped it down on the table in front of Dana. The headline read *The Racist Next Door*.

"Good or bad?" Dana asked, nervously pulling up the V-neck of the oversize sagging T-shirt she had slept in.

"No spoilers," Megan said, grinning. "Just read it out loud."

Dana could tell by her friend's face that it was a positive review. But she didn't know how positive. It was a New York City theater critic, after all, and those folks believed they weren't doing their job if they didn't throw at least some shade. She took a calming breath and began.

"You have been invited into the home of the beleaguered Mrs. Woodbridge, a seemingly quiet play written by Mindy Radler and deftly directed by Nathan P. Thompson."

She stopped to look up. "Deftly! Nathan will be thrilled."

"Read on," Megan said, biting back her smile.

Dana nodded and continued.

"Put upon by a disabled husband, annoying neighbor and world 'gone madhouse crazy' by political correctness—not to mention a toaster oven that can never seem to get it right—the character's racism finds outlets in almost every situation. The narcissism on display might have veered into discomfort for the audience if not for the multifaceted performance of newcomer Kayla Bean in the title role."

Dana stopped to take a quick gasping breath as she broke out in an excited sweat. Multifaceted! She went on.

"Like a young Frances McDormand, she inhabits her character's self-image with grace and pride. Ms. Bean didn't try to oversell here. She simply exposes Mrs. Woodbridge's heart and lets the audience intuit the ache. In the second act—"

"The rest is pretty standard," Megan said, cutting her off. "Except for the last line."

With her heart beating as wildly as a bag of birds, Dana read the rest to herself. The critic had praised most of the cast, and only took exception to the "lackluster" set. Then she stared with disbelief at the last lines.

Not your standard small-theater fare, *Mrs. Woodbridge* might make you rethink some of your own biases. And even if it doesn't, it's worth seeing for the breakout talent of Kayla Bean in the title role.

Dana's fingertips went numb. It was the kind of review she had dreamed of her whole life. But of course, she never imagined the credit would go to a nonexistent version of herself, and that no one could ever know she had received this glorious review.

"I don't even know how to feel about this," Dana said, but as soon as the words were out, she felt her heart crack into pieces, and tears spilled down her face. This could have been her big break. And it would amount to nothing.

She read the review a second time, imagining it from the perspective of a talent scout. "I feel like I'm going to have a stroke or something."

"Don't you dare. You're my only client."

Dana's cell phone rang. It was Nathan. For him, this was a momentous review. Dana wiped her tears and exhaled. This was no time to be petty. No matter how terrible she felt, she had to be happy for her friend. She silently counted to ten before answering the phone.

"*Theatrix!*" she said, instead of hello. And then her emotional damn burst. Dana was racked with sobs, the line between her happiness for Nathan and her own self-pity vanished. Megan handed her a bagel store napkin to blow her nose.

"I was waiting for a decent hour to call you," he said.

"Congratulations, my deft director," she choked out.

He laughed. "Congratulations to you, too!"

"You mean to Kayla," she said, and added a laugh so he wouldn't think she was bitter. She wanted him to be able to bask in this success.

"One day," he said, "this will be an asterisk in your brilliant career—a funny anecdote for a talk show."

When she got off the phone, Dana took several struggling, jagged inhales and assured Megan she was okay. After all, she still had more performances of *Mrs. Woodbridge* to get through, and couldn't afford to be distracted.

"I'll grieve for my career when I have time," Dana said.

Megan shook her head, exasperated. "Your acting career is not over." She held up the magazine. "This is proof that you have the goods. It'll all happen. We just need to have a little patience. Once your two-year contract with the Shopping Channel expires—"

"But this could deliver opportunities," Dana said, grabbing the magazine from Megan's hand. "And I'll never get those back again."

"I promise you," Megan said. "We can use all of this to our advantage. We just have to make a plan."

"What kind of plan?"

"Okay," Megan said, and began ticking off the elements of the plan on her fingers. "One, we keep quiet about your secret identity. Get it? You're Clark Kent. No one can know you're Superman or the consequences will be dire."

"You mean I'll get fired from the Shopping Channel."

"It's more serious than that," Megan said. "Sherry was willing to not shitcan you and keep management off your back. But things are more complicated now. If news gets out that you've been in breach of contract and Sherry covered for you, she'd be neck-deep in it, too. So Sherry would get fired…and you'd get sued."

"In other words, I'm screwed."

"God, no. You're thinking about this all wrong. You've got a great job. A job you're *brilliant* at. A boatload of money. National exposure. And when your contract is up, if you don't want to stay with the Shopping Channel, you just say the word. At that point, I can let it leak that you had this secret identity and kept it quiet despite the rave reviews. It'll be a big story and then…well, then you'll have options. This whole thing can play out in ways you can't even dream of right now. Trust me."

Dana took it all in and knew that she did, in fact, trust

Megan. She took another bagel store napkin from the table and dried her wet cheeks. The sadness and sorrow floated off, replaced by something that felt as light as a feather. Hope.

39

On Monday, Dana was back at the Shopping Channel like it was a regular day. Only there was nothing regular about it. Sherry informed her that Ollie and Kimmo had been taken into custody, and would probably be deported. The station was pressing charges against Adam, who was apparently out on bail.

"And my new segment producer?" Dana asked.

"We're giving Jessalyn a shot," Sherry said, clearly treading more carefully on the whole nepotism thing. She gave Dana a look that warned her not to bring it up.

For the time being, Lorenzo was still there, and he stopped into her dressing room for a private chat before the show.

"I gave notice this morning," he said, smiling.

"Congratulations," Dana said. "When are you moving?"

"Well, that's the funny thing. I might not."

She studied his face, trying to understand. He was happy, so it couldn't be bad news. "What do you mean?"

"They made me a counteroffer. Ten percent more than the QVC job."

"So…you're staying?"

"I'm thinking about it."

"What about the house and the yard and the good schools?"

"Well, yeah. I want all that. On the other hand, I have family here. So, I have some thinking to do."

Dana noticed that he didn't say anything about a possible continuation of their relationship, and any role it might play in his decision. Just as well. Ari was taking up so much space in her heart it was as if he held the mortgage. If only she could find a way to set him straight about her relationship with Lorenzo.

The next morning, she got her chance. She was at home in her apartment when a call came in from the Thirteenth Precinct. Dana tried to tell herself it wasn't Ari. No way. It was probably Detective Lee calling again. Maybe he wanted her to identify Kimmo in a lineup or something.

Still, her hopes were raised. After all, Ari did come to the performance of *Mrs. Woodbridge* Sunday night. So maybe. Maybe.

She took a long gulp of water to moisten her dry throat, and said hello. And there it was—Ari's seductive voice, flooding her with buoyant optimism.

"Congratulations," he said. "I understand you got a glowing review."

Interesting, she thought. *Theatrix* wasn't exactly the *New York Times*. Ari wouldn't have stumbled upon the review. It took detective work for him to find it. This meant…something. At the very least, he was still interested in what she was up to.

"Thank you," she said, and waited for him to tell her he had seen the show.

"Are you still employed?" His tone was hard to read.

"Sherry agreed to keep my secret," she said, "as long as I keep hers."

"So you're working today?"

When she said that she was, he asked if she had any time to see him this morning.

"I do!" she responded, more eagerly than she had intended. If he was ready to listen, she was ready to talk. She knew she could explain everything and make him understand she hadn't lied to him about Lorenzo.

"Great. We need you to come in and make a statement."

"Excuse me?" she said, stalling as she got her bearings. It wasn't what she had expected to hear. She had imagined them sitting across from each other in a coffee shop, bearing their souls. But it was okay. Dana could make this work.

"I said we need you to make a—"

"I'll do it," she said, "on one condition."

"And what's that?"

"I get to talk for as long as I like, and nobody cuts me off."

He paused for only a moment and agreed.

By the time she arrived at the station an hour later, Dana had gone through the story in her head several times. She could imagine Ari's expression. He'd be dubious at first. But by the time she was done, he would understand.

The same surly young man was at the front desk, and she wasn't in the mood for him.

"Excuse me, Officer McBride," she called from her caged position in the entryway. "I'm here to see Detective Marks. He—"

"Name?"

"Dana Barry, but I wanted to—"

"Have a seat."

"I just wanted to say it's important that I talk to Detective Marks. No one else."

"I heard you," he said. "Now have a seat."

She shot him a look and lowered herself into a black plastic chair. After a few minutes, Detective Lee appeared at the gate, and Dana gritted her teeth. This was not part of the bargain. She was here to tell her story to Ari.

"Ms. Barry?" he said.

She crossed her legs, making it clear she was in no hurry to get up. "Where's Marks?"

"He's a little busy right now."

"I'll wait," she said.

"I'm his partner," Lee said, folding his arms. He was smaller and thinner than Ari, but imposing in his fastidiousness. Dressed in a dark blue suit and striped shirt with a carefully matched tie, he looked like someone who insisted on being taken seriously.

"I understand that," she said, and added, "I prefer to give my statement to him."

Lee paused for a moment and then sighed. "Suit yourself. But it could be a while."

Dana shrugged, and he went back to the elevator, leaving her behind on the hard plastic chair. She imagined that Marks was trying to teach her some kind of lesson by leaving her waiting. But she was determined to stick it out, and killed the time on her phone, texting her sister and Chelsea about this latest development.

At last, almost thirty minutes after Lee had walked away, Ari emerged. He looked strained—not a hint of joy at seeing her.

"You ready?" he asked.

"Born ready."

He didn't smile—just held open the metal gate, led her into the elevator, up to the fourth floor and down a hallway to an interrogation room.

"Really?" she said, peering inside. "Isn't this where you take suspects?"

"It's where we have the recording equipment," he said.

"You're recording my statement?"

"Of course," he said. "It goes straight to the DA."

Dana let out a breath. She hadn't anticipated this. But whatever. She'd talk and talk. And if they wanted to listen, so be it.

She lowered herself into the chair at the table and Ari sat across from her. She noted that the wall to her right was almost completely taken up with a mirror, which she knew was a one-way deal, and that it was entirely possible there was an audience on the other side. There was a camera mounted onto the table in front of her, pointed at her face. Another camera was mounted to the ceiling across the room.

Ari began by stating his name and Dana's, as well as the date. Then he addressed her. "I understand that you want to make a statement about your relationship with Oliver Sikanen, as well as the events just prior to and following the death of Kitty Todd. Is that correct?"

"Yes," she said, sitting erect. Dana was well aware of how she looked from the angles of both cameras. She didn't fidget, touch her face or straighten her hair. She kept a calm repose, her hands folded on her lap under the table.

"Is there something specific you want to address, or would you like to start from the beginning?"

Even under the harsh lights, he was strikingly handsome. But his eyes were pained today, ringed in dark circles. She could tell that he didn't want to be there, going through this exercise with her. It was as if he were braced for more hurt. Dana wished she could reach out to lay her hand on his and reassure him. But she glanced at the overhead camera, took a fortifying breath and trusted that when she was done, he'd understand.

"I'll start from the beginning," she said, and then she did, opening with her audition at the Shopping Channel, her first encounter with Lorenzo and her description of the Hector

Comb, which led to her only real encounter with Kitty Todd. She described her first impression of Ollie, and her callback audition the very next day. When she got to the part about going up onto the roof with Lorenzo, she noticed Ari shift subtly in his seat.

"It was a beautiful view," she said, "and I was in a happy mood—glad I'd done well on the air, and anticipating good news."

"What happened next?"

"We heard a gunshot."

"What were you doing at that time?"

She assumed he was trying to get her to say something about the joint, but she still couldn't risk getting Lorenzo in trouble. Even though his parole had ended, he needed to keep his violations a secret.

"We were kissing," she said.

"Kissing?"

"On the lips. Do you need a description?" She knew this hurt him, but she had to take him through the worst of it to come out the other side.

His jaw went rigid. "That's fine," he said. "Go on."

She recounted the details she had told him the day of Kitty's death. When she got to the part about the crowd rushing toward Kitty's office, he asked her to identify exactly who was there, to the best of her recollection.

"And what happened next?" he asked.

She explained about getting the job and how she agreed to take on Ollie as her own personal assistant. She went through every false lead he gave her, from the carefully leaked information about Kitty and Charles Honeycutt, to the sex tape and the visitors' log.

"The one thing he hadn't accounted for was that I would meet Kimmo and be able to identify him as the guy who'd posed as Jason White—the supposed hit man hired by Honey-cutt."

She talked about the sabotage of her show, and how she had wondered if it was the killer coming after her for getting too close to the truth.

"And now?" he asked.

"Now I know it was Adam Weintraub, my segment producer, who thought I might discover his thefts and report him."

"Thank you, Ms. Barry," he said. "I think that wraps it up."

"I'm not done," she said. "There's more you need to know."

He folded his arms and leaned back, as if he were considering it. Or maybe waiting for her to change her mind. She glared, daring him to stop her. Because Dana was determined—she wasn't leaving that room until she'd had her say.

Finally, he exhaled. "Go on."

"During the investigation, you kept pressing me about my relationship with Lorenzo. You suspected him because he has a criminal record. Only he had an alibi—me—and that was a problem for your theory. So you wanted to believe I was willing to lie for him."

"I was only after the truth. And let's not forget—you *did* lie for him."

"Only the part about not having a relationship. The alibi was true. You know that now. I'm sorry I had to lie to you about Lorenzo and me, but I stand by that decision. If I had it to do over again, I'd probably play it the same way." She paused and leaned toward him. "I just couldn't let him go to jail, Ari."

He furrowed his brow at the use of his first name.

She continued speaking to him, not the camera. "I met his little girl." Her voice was slow, gentle. "She's so tiny, Ari. So young. Can't even tie her own shoes yet, and Lorenzo is all she's got. He takes such good care of her. You'd be impressed."

"Are you finished?"

"No." She paused to make sure she had his full attention. "We got into a fight. Me and Lorenzo. You need to know that."

"About what?"

She shook her head. "It doesn't matter. Point is, we didn't speak for days. He kept trying to explain himself to me, but I was too hurt to listen."

For a second, his eyes softened, and she couldn't help adding, "Sound familiar?"

She thought he would reply with a grunt, but instead he said, "Maybe."

She went on. "When I finally let him tell me what was happening, he explained that he had a chance at a better life for him and his daughter—a job out of state. He was just waiting for his parole to end so that if the job came through, he could move." She was cagey in the way she presented the details, not revealing that Lorenzo had traveled out of state for the interview while still on parole. If Ari noticed, he didn't let on.

"And this was a great job," she continued. "Higher pay, terrific company, easier lifestyle. At that moment, I forgave him. It was over between us—it was never really right, anyway. But I was excited for him to have a chance at a better life. And then he told me the big news—the job offer came through and he accepted. I was so thrilled for him I threw my arms around him. He spun me around in a celebratory whirl and..."

"And that's when I walked in."

"Exactly."

"Are you done *now*?" he asked.

She searched his face, looking for any indication that he

forgave her. But he was so stoic she was sure she had been unsuccessful.

"Yes." She felt like a failure, and sorrow washed over her. But at least she had explained herself. At least there was that. "I'm done."

She sat there, her head down, as he got up to shut off the cameras. He pulled back his chair and sat down again. Then he leaned forward, snaked his fingers under the table and grabbed her hand.

She looked up into his eyes and saw it. He forgave her.

40

Dana and Ari went on a real date—dinner and a much-too-long experimental theater production starring Gwendolyn Monk, an old friend of Dana's. Afterward, they went backstage and Dana found things to gush over. Ari was polite enough to say he'd never seen anything like it. When Gwendolyn introduced Dana to the other cast members with a reference to her job as a nationally known host on the Shopping Channel, the backstage energy shifted, and Dana found herself the center of attention. Not wishing to steal her friend's thunder, she told Gwendolyn again how brave her performance had been, and made a quick exit.

"Watch out for cats, Scar!" Gwendolyn called as the door closed behind them.

Before Dana could explain the inside joke to Ari, he took her hand and kissed it.

"What's that for?" she asked.

"I think you know."

She did. Somehow, he had intuited exactly why she had made a beeline for the exit. "If you're under the impression I'm some kind of a saint," she said, "you're going to be sorely disappointed."

"Is that a warning?"

"I just want you to know I'm not always so well-behaved."

"Actually, I was counting on it."

This time, when she invited him into her apartment, there was no mysterious bouquet in the doorway, no specter of another man getting in the way. It was just Dana and Ari, ravenous and eager, unable to get enough of each other.

And in the weeks that followed, the heat didn't diminish. If anything, it intensified. Dana felt herself swept into the delirious current of new love. Yet despite her joy, she was aware of a subtle but insidious undertow—the fear of heartbreak.

So when she got the invitation to her father and Jennifer's wedding—addressed to *Ms. Dana Barry and Guest*—she didn't know what to do. Sure, she wanted Ari to come with her. In fact, the idea of it was like a dream. She wanted him there, by her side. Drinking with her. Dancing with her, especially if a Motown song came on. He had a strange obsession with that genre. Fortunately, it was the only trait he seemed to share with her father.

But she was afraid to even bring it up. Because it seemed like just the kind of thing that could jinx a couple. It was exactly what had derailed her last two serious relationships. At least, that was the way it felt to Dana, as there were family events on the horizon when her last two boyfriends had cheated on her.

She tried to tell herself she was creating a superstition out of a coincidence, but it didn't help. And so she tucked the invitation in a drawer, and vowed to ask Ari about it later, when their sapling of relationship had grown deeper roots, and was strong enough to support the weight of a commitment.

"What's wrong?" Chelsea asked Dana a week later as she poured coffee from a French press into an oversize mug. She turned and handed it to her sister.

Dana took the filled-to-the-brim cup from her and set it carefully on the granite counter. "This isn't decaf, is it?"

"It's not decaf."

"Last time you gave me decaf and—"

"Three sips and you'll be bouncing off the walls," Chelsea said. "I promise."

Dana slurped off a sip and poured in a splash of milk before tasting it again. It was earthy and just bitter enough, with a roasted nutty finish. "It's good," she said.

"See? Now tell me what's wrong."

"Nothing is wrong."

"With Ari, I mean," Chelsea said.

As far as Dana was concerned, her relationship with Ari was wonderful. Sublime. They couldn't get enough of each other. But Chelsea was right, there was…something. Something that was still keeping her from bringing up the wedding invitation.

"Everything is great with Ari," she said.

Chelsea took the stool opposite her at the grand island in the middle of her pristine designer kitchen and blew across her coffee. "Except?" she prodded.

Dana sighed. "I don't know. I can't relax. I think the problem is that we had a fight before we even started."

"But he's committed now. He gets you. And he's not an unreasonable man."

Dana nodded. Her sister was absolutely right. Still, she couldn't quiet that rumble of uncertainty.

Chelsea took a small sip of her hot black coffee and made a face. She went to refrigerator, where she pressed on the ice dispenser and let a cube fall into her hand. "I know what the problem is," she said as she dropped it into her coffee.

"You do?"

"Deep down, you think you like him more than he likes you."

Dana looked up at her sister, whose back was to the window. The late-afternoon sun sat low and white on the horizon, making Chelsea's blond hair seem almost colorless. It hurt Dana's eyes, and she had to look away.

"It's true," she whispered, and it felt like the very admission she'd been hiding from herself.

"But it's *not*," Chelsea said. "That's my point. The guy is crazy about you. It's just that there's a part of you that thinks you don't deserve it."

"So how do I fix this?" Dana asked, feeling more like the little sister than she had in a long while.

"Just give it time," Chelsea said. "Your heart's a little stupid. It needs a chance to catch up."

Dana knew her sister was right, and within a few weeks her heart was just starting to get it. By then, the wedding was perilously close, and she hoped Ari would be able to laugh over how foolish she had been about bringing it up.

"Next weekend?" he asked, incredulous. They were in her apartment, getting ready to go out for breakfast.

"This can't be a complete surprise," she said. "You heard me talking about it. You knew I was buying a dress."

"But you never said anything, so I assumed I wasn't invited."

"I should have, I'm sorry." Dana paused, and decided that if she was honest, everything would be okay. "I was…afraid."

"Afraid of what?" he asked, his face strained with confusion.

"It felt like a bad omen. I know that's stupid. But Benjamin cheated on me a week before my cousin Zoe's wedding. And Chris started sleeping with his ex-wife just days before we were supposed to have Thanksgiving with my mom in Florida."

Ari's brow tightened, and it took a few minutes for him to respond, as if he needed to calm himself. "Dana, there is *always* something on the calendar for a couple."

"Well, it sounds so stupid when you put it like that."

"It *is* stupid," he said. "Don't you trust me?"

"Of course I do. I was just worried about our relationship. I didn't want to do anything to jinx it." She paused and took his hand. "Can you forgive me?"

"Of course I forgive you," he said, pulling her in for a hug. "But there's one problem."

She backed up to look at his face. "What's that?"

"I'm on duty next weekend."

Dana's heart plummeted. "Can't you get someone to cover for you?"

He shook his head. "Two of the detectives are away, and I'm already covering for Lee. He asked me to do him the favor, and since you hadn't said anything about the wedding, I agreed. At this point, it's too late. I'm committed."

Dana stared at him, wondering if it was really too late, or if a part of him wanted to punish her for stalling. But there was nothing she could do. He was resolute. Dana sighed and grabbed her purse.

"I wish I had your police academy training," she said as she hitched the strap over her shoulder.

"And why's that?"

"Because I might have learned to stop shooting myself in the foot."

41

Kenneth Barry's backyard—with its expansive view of the Long Island Sound—had been set up for a party and a ceremony. To the right, there were tables and a makeshift dance floor under a large tent. Straight ahead, in the open air, a chapel had been created with white chairs set up in rows, facing a canopy draped in billowy gauze. Dana tiptoed across the lawn, trying to keep her narrow heels from sinking into the earth, and found her sister, Brandon and Wesley sitting in the front row. Chelsea patted the empty seat next to her, and Dana settled in.

Kenneth already stood beneath the canopy, waiting to begin. As the music started, the crowd turned to see Jennifer walk down the aisle—in a silvery white satin gown—escorted by her elderly parents. They took seats in the front row as the bride went to stand beside her groom.

Dana had been told it would be a nonreligious ceremony, officiated by a woman Jennifer had known for years—an old friend who had been ordained. Dana wasn't sure what it took to be ordained, but she had pictured a plain woman with a bad haircut and a dull suit. Like a nun in street clothes. But the person who stood before them was more like an aging hippie guru goddess, swathed in something that resembled a sky blue toga.

"Did Dad agree to this?" Dana whispered to Chelsea, who shrugged.

Soon, Dana understood why Jennifer had chosen this fully bloomed bohemian to perform the ceremony. She was good. Inspiring. She delivered such a beautiful speech about the transformative power of love that the entire congregation of family and friends hung on her words. Dana felt herself choking up.

The biggest surprise was that her father and Jennifer had written their own vows. Dana braced herself, because she couldn't imagine anything heartfelt and romantic coming from her dad. Sure enough, his little speech made her wince, as he had written it in a forced and singsongy rhyme, with a meter inspired by Dr. Seuss. She glanced at her sister to see if she was laughing. Chelsea's head was down as she tried to contain herself.

Dana looked around and saw that most of the attendees seemed charmed, and she decided that there was indeed something endearing about the clumsy effort. By the time it ended she was dabbing at her eyes.

Afterward, Dana stood on the patio sipping a mimosa, talking over the three-piece band as she agreed with relatives that yes, it was a beautiful ceremony. They treated her like a celebrity, peppering her with questions about what it was like to be on the Shopping Channel, and she was grateful they were distracted from asking about her love life. As it was, Dana barely managed to tamp down thoughts of how stupid she had been to stall over inviting Ari to the wedding. If only she had brought it up sooner.

And now, the part of her that Chelsea had mentioned—the part that assumed she simply wasn't lovable enough—

threatened to make another appearance. In fact, she kept hearing a line of poetry in her head—something from an old Dorothy Parker verse—that played out like a prayer.

Let me, for our happiness,
Be the one to love the less.

It depressed her. Because she couldn't help thinking that if Ari was more serious about this relationship, he would have found a way to be with her at this wedding.

Dana took another sip of her drink, and her aunt Lillian came rushing over.

"There's a man in the house looking for you!" she gushed.

"A man?" Dana asked, her heart thudding.

"I don't know what you did to this one, honey," Aunt Lillian said, "but he's got stars in his eyes. Something tells me you might be next."

Oh God, Ari *had* come! Dana was so excited she didn't even bother resenting her aunt for the presumptuous comment.

"Where is he?" she asked.

"In the living room—on the sofa talking to your cousin Becca."

Dana handed her drink to her aunt and rushed into the house, nearly crying with joy. She stopped short when she reached the living room, where she found Becca talking to the man who had been asking about her. Dana blinked as she reconciled the sight before her with what she had expected to see.

"Dana!" cried the man, looking her up and down with lascivious attention.

It wasn't Ari.

Dear God, it was Rusty Lindemuth. She tried to reply, to choke out something as simple as *hello*, but she couldn't get her voice to work. Dana turned away and rushed to the bathroom, where she locked the door. Damn Aunt Lillian. This was all her fault for raising Dana's hopes.

There was a gentle knock on the door. "You okay?" Rusty said.

"Go away!" she yelled, and immediately regretted it. Poor Rusty. It wasn't his fault Ari didn't love her enough.

Dana took a cleansing breath and steadied herself. She had to go out there and face the rest of this party with a smile. And she had to apologize to Rusty Lindemuth.

By the time she opened the bathroom door, he had retreated. But Chelsea was standing there, holding two mimosas. She handed one to Dana.

"You okay?" she asked.

"Not really."

"Let's find a private spot," Chelsea suggested, and led Dana out the front door, where her father kept the old porch swing from their childhood home. They sat down and began rocking back and forth as Dana told her sister that she didn't want to talk about it. Everything was fine. She had worked herself into a froth over nothing.

"You mean because you think Ari doesn't love you enough to rearrange his work schedule for you?" Chelsea asked, smirking.

Dana stared down at her drink. "I'm glad my heartache amuses you," she said, wishing she had something stronger than a mimosa.

Chelsea's smile erupted into a laugh.

"What's so damned funny?" Dana demanded.

Chelsea pointed, and Dana followed the line of her finger to the car that had just pulled up in the driveway, where one of the parking valets her father had hired stood at attention. She recognized the car first—a white Explorer. Then the driver. The door opened and he emerged, tall, dark and devastating in a trim charcoal suit and a silver tie. God's version of the perfect wedding escort. Or Dana's version, anyway.

Ari. Her heart seemed to stop beating.

Chelsea gave Dana's hand a squeeze and left them. And then it was just Dana and Ari and a twenty-year-old kid earning some extra money on a Sunday afternoon. Ari tossed him his keys and approached the porch.

"You came," she said.

He shrugged. "It was important to you so... I rearranged some things."

Dana looked at him. She knew it couldn't have been easy. He had a serious job. It was, *literally*, life and death. And yet here he was. For her.

Ari slung his arm over Dana's shoulder and they walked into the backyard as she pressed him for details on how he had managed to get out of work. But they didn't get to talk for long, because all at once her father and Jennifer stood before them, waiting for an introduction. Dana complied.

"You're not an ex-con, are you?" said Kenneth, taking in Ari's imposing height. Dana could tell he felt ready to dismiss him as unworthy.

"No, sir."

Kenneth's brows moved together, as if preparing his face for a scowl. "An *actor*?" He pronounced the word like it was something that required a dose of antibiotics.

Ari laughed. "I'm a police detective," he said, and Dana watched her father's face soften.

He nodded in approval, then got distracted by the band, which had just started a Motown set with its version of the Temptations' "Ain't Too Proud to Beg."

"Would you excuse us?" Jennifer said, and led her new husband off. Before they were even out of earshot, though, Kenneth said to her, "Why would she choose a cop over a doctor?"

Dana looked at Ari, who seemed more amused than offended. And she was, too. Because she knew that, despite everything, her father was growing and evolving. She also knew that it was hard to change. In the end, the best you could do was try.

"Dance?" Ari asked her.

She didn't answer. She just took his hand, and they began.

★ ★ ★ ★ ★

ACKNOWLEDGMENTS

It's always an exciting moment when a book finds a home. But when that home is with one of the smartest senior editors in the business, it's time to celebrate. So to Kathy Sagan, my happiest and humblest gratitude. Special thanks to editorial director Nicole Brebner, as well. I'm thrilled to be part of the MIRA Books family.

Before a book makes it to the editorial stage, writing can be sad, lonely and anxious. Sometimes all at once. That's why it helps to have supportive writer friends. I'm so grateful to Saralee Rosenberg, whose wisdom, clarity and feedback make me a better writer and a better person. My other beta reader, Susan DiPlacido, also came to the rescue when I was feeling shaky, and I thank her from the bottom of my heart.

To the other literary friends who inspire me daily, including Myfanwy Collins, Susan Henderson, Robin Slick, Amy Ferris, Debbi Honorof, Carol Hoenig, Peggy Zieran, Jordan Rosenfeld, Lydia Fazio Theys, Brenda Janowitz, Victoria Burgess, Eric Saiet, Anabel Graff, Debbie Markowitz, Mary Ellen Walsh, Alix Strauss, Dina Santorelli, Greg Correll, and Devan Burton, thank you.

I also need to acknowledge the adult writing students I've been working with for several years. Somehow, they think

I'm the one teaching them, rather than the other way around. I'm honored by their trust, and awed by their talent and dedication. My warmest gratitude to all of them, including Louis Cornacchia, Ivan Debel, Ruth Eichacker, Keith Furino, Madeleine Ganis, Anne Kenna, Diane Lazuta, Michelle Levine, Melissa Moss, Jayne Isabel Potter, Olga Kontzias Psillis, Darlene Record, Connie Ring, Kate Shaffar, and Jeffrey Siegel.

I'm lucky enough to have dear friends who know the world of theater and acting, and were able to offer their input. Thanks, love and hugs to Wendy Baila DeAngelis and Stephen DeAngelis. Affectionate thanks to Jay Bloomrosen, too, who gleaned quite a bit of tech expertise since our junior high days.

To the hosts, staff and management at HSN, QVC and other real-life shopping channels, my humblest thanks for the inspiration and apologies for the creative license I took with your business model. I hope you can accept this fictional world as an homage to the work you do so very well.

Love and gratitude to my agent Annelise Robey, who thrilled me with her enthusiasm for this book from the very start and provided exactly what I needed to get it into shape. I couldn't have done it without her. I'm also grateful to my other superstar agent, Andrea Cirillo, who always has such savvy advice and helpful answers. In fact, I tip my hat to the whole team at the Jane Rotrosen Agency. I'm so lucky to have you.

I don't know what I would do without my mom, whose favorite question—when can I read it?—warms me every time.

To my kids—Max, Ethan and Rook—love and thanks for keeping me laughing and living in this actual century. And most of all, thanks to Mike, for everything.